HORACE DORLAN

[redacted]

By the same author

The Depository
The Secret

ANDRZEJ KLIMOWSKI

HORACE DORLAN

faber and faber

First Published in Great Britain in 2007
by Faber and Faber Limited
3 Queen Square London WC1N 3AU

Designed by Jeff Willis

Printed in England by T. J. International Ltd,
Padstow, Cornwall

A CIP record for this book
is available from the British Library

ISBN 978–0–571–23221–5

2 4 6 8 10 9 7 5 3 1

Dedicated to my mother
Melania Klimowska

ACKNOWLEDGEMENTS

The author wishes to thank the Research Department and the Communication Art and Design Department at the Royal College of Art for their support, and the following individuals for their collaboration and inspiration:

Angus Cargill, Ron Costley, Dan Fern, Ian Gabb, Ben Hooker, Shona Kitchen, Dominik Klimowski, Natalia Klimowska, Deborah Levy, Nicholas Lowndes, Danusia Schejbal and Jeff Willis.

HORACE DORLAN

CHAPTER ONE

'Hori.

Hori, darling, we must help them.

Only you and I can help them.

We alone know; it is up to us. We understand.

They will disappear, like us, into thin air, never to be seen again.

But we are tireless. Therefore it can be done.

That is why I am talking to you.'

The words were spoken in a slow, broken yet forthright voice. Like a mantra, the phrases were repeated for what seemed like minutes; then a long pause. Dorlan did not know how to respond. What could he say? How was he to react to such rambling? The voice was vaguely familiar, like his wife's. Only deeper, hoarser, like that of a heavy smoker. The words were spoken with such determination that he found it hard to get a word in edgeways, interjecting only the odd 'yes' and 'I see'.

After he had put the phone down he felt afraid. A deep sadness consumed him. He remained seated by the telephone for some time before he got up and went over to the window to stare across the street. From the third floor he could see the city stretching before him.

– My God, what is happening?

Eventually he returned to bed, still very tired. He fell into a deep sleep the minute his head touched the pillow. It was not long before the phone rang once more.

'They have come in again today. They give me no peace, barging in like this, searching the place, leaving nothing unturned. They take everything out of the locker. It's embarrassing. One of them looks under the bed, while the other searches behind the screen. They ask me questions. All I know is I have to rest, I need to be left alone. I have no time for them. I must sort out my own thoughts. Everything is racing ahead. Where am I in all of this?

Once they have gone it takes me a while to calm down. How long will this go on for? I'm so stiff, I can't even reach my glass of water. Even if I did reach it, my hands are shaking so much that I would spill it all.'

She sighed, once, twice, and then a long silence ensued.

The croaky voice resumed as suddenly as it had broken off.

'Hello, are you still there?'

'Yes, yes I'm listening.'

'So then little Minnie comes in. After they have left, that is. She is standing by the door, so small, wearing a white dress, the one I made for her last summer. You know the one? The one before . . .'

'Before?'

He could hear her breathing into the receiver.

'She came in and crouched down to look under the bed. For a while I could not see her at all until she popped up and stared at me. She smiled, her eyes wide open and sparkling.'

'It's safe,' she said, 'our secret is safe!'

After the second call Dorlan could not return to bed, he would never fall asleep. Instead he went out onto the balcony. The first aeroplane flew over, heading towards the airport. Dorlan stepped back into the room; it was still quite cold so early in the morning. In the kitchen he put some coffee into the percolator, poured in the water and lit the stove. Half asleep, he shuffled towards the bathroom, knocking into the walls of the narrow corridor.

– What the hell is going on?

He emerged from the bathroom refreshed, the pleasant smell of coffee took his mind off the telephone calls. He loved the ritual of making and serving coffee, even if now it was only for himself. The small porcelain cup and saucer, the glass of water with a slice of lemon; he positioned them carefully next to each other on the coffee table in front of the leather sofa. Automatically he brought out the ashtray. He felt a pain in his chest. It had been a long time; only now did he feel his loss so strongly.

The phone was ringing. This time he would not answer it. He drank his coffee slowly, then took a sip of water. The effervescent bubbles tickled his nose. The ringing broke off. Dorlan tried to relax but found it difficult. Taking his coffee, he walked across to the window. The leaves were shimmering in the morning light and cast intricate shadows onto the tree trunks and the lawn below. He was surprised that even at such an early hour birds were already trying to outsing each other. He watched them impatiently jumping from branch to branch. A second aeroplane crossed the sky. He downed his coffee, placed the cup on the table and, with the back of his hand, wiped his moustache. He realized then that he had not done a good job of shaving; with a goatee beard it is imperative to shave well around it, across the cheeks and under the chin.

He strode into the bathroom and inspected his face at close quarters in the shaving mirror.

– Not a good job; small wonder after those phone calls. He would have to go through the ritual over again. He filled the washbasin with hot water and turned off the taps. The sound of the ringing telephone reached him from across the corridor, but again he would not answer it. With great dexterity Dorlan guided the razor across his cheeks.

He made and ate breakfast in the kitchen while listening to the radio, then retired to his study. Surrounded by books and insect specimens in glass cases, he began to write. In no time he was encircled by stacks of notes and diagrams. Files were taken off the shelves, opened, referred to, closed and replaced. Occasionally the faint ringing of the telephone reached his room. He raised his head from his desk and looked through the window into the distance: trees, rooftops, part of the road and the clear blue sky. For a few seconds his mind was drifting, then his eyes returned to the study, to the desk calendar: June, a few crossed-off numbers, today's date.

– Good gracious, the meeting!

*   *   *

Still no reply. Where could he be?

After putting down the receiver I joined my colleagues back at the bar.

'Well, where is he?'

'I don't know, there was no reply. It's not like him to disappear like this.'

'Who said anything about disappearing? He's just not answering the phone,' said George.

'That may be so, but I've been phoning him all morning, even before I met up with you chaps.'

Amadeo leaned over and asked me whether I had phoned the academy. I hadn't.

'Well, there you are then,' retorted Dorlan's young assistant.

'Yes, but I phoned him earlier, at home, just as he had asked me to, and every time there was no reply. Come to think of it, the answering machine should have turned itself on. Maybe he is ill.'

'Don't be daft,' George dismissed my speculation. 'I think Amadeo is right, he must have gone to the academy early in the morning. He's got his own keys to the department. He probably wanted to sort out a few things before meeting up with us; prepare himself.'

I nodded my head and suggested we go through to the restaurant.

'But aren't you going to try the academy first? It'll set our minds at rest,' said Amadeo.

I agreed and rose to go back to the telephone kiosk by the cloakroom. Amadeo pulled out his mobile phone.

'Here, use this! You really must get yourself one, Ed.'

I fiddled around with Amadeo's gadget.

'Let me.' Amadeo went through the appropriate actions, then handed me the phone. Dorlan's secretary answered and said she had not seen nor heard from the professor all morning. Amadeo took back his mobile and swiftly dialled another extention: no news of Dorlan.

George got up from the table. 'I don't know about you chaps, but I am starving. If I don't eat something now, I'll go mad.'

We gathered our briefcases and moved through to the restaurant. It was empty save for a couple occupying a table at the far end by the window. We sat down at a table and George pulled out some papers. A waiter arrived with the menus; it broke our concentration, but did not deter George, who continued laying out his papers. The waiter returned to ask us if we would like any drinks. We ordered white wine and mineral water. George resumed his presentation. Just as we began to probe him with questions, the waiter reappeared, ready to take our orders. We had to tell him we were not yet ready. Thus interrupted, we found it hard to return to George's exposé. Instead we studied the menus.

After ordering our food we discussed Dorlan. Everyone was genuinely puzzled by what could have happened to him. Sam, who up until then had not said a word, raised a question about Dorlan's wife. Why was Dorlan never seen with his wife? They were always so close, but in recent months he was never with her. What is more, he never mentioned her in conversation. It was as if she stopped existing. George would have no more of this. First of all we were talking about Dorlan disappearing; now his wife.

I vaguely remembered Dorlan telling me something about how Angela had had to go abroad to visit her mother, who was ill and spending time in a sanatorium. That was some time ago, however, just after Christmas. I remembered inviting Dorlan to spend New Year with me and my uncle. He had declined the offer, telling me that he was going to join Angela and his convalescing mother-in-law. I don't think he did, because I saw him about town when I was travelling to my uncle's. It was only a glimpse, through the window of an underground train. My train was pulling out of the station and there he was, sitting on a bench in the middle of the platform. I am sure it was him. I kept all this to myself as we sat there eating our hors d'oeuvres.

'I saw Mrs Dorlan just after we broke up for Christmas. Professor Dorlan asked me to take him some essays he had left at the academy. I arrived at his apartment that evening and he invited me in for a drink. I told him I was in a hurry but he said he wished to give me a small Christmas present, in appreciation of all the hard work I had put in over the term, and it would only take a minute, I could wait in the hall. As I stood there I saw a woman at the end of the corridor. In the light of an open door I could see it was Mrs Dorlan. It was only for a second that I saw her, but I noticed that she looked terrible. Most of her face was covered by her hair, but I could see that she was without make-up, standing in her bathrobe. I wanted to get away as quickly as I could. Eventually Professor Dorlan appeared. He handed me the present and wished me a happy Christmas. Seeing me to the door, he patted my back and told me not to work too hard. I thought of calling the lift, but decided to run down the stairs. Once outside in the cold air I felt better, but my heart was beating so fast I thought it would burst.'

Amadeo was staring at his plate as he recounted this event; our eyes were fixed on him. Waiters cleared our plates and brought in the main course. I ordered another bottle of wine. An uneasy silence followed. It was broken when George started choking on a fish bone. I slapped his back, but it only seemed to aggravate his condition. His face turned from red to violet. Amadeo was the only calm person around. He took a pair of tweezers from his breast pocket and with a steady hand extracted the fish bone from George's throat. It was a big one. He wrapped it in his napkin. I supported George, who had slumped back across his chair. Sam gave him a glass of water. George spluttered and coughed but was soon visibly relieved. We had created a commotion, waiters were running to our aid, but we had the situation under control and just asked them to take some of the plates.

I could not help asking Amadeo how he happened to be carrying tweezers in his pocket. The answer was simple: for handling insect specimens. He had a pair in every jacket, they were as important to him as a writer carrying a pen. We ordered coffee, still hoping that the professor would turn up. George asked for a cognac: 'To disinfect my throat, you understand,' he said with a twinkle in his eye. The drink put colour back in his face. He downed it in one go and then insisted he buy us all one. We needed little persuasion. The waiter poured out the drinks and left the bottle on the table.

'Here's to Horace!' exclaimed George in a hoarse voice. Clearing his throat, he added, 'And to his lecture.' We all clinked glasses. The vibrations continued for a second longer; it was Amadeo's mobile phone. The three of us looked at him as he pressed the apparatus to his ear. The talking was done at the other end, and judging by Amadeo's expression, it was serious news. Finally Amadeo switched off the phone.

'There's been an accident.'

*   *   *

Realizing that he would be late for the meeting, Dorlan had sprung into action. He rushed out of his study to the bathroom, where he brushed the back and sides of his head, checked his beard and splashed some cologne around it. For good measure he put some about his armpits and ran to the bedroom, where he threw on his jacket and tied his bow tie, hardly needing to look in the mirror, his thoughts on where best to catch a taxi. Locking the door to his apartment, with his briefcase wedged under his arm, he saw the lift descend past his floor. Through the grating of the caged lift shaft he managed to discern three silhouetted figures crammed inside the narrow, wood-panelled box; the bevelled edges of the windowpanes caught the light from the floor below. Dorlan started to run down the stairs, determined to reach the ground floor before the lift got there. He accelerated, jumping over every other step. On reaching the second floor, he almost collided with a midget dressed in black and a bowler hat on his head. The tiny man was attempting to reach the front doorbell to one of the apartments. He made way for Dorlan and automatically tipped the brim of his bowler, in a gentlemanly manner. These details were registered by Dorlan within a split second but he did not dare to look back at the midget for fear of falling down the next flight of stairs.

Before reaching the ground floor, however, the lift stopped on the first floor and the door swung open.

There was no way of avoiding a collision.

CHAPTER TWO

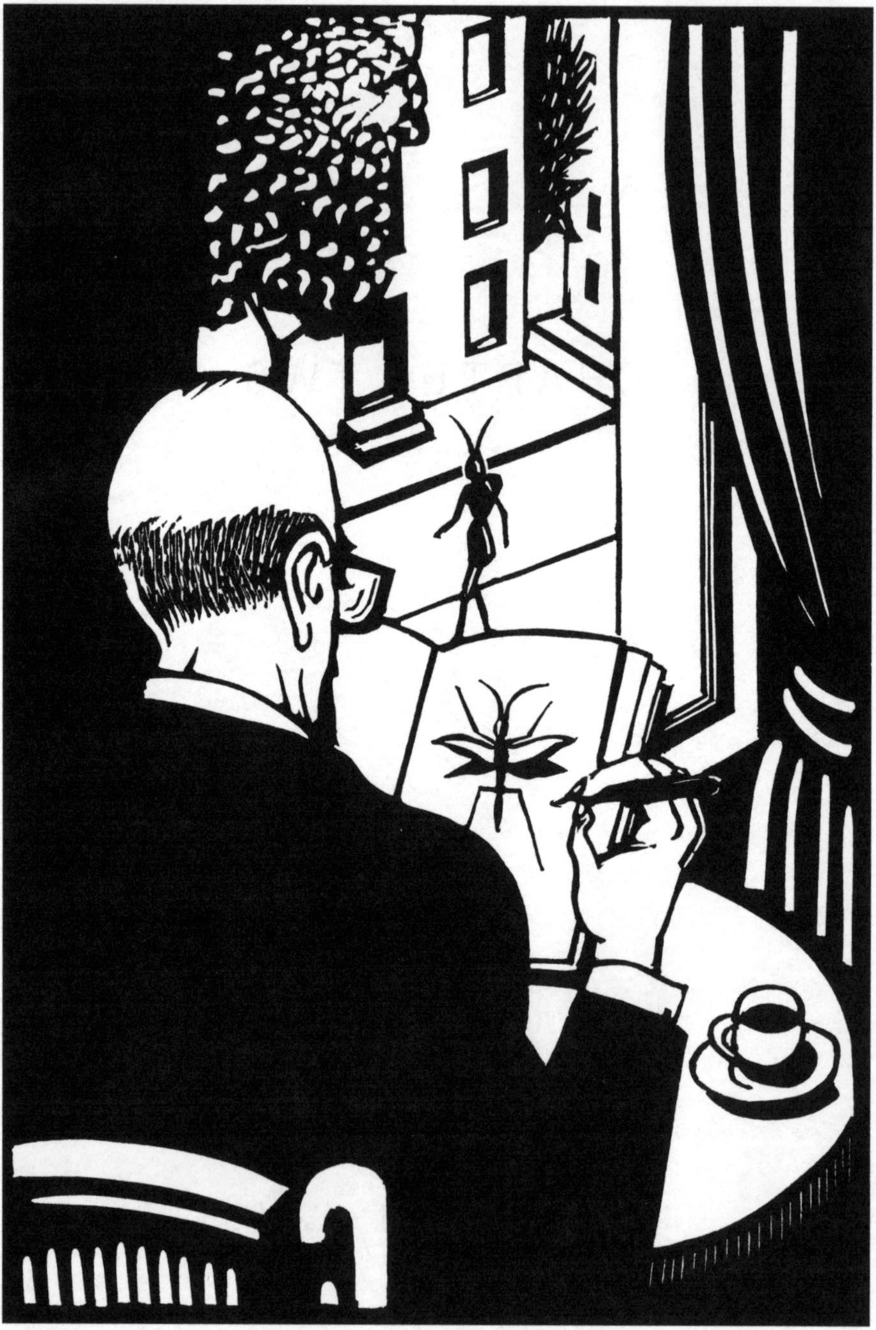

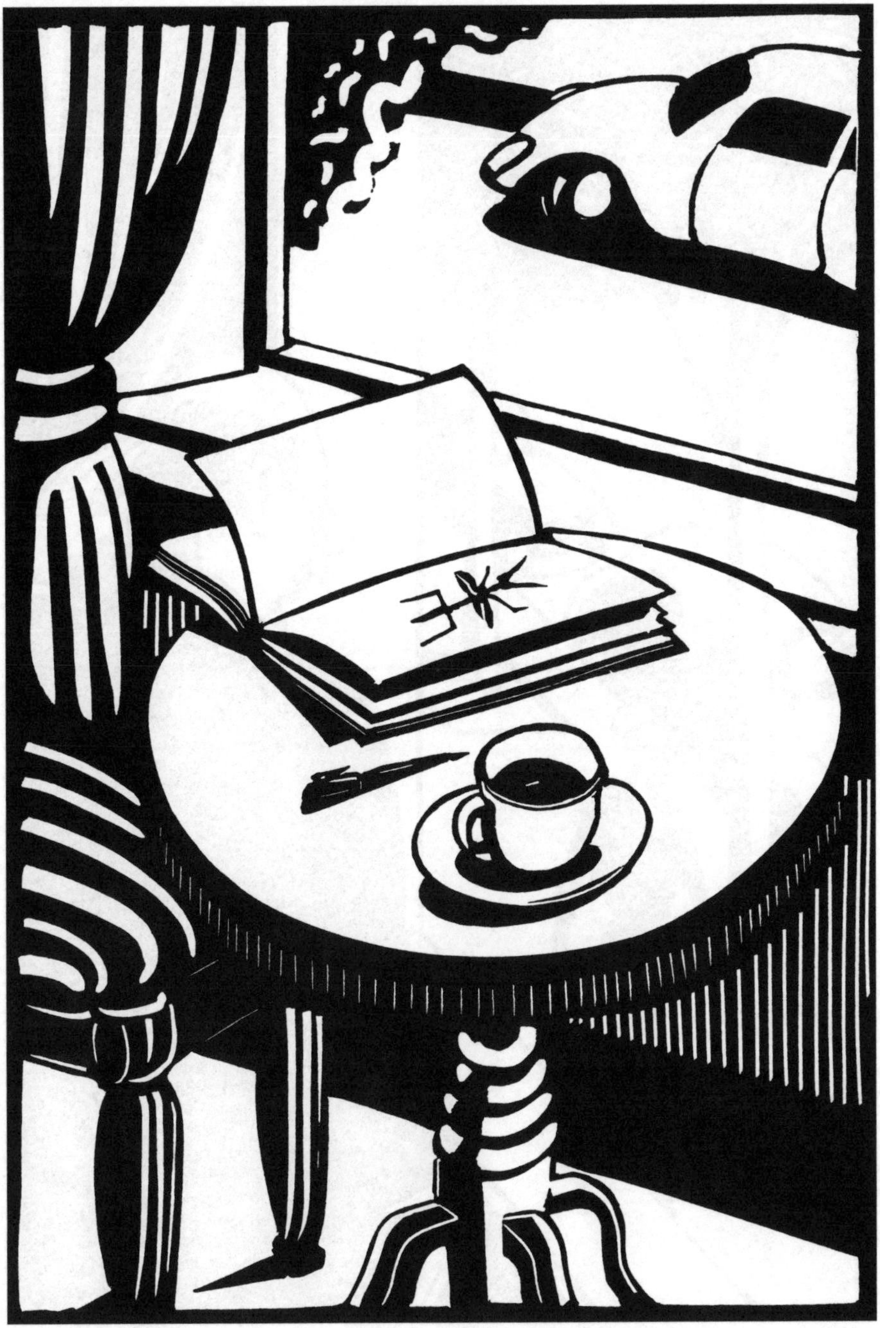

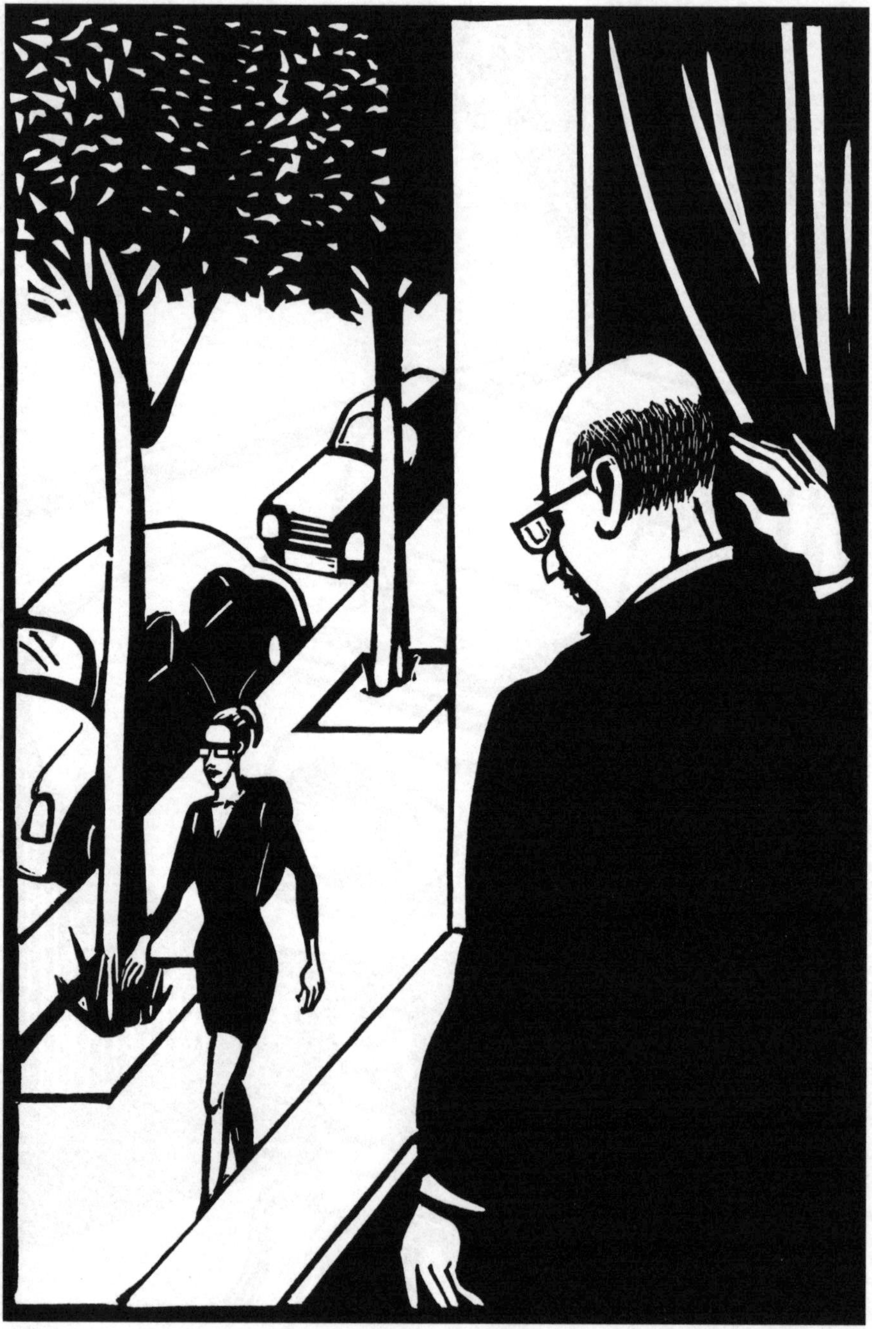

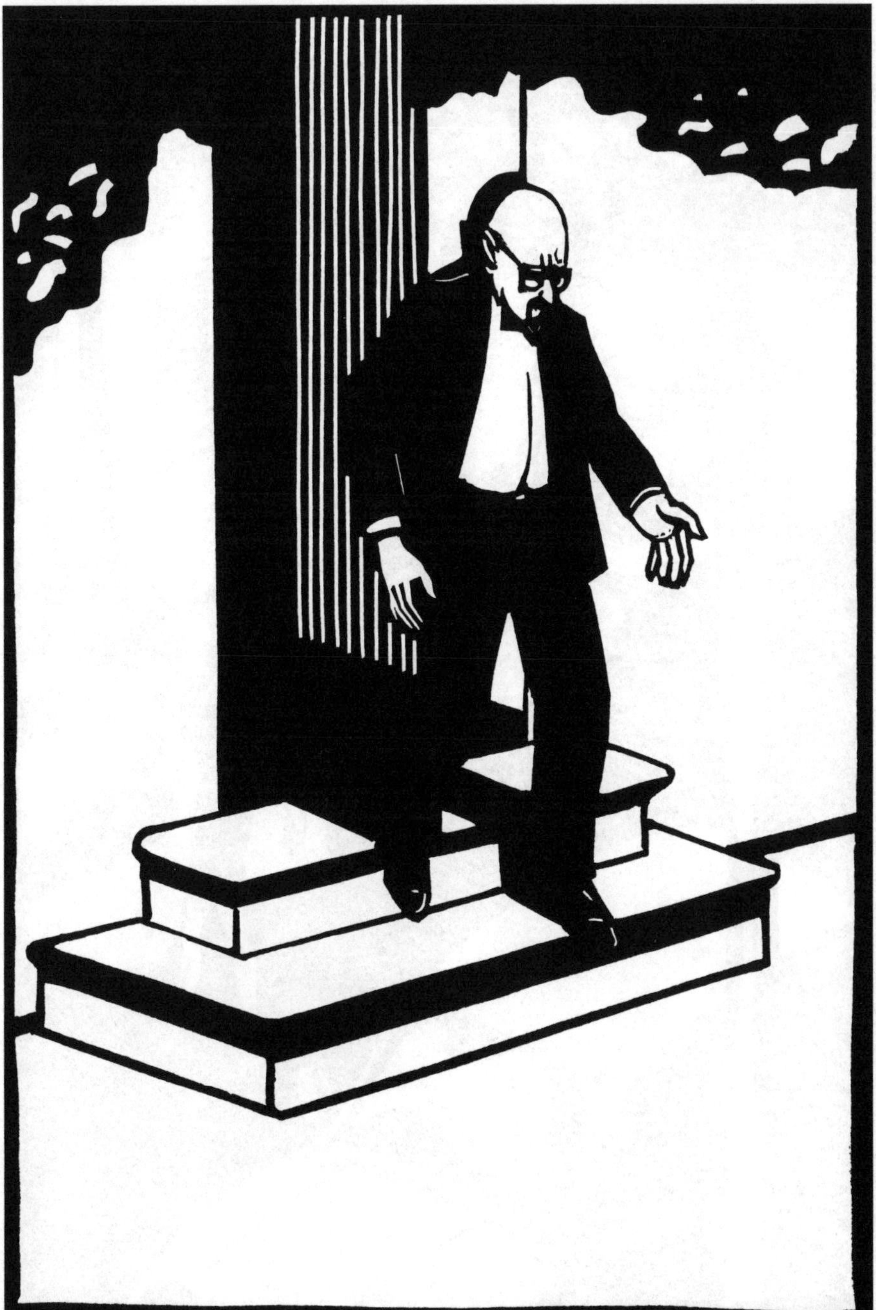

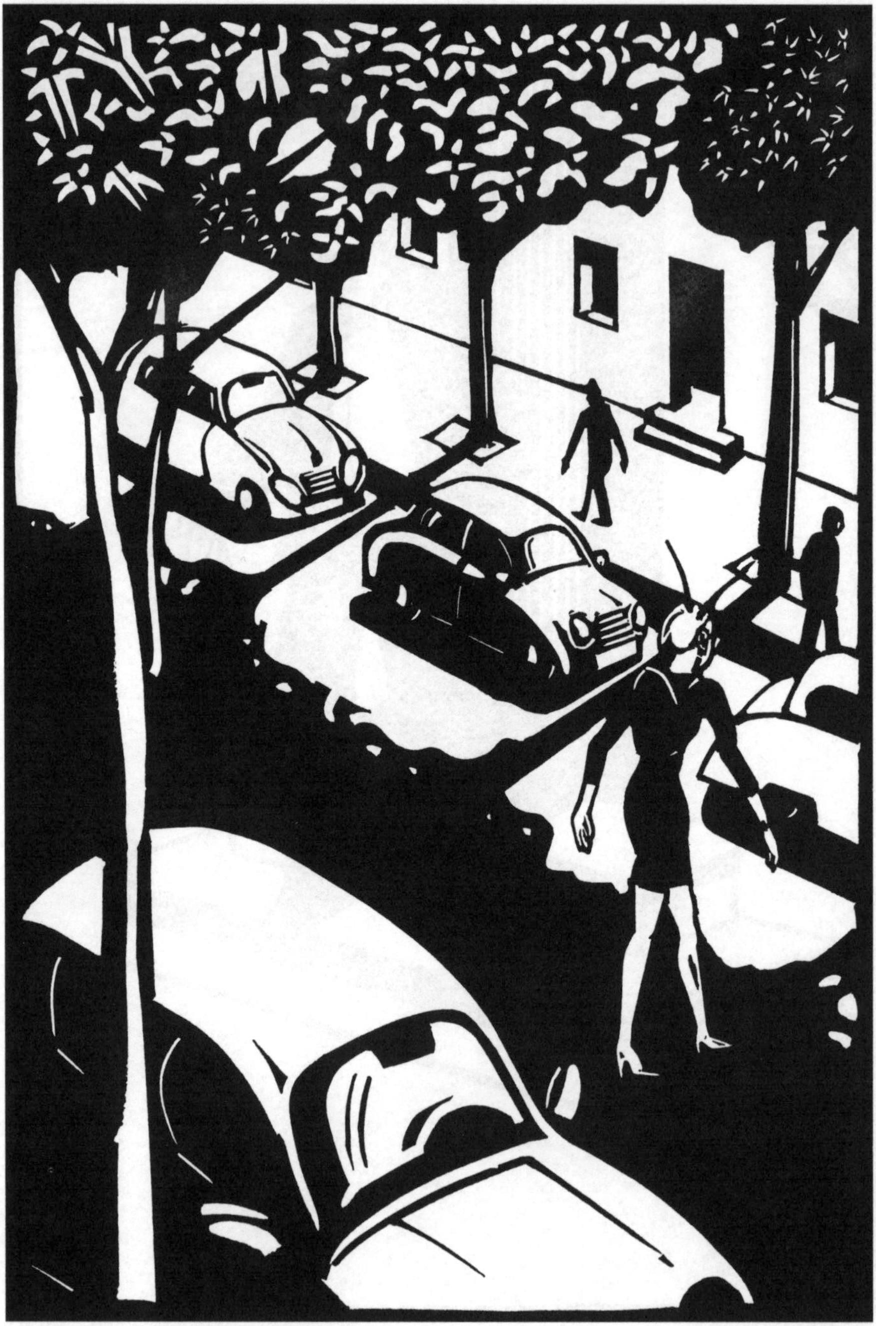

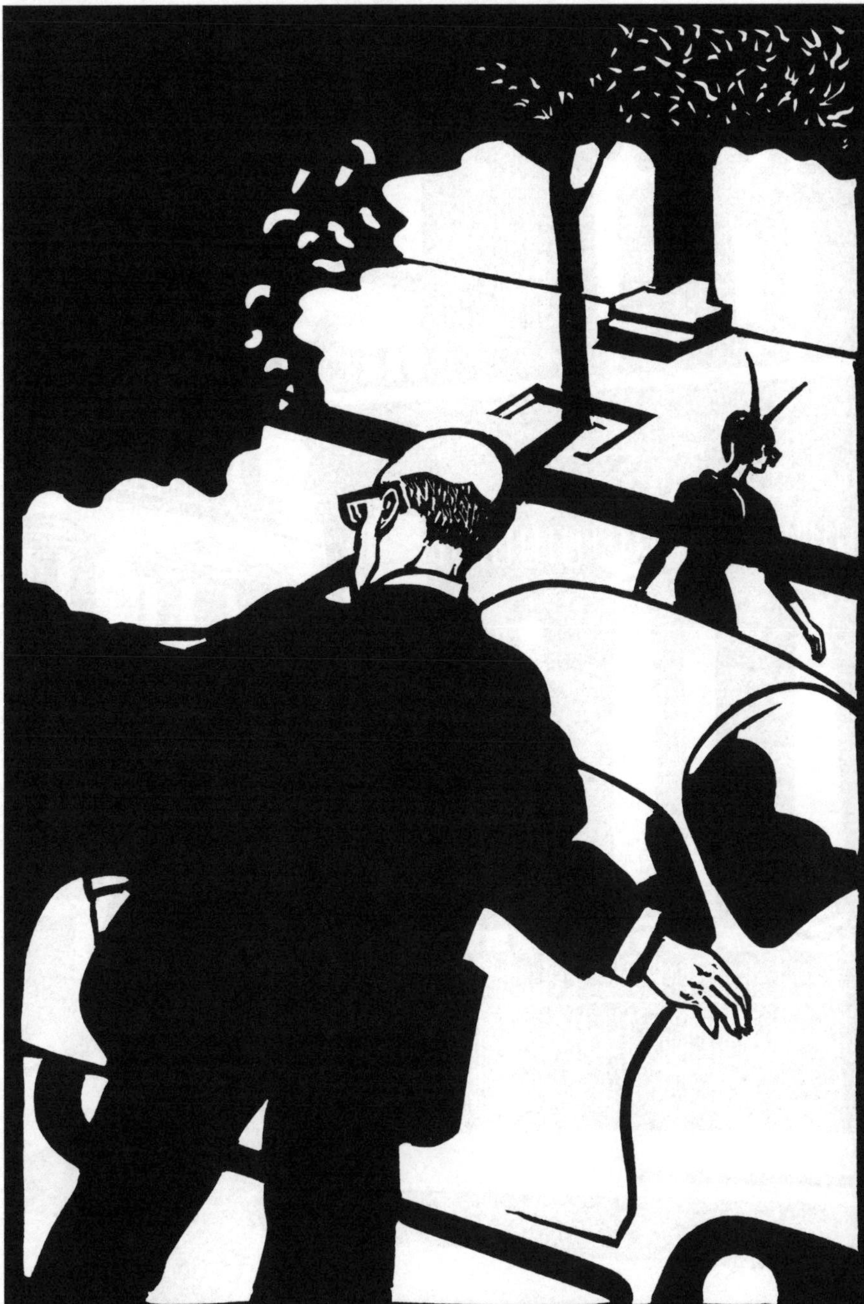

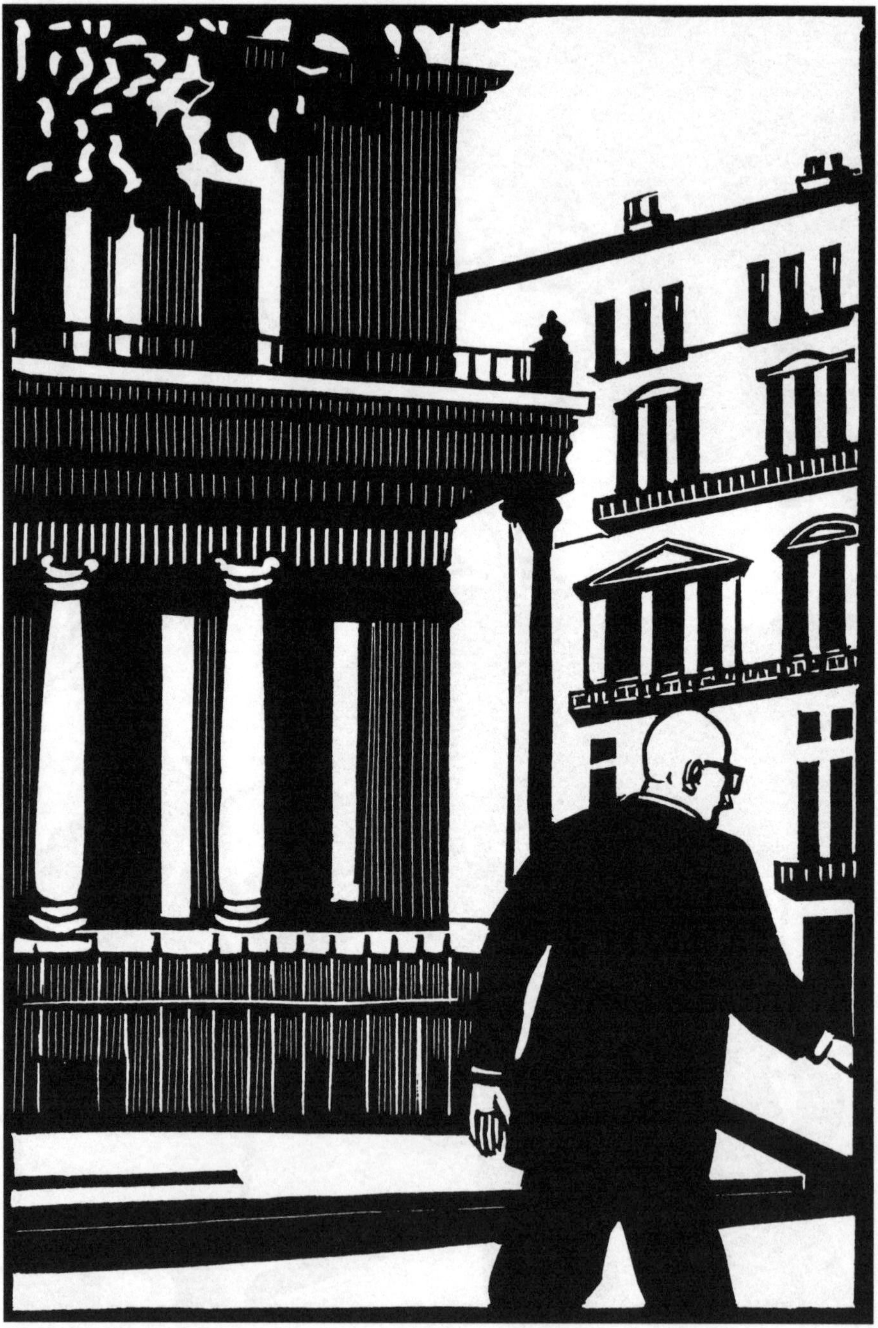

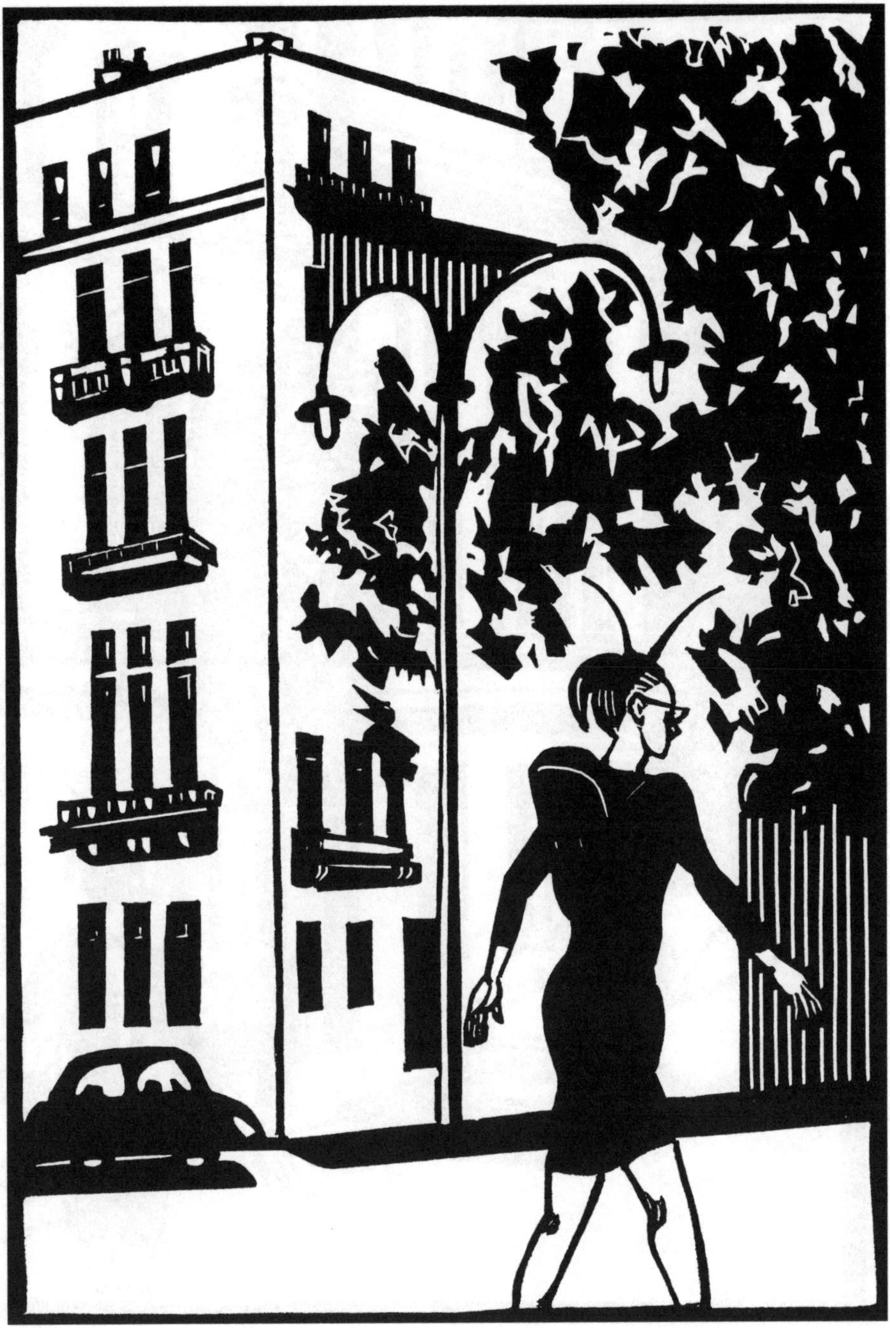

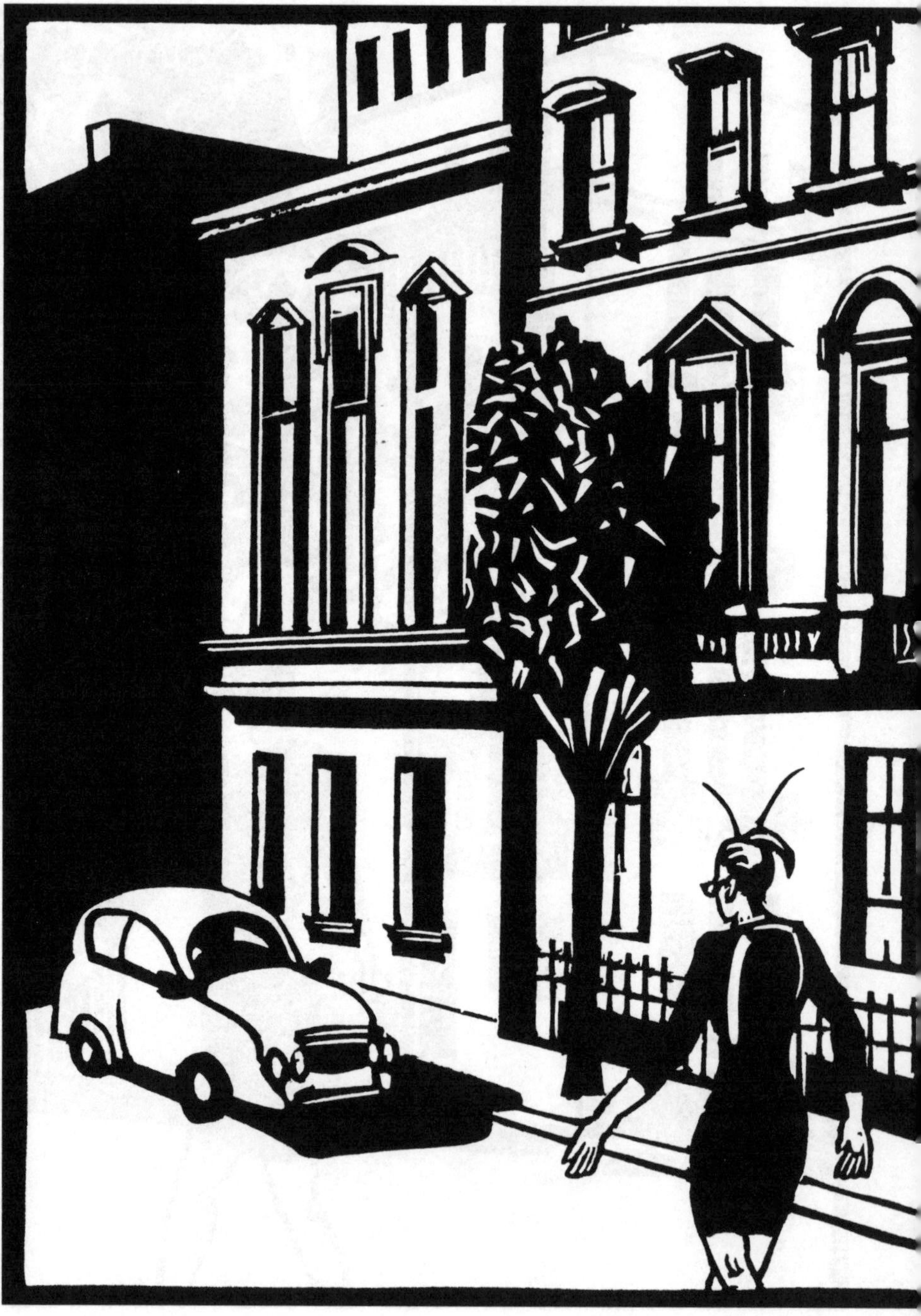

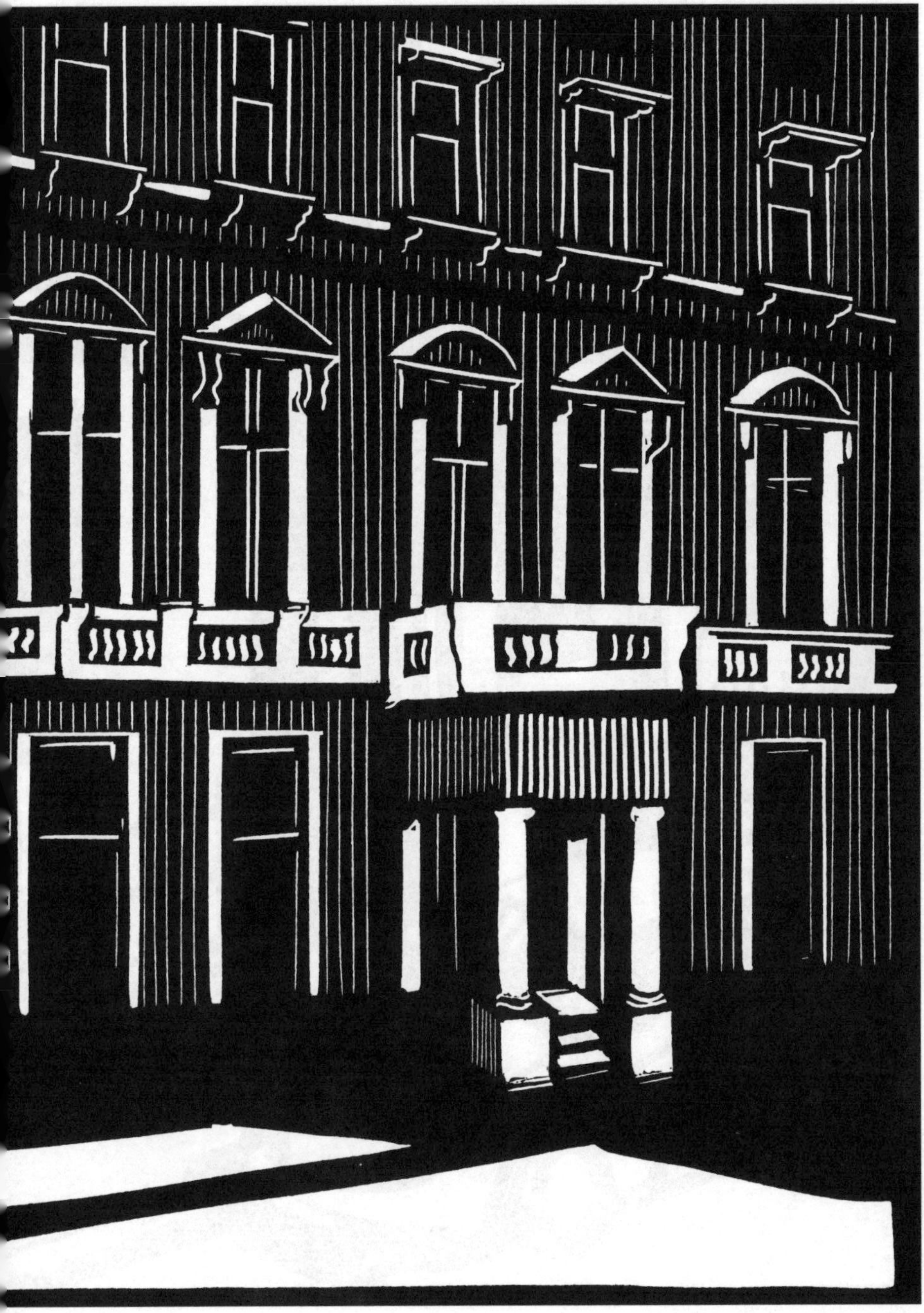

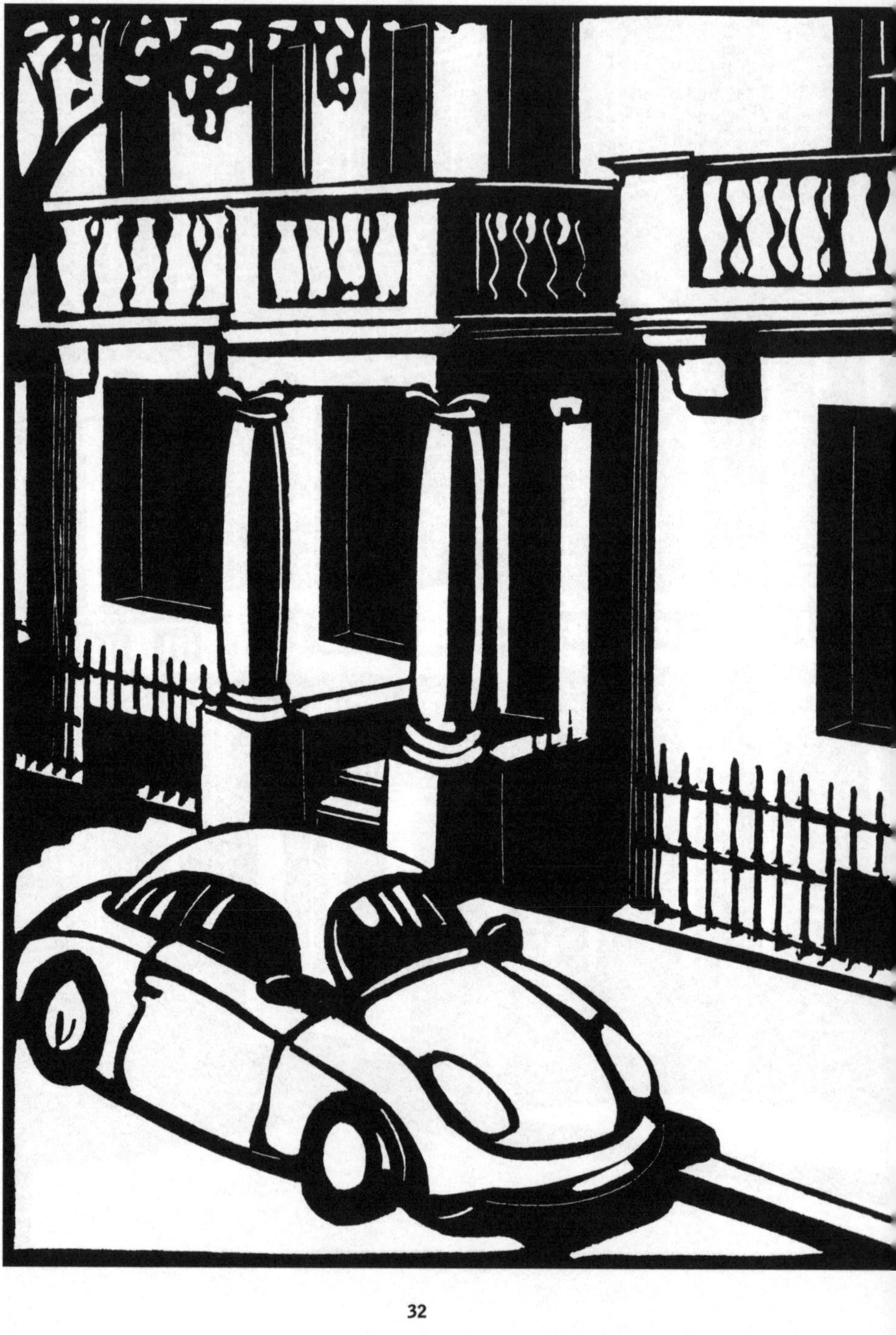

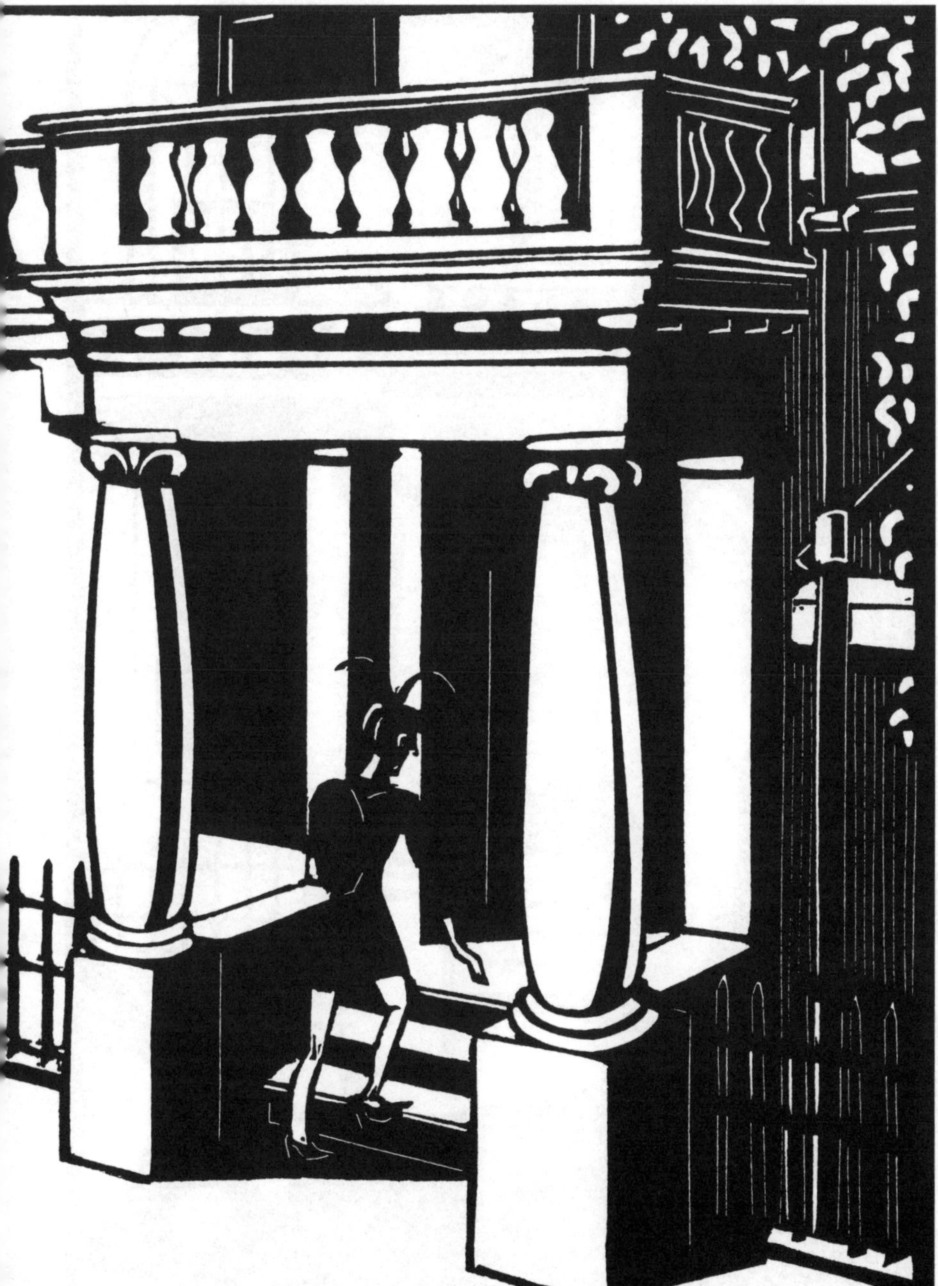

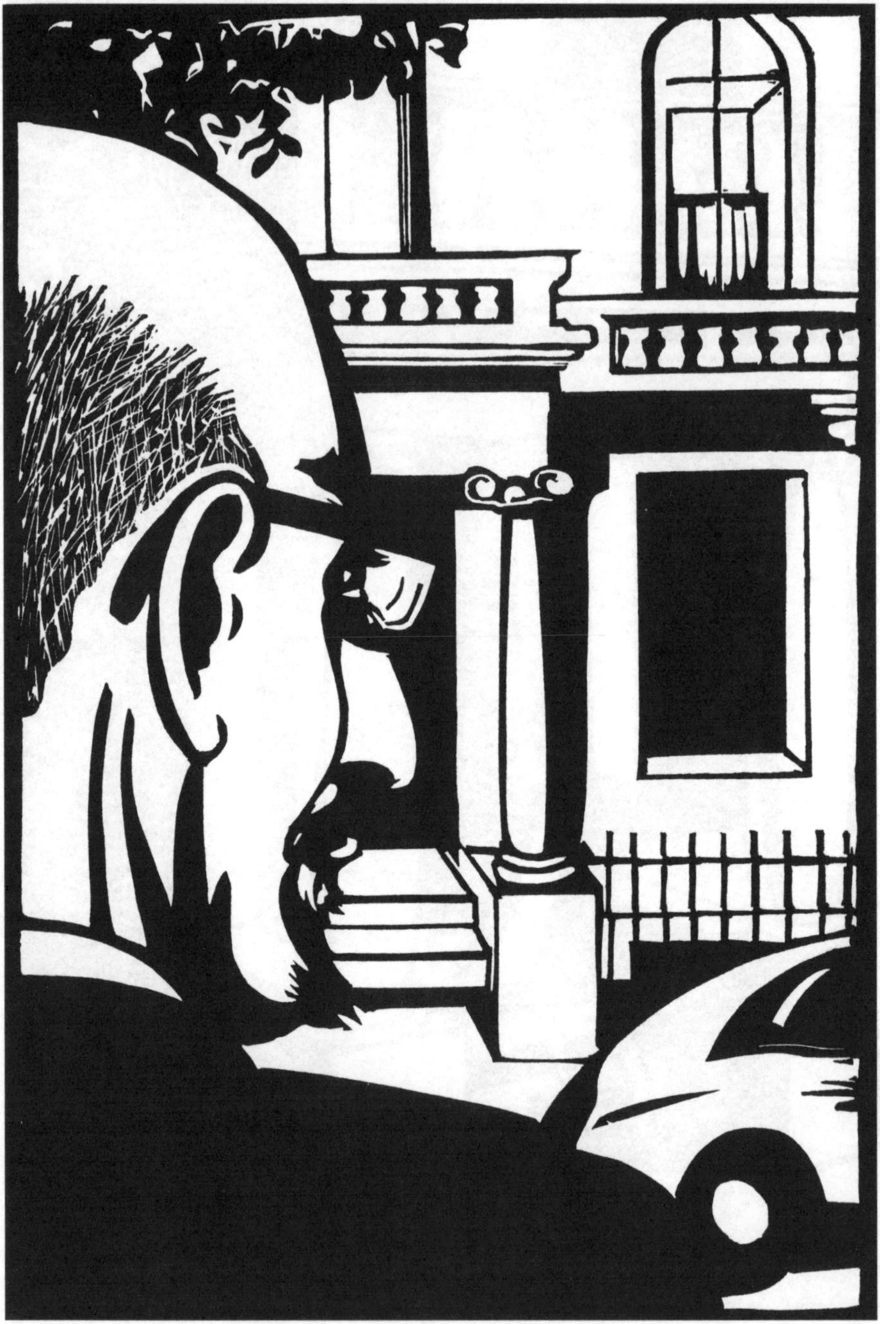

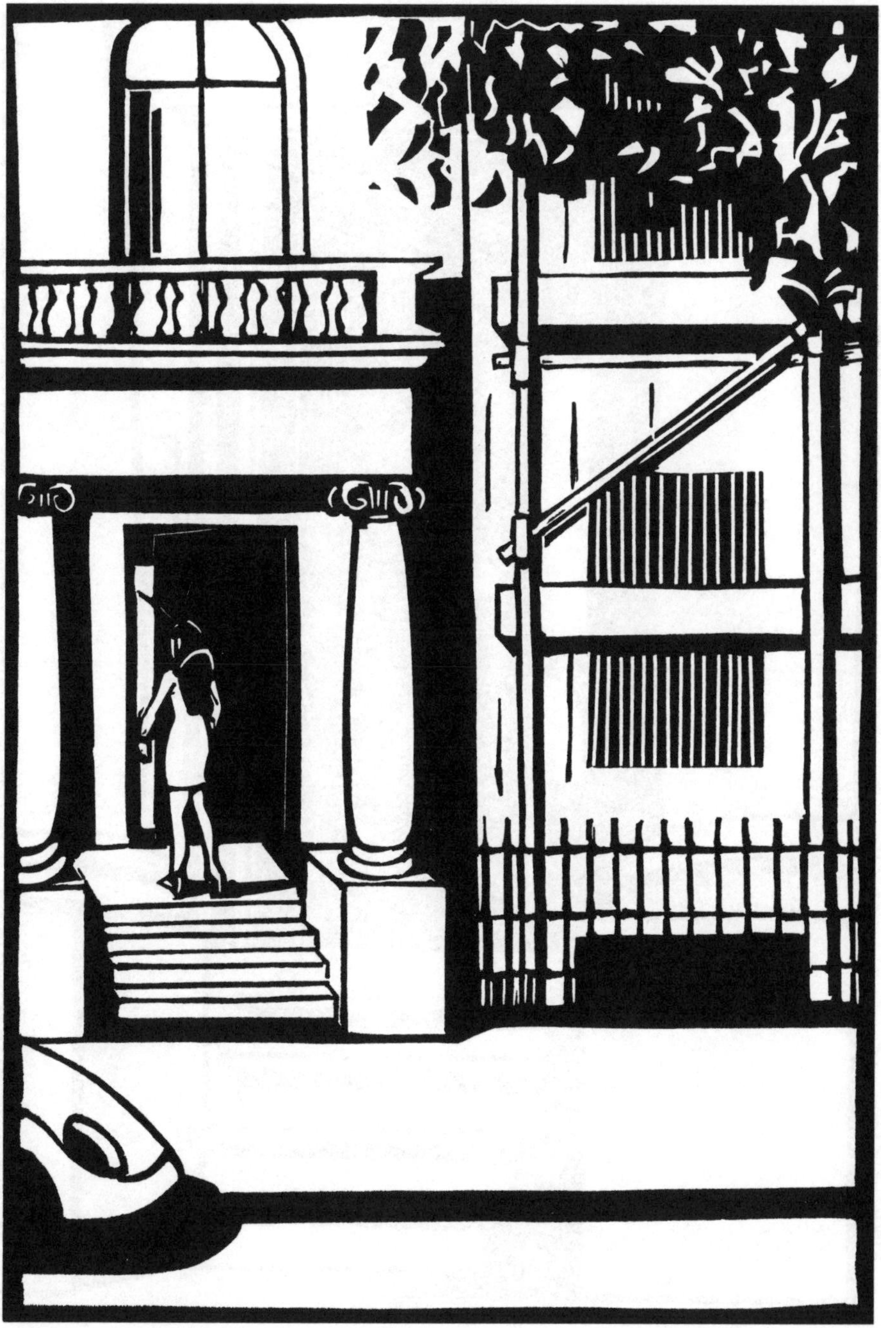

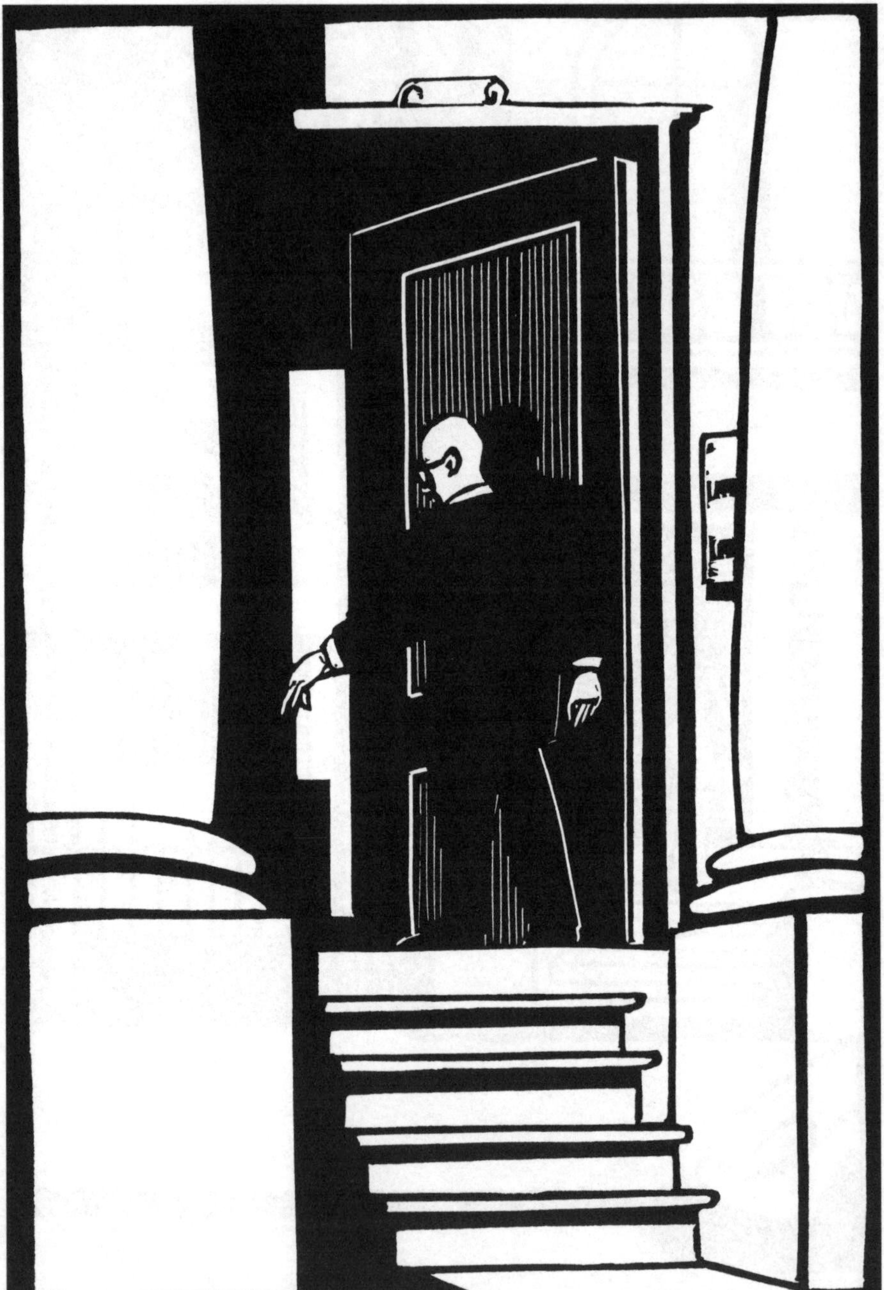

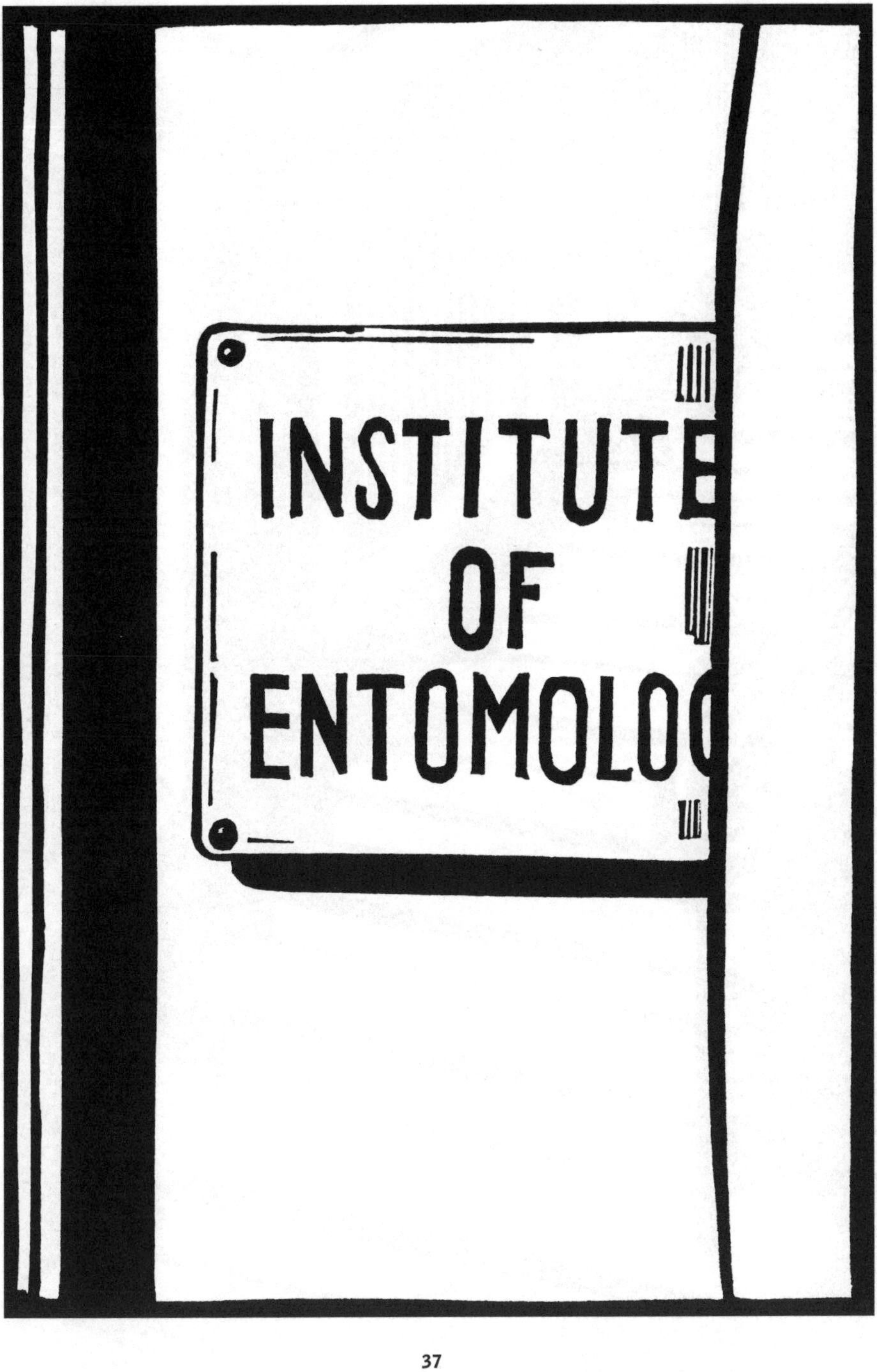
INSTITUTE
OF
ENTOMOLOG

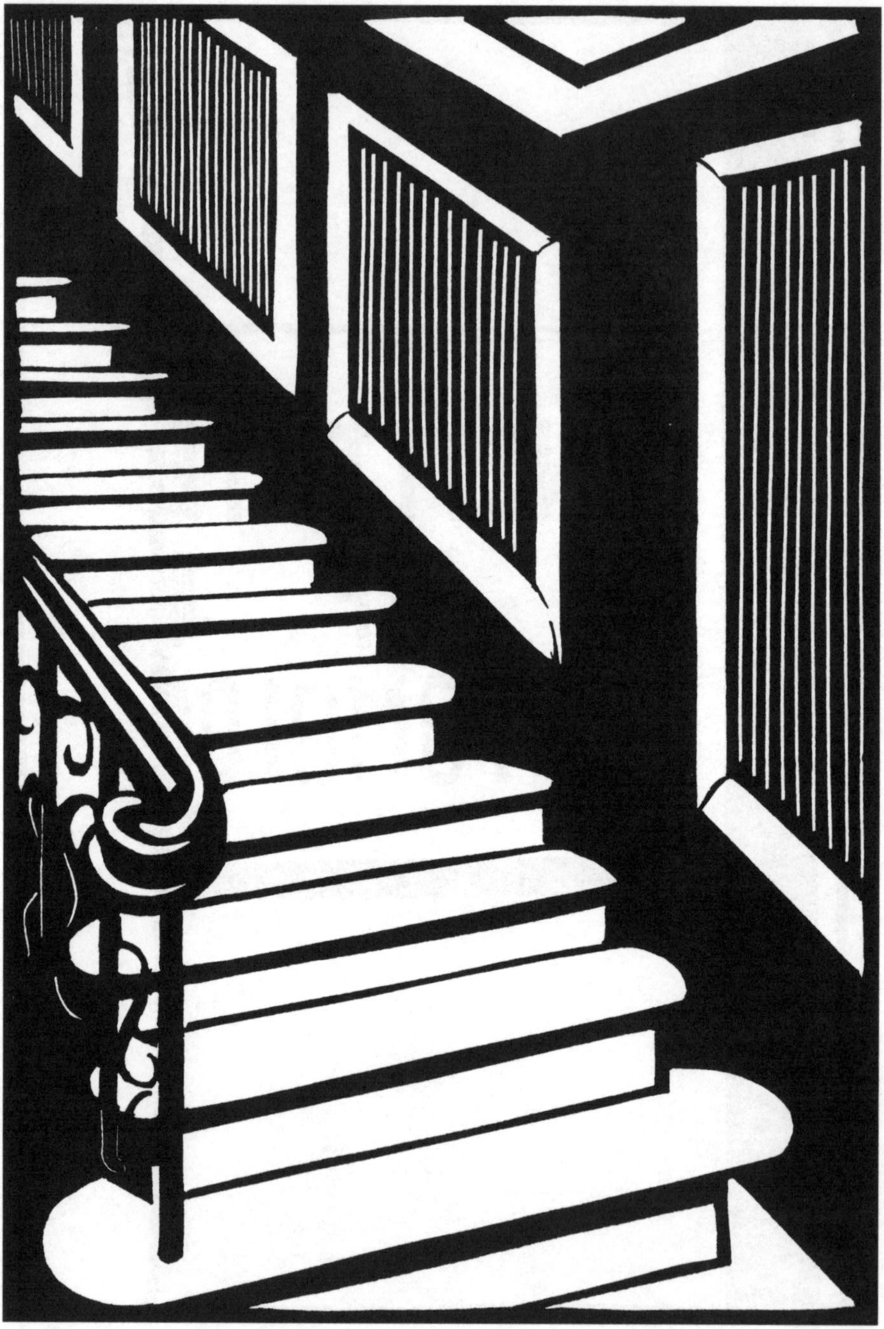

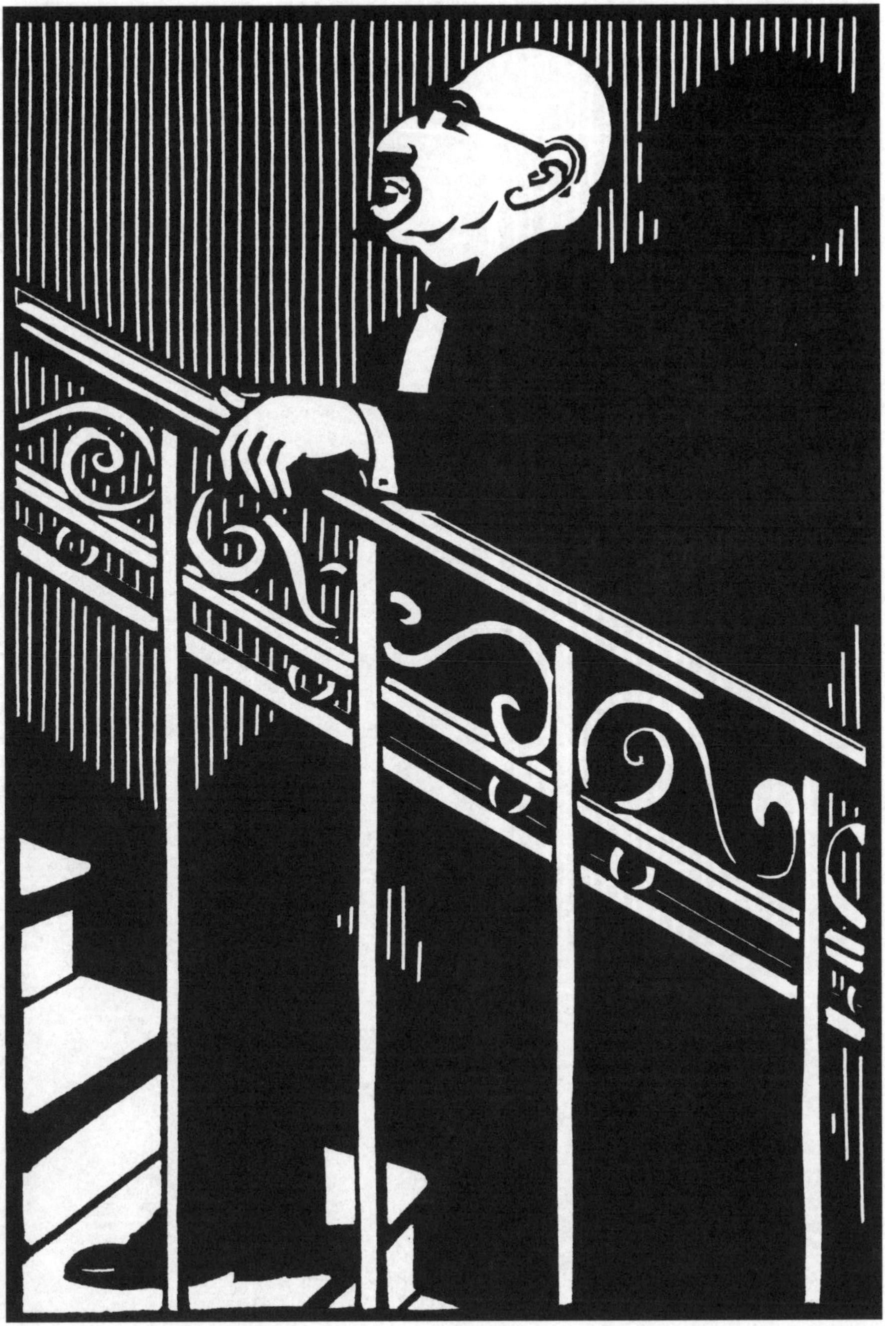

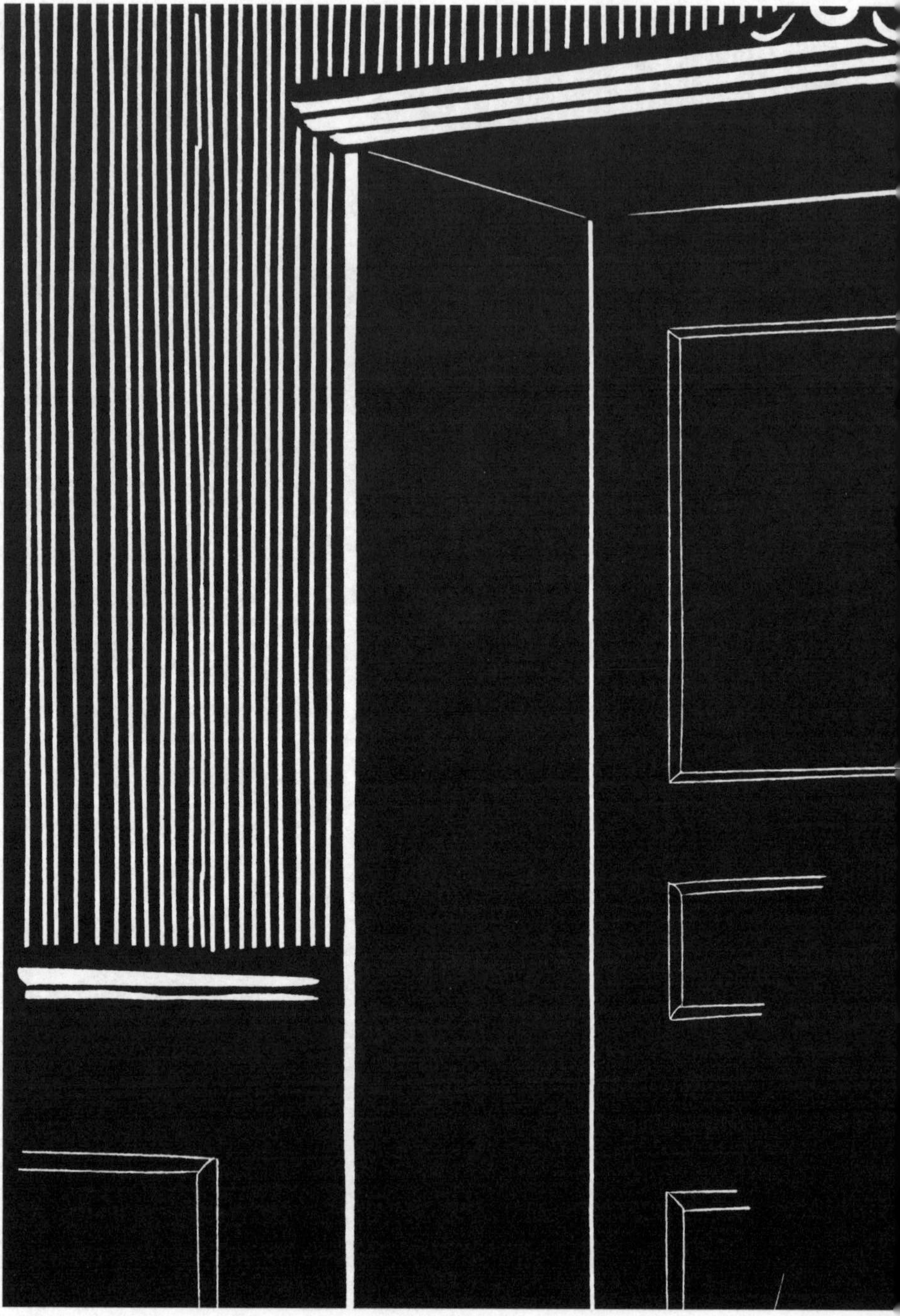

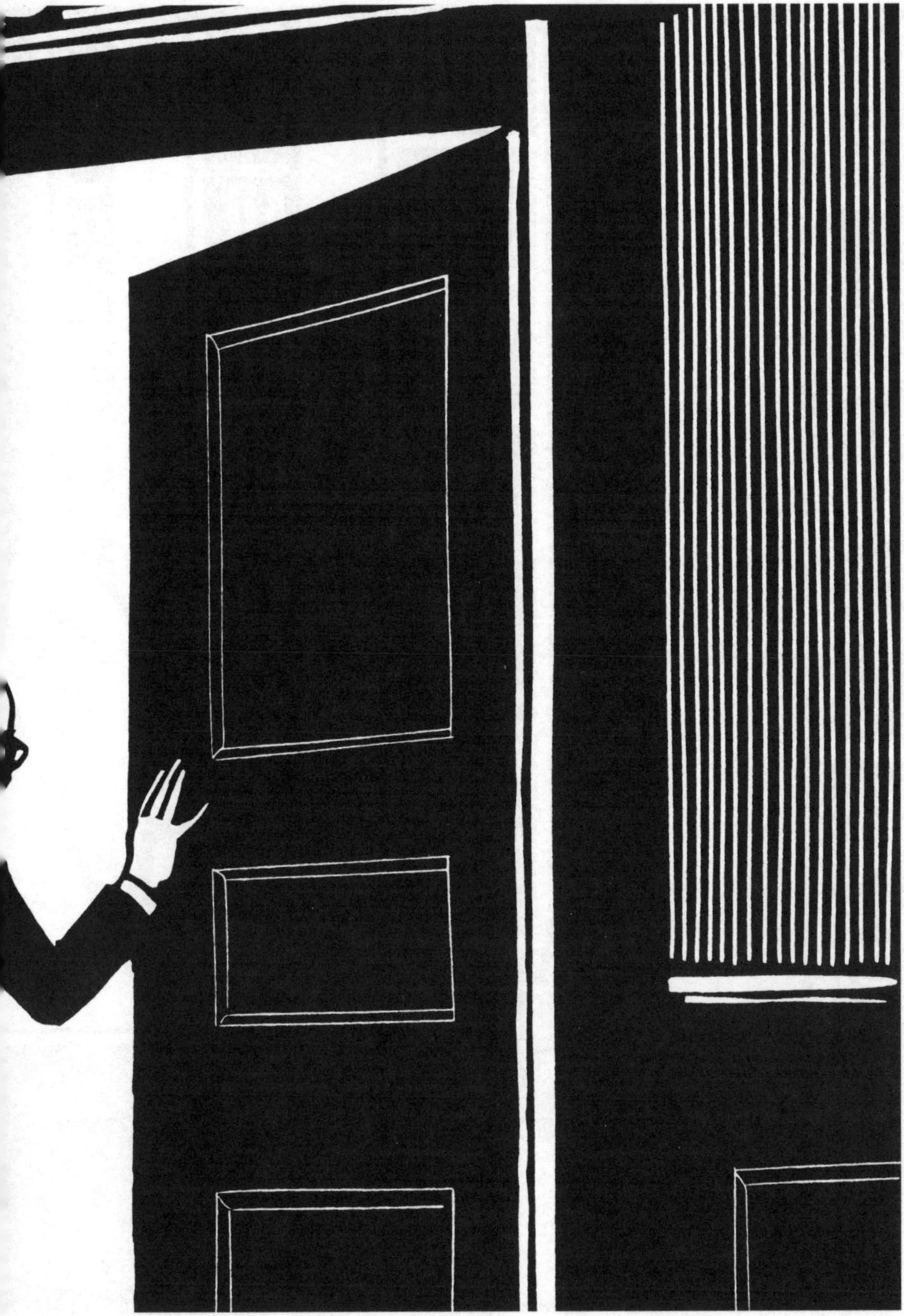

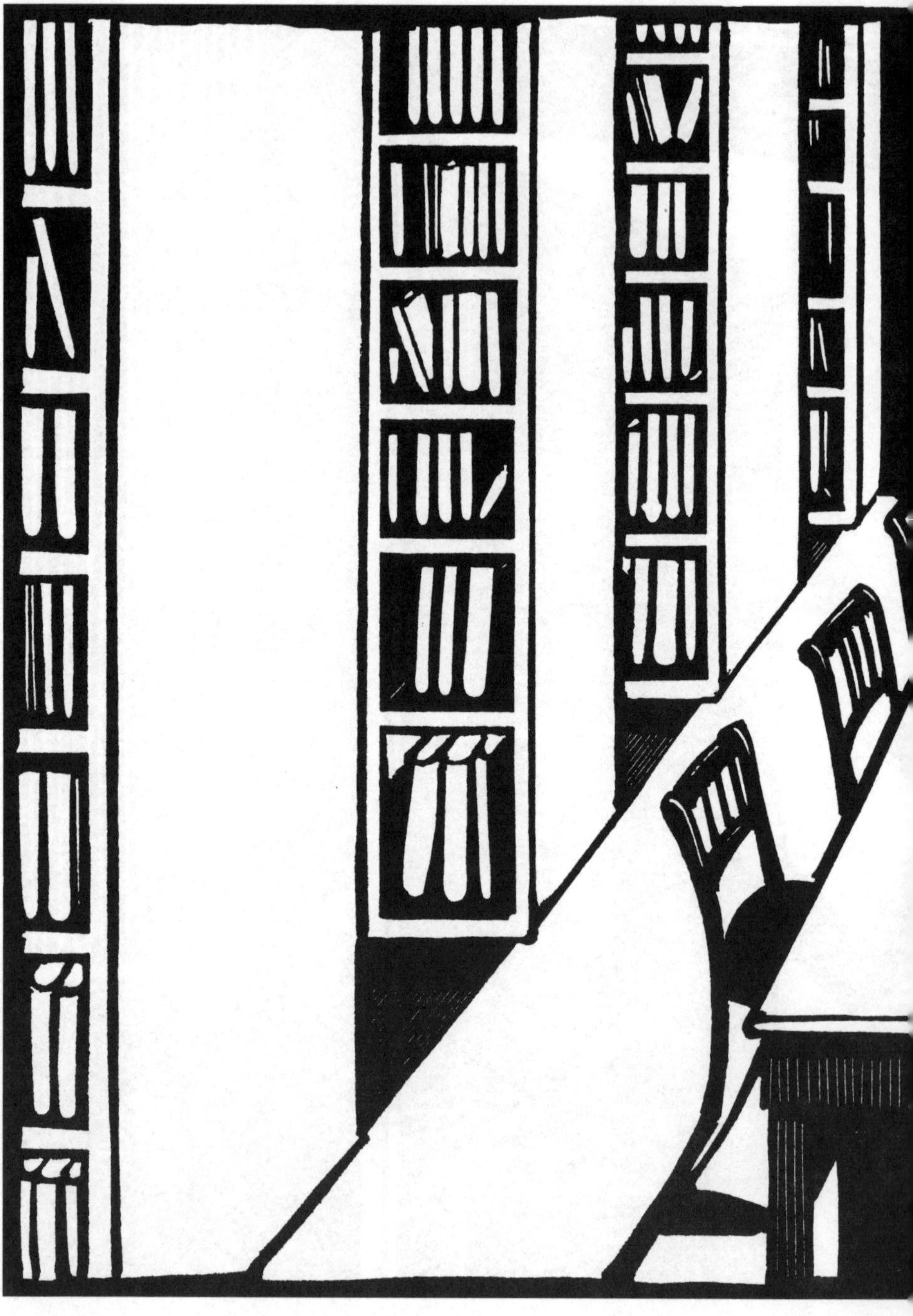

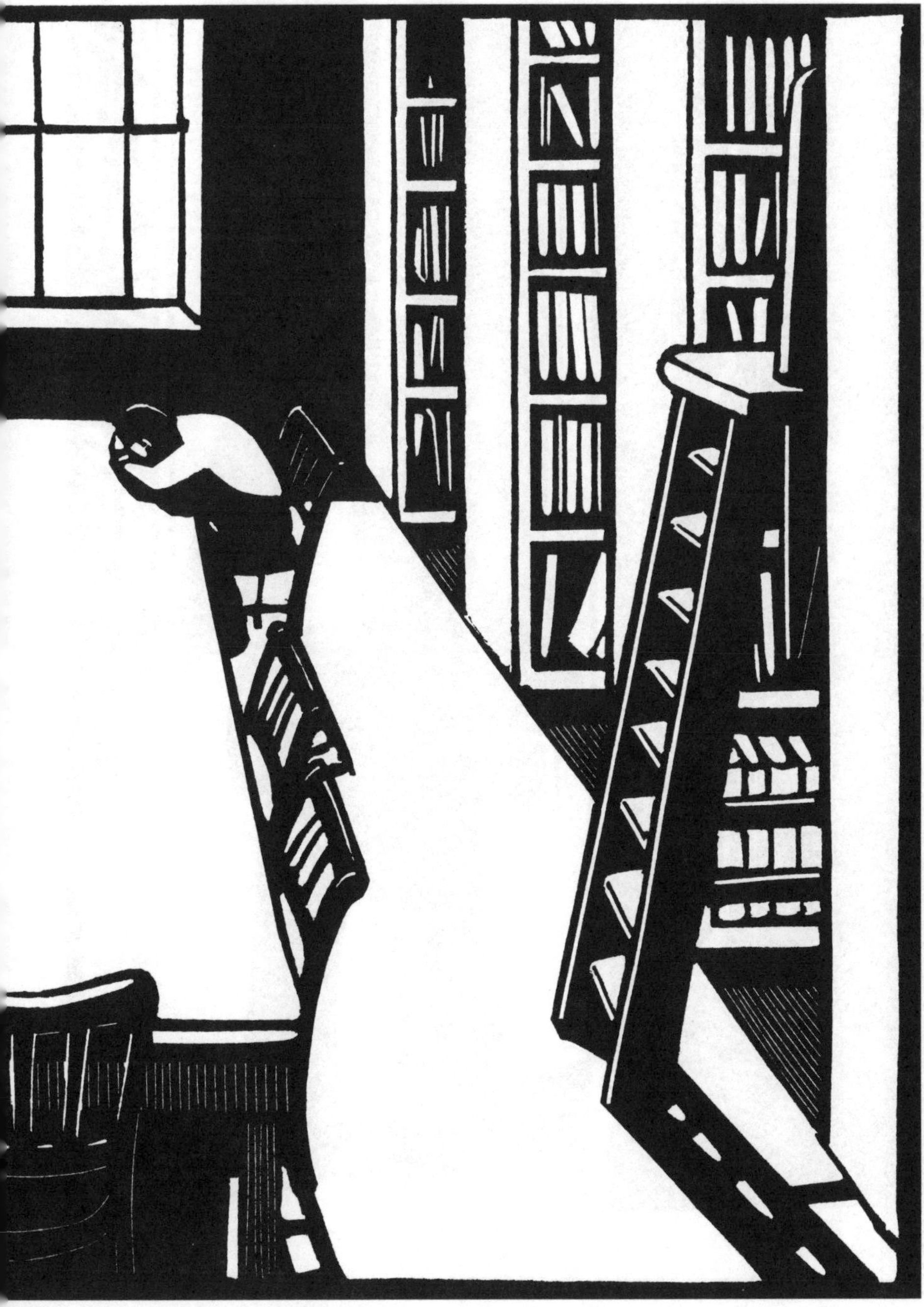

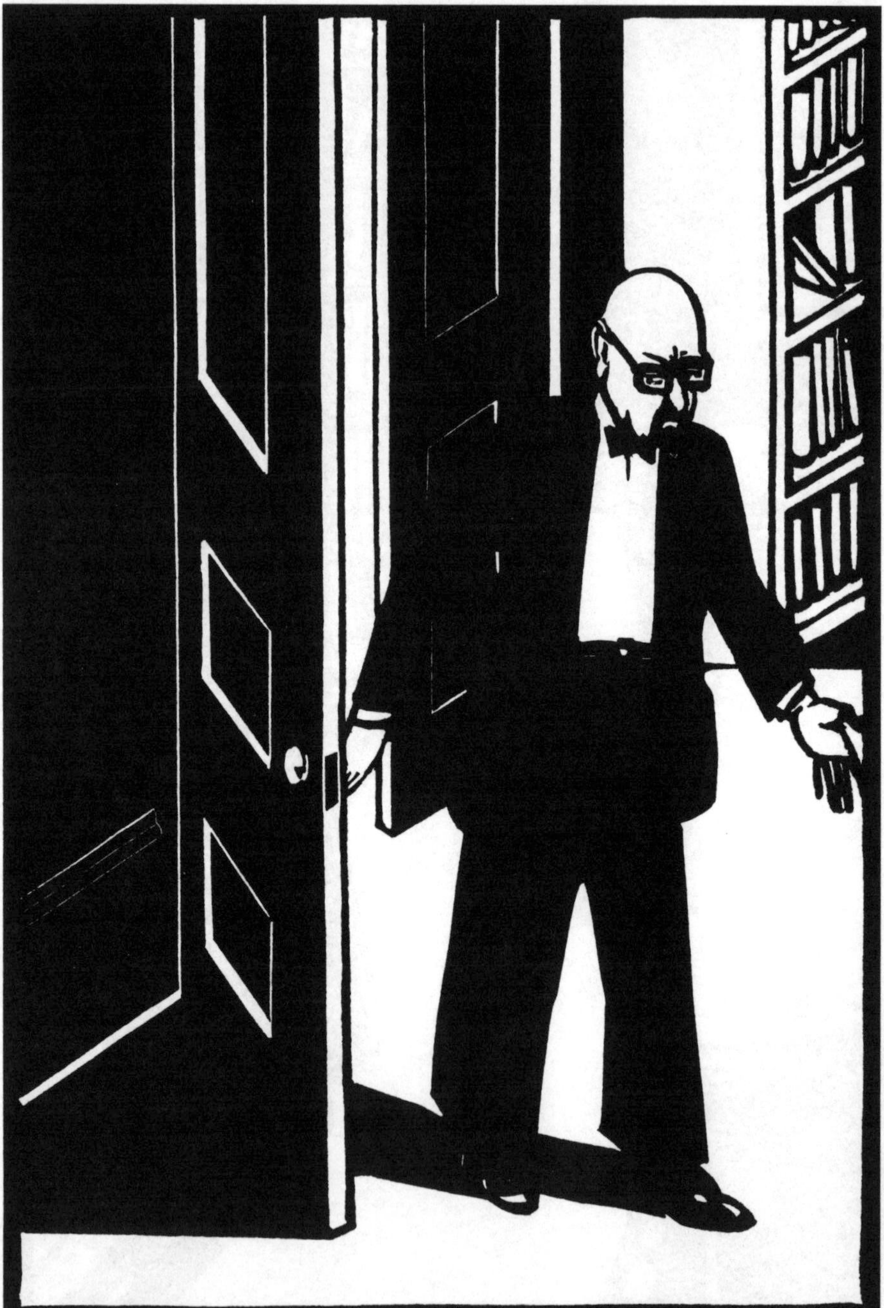

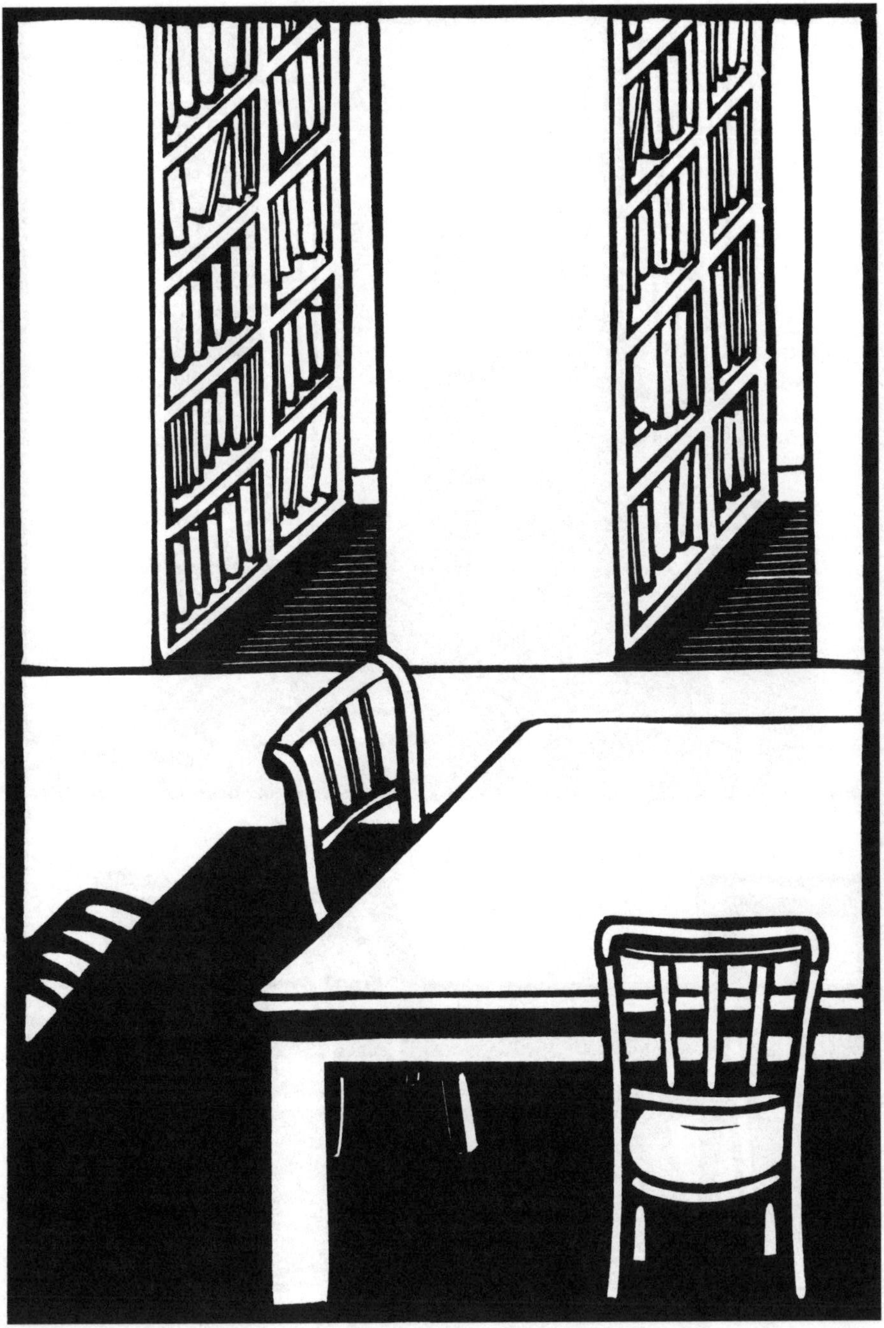

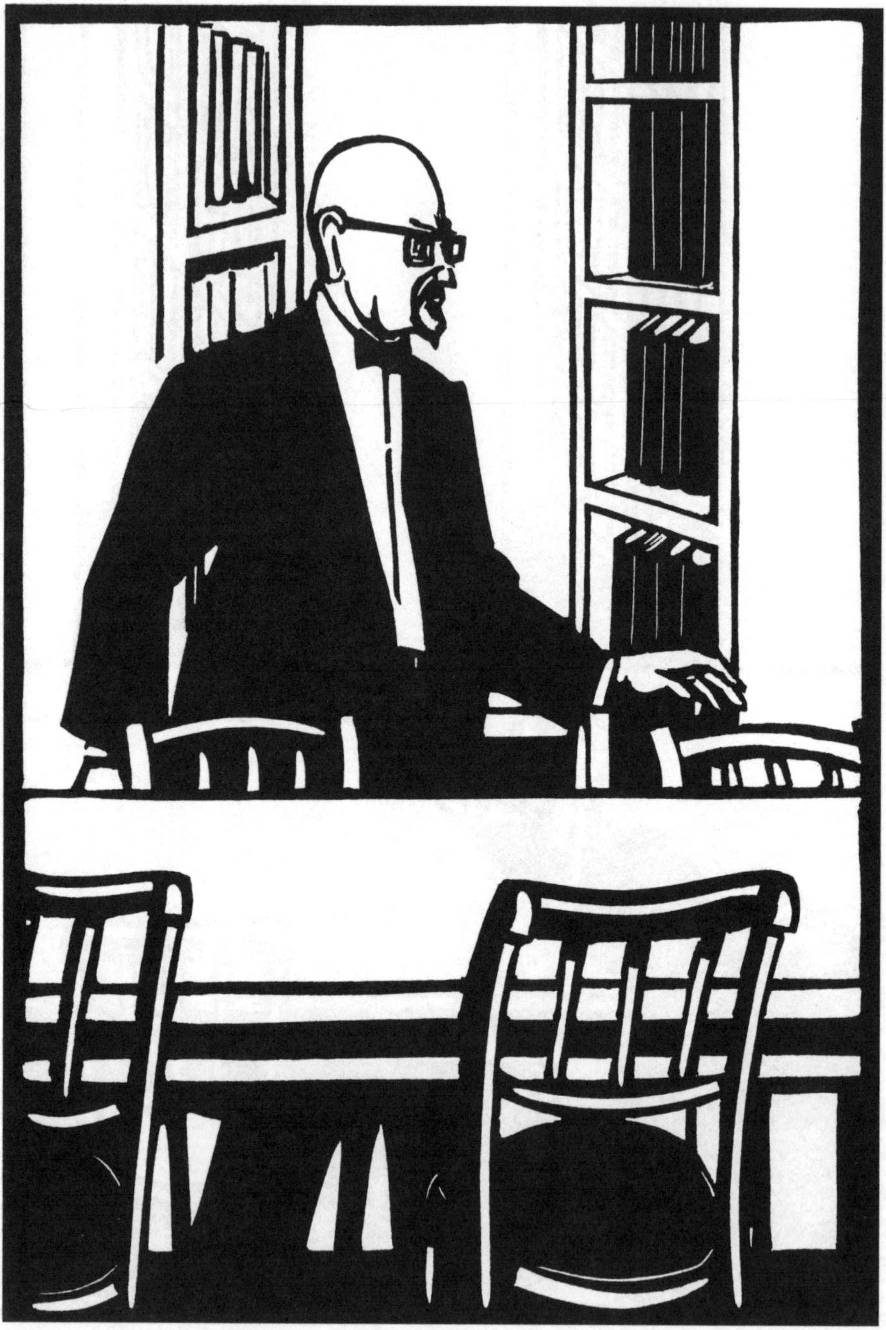

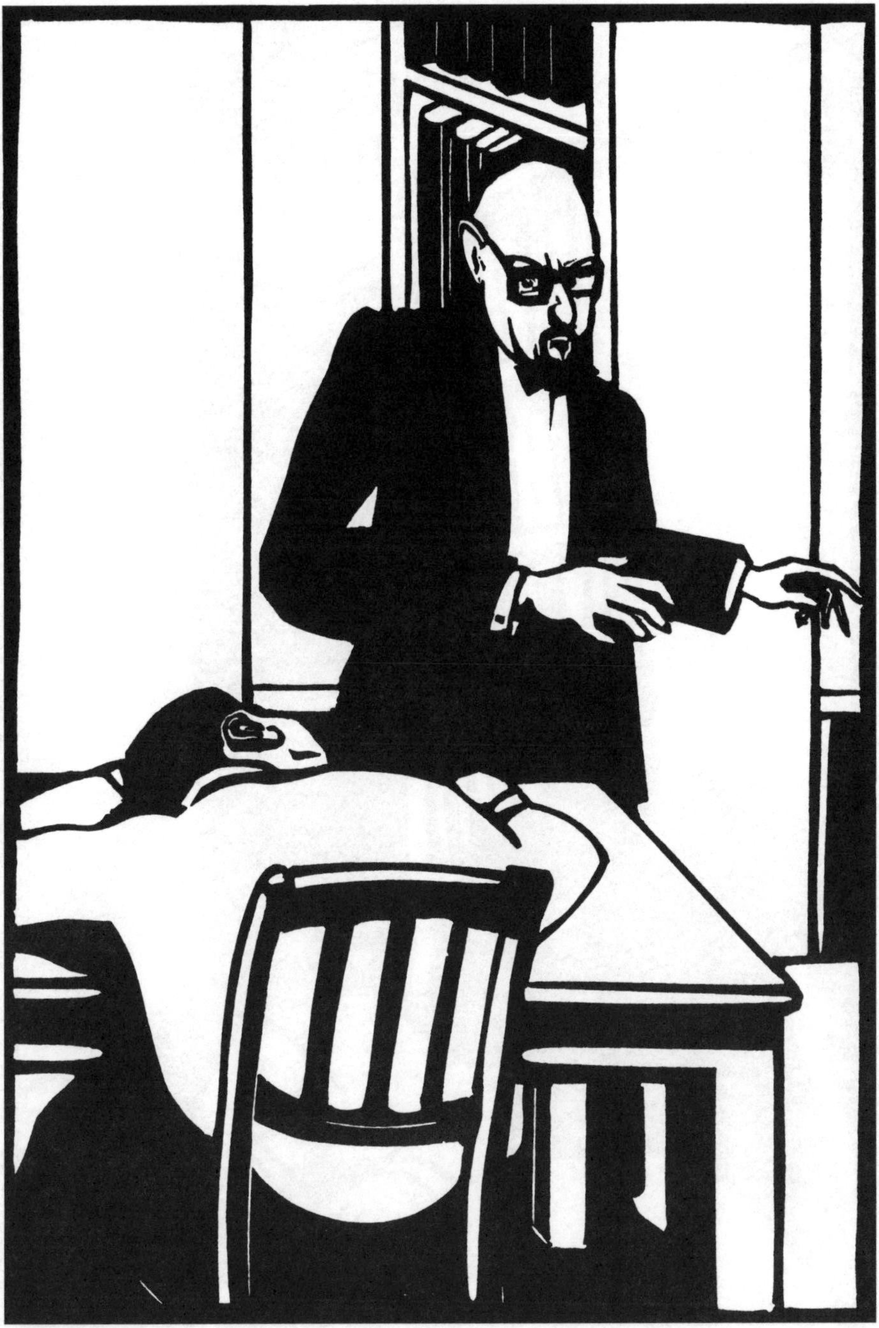

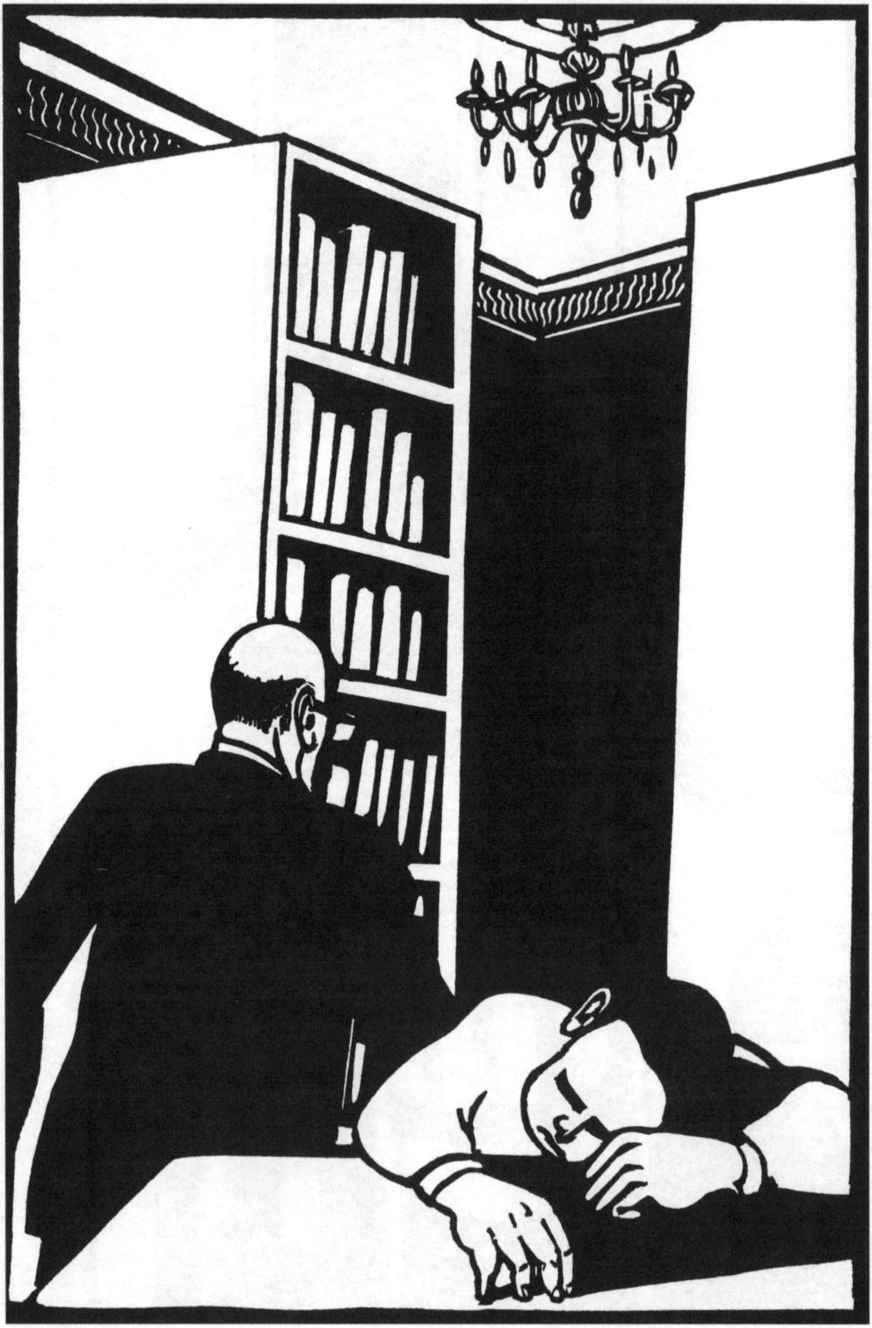

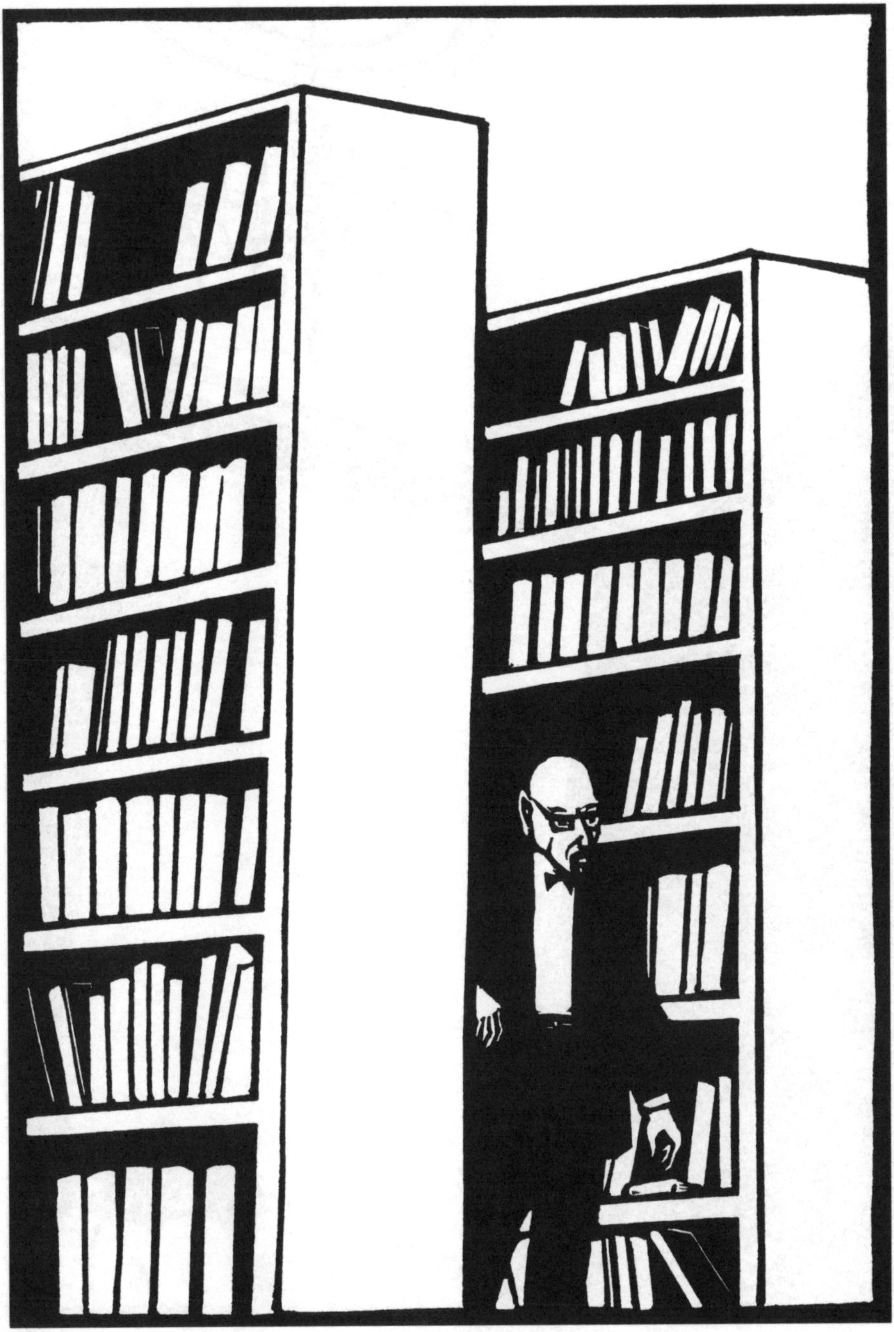

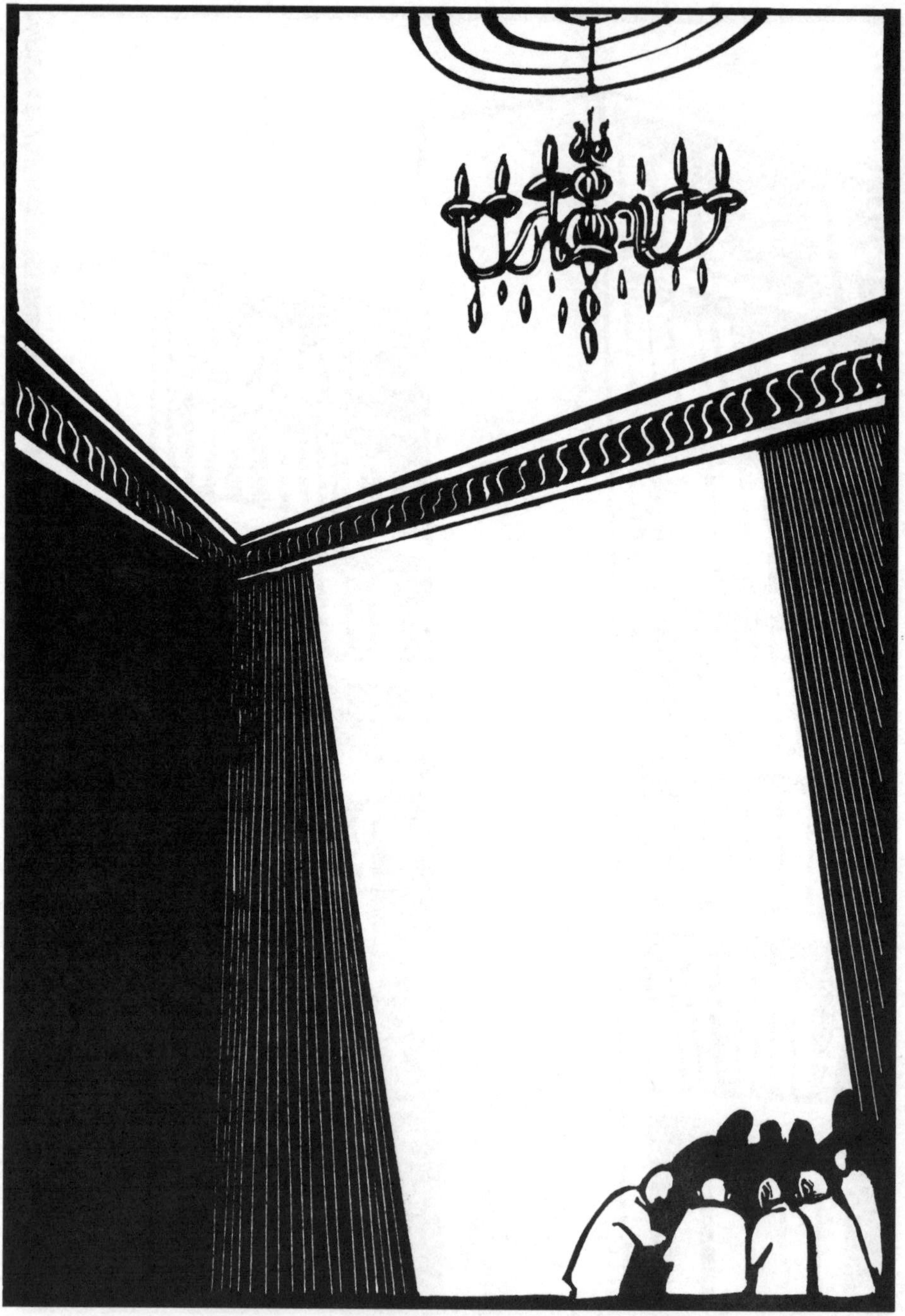

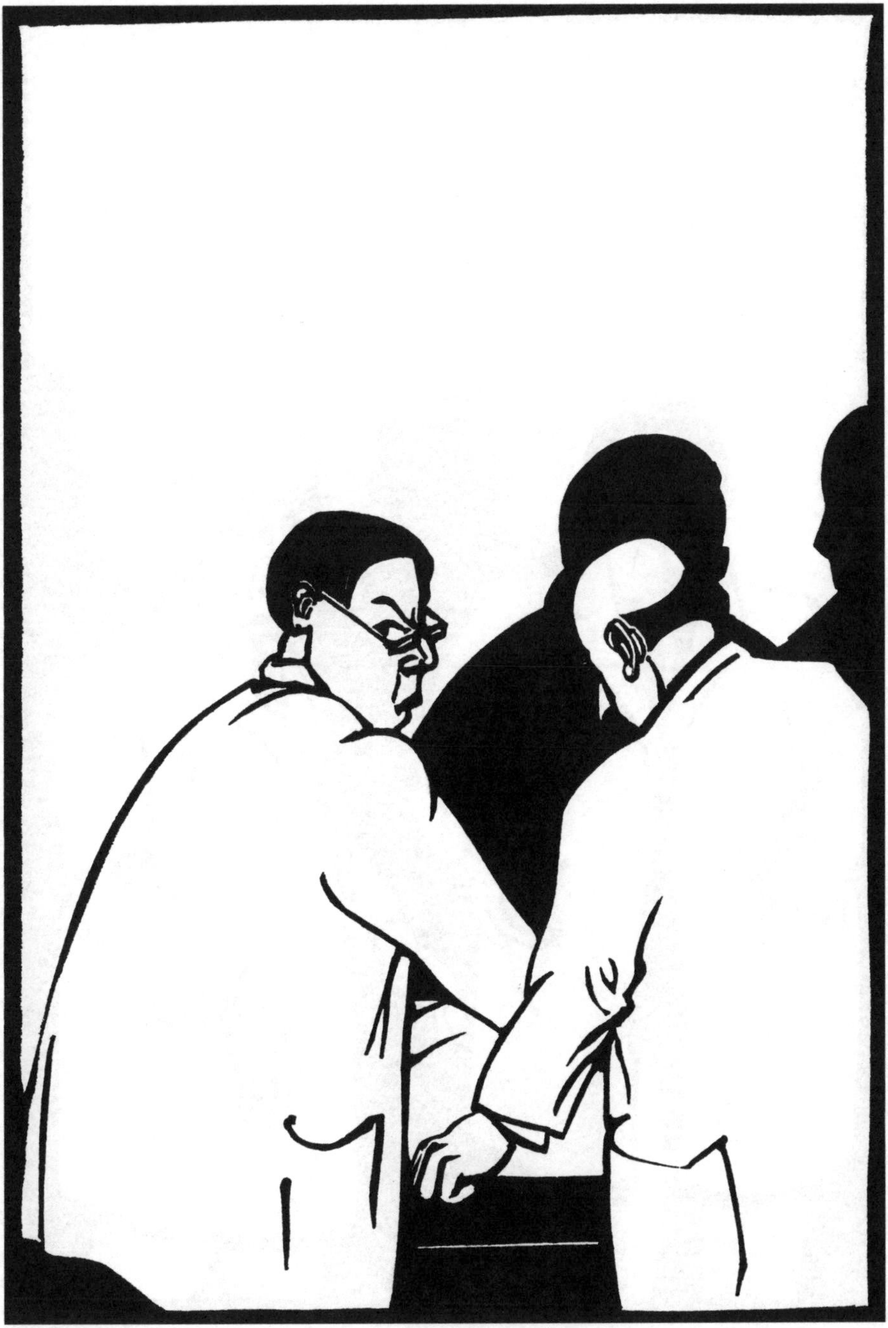

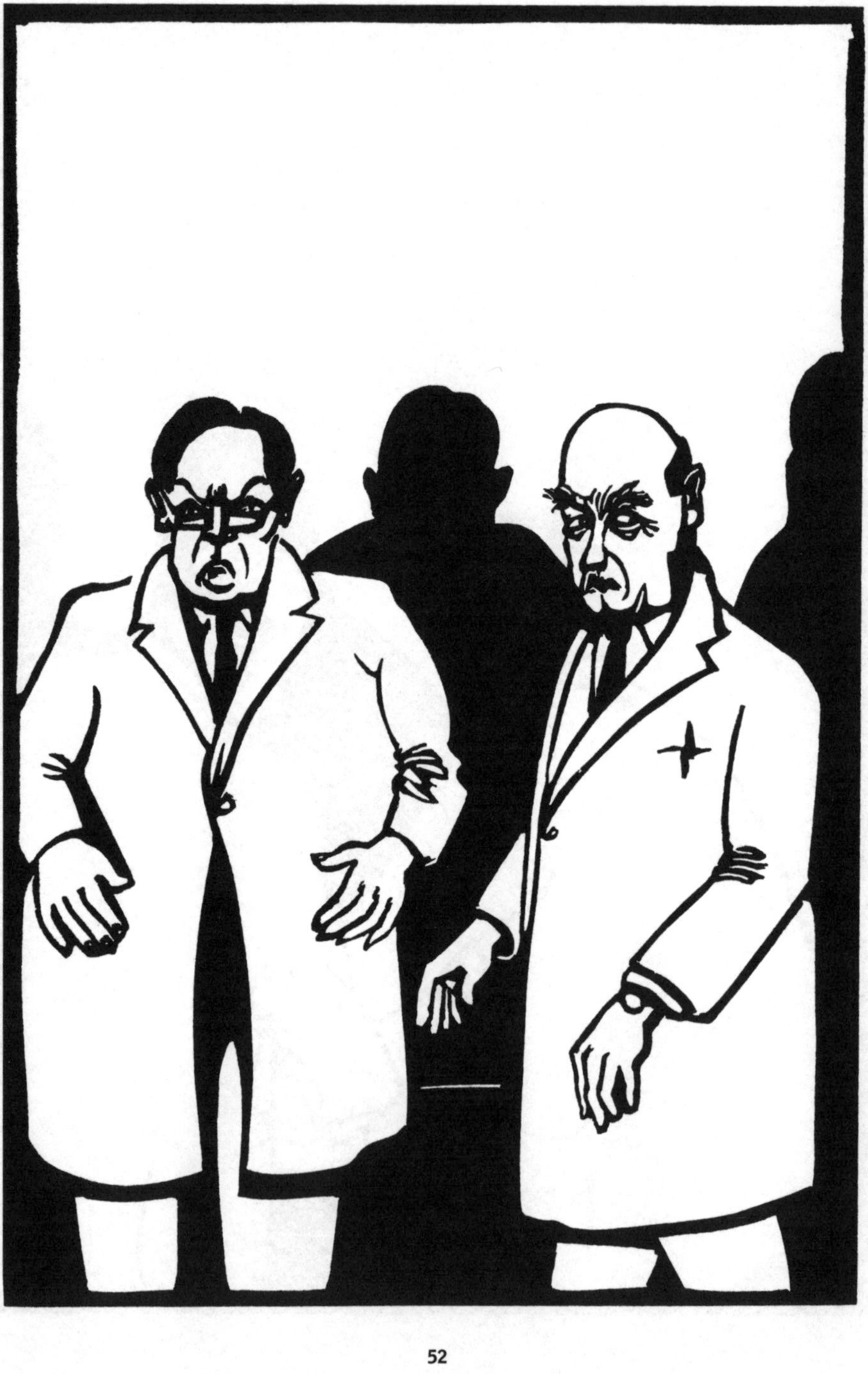

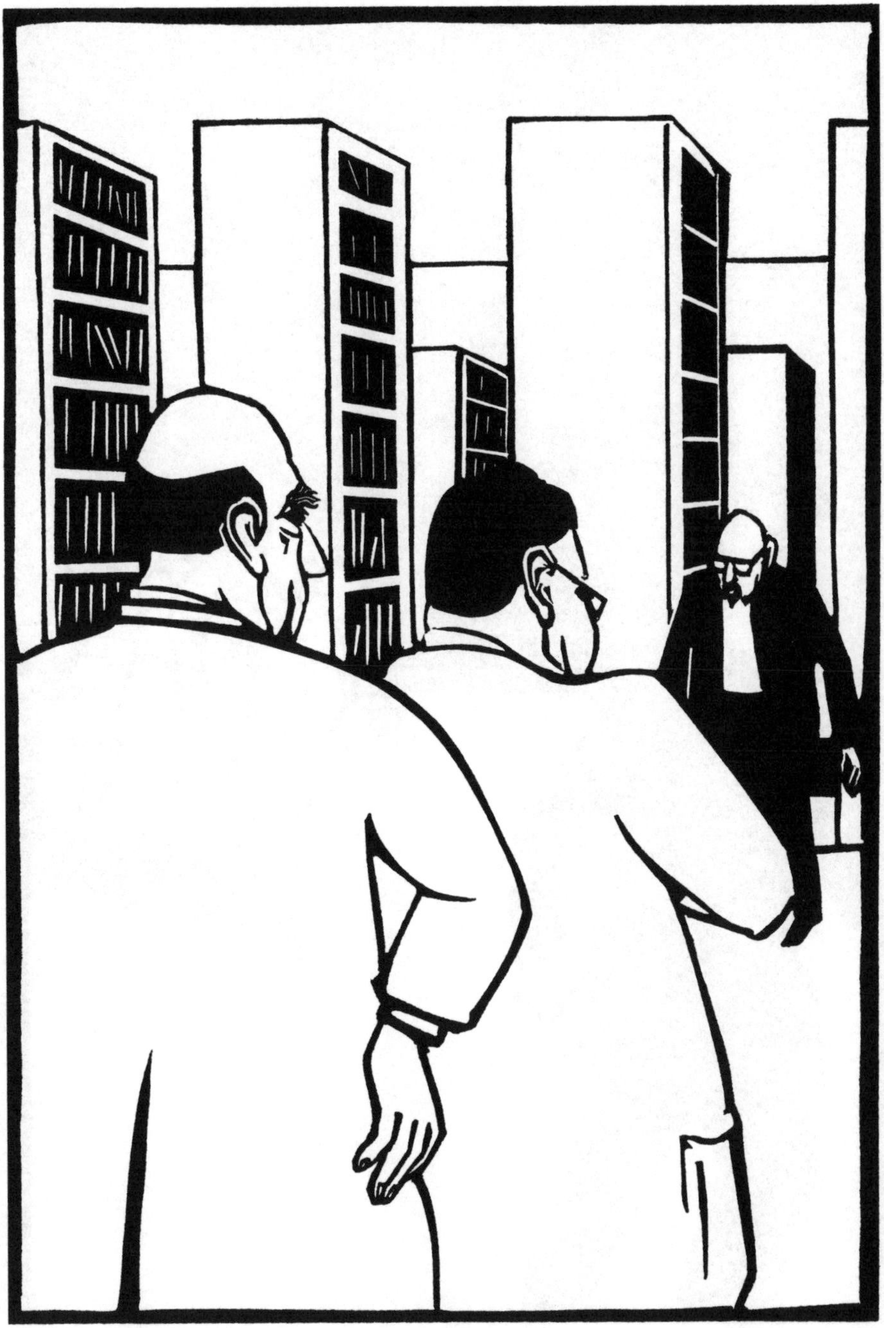

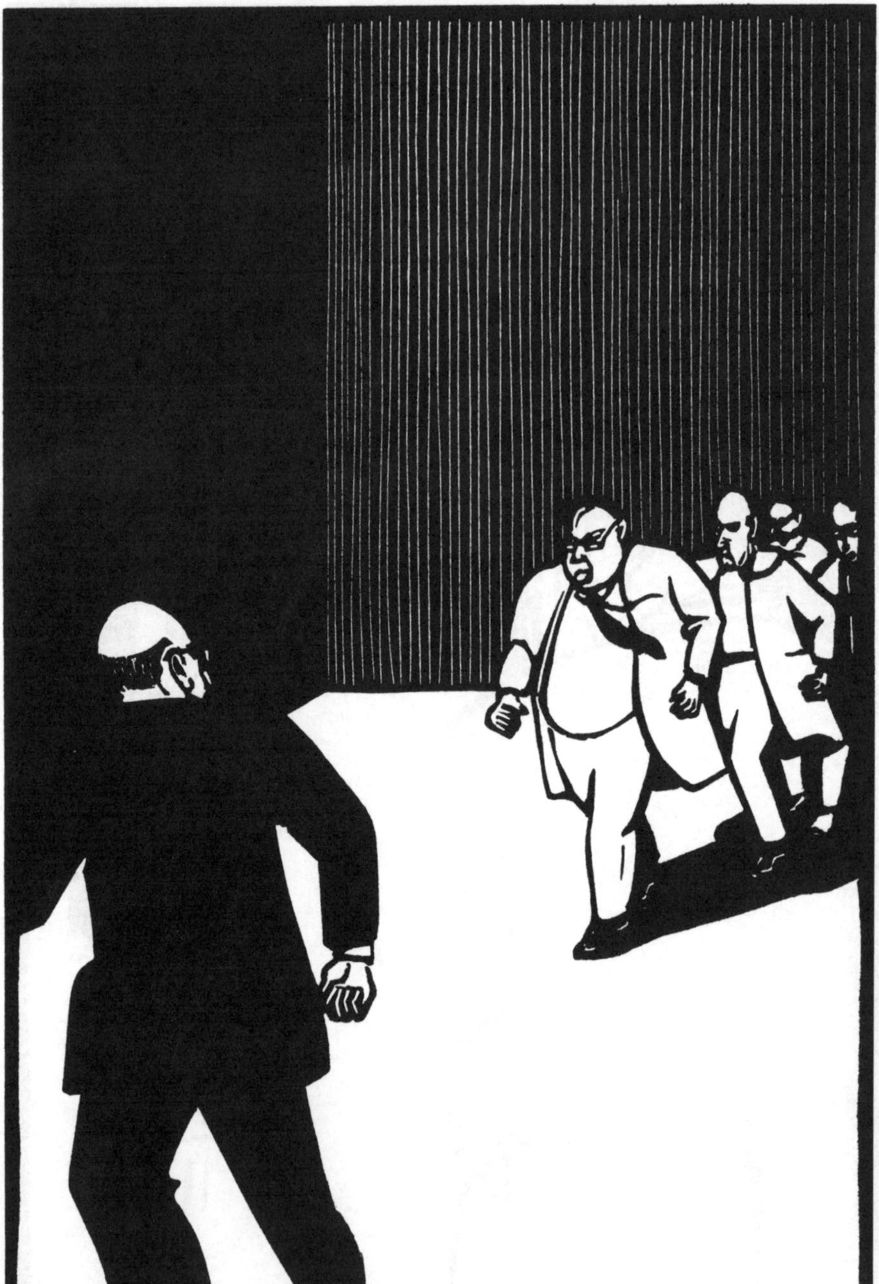

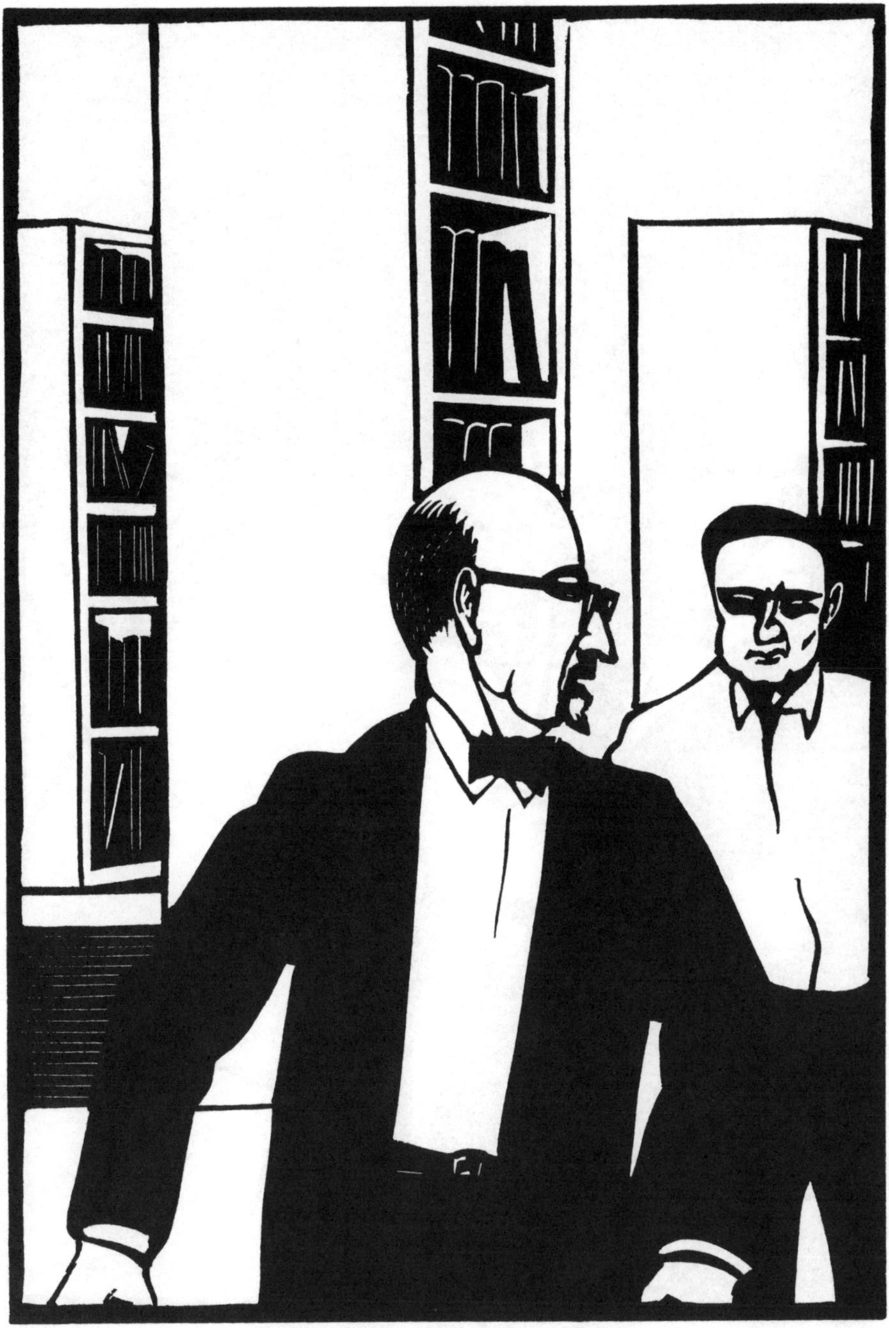

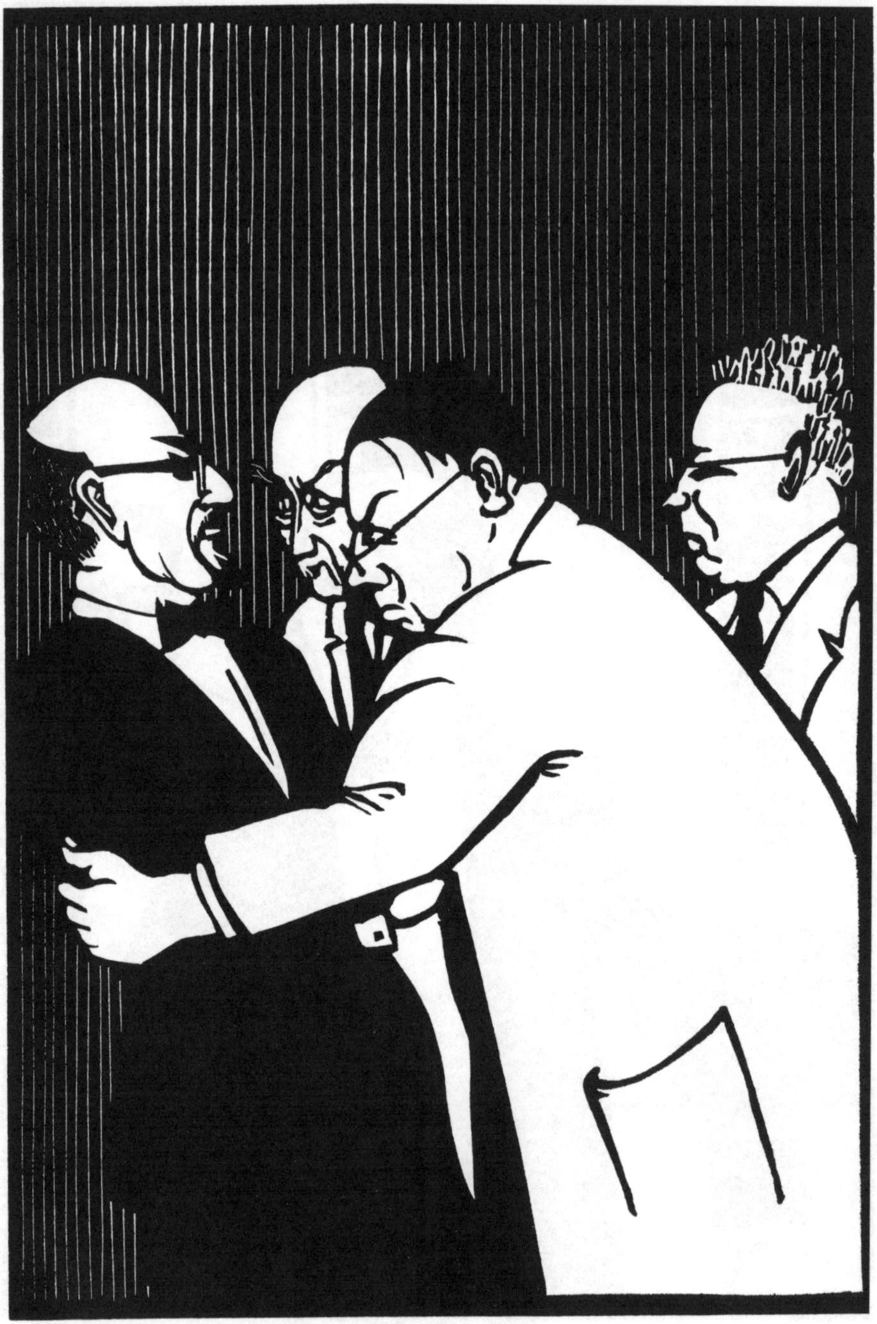

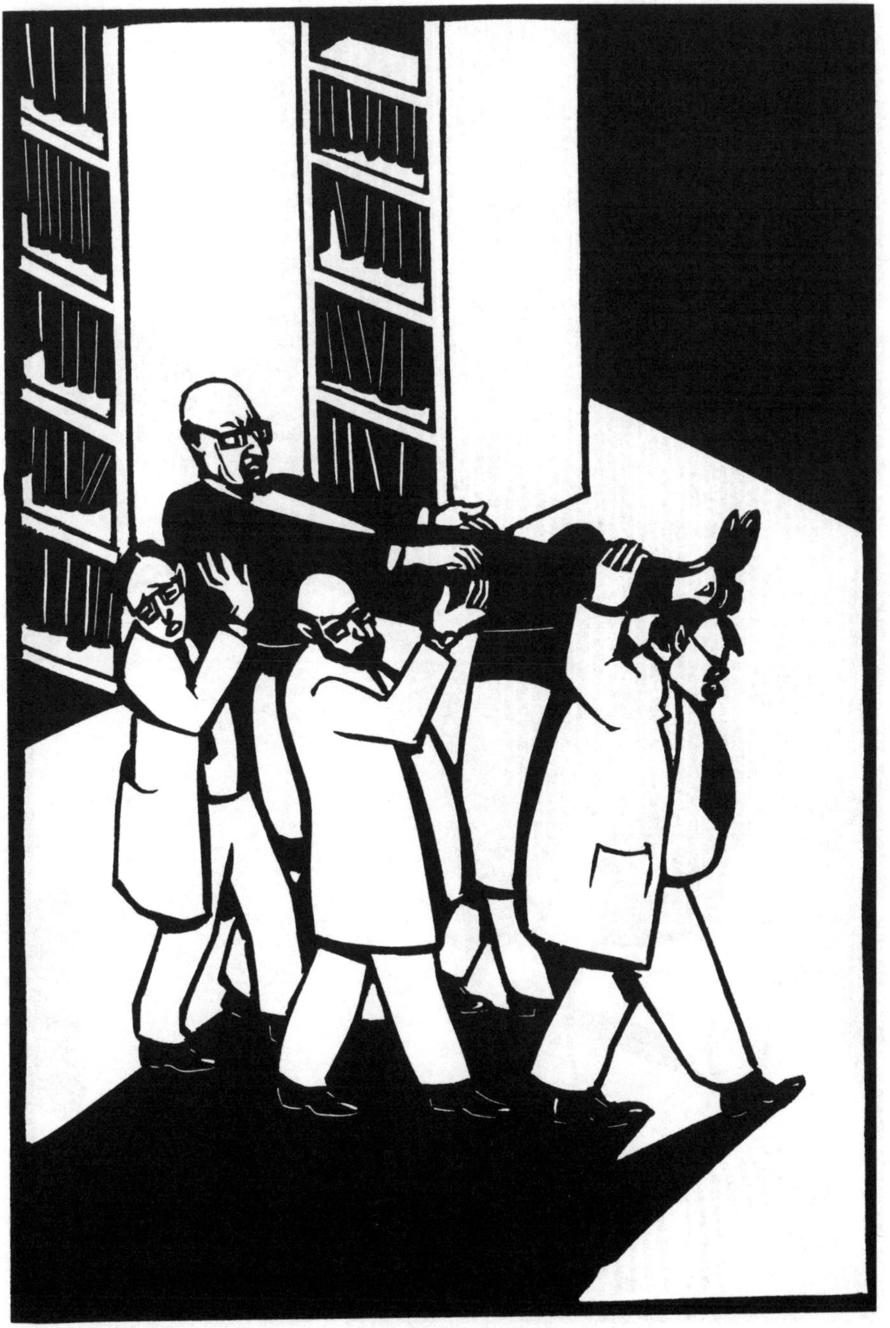

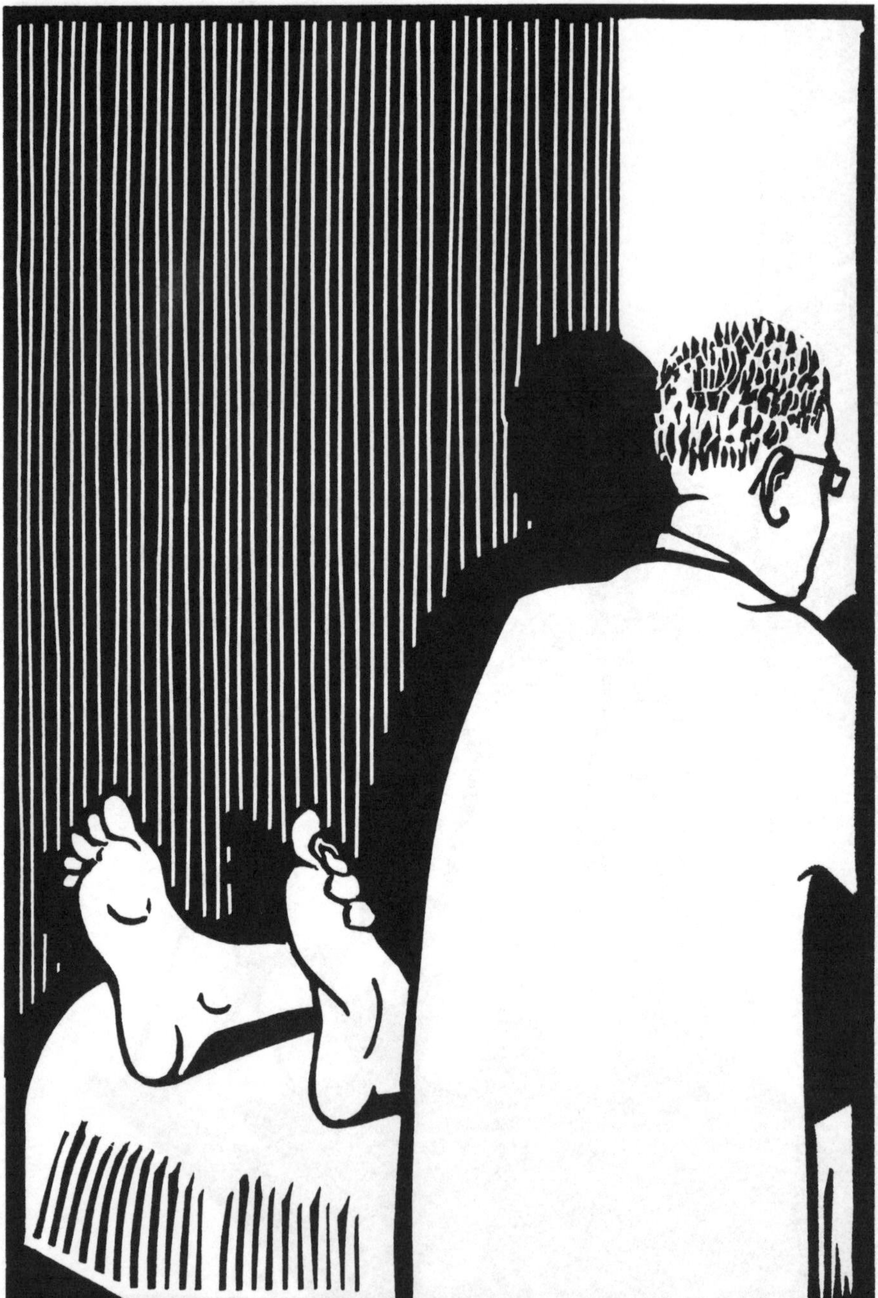

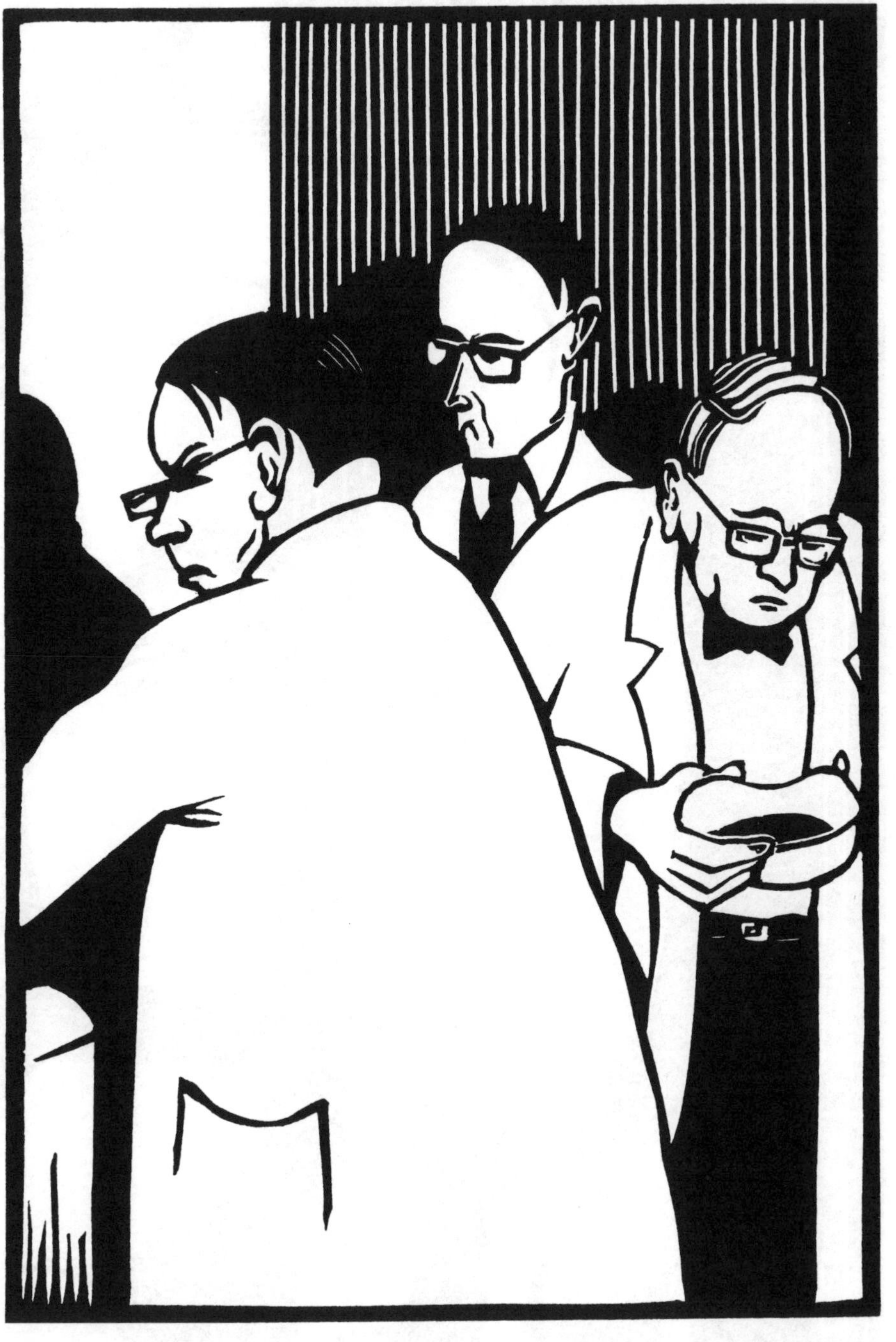

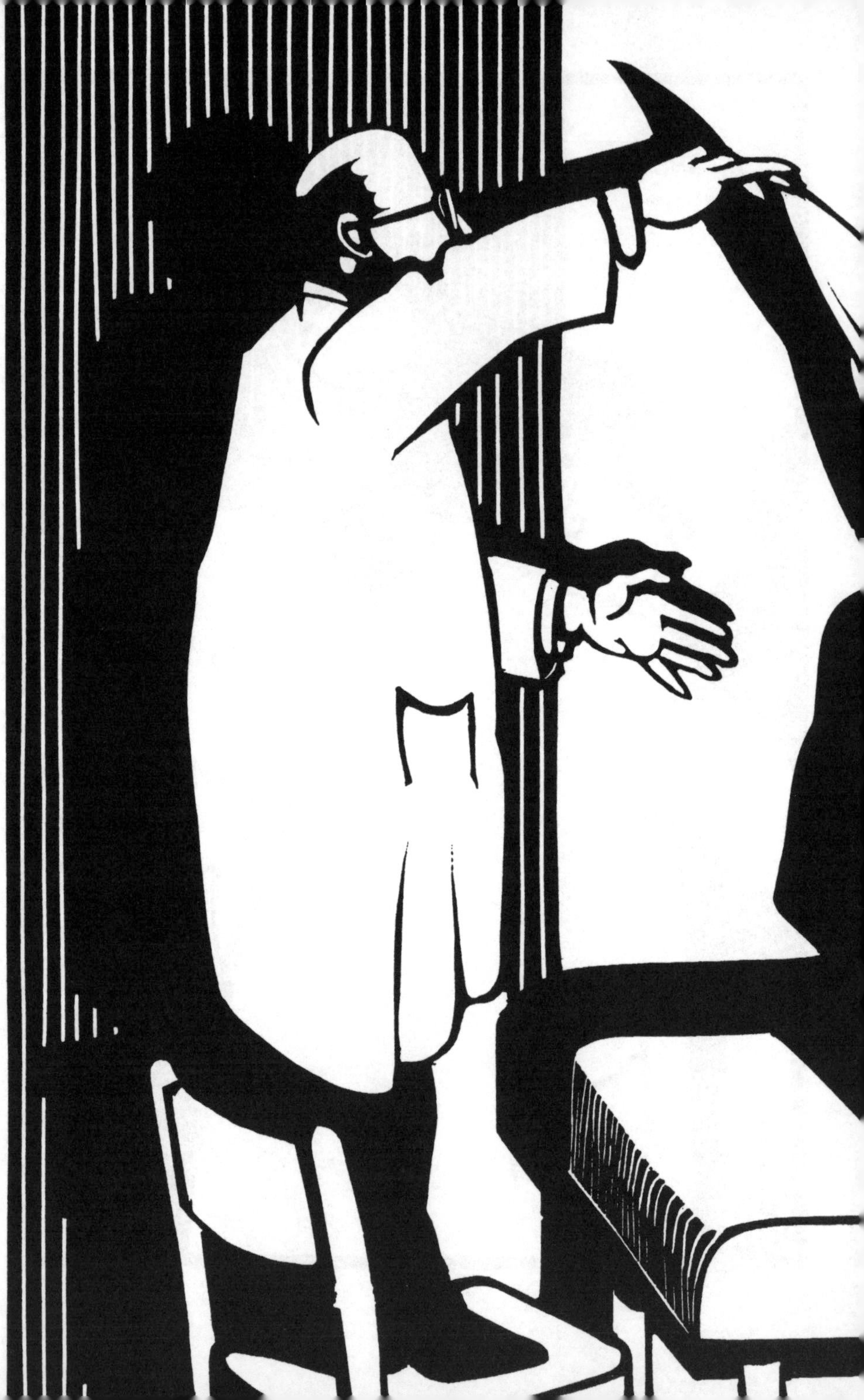

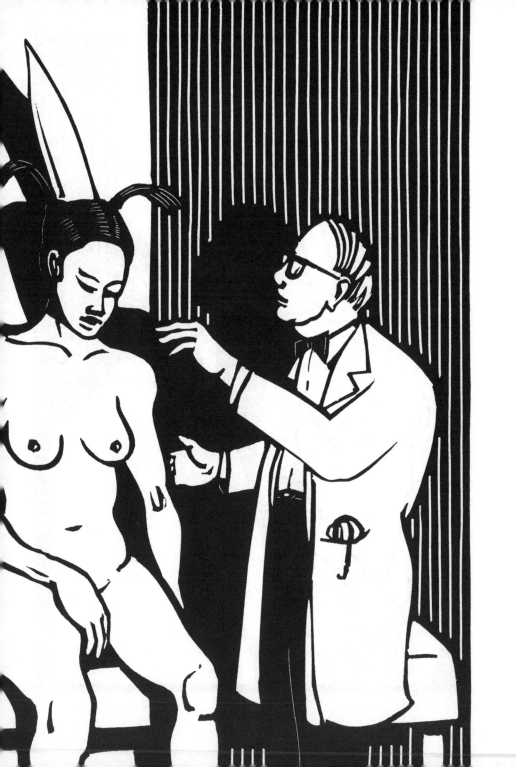

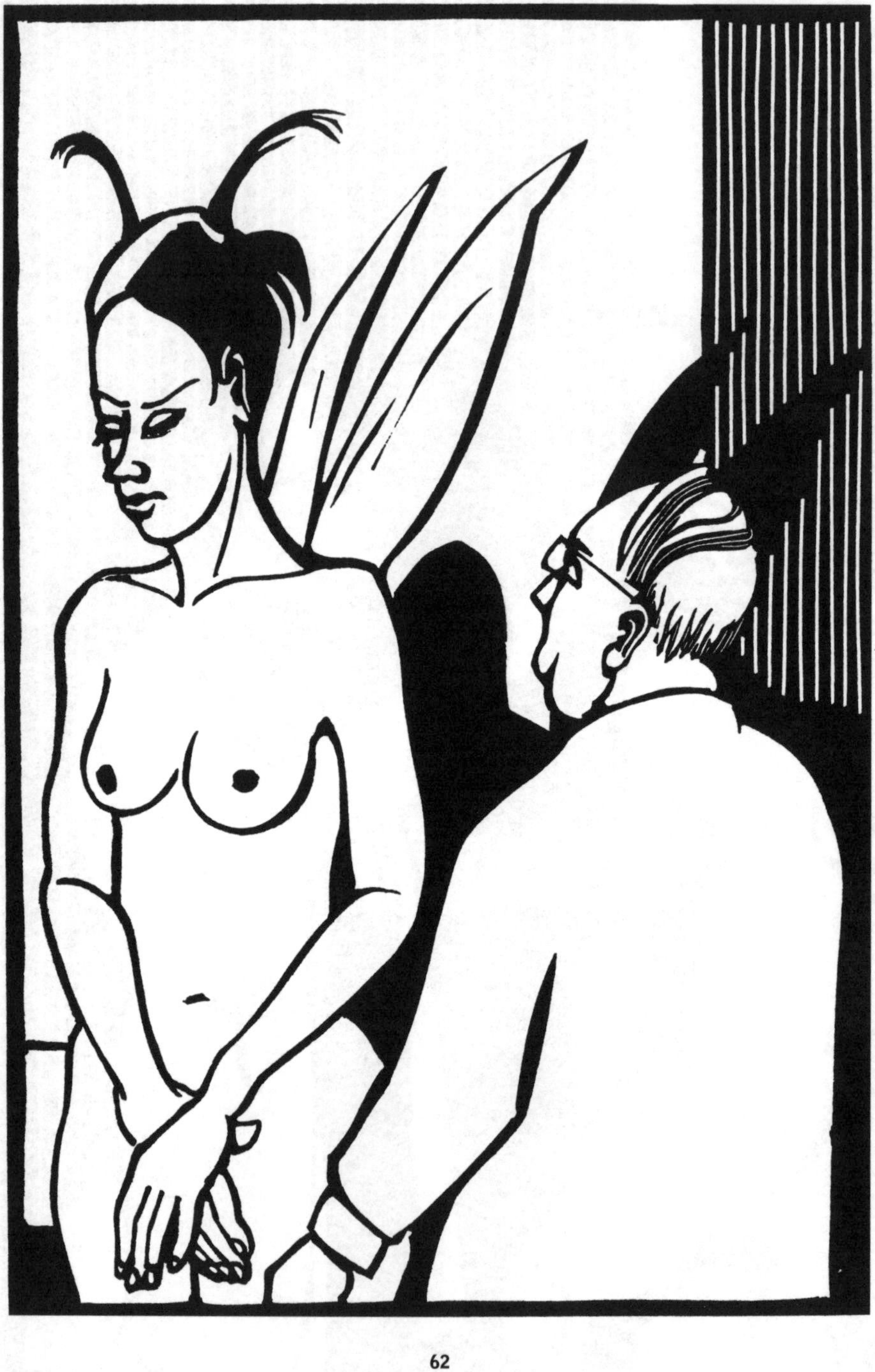

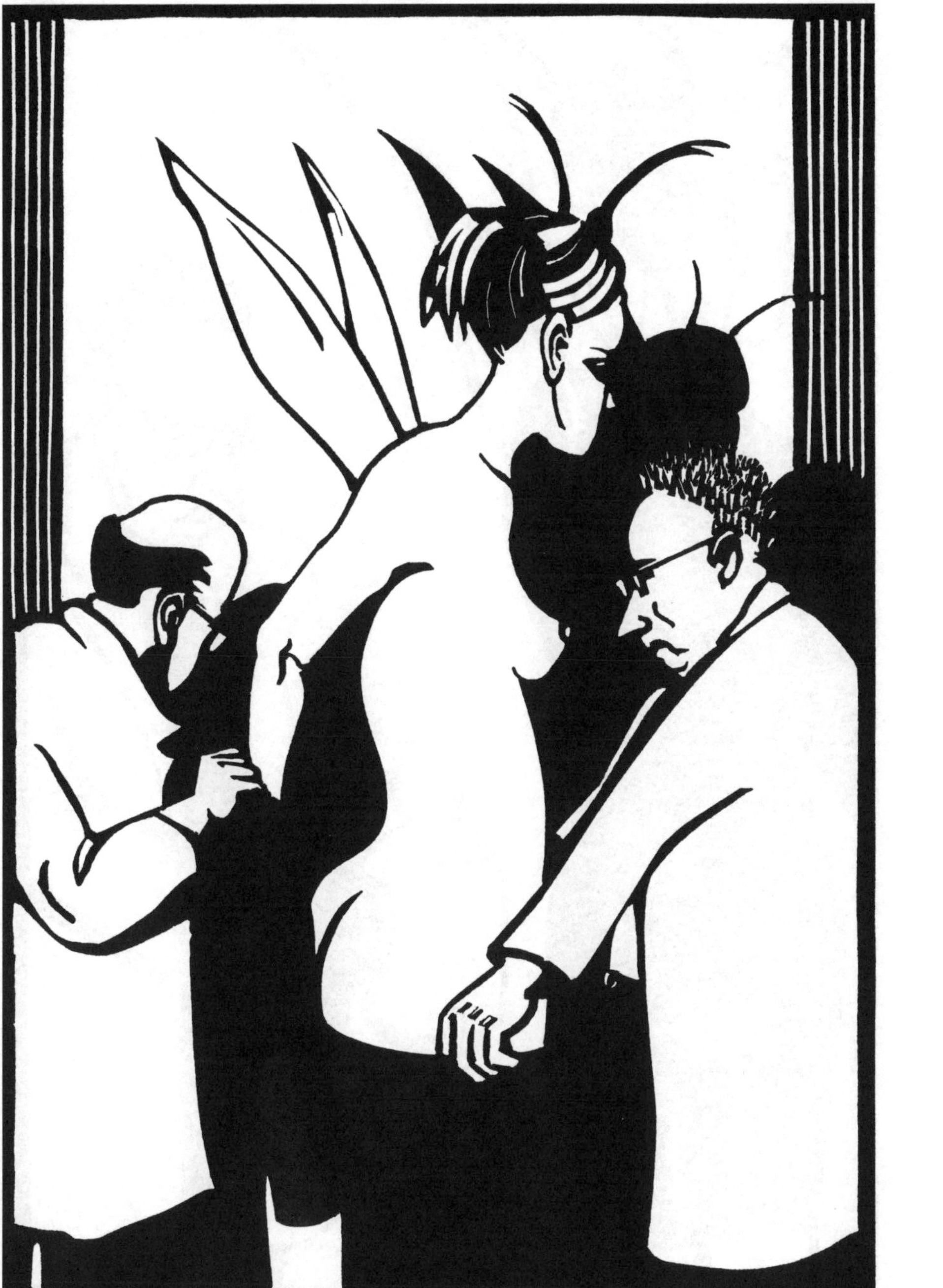

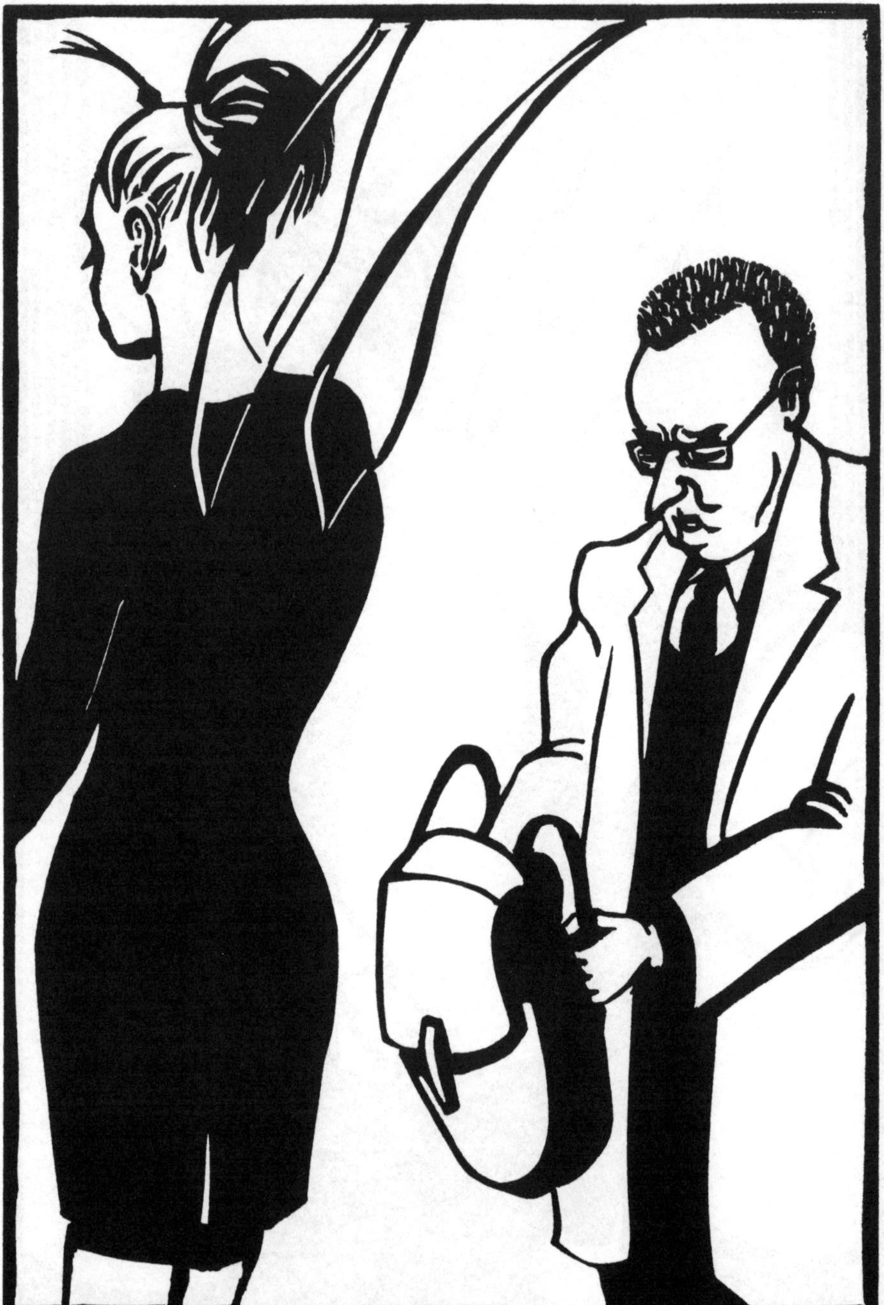

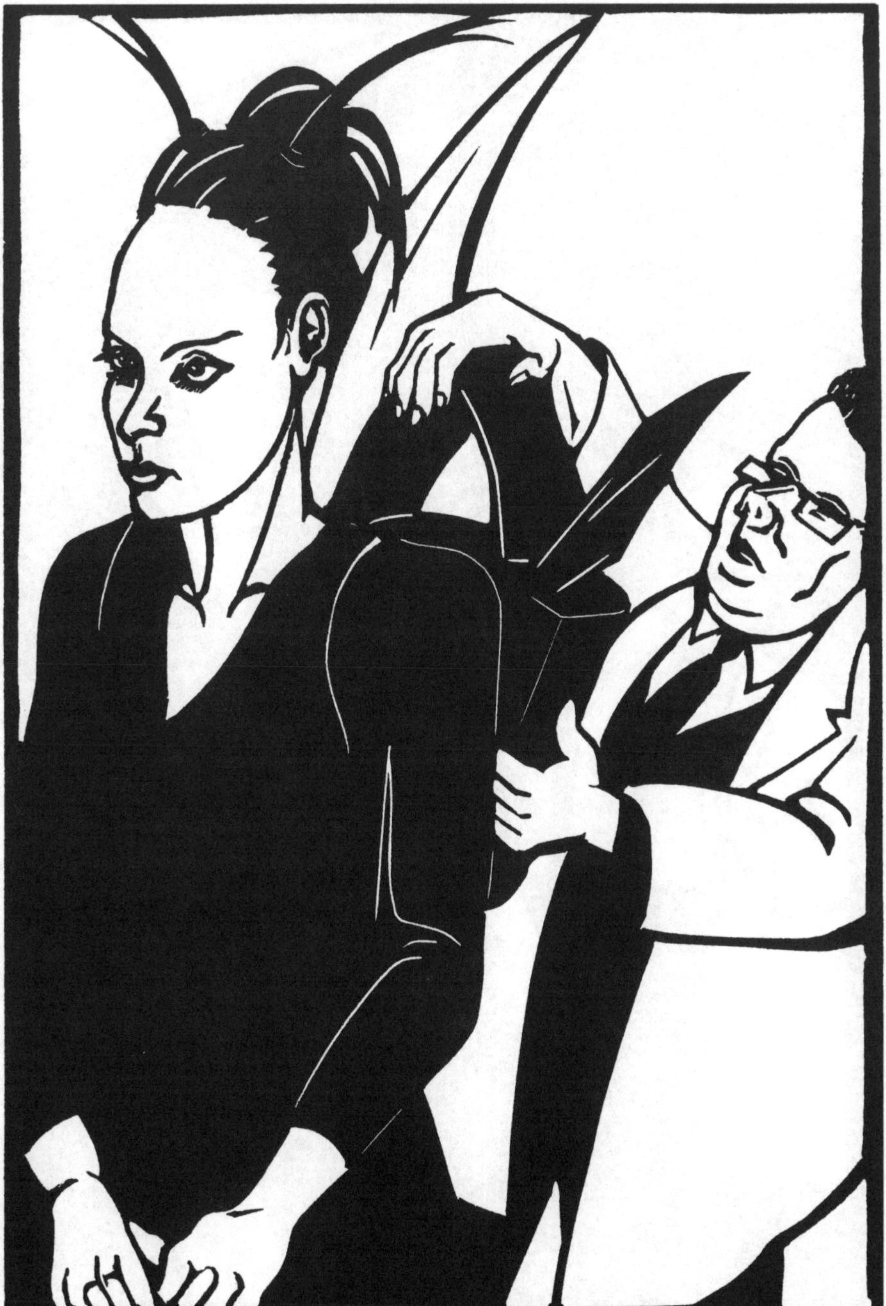

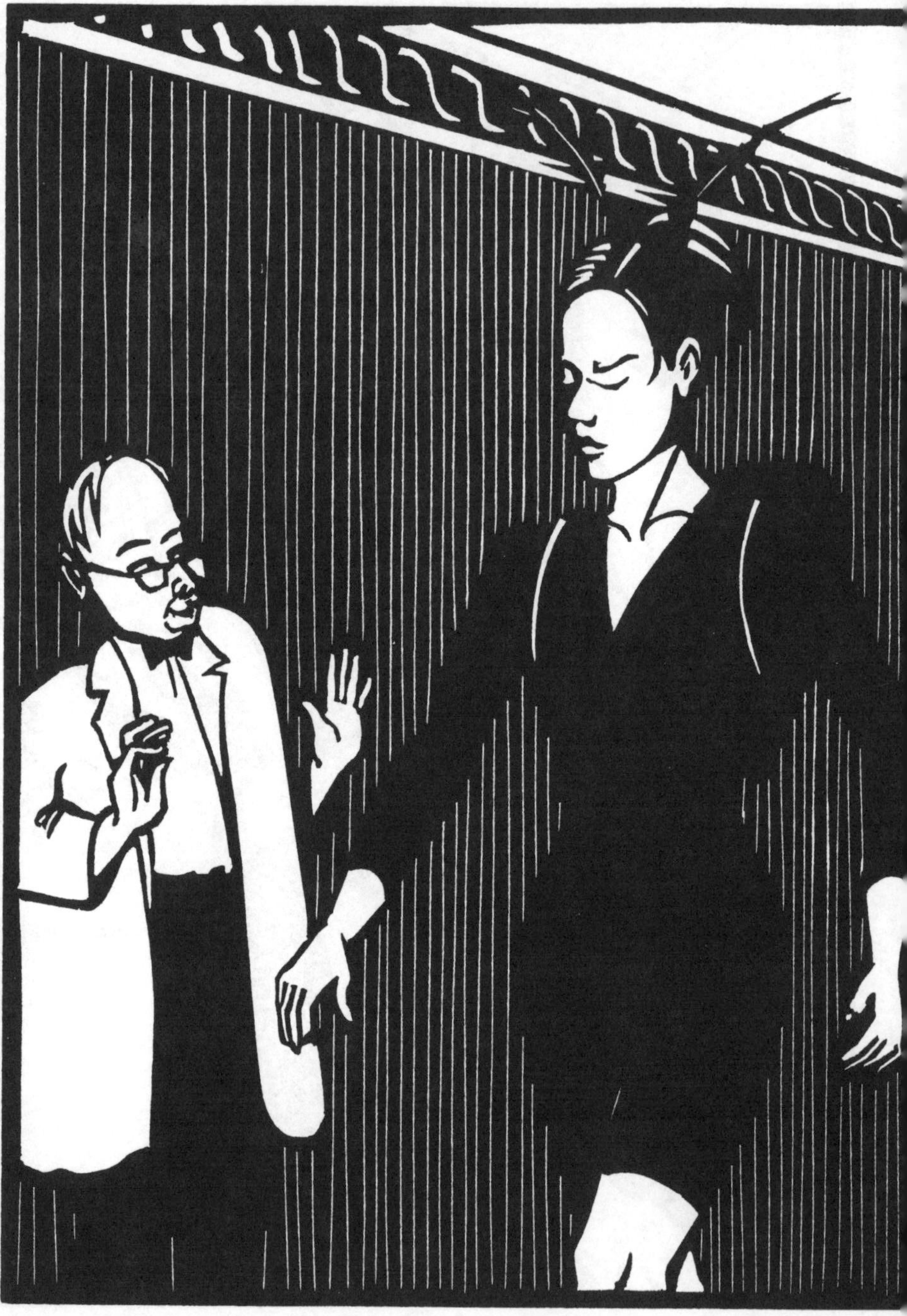

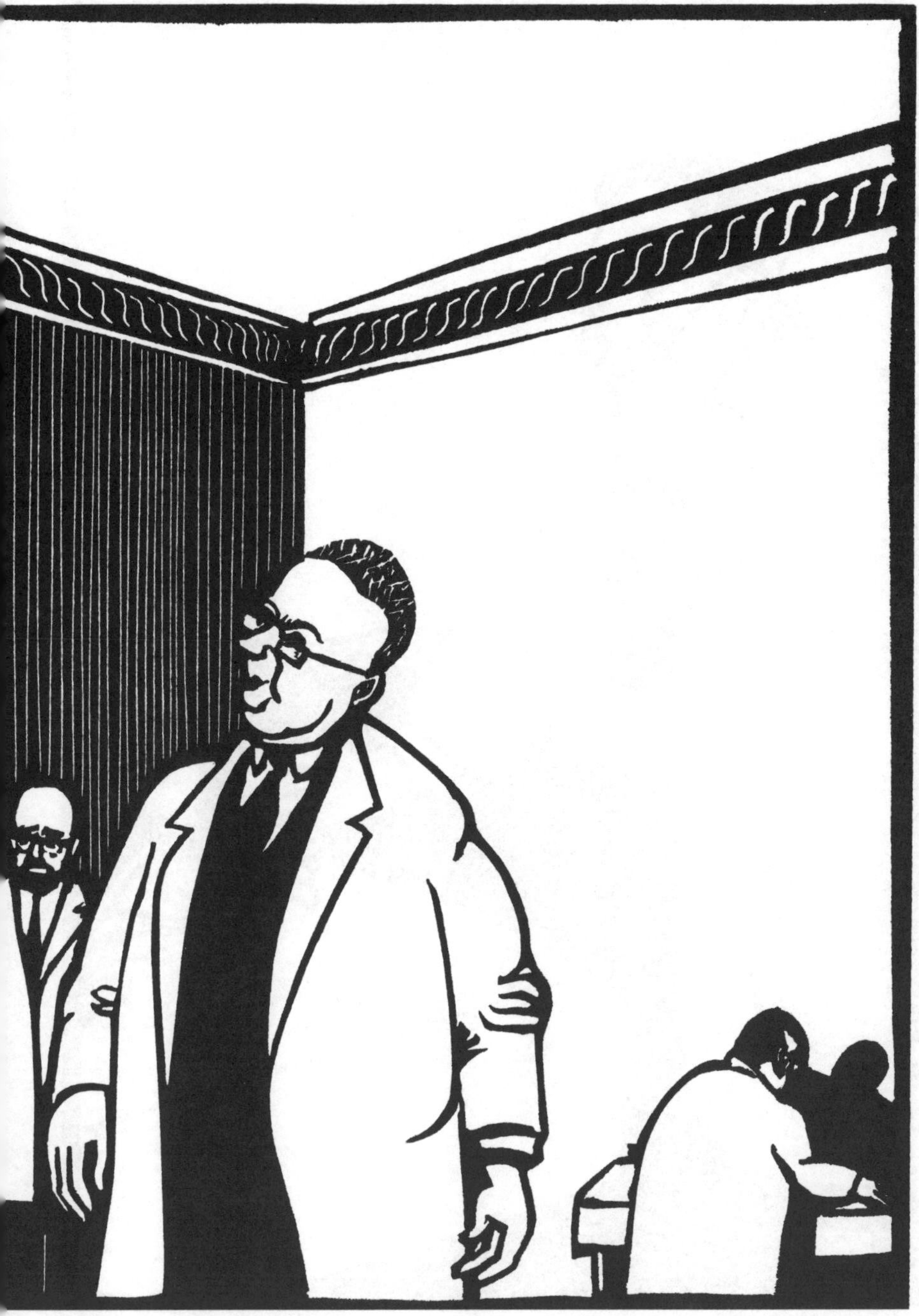

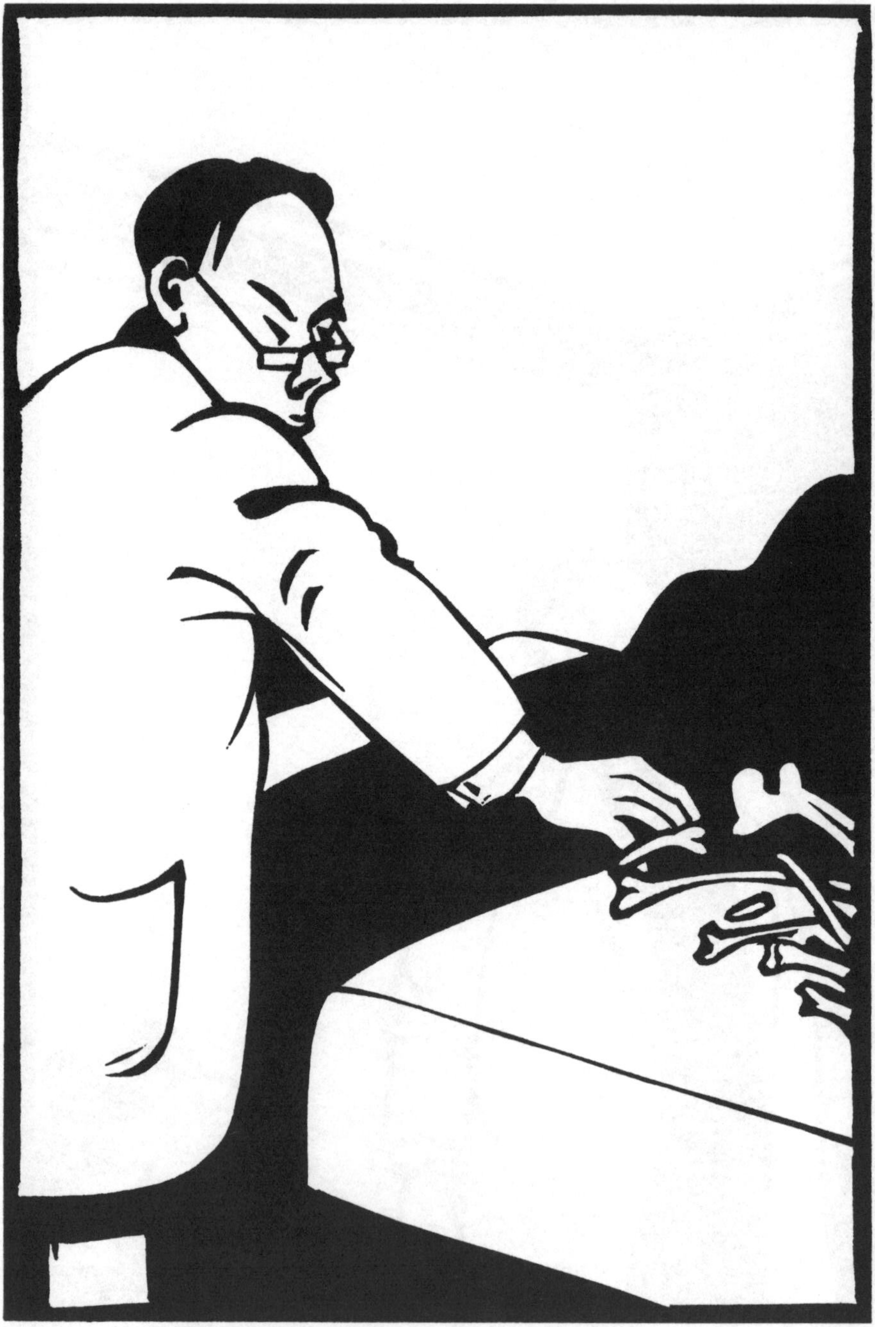

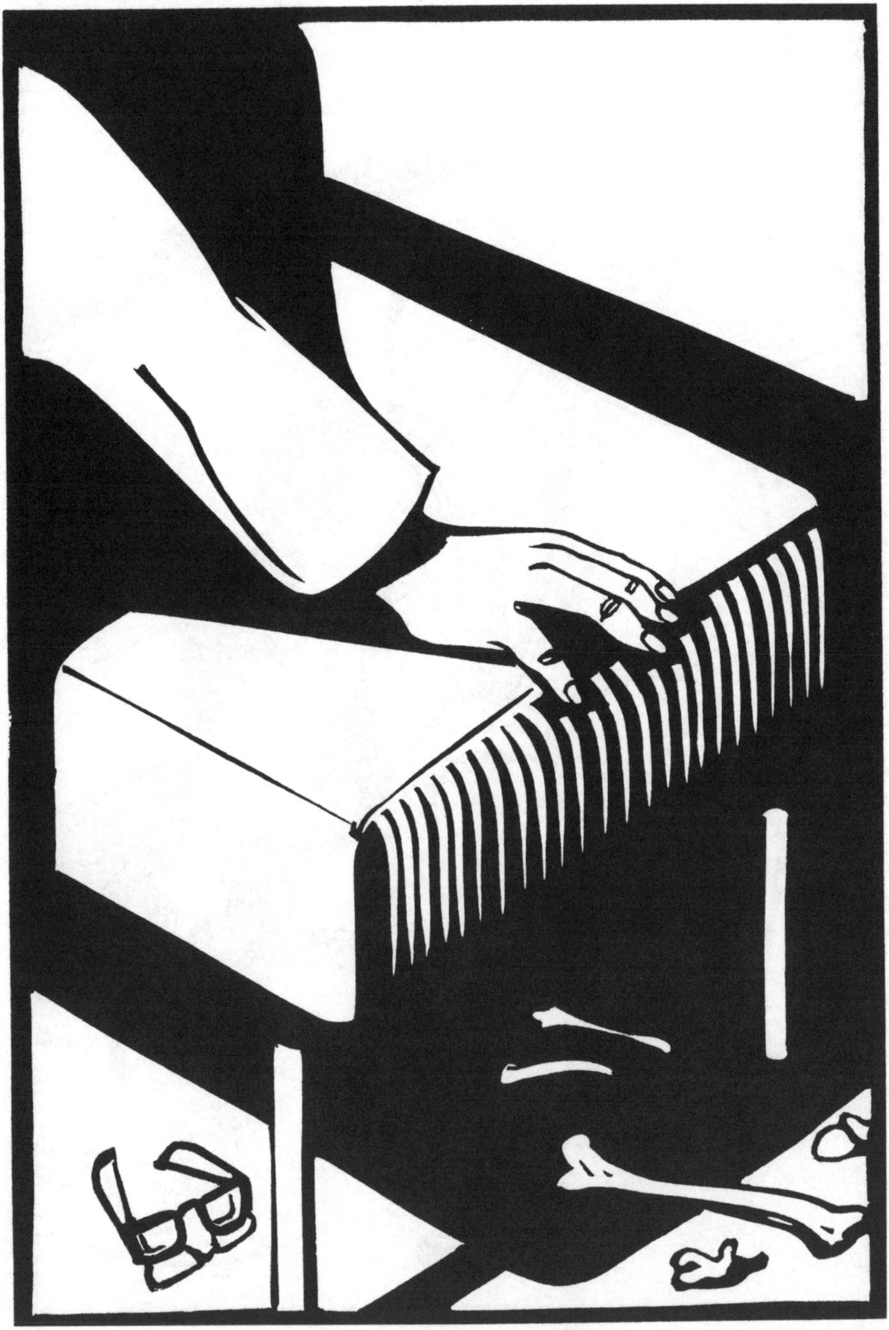

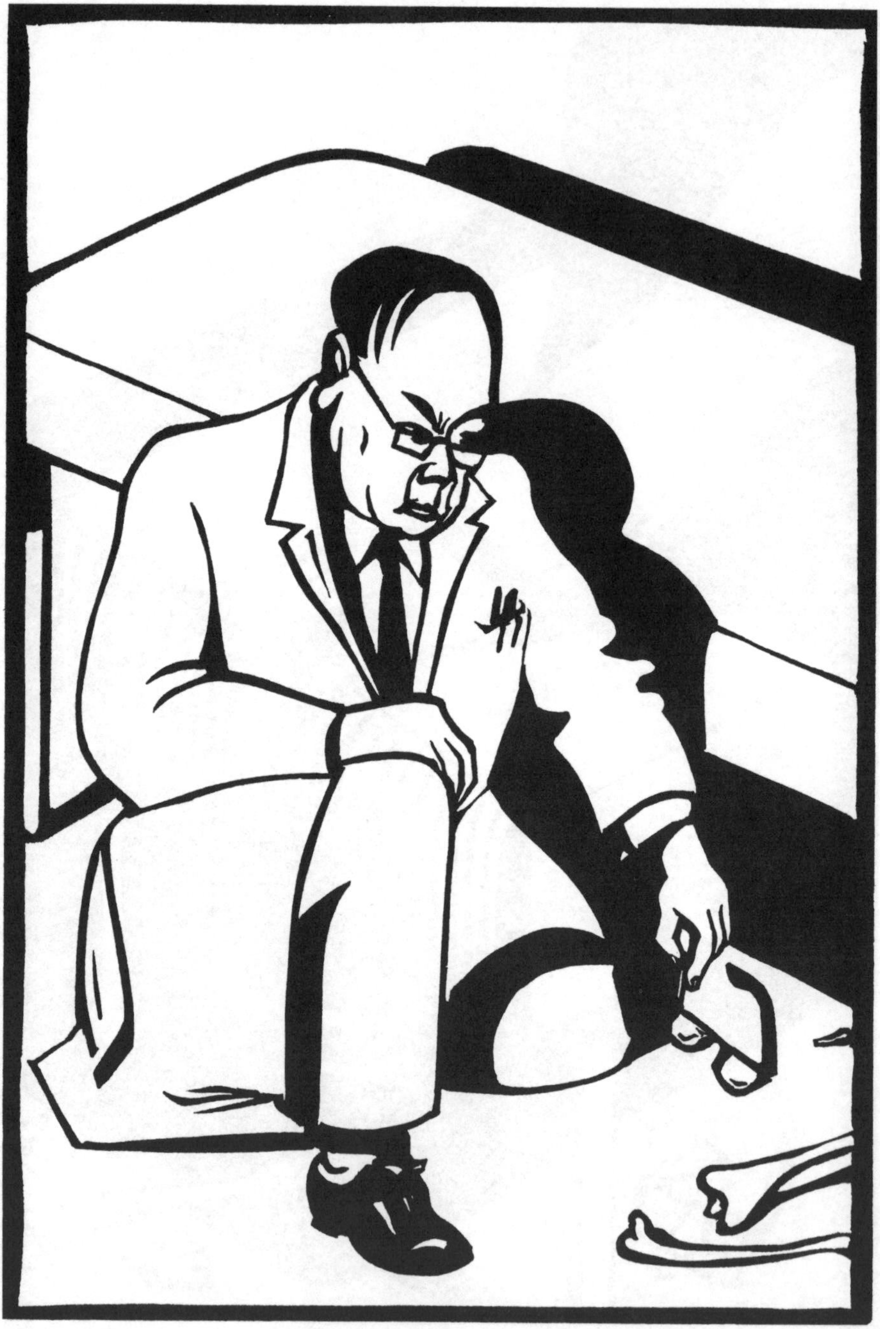

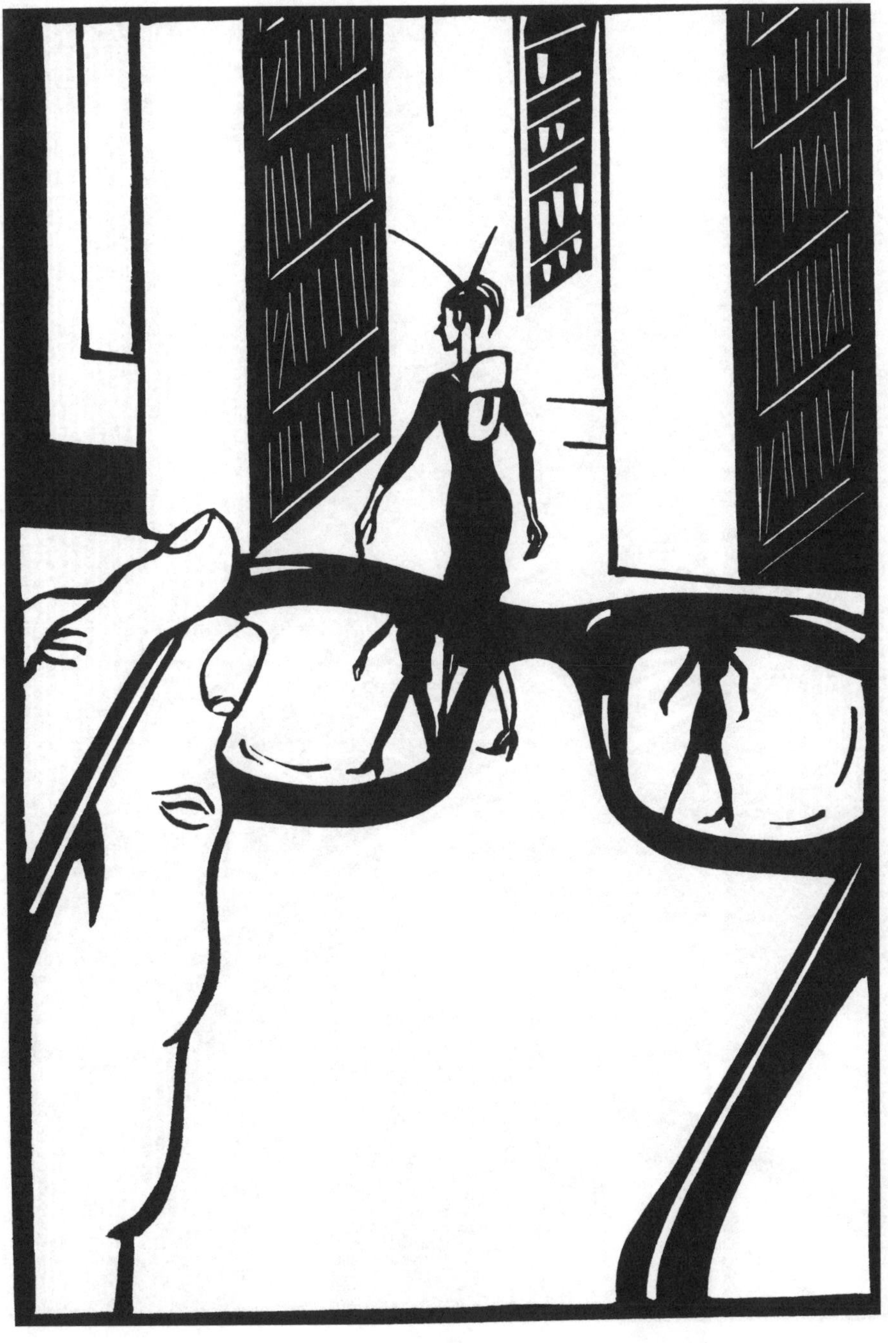

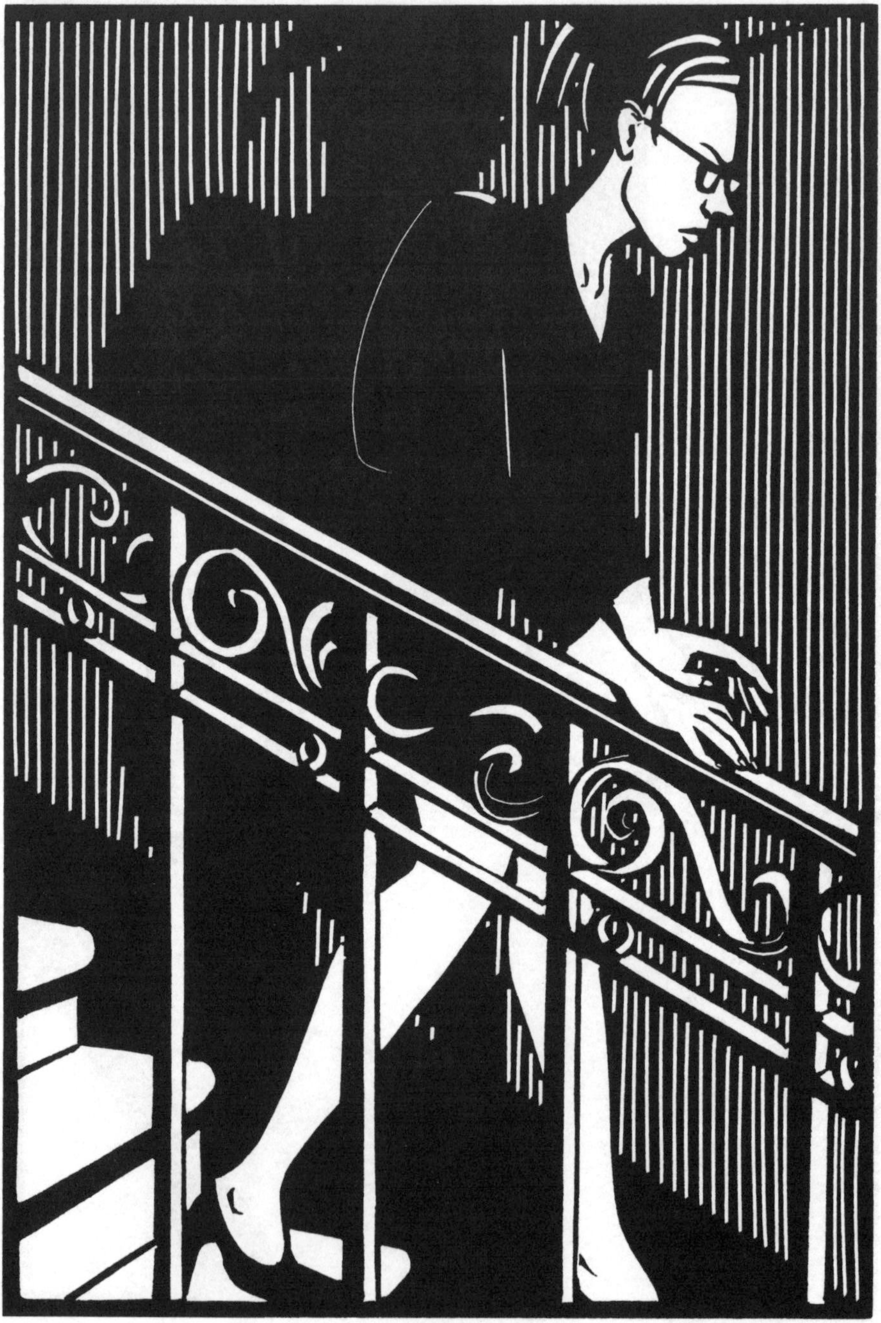

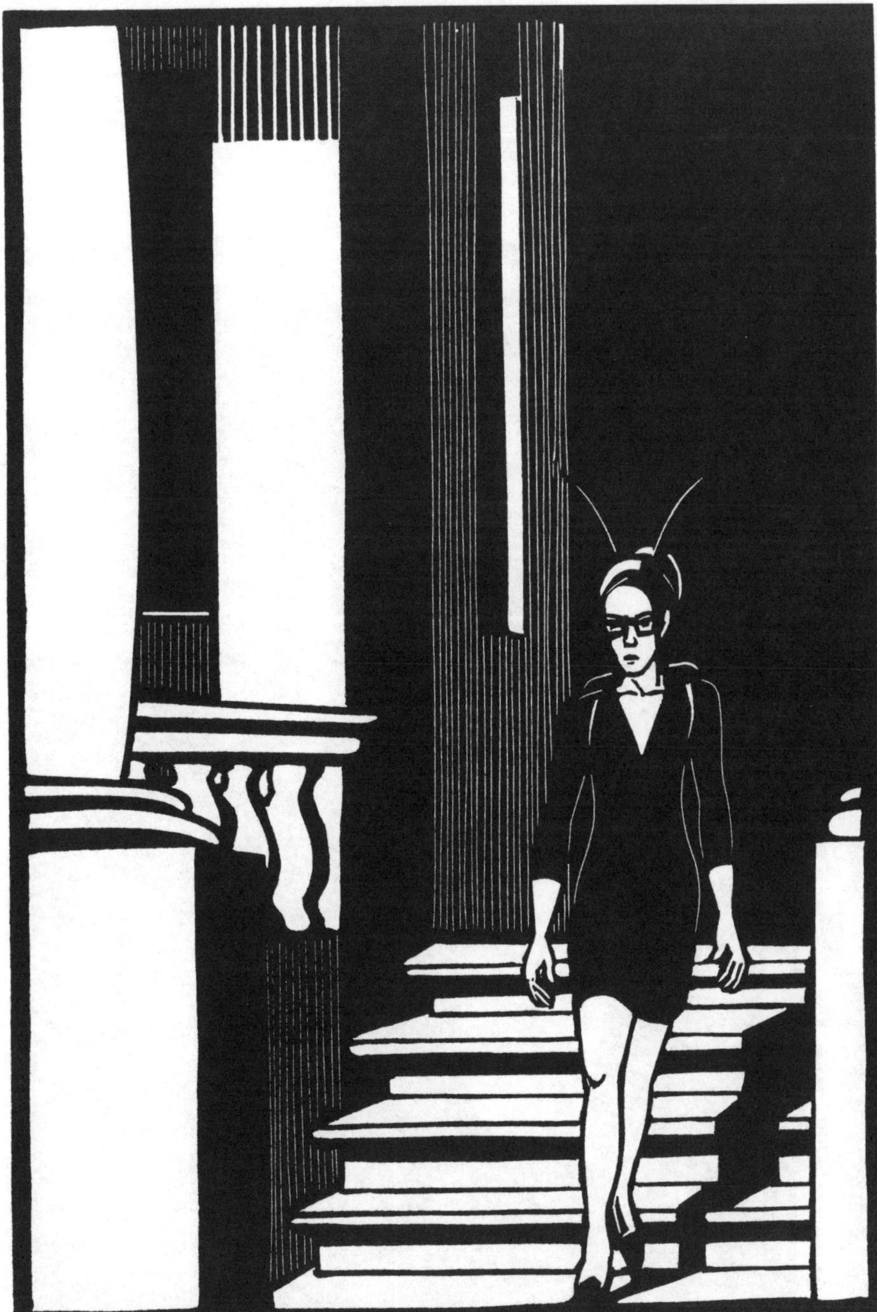

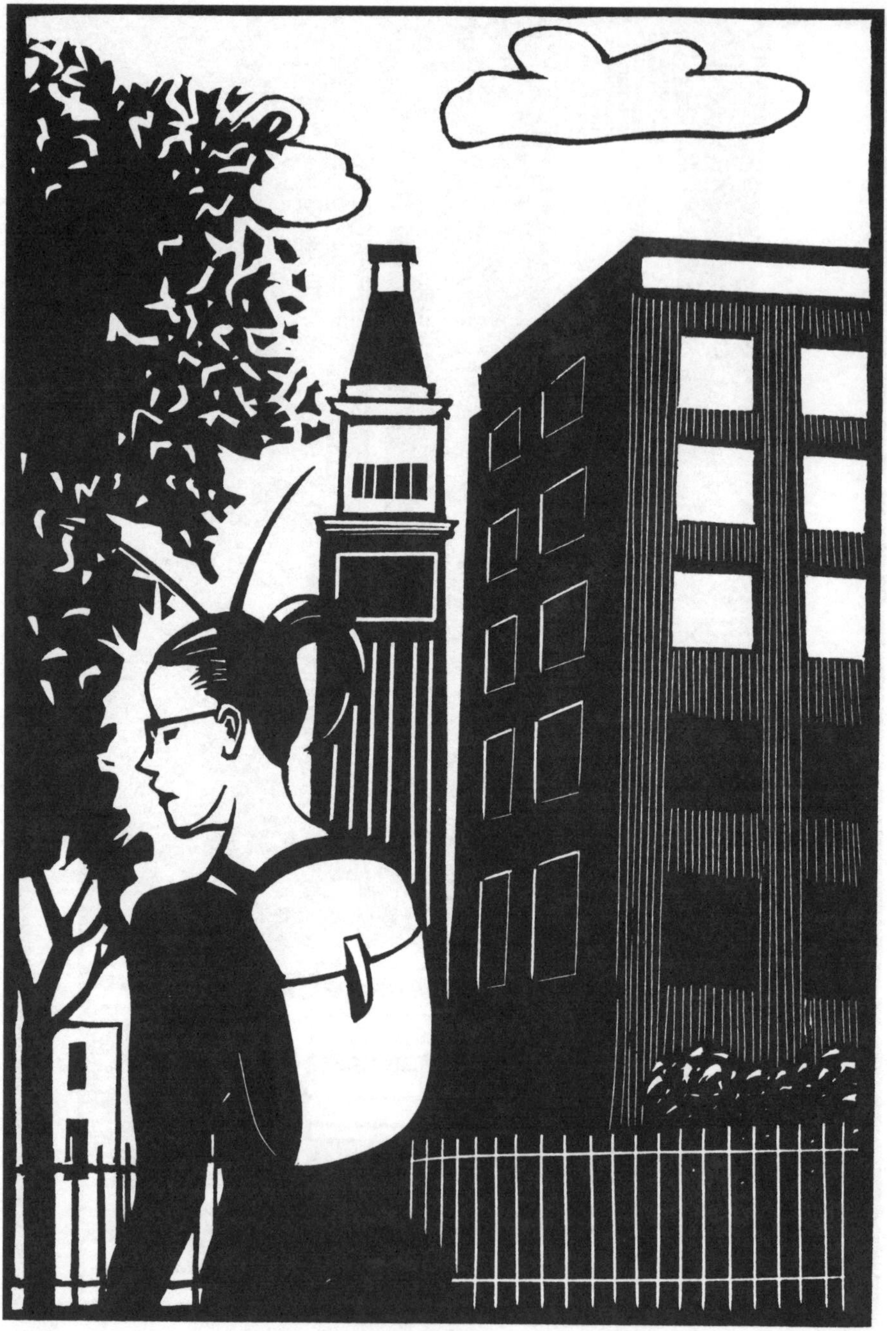

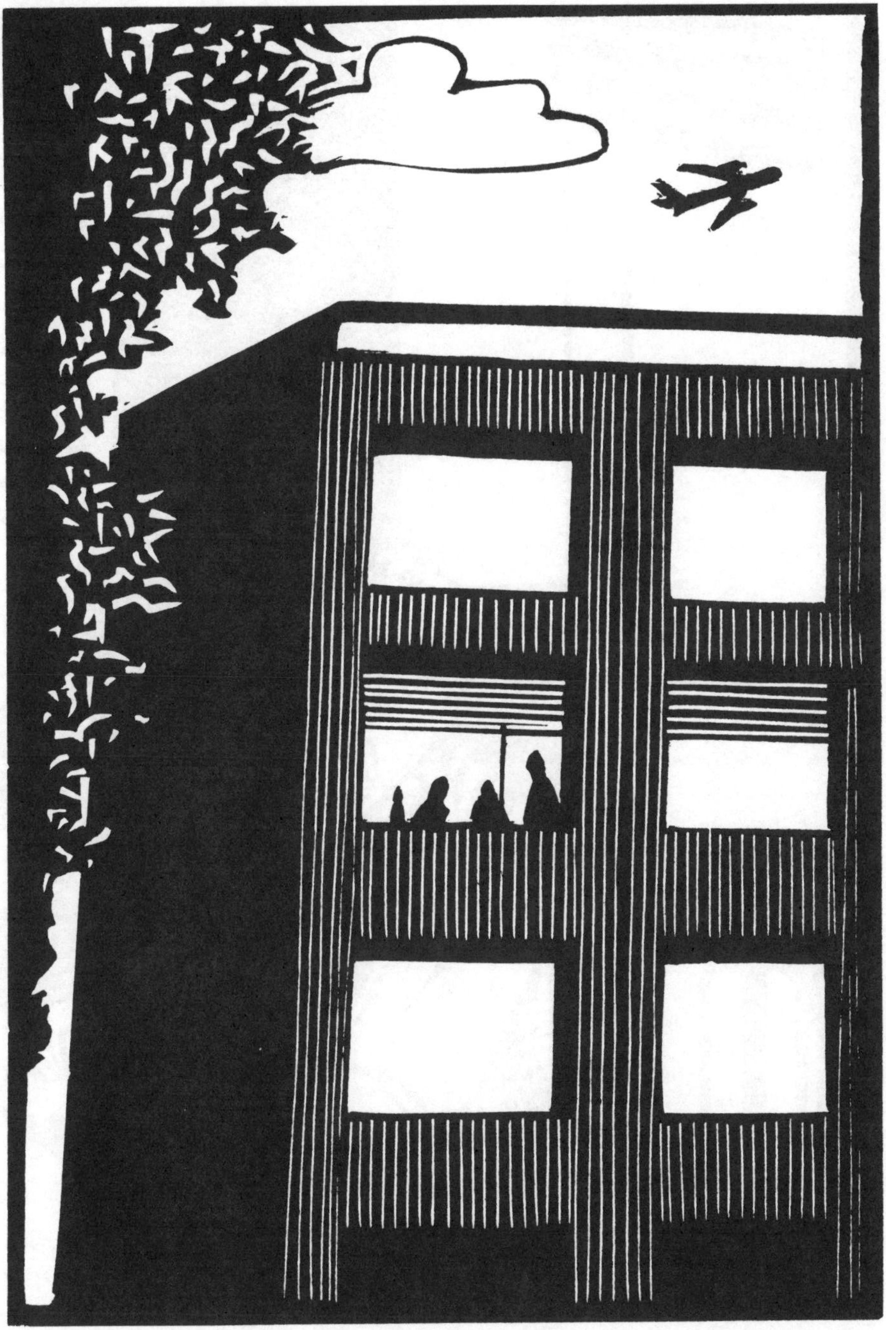

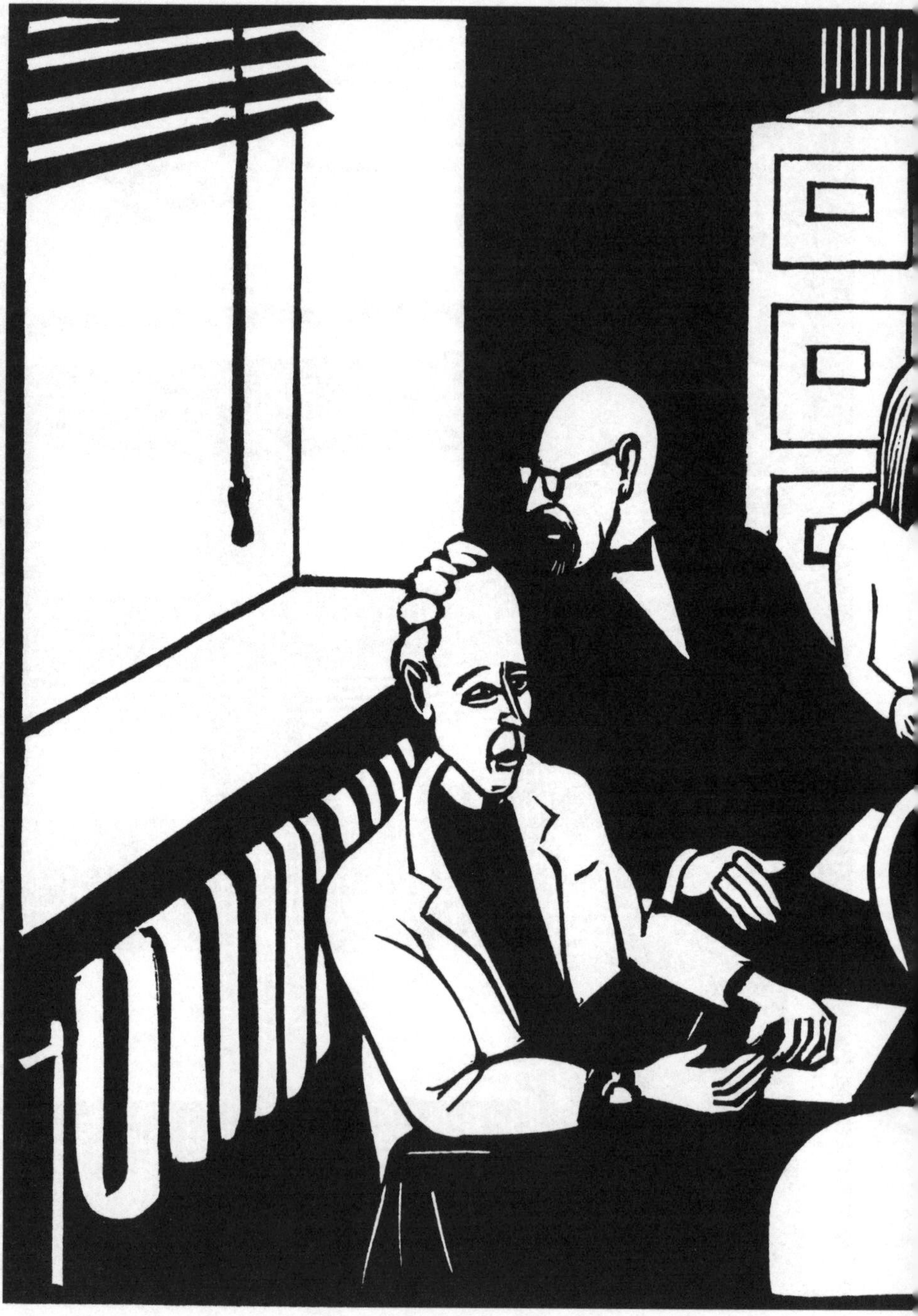

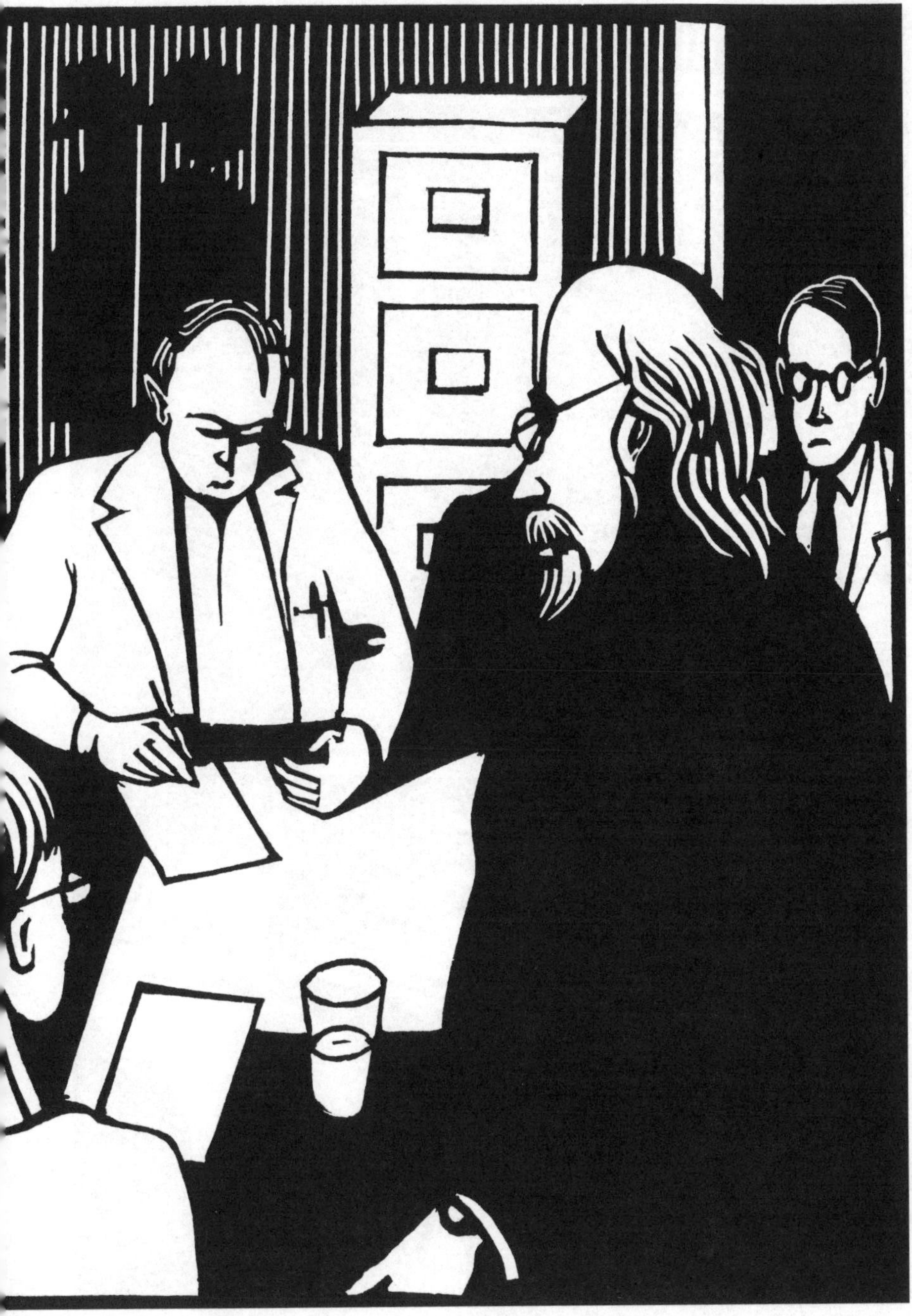

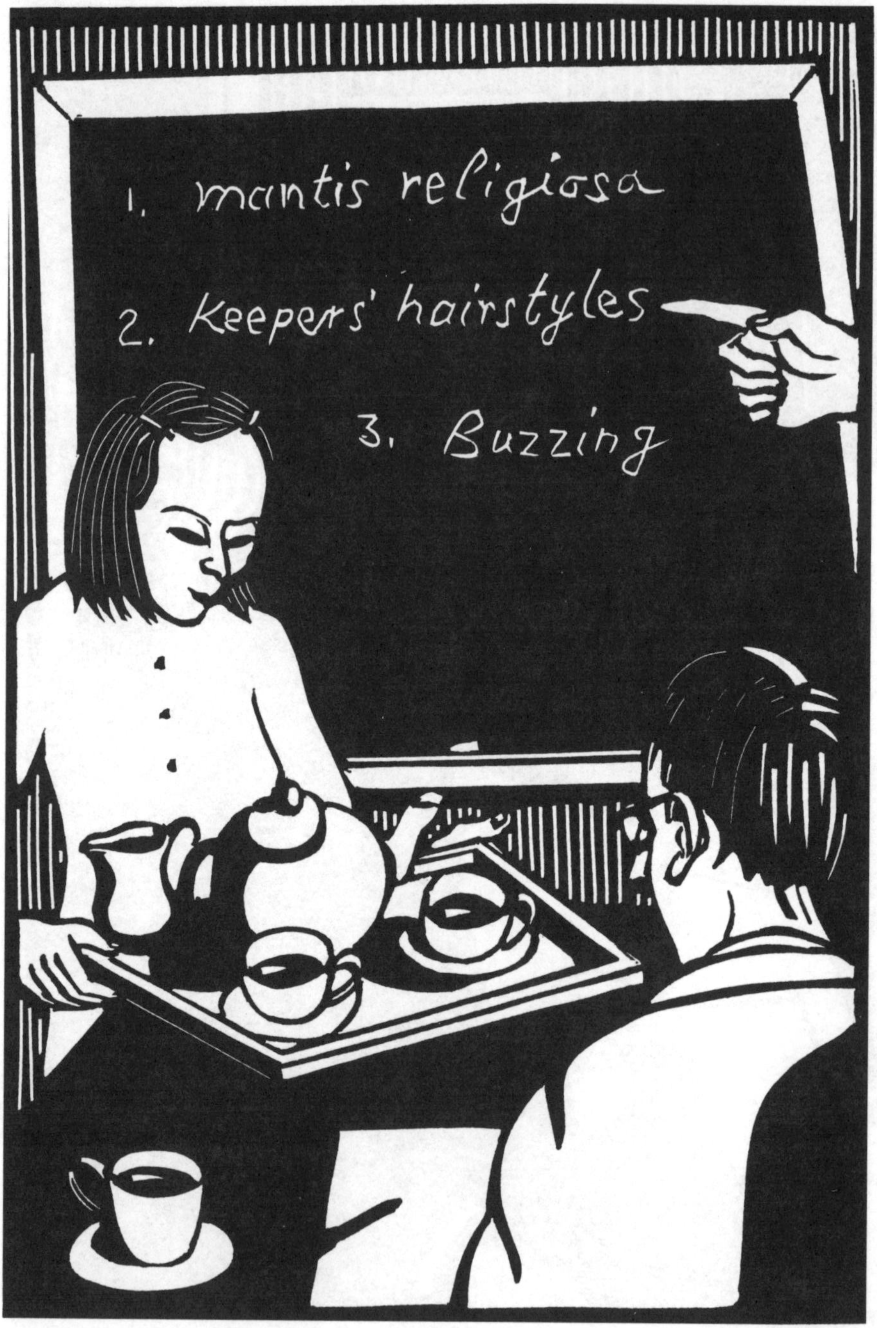
1. mantis religiosa
2. Keepers' hairstyles
3. Buzzing

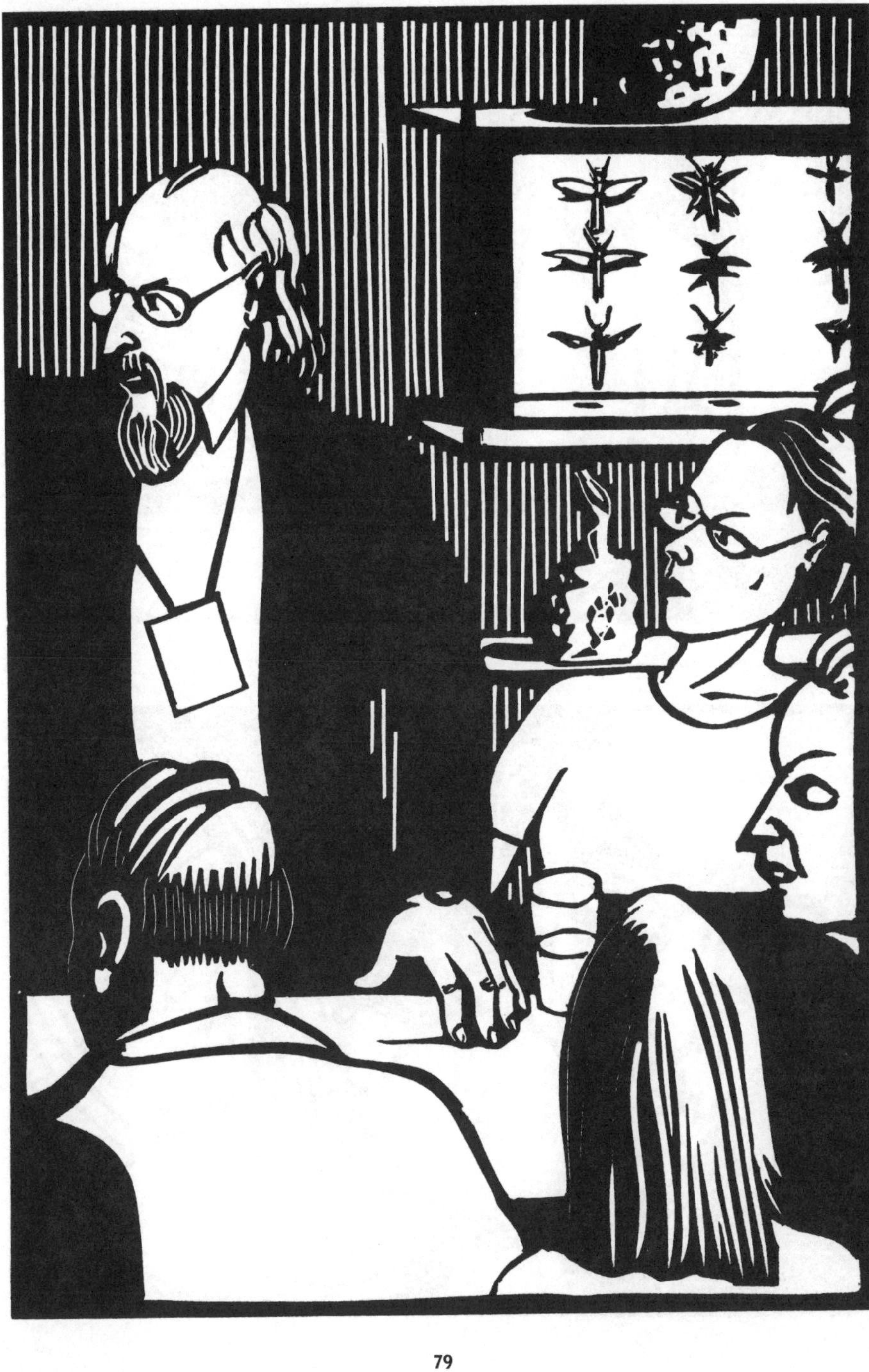

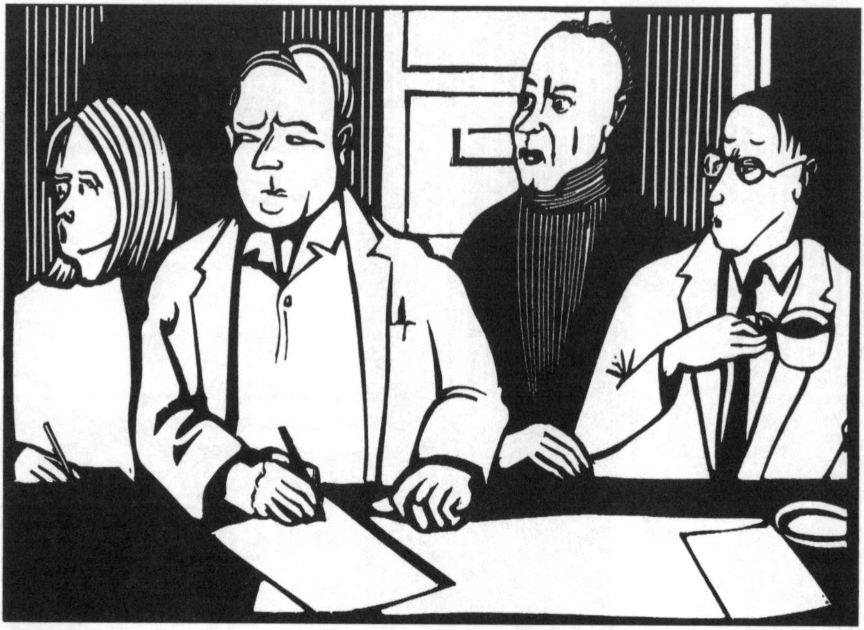

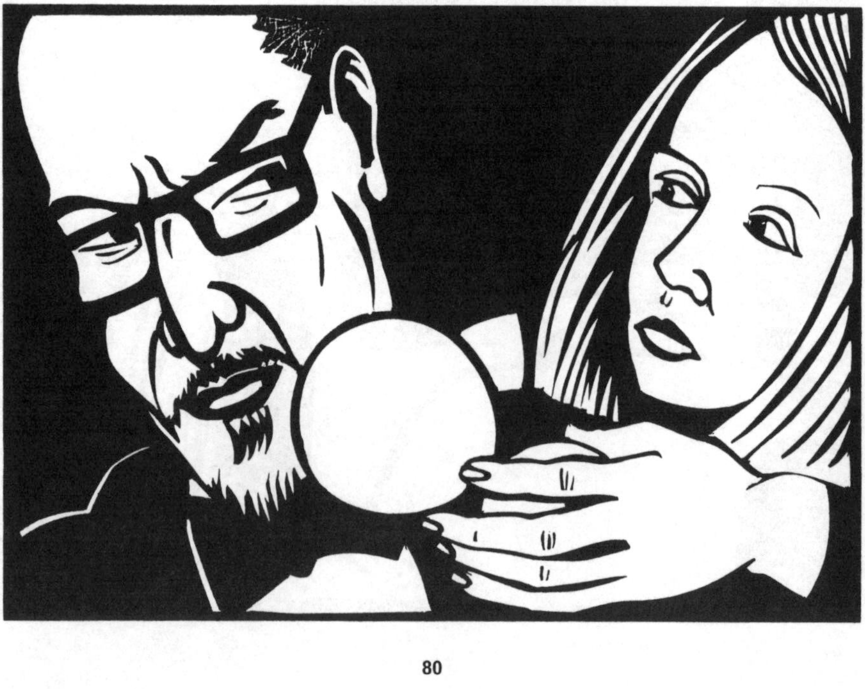

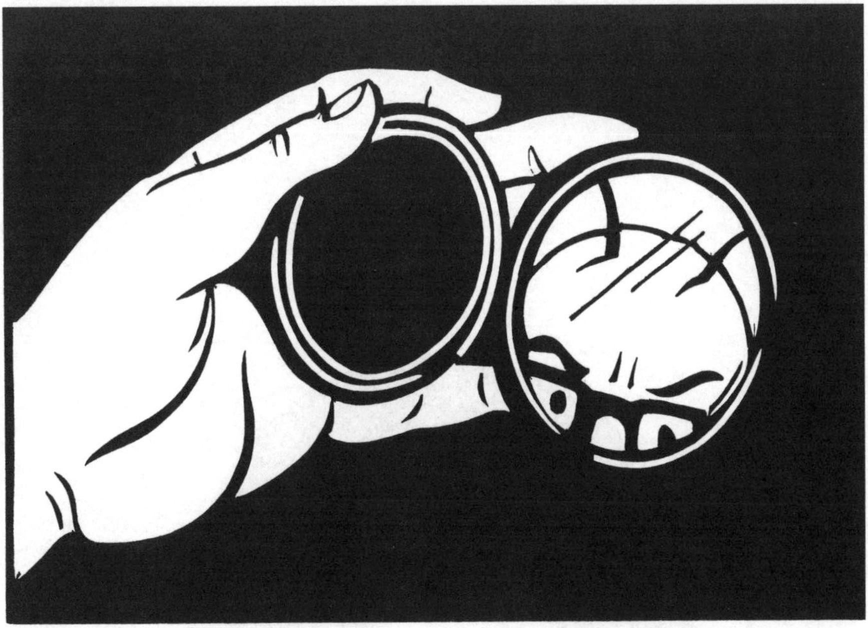

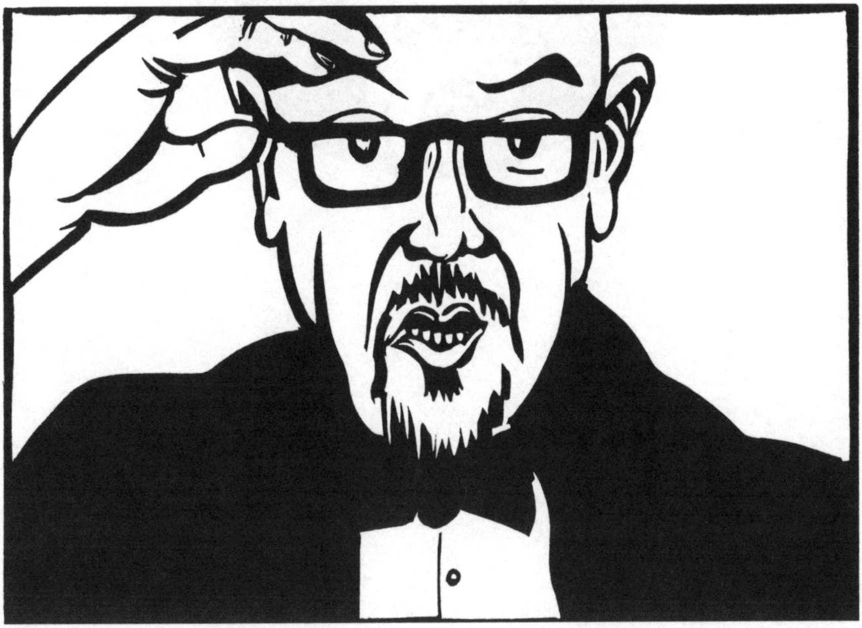

CHAPTER THREE

Everyone was looking sombre; after an enthusiastic start to the project, we were facing an impasse. In our individual ways we would still be able to prepare and research material for the event, but without Dorlan there seemed little point. This was why we arranged to meet; we had to decide whether to continue with the project or not.

George was the most decisive. To him it was clear. Dorlan was indeed lying unconscious in hospital, but the doctors were of the opinion that the situation was temporary; they expected him to regain consciousness soon. We should therefore continue. Sam countered by pointing out that with every passing day there was more chance of Dorlan sliding deeper into a coma. Amadeo recalled how a distant acquaintance of his had slipped on the kerb of a paving stone, hitting his head, and had spent over a year in a coma.

'And what happened to him?' inquired George.

'He died.'

The brutal fact put an end to the discussion, and it was into this silence that I entered the club and saw my colleagues sitting there like statues.

'How miserable you all look!'

'What would you expect, Ed,' uttered George with a sigh. 'Our friends here seem to think that Horace is sliding into a coma.'

'Let me reassure you, then. Horace has regained consciousness. The hospital phoned me this morning.'

Everyone sat up in anticipation.

'What else did they say?'

'It appears that a nurse noticed him moving his eyes; he was following a fly around the room with his eyes.'

'Anything more.'

'That was all, but it's a start. They told me to phone this afternoon for further developments.'

'Or relapses.'

'Why the pessimism, Sam? I'll make the call just as soon as I have had some coffee.' I waved my hand in the direction of the bar.

Amadeo passed me his mobile phone. I took out my address book and tapped in the numbers. I asked for the neurological ward and was soon speaking to one of the medical staff. The barman came up with his tray and placed my coffee on the table. Occasionally I looked over to my friends, their impatience was obvious, so I nodded my head a few times but this made them more impatient; was it good news or bad?

Finally I uttered a few words of thanks and handed Amadeo back his phone.

'Well?'

'Horace has been asking for paper.'

No one knew what to say.

Dorlan had lost the power of speech; he was not responding when spoken to and was communicating with the medical staff by writing messages. After a detailed otolaryngological examination, the doctors concluded that there was no evidence of any damage to his ears and could not understand why the patient behaved as if he was deaf. What was more intriguing was that Dorlan did not use the paper solely for writing messages. When left alone in his bed he was drawing, continually drawing, and covering one sheet after another; when he ran out of paper he would press a button to call a nurse, who on arrival would see him holding up a written message: MORE PAPER!

Through the porthole window of his room, the medics could observe him drawing. He would never look at his designs; only stare straight ahead as if in a trance, drawing automatically, the tip of his pen never leaving the page. Some pages were covered with intricate lines, like the veins of a leaf, whilst others had no more than three or four lines on them. There was no telling how long a drawing session would last, nor was there any clue as to how frequently Dorlan would take up his pen.

Later that afternoon when I visited the hospital, I could see that his output was prodigious; the floor around his bed was covered in paper. He was drawing at a steady pace. Not wanting to interrupt him, I stood by the door motionless, curious as to what he was drawing. Eventually I approached the bed to look over his shoulder. He was drawing a design so complex that it was hard to decipher. He was going through the motions dispassionately, like an automaton. I knelt down to see what the other images on the floor looked like. They varied, but there seemed to be something linking them to one another. I had the feeling that if configured in the right way they would form one meaningful picture. As I was sifting through the scattered sheets, the drawing I had seen Dorlan making fell delicately to the floor. I rose to see him with a written message in his lap:

HELLO, ED.

He turned to face me and smiled. His eyes were bright.

'Horace! How are you? You look well.'

I soon realized that I needed to write this down and did so in a nervous handwriting that betrayed my emotion. We exchanged a few pleasantries, after which Dorlan closed his eyes and fell asleep.

Once I had collected the many drawings that were scattered about the bed, I left the room and looked for the nurse. The nurse did not mind me taking the papers with me; they meant nothing to the patient, she said, he never looked at them while he was drawing and never asked for them afterwards. She asked me if I would like a cup of tea, but I declined, telling her that I was pressed for time. I was eager to leave the building. I was in need of fresh air and I was yearning to be walking through the park on my own; the sooner I got the drawings over to Amadeo at the academy, the better.

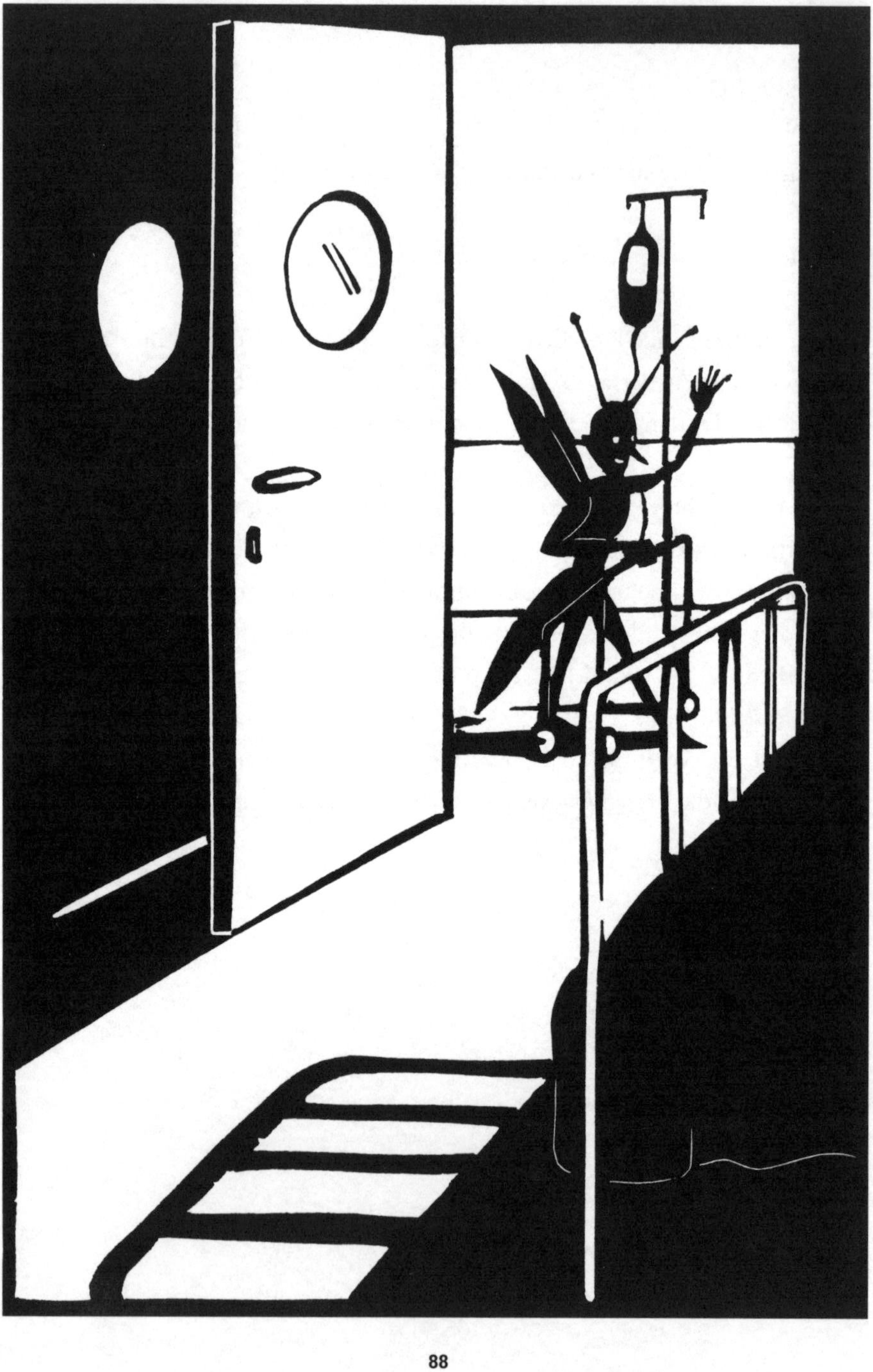

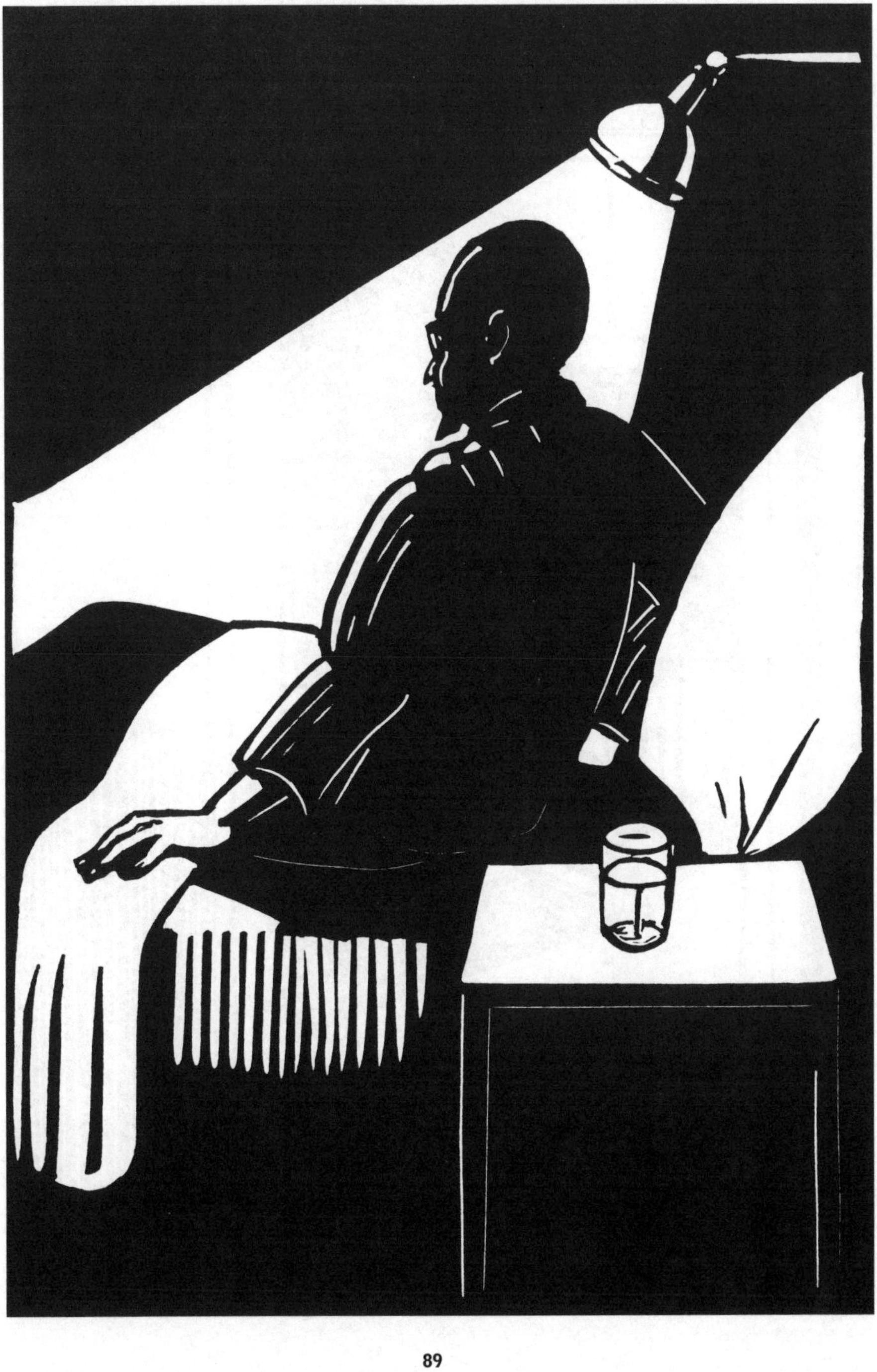

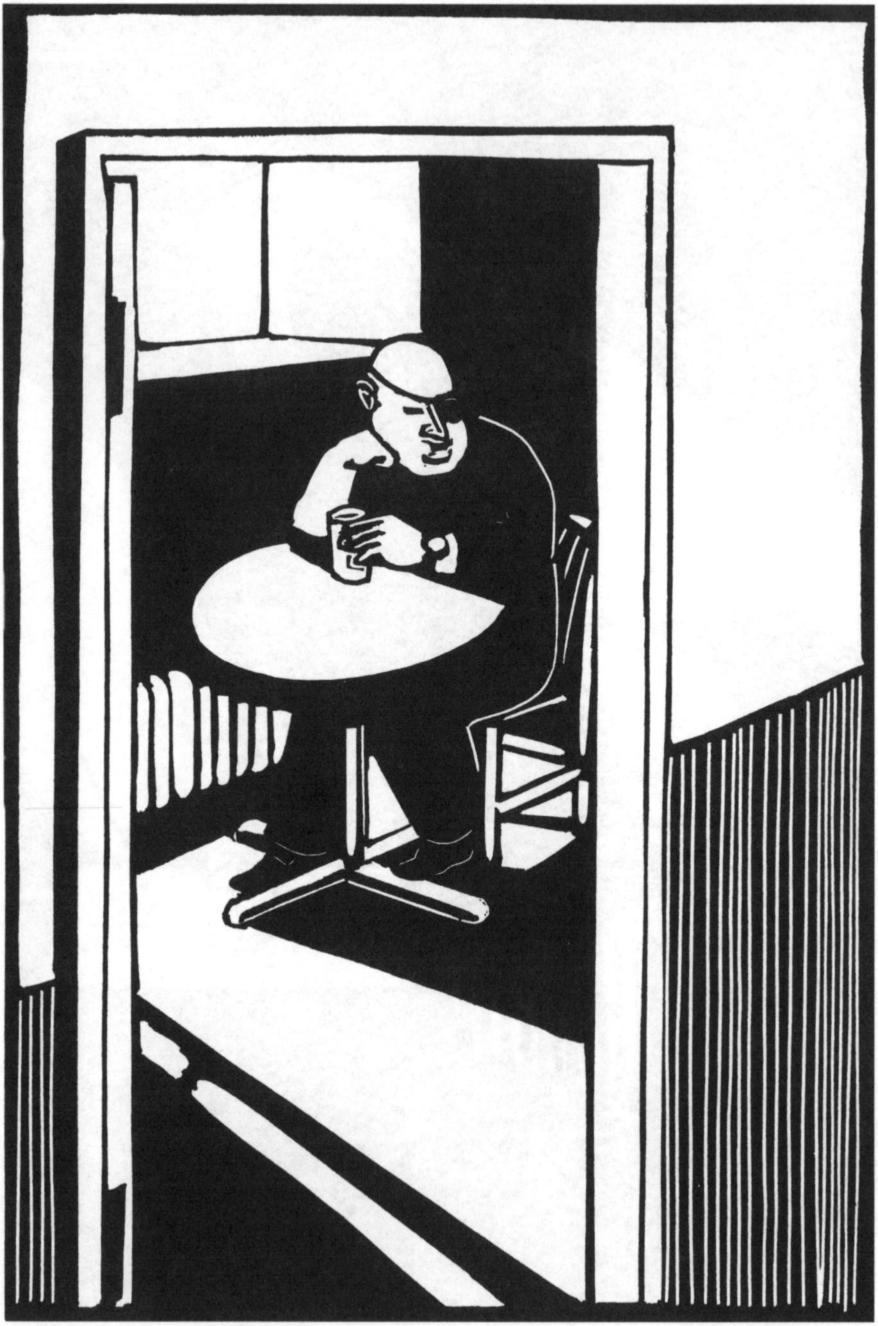

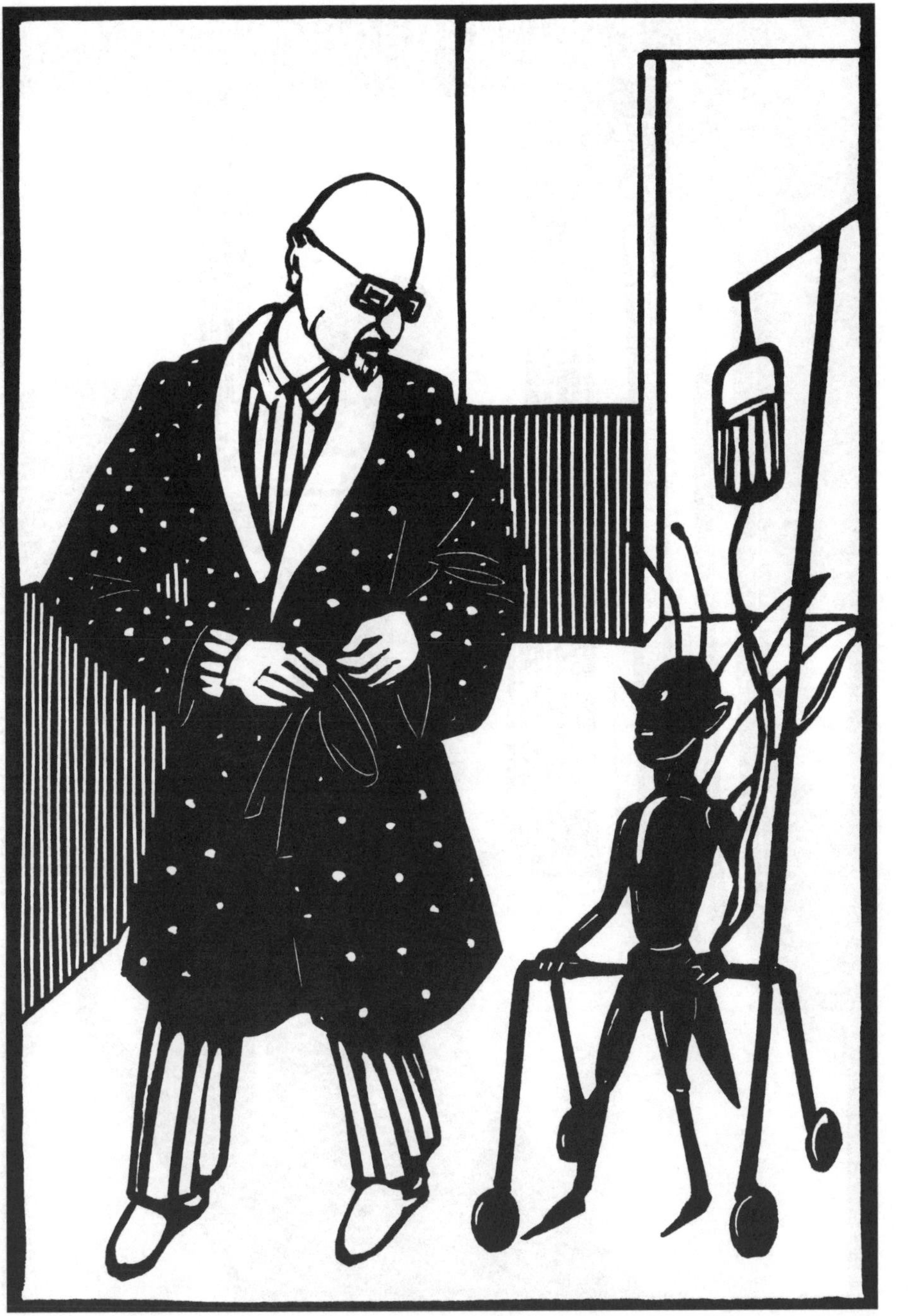

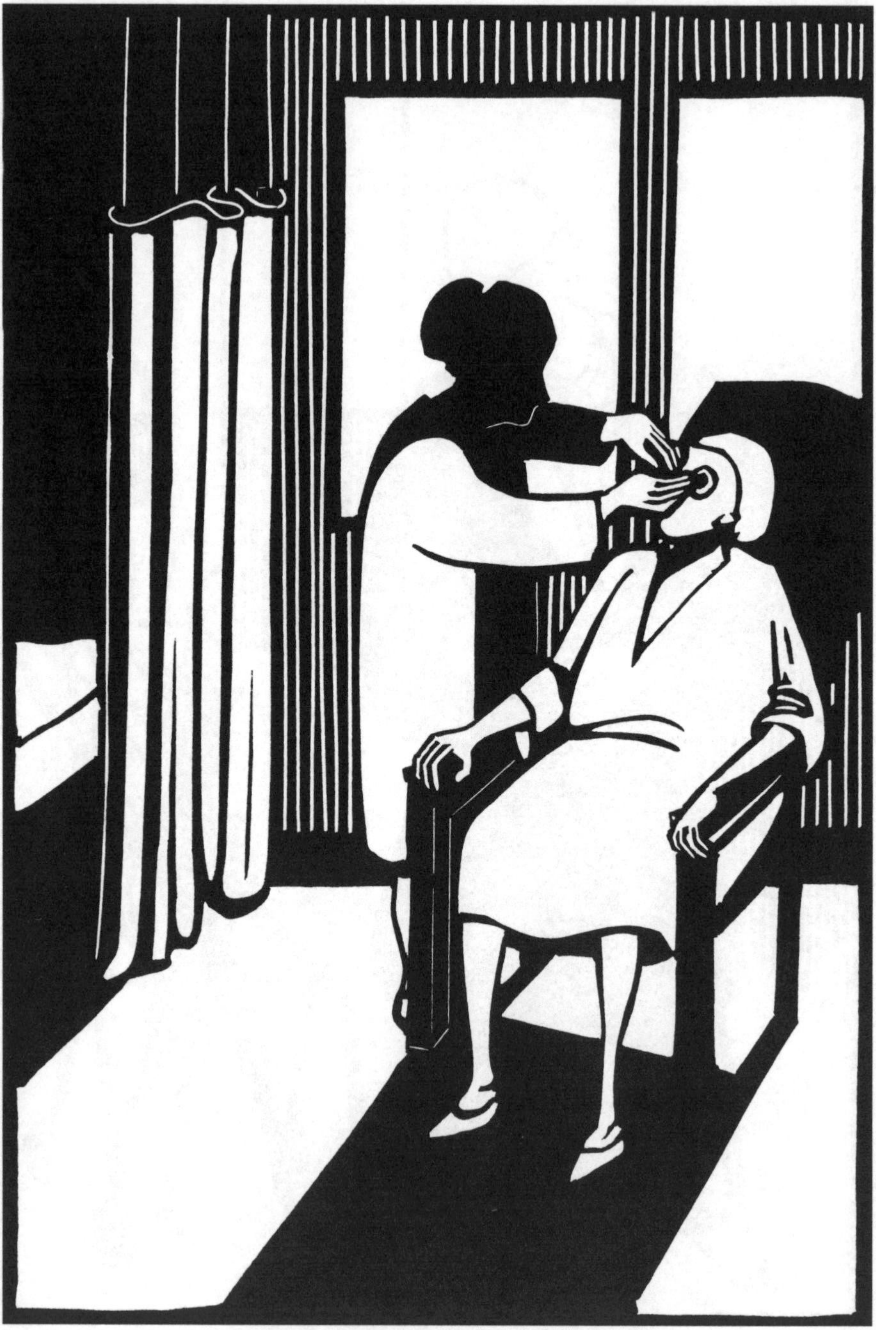

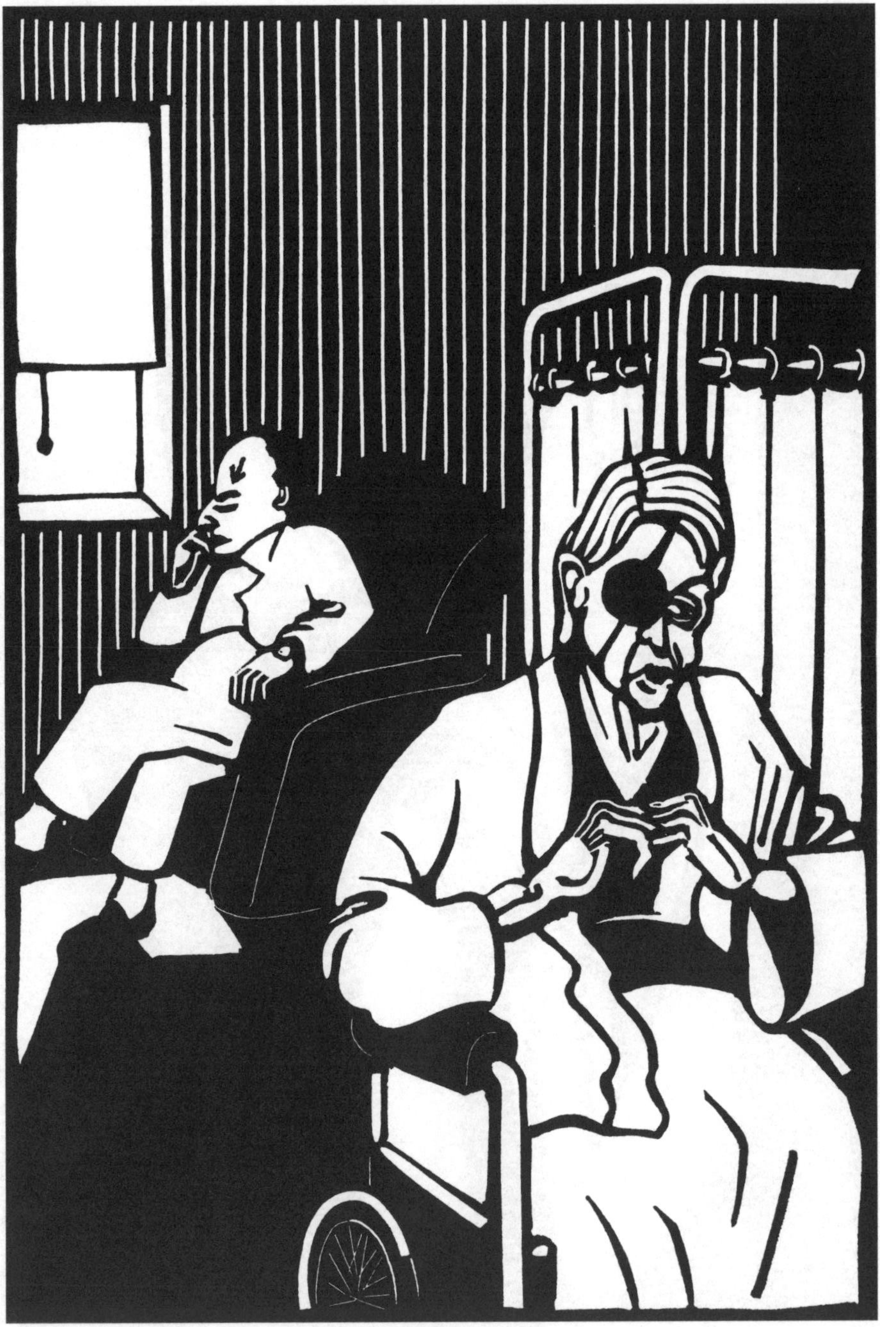

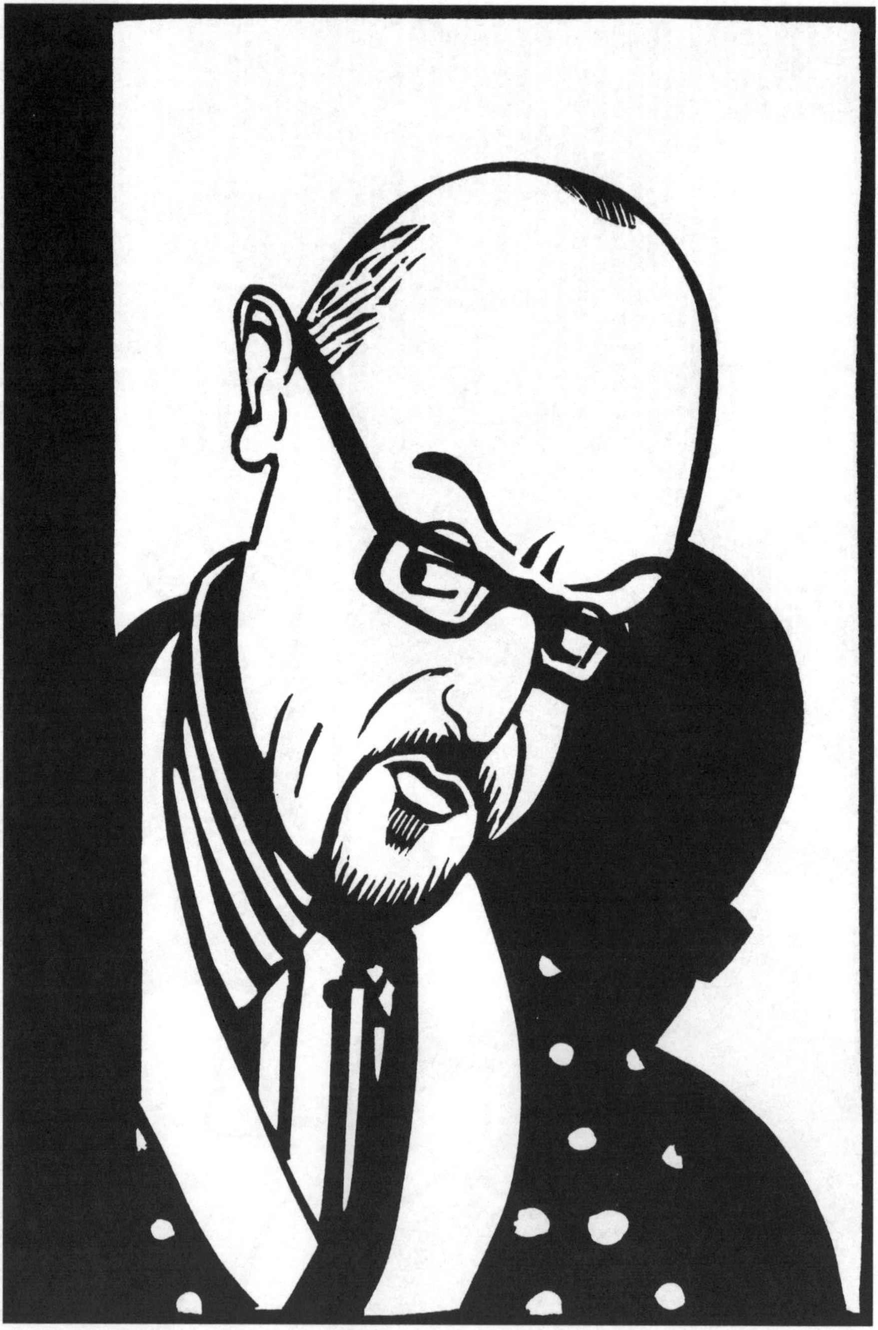

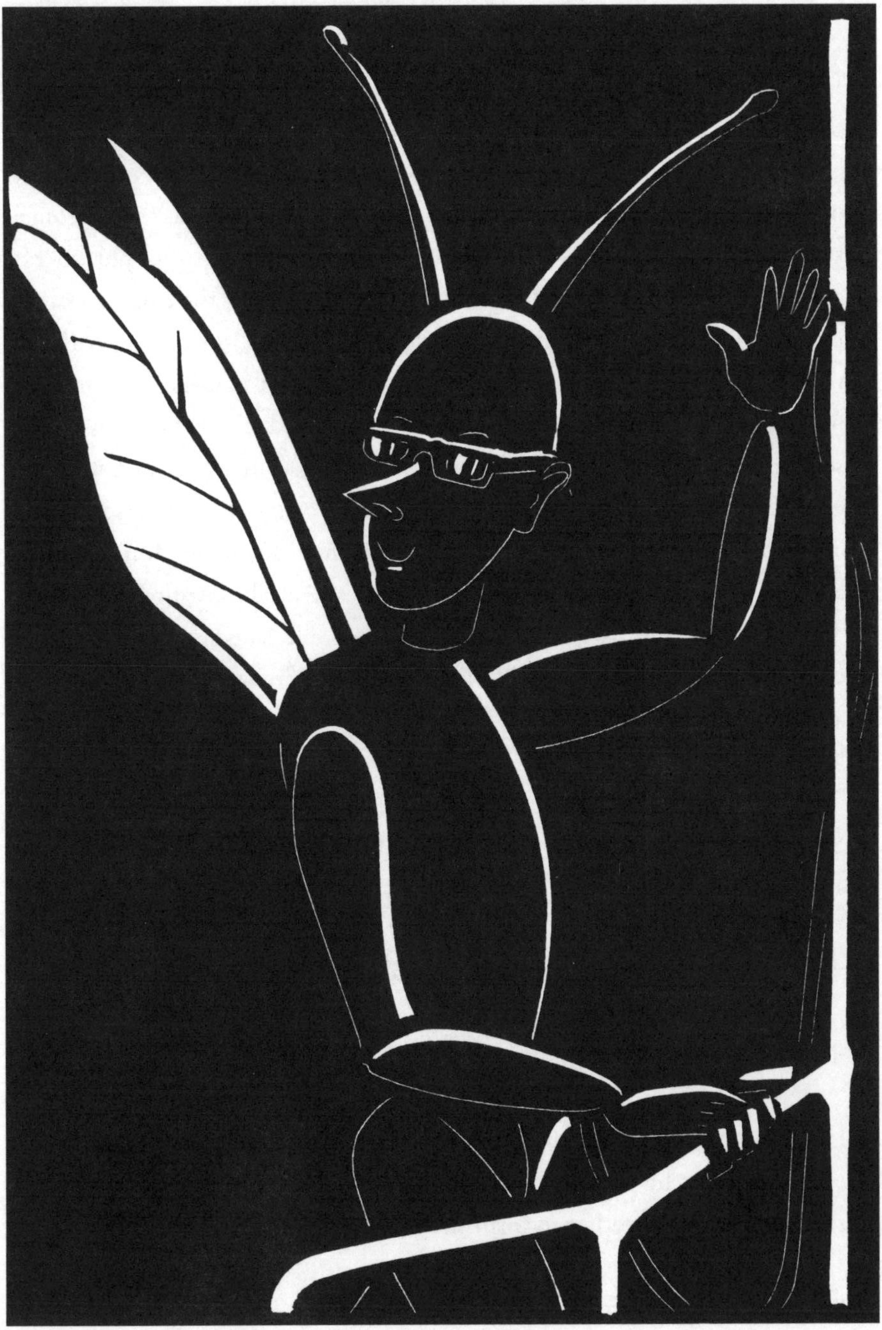

It was a good idea to have given Dorlan's drawings to Amadeo. As we sat together at the club, he took out a file and placed it on the table. He apologized for having taken so long; it had been hard to make much sense of Dorlan's scribbles. However, he had persevered and this was the outcome: two computer printouts. We drew up our armchairs. George put on his spectacles and picked up one of the prints; it was a giant close-up of an insect's wing, detailing all the minuscule fibres holding it together. With the next print he thought he was looking at an abstract painting – a piece of modern art – but on closer inspection he realized it was nothing of the sort; it was part of a bat's ear. What Amadeo had done was to assemble the cryptic drawings as one would the pieces of a jigsaw puzzle, separating detailed pictures from the sparser ones, and then slowly building up small areas. Halfway into the work he realized he was dealing with two images. This made it easier to proceed with the task. He laid out the completed compositions on the floor of a seminar room and photographed them with a digital camera from the top of a stepladder. These were the prints we sat looking at.

Sam congratulated Amadeo with a vigorous handshake, nodding his head in affirmation.

'Don't congratulate me,' responded Amadeo.

'It's the professor's work, not mine.'

He was right. Just think how Dorlan could have done all this when he wasn't even looking at his drawings as he made them. How could he have foreseen them all coming together to form such stunning images?

'At what time is he arriving, Ed?' asked George.

'You know, I still can't believe it,' Sam spoke softly. 'To be staring at the wall while drawing such complicated patterns!'

'I know it may sound incredible, but I have a theory.'

'Mr Green has a theory!' exclaimed George.

'Don't be cynical, George.' Amadeo then turned to me: 'What is your theory?'

'The wall facing Horace's bed was covered in tiles. If you look closely at any tile which is old, like the ones in the hospital, you will invariably find many little hairline fractures. Like these ones.'

I picked up the saucer from under my cup. George let out a long sigh. Sam asked Amadeo whether he had brought the original drawings with him. Amadeo took one out of the second file that he had in his briefcase and handed it to Sam, who stood up and raised it to the light, comparing it to the saucer. Before he managed to sit down he exclaimed, 'There's Dorlan! Look, he is walking up to the club.'

We all looked out through the window to see the old professor, sprightly dodging the traffic, as he crossed the street.

'Listen, George, I must just tell you something before Horace arrives . . . You may find him odd; he's changed somewhat.'

George could see I was struggling with words, but made no effort to guess what I was trying to say.

'On my last visit . . . on my last visit to the hospital . . . Well, what I am trying to say is that he . . . he told me he wanted to include George Reyes on the team.'

'What!' roared George.

'Yes, he sees an important role for him.'

'Well, that's all I need to hear,' George pulled himself out of the chair and with a nervous gesture adjusted his tie.

'Wait, George, what are you doing?'

'Can't you see, I'm going.'

'What do you mean? You can't go. Horace is coming.'

'If Horace is engaging that moron, then there is no point in me staying here.'

'George, you can't go. There's no way in which the project can go on without you.'

'There's room for one George, but not two!'

'Listen, just wait for Horace. It may become clear when he explains.'

George was not convinced, but Dorlan had come in through the door and we all stood up to welcome him back into our midst. George succumbed to the convivial nature of the occasion and joined in the embraces that followed. We ordered drinks and showered Dorlan with good wishes, complimenting him on how well he looked. The manifestations of joy went on for a while, until Dorlan asked after George Reyes. I glanced at George Sudok, who was wriggling in his armchair with his hand around his neck.

'What role do you see for Reyes?' asked Amadeo.

'Gentlemen, I have been doing a lot of thinking while away in hospital and have decided that, as it stands, our project is too narrow; we must embrace the spirit of surprise. We must engage the audience totally, reach to the core of all their senses, not just their brains. To do this it's not enough to explain how one insect lives longer than another, how this one breeds, how that one feeds. We must be the insect!'

We all sat quietly, listening to the professor, who with every second was turning into a guru. To cap it all he took out a packet of Turkish cigarettes, lit up, then exhaled a cloud of smoke towards the ceiling. No one had ever seen him smoke before.

Dorlan was about to enlighten us further with his wisdom when an operatic voice echoed in the hall. Reyes's large frame filled the door; he opened out his arms to us. Dorlan rose from his chair and introduced him to us. We knew him by reputation; only George had actually met him before. When all the greetings were over, Reyes stood back and, with one hand outstretched, the other on his chest, sang out a couple of stanzas.

'Bravo, bravo! Sit down, old chap.' Dorlan drew up an extra armchair for the new arrival.

'What was all that about?' I whispered to Amadeo.

'He just sang out the names of some insect species; their Latin names, that is.'

Seeing how enthusiastic Dorlan was, Reyes tapped him on the knee to indicate that that was not all and, sitting upright on the edge of his seat, burst out singing.

'This time it's the name of a bat species,' whispered Amadeo.

'This is excellent!' Dorlan rubbed his hands and waved over to the barman, ordering Reyes a drink.

Everybody started to talk, Dorlan with Reyes, Sam with Amadeo; meanwhile Sudok came over to my armchair and said through his teeth: 'I see what you mean about Horace having changed; he's completely batty. Batty! And he's brought bats into the equation. What is this lecture turning into?'

There was a commotion in the hall. A cacophony of voices, snatches of conversation and enthusiastic greetings put an end to our discussions and we looked towards the door. It took a while before the new arrivals started to trickle into the room, vying for positions by the bar. They were very old, some just barely making it to the nearest armchair, but they were extremely animated, like children on a school outing.

From behind the giant plant that stood in the archway separating the bar from the dining area, a waiter appeared and timidly approached Dorlan. He advised the professor to go through to the restaurant before the old guests made their way there. He had found us a table in the corner behind the pillar. Dorlan thanked him and we made our way over, taking a last look at the jovial octogenarians chattering like birds by the bar. Several tables were joined together in the middle of the room and elegantly laid as one long table, decorated with bouquets of flowers and paper flags. The old guests were no doubt celebrating an anniversary; perhaps they were veterans.

Dorlan outlined the changes he intended to make to the lecture and suggested how we should deal with them. Some kind of revelation must have come to him in hospital, but it was difficult to prise anything out of him; he gave us no opportunity to interject with a question but continued to elaborate on new material that he was working on. His new vision was inspirational. I felt elated but an uncomfortable thought began to gnaw at the back of my mind; were we no longer to be his collaborators but merely unquestioning assistants? He asked Amadeo whether he had the hospital drawings; some of these he then arranged on the table before the food arrived. He was particularly interested in George Reyes's reaction. Reyes was beaming, as their eyes met, their minds in perfect harmony.

Before we left the club Dorlan sprang another surprise which further irritated Sudok. He told us that he was in contact with a group of musicians whom he was hoping to include in the project. He was to meet up with them at the Arts League that evening for a rehearsal of his 'readings'. He suggested we all come so as to be, as he said, 'au courant' with the project.

On the way back to the underground station Sam told me that Dorlan was going to meet him in the morning to discuss new recordings he wanted made and that he would no doubt contact me about alterations to the podium. I expressed my enthusiasm for Dorlan's new vision but confided to Sam how strange I thought it was for a methodical man like Dorlan to be making so many last-minute changes, some of them major ones like incorporating jazz music.

'That is why we should be at tonight's rehearsal,' emphasized Sam.

'You go Sam; I still have a lot to do in the workshop. You can tell me how it went when we all meet tomorrow. You know, I can't help feeling sorry for old Sudok and for Amadeo. They're so pragmatic; for them everything must be logical, all ideas have to be based on concrete, scientific principles'.

Our trains were approaching from opposite ends of the platform, so we quickly set a time for tomorrow's meeting before saying our farewells.

*   *   *

A roll of the snare drum, then the timpani was followed by one sharp clash of the cymbals. Shaking his head, the percussionist counted out the bars of silence, then, together with the pianist, drifted into a dreamy melody. The saxophonist was leaning against the wall with her eyes closed and dark glasses perched above her fringe. The horn player stood upright with his trumpet close to his chest, while the double bassist was embracing his instrument like a dancer holding his partner, about to make the first step. Dorlan stirred about in his armchair, then closed his eyes and smiled.

Aniela slipped her shades onto the bridge of her nose and pursed her lips around the mouthpiece of her saxophone. Swaying her hips, she exuded a long wailing sound into the room. Soon the trumpeter joined in; Dorlan slumped deeper into his chair almost to a horizontal position, his elbows on the armrests and level with his head. Occasionally he waved his right hand to the beat. The slow, dreamy number was followed by a racy, funky tune. Dorlan straightened up and began to order his papers. When the music came to an end, he rose quickly and, with his wad of notes, walked up to the musicians. They huddled around him as he proceeded to read them excerpts from his text. There was much animation and laughter; Aniela lit up a cigar.

Sam was sitting quietly observing the scene from the other end of the room. His eyes met Aniela's; her sunglasses were once more perched on her head. She winked at him. Dorlan was jubilant. 'This will be fantastic. Yes, it will be fantastic!'

*   *   *

We did not have much time before the students would start arriving. I made use of the blackboard; working from my blueprints, I drew up the plan and elevation of the podium that was to be erected in Pisa. It would give the others an idea of how their elements would fit in. George Sudok was delighted by what he saw; the drawing was clear and functional, in contrast to all the artistic talk, for which he felt an ever greater aversion. When Sam elaborated on the score, Sudok ignored him, preoccupying himself by taking measurements from the blackboard and writing in his notebook.

'So what we have here is a score. All those drawings Dorlan was making in hospital constitute a score that George will interpret musically, while the other George will project them as images onto the podium that you, Ed, are constructing and have just shown on the blackboard. In the meantime, I will be overlaying the sound effects that will counterpoint Aniela's quintet, about whom I'll talk to you in a minute. George's singing voice will form a duet with Dorlan's recital.'

Sudok mumbled something with his back to the group.

'What did he say?' inquired Sam.

'I think he said, "Where's the science?"' answered Amadeo.

Sam made a dismissive gesture and continued.

'Everything, as you can imagine, will have to be perfectly timed. Synchronization is the key to the success of the event. Now, there are still things that need work on. Ed, Dorlan told me that your uncle has an early version of the theremin which he himself designed.' I nodded my head. 'Do you think he would be willing to lend it to us?' Again I nodded my head.

Sam was describing Dorlan's gig from the previous night when a bell started ringing in the corridor. He stopped talking and took out his diary to arrange the next meeting; it would be our last before leaving for Pisa. We would travel ahead of Dorlan in order to set everything up, giving him a few more days to finalize his lecture. Students started walking into the room; I quickly grabbed the duster and wiped off my chalk diagrams.

CHAPTER FOUR

He knew it was inevitable; it was creeping up on him and soon he would no longer be able to resist. It was unbearably hot, the air conditioning was not working and the fans were turned off; they would interfere with recording. Dorlan, however, was shivering and was horrified by his own reflection in the glass wall separating him and the sound engineer from the musicians. His face was white as a sheet.

Then it happened. He fainted, collapsing onto the floor. Aniela was the first to stop playing. Putting aside her saxophone, she ran up to him in her bare feet, lifted him by the shoulders and, with the help of George Hanson, her bass player, carried him over to a chair in the corner of the studio. George quickly brought over two more chairs and they lay Dorlan across them, slipping George's jacket under his head. Aniela went to the water dispenser.

By this time Dorlan had opened his eyes and saw the musician approach him in her black underwear, carrying a plastic cup of water. But she stopped midway as a door opened behind her. She turned her head and saw a woman entering the studio. The woman looked so much like her: the same hair, the same complexion – only she was in white: white knickers and T-shirt. The two women blended into each other.

'Angela?' murmured Dorlan as he rubbed his eyes, fearing he was suffering from double vision. 'What's that?' he whispered.

'Tickets please!'

Instead of the black and white woman, it was a balding, bespectacled ticket inspector who was staring down at him.

'You'll have to be collecting your baggage sir. We are approaching the airport.'

*   *   *

His case was the first to appear on the conveyor belt. With his jacket slung over his shoulder and briefcase tucked under his arm, he wheeled his case across the hall and stepped out into the sunlight through the sliding glass doors.

'Hotel Bologna.'

Within minutes the taxi pulled up at the hotel. His room was small but it felt spacious due to the high ceiling. It was very dark; Dorlan went up to the window, pulled aside the net curtains and opened it. With an outward movement of his arms, he opened the shutters onto the street. Looking down from the second floor, he saw two motor scooters pass each other in opposite directions; their high-pitched engines disturbed the stillness.

Dorlan's gaze lingered on the street for a few seconds. As he was about to turn back into the room, he caught sight of an old couple in the apartment across the street, directly opposite his room. They were like immobile shadows. The woman slowly got up from the table at which they were sitting and shuffled across the room, disappearing into the darkness. After a while she re-emerged, carrying a steaming bowl which she carefully placed before the man, who proceeded to eat from it with a spoon. Dorlan was fixated by this theatre of shadows. The couple was unaware of being observed; probably they were oblivious to the rest of the world as they acted out their daily routine, which with every day would become that little bit slower.

Dorlan started to unpack, then changed his mind in favour of going out and reacquainting himself with the city. He walked down a network of narrow streets towards the river. Soon he caught sight of the tiny church of Santa Maria della Spina. The tops of its miniature, Gothic steeples reflected the light of the sun. Turning left at the church, he walked along the embankment towards the west bridge. With the bend in the river he was in the sun, his long shadow preceding him on the pavement. He stopped in the middle of the bridge and, leaning his arms on the railings, looked across towards the city centre. Beyond the facades of the north embankment, behind the towers, he saw the distant foothills of the Apennines. From the highest hills thin radio masts protruded into the sky.

He walked on, before him two stone lions were guarding the north end of the bridge. Then he saw the modern apartment block curving towards the junction of two streets, the river bank and the bridge. He stood still for a while on the bridge, starring at the building in front of him. A man stepped out onto the balcony on the second floor. The man lit a cigarette and looked straight into the sun. His figure cast a crisp shadow onto the wall behind him. He remained perfectly still. Dorlan stood transfixed. For a moment he felt as if he was looking at himself. The man moved, took a few drags of his cigarette, then finally discarded it over the balcony and re-entered the apartment. The apartment that Dorlan himself had occupied all those years ago.

Once on the other side of the river he proceeded back towards the centre of the city. He was in no hurry. He was pleased to have taken the earliest flight from London; he now had the time to aimlessly roam the city and rediscover his old haunts. He stopped again and looked into the sun, which reflected off the surface of the river. Squinting his eyes, he barely made out the silhouetted buildings but had no desire to clip on his shades over his spectacles. In fact he removed his glasses and in the silence enjoyed the warm light spreading across his face. This is what cats do, he thought; face the sunlight and squint their eyes.

Continuing his promenade along the Lungarno, he passed the Palazzo Reale and, before reaching the central bridge, decided to go into the Caffé dell'Ussero, a place he frequented as a student.

It had not changed much. He half hoped that the man at the bar would be the same barman from years past, but that would be too much to hope for; even in his student years the man must have been pushing sixty. Dorlan ordered a coffee and mineral water at the bar and carried them over to one of the booths. He placed the cup and the glass on the table and carefully squeezed his way between the marble slab and the seat, making sure not to upset the coffee as he sat down. The seat gave way under his weight, bringing the table surface high up to his chest. It was too soft and the upholstery was different, no longer the weathered tan leather that he remembered but red velour, trimmed with gold. Much too vulgar, thought Dorlan, as he wriggled about, trying to make himself comfortable. Inevitably he managed to disturb his coffee, which spilled into the saucer. Suppressing his annoyance, he mopped up the spilt coffee with a paper serviette.

He thought of reading the newspapers which hung on the stand by the bar. Another tricky manoeuvre was required, this time to get himself out of the seat. Dorlan had to swing forward with enough momentum to lift himself out of the soft seat. On the second attempt he managed to half stand with knees bent, but his thighs could not avoid knocking against the edge of the table, again spilling more of the coffee and some of the mineral water.

'Blast,' Dorlan cried. At least he had ordered a cappuccino, had he taken an espresso there would be nothing left of it by now. He selected a local newspaper and brought it over to his table. The next couple of hours were taken up by acquainting himself with the local news. Dorlan also scanned the national dailies. When he emerged from the café the sun was directly overhead and it had become unbearably hot. He was hungry, but when he looked up at the clock tower across the river he realized it was still too early for lunch. What was he to do? He walked towards the bridge. It made no sense returning to the hotel, so he went in the opposite direction and proceeded down the Borgo Stretto, where he found a seat at a pavement café. He ordered an aperitif and watched the crowds drift lazily to and fro. With so much time to spare he regretted not having taken his notebook with him; he could have studied the diagrams.

The waiter brought him his drink. Dorlan asked whether he could recommend any restaurants in the vicinity. He recognized some of the names, but it was only when the waiter mentioned the Vecchio Teatro restaurant that Dorlan's eyes lit up. It was only a little further off, past the marketplace.

The square was exactly as he had remembered it: the same dilapidated facades, with brickwork showing through exposed patches of crumbling plaster. Only the majestic edifice of the city bank shone in full splendour behind two gigantic palm trees planted on either side of the entrance. And there it was, the tiny entrance to the restaurant, tucked away in the corner of the square. Above the arched portal, the words 'Vecchio Teatro', spelt out in flowing neon: underneath it the word 'ristorante'. The door was closed. Dorlan gripped the handle and pushed hard, but in vain. How could this be? One o'clock in the afternoon: why would they be closed at lunchtime? He looked through the glass panel running alongside the door; it was dark, no sign of life.

What a disappointment, Dorlan was deflated. Looking across the square, he thought of walking back to the marketplace. However, behind the vine leaves he found a notice: the restaurant was only open in the evenings and not for lunch. At least the news was not all bad; Dorlan decided to take his friends there after the reception at the rectorate which was to take place in the early evening.

He had a light meal in one of the market square restaurants, then strolled back to the hotel and took a long nap.

The telephone rang; it was the university. His team was there, ready for his instructions. It took Dorlan some time to wake up from his deep sleep. He listened without really absorbing what was being said to him. Only when the receiver was handed over to me did he realize whom he was speaking to. We arranged to meet and go over our schedule.

We met at the university gates, shook hands and walked across the spacious courtyard to one of the lecture theatres at the far end of the building. Dorlan glanced at the huge clock above one of the galleries.

'Is that the real time?'

'It is a bit fast. I think it is just after six.'

Dorlan could not believe that he had had such a long siesta; he never wore a wrist watch and did not bother to check the time by the clock tower when crossing the river. Ever since landing at the airport he had felt as if he was in a daydream. He was like a ghost, unattached to this world. What is more, he liked being in this state; such a contrast to his usual, ordered self. 'Pisa, the city that dreams!' he thought to himself.

The wooden structures for the podium were not yet completed, but most of the sound equipment was in place and the technicians were in the process of testing out the acoustics. This procedure was conducted so loudly that Dorlan suggested that we take our blueprints and make for the Caffè dell'Ussero to work out the running order of the performance. I tucked the scrolls under my arm and we strode out into the evening air towards the river.

Our conversation was animated as we pored over the plans laid out before us on the table in the café. The long preparations were all but behind us; now the lecture was close to becoming a reality. A scientific lecture delivered with the backing of a musical quintet, with electro-acoustic interventions and a digital light show, was to me unprecedented. I told Dorlan that it would not take me long to finish assembling the podium. I had resolved most of the technical difficulties and this set his mind at rest. I then eulogized about how visionary his project was; he was more measured, as he had witnessed similar events conducted by his artist friends at the academy, but he was aware that it would create a stir among the scientific community. All the planning was conducted in utmost secrecy, but rumours were rife along the corridors of the science department about Dorlan's recent activity. He knew he was taking a risk; after all, his audience in Pisa would be made up of distinguished scientists with international reputations. He was spurred on by his artistic collaborators and his self-confidence grew. But what if it failed? He did not even contemplate such a possibility, driven by the strong desire of just wanting to experience the event for himself. Thus he had no fear; he was living for the present and for the present alone. We had absolute faith in him. The musicians relished the experience of working with a scientist. The rehearsals in London had been great fun. They did not pretend to understand the scientific jargon, but the way Dorlan delivered the text was inspirational. It was like listening to a poet reciting verse in a foreign language. They went with the inflections and tone of his voice and created an accompaniment any singer would envy.

After going through the plans for the rehearsal I suggested that we should have a small brandy with our coffee before going to the rectorate. Downing the brandy was like putting a full stop to our deliberations. Now we could face the reception and meet all the guests.

As we approached the rectorate people were already climbing the front steps of the palazzo. Some men wore diner jackets, others were more casually dressed. The women accompanying them were elegant, some were glamorous. Once inside the building, the sound of laughter and polite conversation pervaded. We were soon identified by a woman dressed in black wearing a pearl necklace. She led us to the rector, who was extremely pleased to see us. He asked Horace about his journey and whether his accommodation was satisfactory. The vestibule was filling up with more guests; pressing up against us was a group of academics which included Dr Rissi. Bearded, bespectacled, with thinning grey hair and dressed in a corduroy suit with leather patches around the elbows, he looked like a real professor.

'Dr Dorlan, let me introduce you to Dr Rissi, Professor of Genetics at Florence University. Dr Rissi will also be delivering a lecture, but in the university building.'

'We are all very much looking forward to your lecture, Dr Dorlan,' Rissi whispered in a soft Italian accent. 'I have a particular interest, as I have long studied the genetic lineage of *Chiroptera*.'

'Then I hope I will not disappoint you,' responded Dorlan.

At this point a group of young people descended upon us, firing off questions. Overwhelmed, Dorlan was lost for words; how to begin to answer so many questions in such a crowded space. Soon he found himself moving up the ancient, wooden staircase; he was part of a human river flowing steadily forward. On reaching the first floor the tightly packed crowd was approached by waiters and waitresses carrying trays laden with drinks. Judging by their young age, they must have been students working part-time. This turned out to be true, as the young people surrounding Dorlan exchanged greetings with them. While ascending the staircase, Dorlan realized that his youthful company were research students, some of whom would be helping out with his event. He was pleasantly surprised by their knowledge of his subject and sensed their enthusiasm. It was reassuring for him to be in the company of such empathetic assistants. Dorlan took a glass of champagne and raised it to his lips.

A loud tap on the microphone turned all heads towards the centre of the hall. The rector cleared his throat and proceeded to greet the guests. He then said a few words about the scientific symposium and introduced the main speakers and participants. He emphasized the importance of international cooperation in the world of science and expressed how proud he was that Pisa University was this year's chosen venue for the event. He outlined the history of the university and its achievements over the centuries, every so often interjecting that this was the birthplace of Galileo.

We stood on the periphery of the crowded hall, near one of the large windows, and as is often the case guests standing far from the centre of the congregation had already started to talk in whispers among themselves. This behaviour irritated Dorlan: however boring a speech might be, a measure of respect was called for. He tried to listen to the rector but could not avoid overhearing his neighbours discussing his forthcoming lecture; they did not realize who was standing right next to them.

'. . . I have always followed Dr Dorlan's research on bats, but the lecture I hear he will be delivering tomorrow will be something of a farce. He's been experimenting with artists from his university.'

'. . . and with musicians,' said another.

'He has always been so methodical and rigorous in his approach. Everything he published always had an air of authority about it. You could trust his conclusions and base your own research on his findings. Now I hear he is relying on improvisation and the theatrical. I know it is important to encourage the younger generation to engage with the sciences, to whet their appetite for the subject, but this is really going too far.'

'I agree, but I do think we should give him a chance. After all, this is the Dorlan who disproved all those theories from the previous century which we now know were rooted in dubious experiments. I find that his own field experiments were very sound and have certainly contributed to the world of knowledge.'

'But that was ages ago . . .'

At this point the rector had concluded his speech and the audience responded with applause. A string quartet situated in the far corner of the hall started to play a piece by Vivaldi; the guests resumed talking and drank more of the champagne being served by the student waiters. Dorlan and I turned towards the window which overlooked the river and gazed into the cloudless sky, the setting sun illuminated the clock tower across the Arno.

The clock struck eight.

I moved closer to Dorlan. 'We may be in for some confrontation.'

'Confrontation? We will give them a performance they will never forget! I just can't wait! And this element of uncertainty . . . This is what really excites me.'

I had to smile. A beautiful waitress carrying a bottle of champagne wrapped in a linen napkin approached us and replenished our glasses.

'Listen, Ed, let's not hang around here for too long. I know of a charming little restaurant off the square behind the university.'

'Good idea, I'm famished!'

'Do you think we can find the others? I caught sight of Amadeo, when coming up the stairs, but . . .'

I stood on my toes and soon spotted our colleagues.

'I can see them! They're at the far end, close to the musicians. I think they are all together.'

'Let's go, then!'

The Dorlan party descended the steps of the palazzo and walked along the river. There were eleven of us: Dorlan, Amadeo, Sam the sound engineer, the five musicians, the two Georges, and me.

'Good God, I couldn't wait to get out of there!' gasped Aniela.

'So where are we going?' asked Sam.

'To the Ristorante Vecchio Teatro, dear boy!' replied Dorlan, leading the way.

We passed the university and turned right before the Palazzo Reale, entering an oddly shaped square in the middle of which stood the illuminated statue of Cosimo III. Aniela remarked that this square was like a De Chirico painting. We walked in small groups in the shadow of the statue, which stretched to the far end of the square and directed us to a hidden alleyway which opened out onto a much larger square and the restaurant.

From the outside it looked shabby and small, but on entering we found ourselves in a charming interior; half a dozen round tables were neatly laid for dinner. The walls were covered with pictures of all sizes. Some were paintings of local landscapes; some were still lifes depicting food, mostly fruit and fish. There were also many photographs, all related to the theatre: faded shots of the old theatre after which the restaurant was named, its small auditorium looking like a miniature La Scala. Taking off his jacket, Dorlan inspected the framed photographs of actors from a bygone age. I asked the waiter if he could join two of the tables together and we took a little while to settle down.

Once seated we began to relax. Aniela was laughing at an impromptu comment Dorlan had made. A waiter started to lay the table; he was soon followed by a short, balding man who introduced himself as the owner. He handed out the menus, which were nothing more than photocopies of a typed-out list, and left us to study the promising culinary delights.

Apart from a couple sitting by one of the windows, we were the only ones in the restaurant. The rustic intimacy of the place appealed to everyone, even the primitive photocopied menus had their own charm. At the top of each menu was the name of the restaurant and a small engraving of a view of Pisa which was indistinct due to over inking from consecutive photocopying. Beneath the image a poem was printed in very small type. Dorlan had to take off his spectacles, while Aniela had to take hers out of her bag to attempt to read the lines of verse. Even then, both were hard pressed to decipher the meaning of the text. Dorlan exclaimed that it was written in archaic Italian, most probably a Pisan dialect, and he read the last line out in English:

'Pisa, the city that dreams.'

'I like that!' said Sam. 'The city that dreams; it's romantic, magical. It sets the mood.'

I was frustrated. 'That's all well and good, but I can't make heads or tails of the menu. Where are the prices? And all the dishes seem to blend into each other. There is no separate list for starters, no list of main dishes or desserts. We get this block of text which looks like a never ending hors d'oeuvre.'

At this point the owner returned from the kitchen with a small notepad and pencil. He took off his glasses and left them suspended on a thin cord around his neck.

'Are you ready to order, signore, signori?' He uttered in a thick Italian accent.

'Well, we are not quite sure which are the starters and which the main courses.'

The owner's answer was hard to understand and Dorlan repeated the question in Italian. On hearing that one of the party spoke Italian, the proprietor's disposition became much more animated and cordial, and he embarked on an elaborate explanation. He gesticulated like an orchestra conductor waving his baton, his voice ascending and descending in a melodic fashion. The rest of the party had to wait in anticipation for Dorlan to translate.

'Capito, grazie, signore,' replied Dorlan, and turned to his friends around the table. 'He said that it's a fixed menu.'

'What do you mean it's a fixed menu?' I cried. 'All that stuff? Besides, he was going on for hours. Surely he said something else than that it's a fixed menu?'

Aniela took off her glasses and pointed to the menu with them. 'Horace, I can't see myself eating all this. It's much too much.'

'Don't worry,' responded Dorlan. 'They are small portions, it's all carefully worked out.' He turned to the waiter and said, 'Va bene, signore. Prendiamo tutto.'

'E il vino?'

'He's asking what wine we will be drinking.'

Dorlan ordered a local Pisan red wine and the restaurateur retreated to the kitchen, shaking his head from side to side, mumbling something to himself.

'I think he thinks we are mad to choose red wine, as all the dishes are fish and seafood,' said the sound engineer.

'You may be right,' replied Dorlan. 'He strongly recommended some local white wine. But we like red, and red it will be. Who cares what he thinks?'

'But listen, Horace,' I cut in. 'He was talking to you for hours. What else did he say?'

'I've already told you. He was going on about all the dishes and where they come from, how they originated. That his mother runs the kitchen etc., etc. Actually some of the history is quite interesting. For example,' Dorlan pointed to the menu, 'this one here, the fish, it is wrapped in smoked ham, a recipe originating in the Renaissance, when one member of an influential Pisan family hated fish, but since fish was very much part of the staple diet, this dish was invented especially for him. The ham of course disguised the fishy taste and accommodated the aristocratic palatte, thus becoming a very popular recipe. And there are a few others.'

'Well, let's hope they arrive soon. I'm hungry,' exclaimed Aniela.

Everyone was so excited to be in each other's company; only the two Georges seemed reserved. We had all put a lot into the project, working hard over the last few months. Now was the time to relax and look forward to the event itself. Aniela, who was seated next to Dorlan, leaned forward and whispered into his ear.

'That couple by the window.'

'What about them?'

'The woman keeps staring at you.'

Indeed at that very moment the woman threw a brief glance at him as she was talking to her male companion.

'Do you know her?'

'I don't think so. Mind you, she does look vaguely familiar.'

The dishes started arriving, to everyone's delight. Both the waiter and the proprietor were busy hovering around the two tables, positioning their plates among the bottles and glasses. Each plate carried a small but elegantly prepared dish, a feast for the eyes. The party started reaching for the cutlery. Dorlan made sure that everyone's glass was full. When it was time for the next dish to arrive, Dorlan ordered another two bottles of wine.

'You know Horace,' cried Amadeo, 'I am Italian but I have never eaten such exquisite food in my life; you were right to bring us here! Has it changed much from the time you were a student?'

'I think it's even better than I remember. I'm glad you like it.'

Dorlan was so excited that he had to undo his bow tie and roll up his sleeves. Aniela was talking with members of her band, while Sam and I were expressing our enthusiasm for Pisa. Dorlan proposed a toast to his colleagues: he thanked us for our hard work and dedication. We responded in chorus, cheering our leader on. Aniela got up from the table on wobbly legs, already affected by the wine.

'Here's to Doris Horlan!'

Everyone burst out laughing. Aniela, realizing what she had just said, put her hand to her mouth in embarrassment and fell back into her chair, laughing uncontrollably. Jokes followed in abundance; we let go of all our inhibitions.

Dorlan looked at the woman by the window and saw her staring straight back. Without taking her eyes off him, she was still in conversation with her companion. She was very elegant and sat erect, with her forearms against the edge of the table. Several silver bangles jangled about her wrists. She was dark-skinned and her jet-black hair was pinned back, leaving the nape of her neck exposed. She wore glasses which were similar to Dorlan's, only narrower.

Dorlan's mind was working hard: did he know this woman, and if so where had he seen her? He had little idea of how old she might be; most probably she was in her forties, but from a distance she looked younger. Then again her hair was most probably dyed black; no one could have hair that black, although she had a dark, Mediterranean complexion. Dorlan's eyes were scanning her face, then her whole body. It was firm, no droopy arms. Then the scanning stopped. He had found a vital clue: the neck. Its wrinkles betrayed signs of ageing and he sensed that he was close to discovering her identity.

At that very moment the woman stood up, brushed invisible creases out of her skirt and made her way directly towards Dorlan. Dorlan, in his embarrassment, reached for a glass of water, hoping the woman was going to the toilet.

'Horasss! Horasss Dorrrlan!'

Dorlan put down his glass and reluctantly looked up at the woman, who was towering over him. With both hands on her hips, she was staring into his eyes, awaiting his response. His companions stopped talking and turned their attention to Dorlan, who clumsily took a handkerchief out of his pocket to wipe his forehead. He was sweating profusely. Dorlan's eyes could not rest on the woman's eyes for long, but slipped down to her right hand; her fingers were drumming a silent beat on her hip.

'It's me! Carmelita. Don't you recognize me?'

With no response coming from Dorlan, she inched her way towards him and extending her arm, clenched her fist, imitating a claw; simultaneously she opened her mouth pretending her teeth were fangs.

'I am Dracula.'

Dorlan's friends sat bemused, but Dorlan's eyes suddenly sparkled. He smiled.

'Of course. Carmelita. Carmelita Ruiz.'

'Carmelita Rignoli. I am a married woman. That's my husband over there, Roberto Rignoli.'

The man by the window nodded his head.

Dorlan rose to his feet and embraced Signora Rignoli. He pulled up an empty chair from a neighbouring table. Carmelita sat down, again smoothing her skirt with her hands; the silver bangles added a musical accent to the manoeuvre. Dorlan introduced Carmelita to his companions and in turn presented his friends to Carmelita. There was much hand-shaking and soon the boisterous conversations resumed as the dancing waiters brought in another set of dishes.

'Why doesn't your husband join us?'

Carmelita waved her hand at her companion, who gesticulated a response that seemed to suggest he had to read something.

'Roberto is going over a lecture he has to deliver tomorrow at the university.'

'Really! That's exactly what I'm doing tomorrow.'

'I know. That's why I asked Roberto to take me with him. I don't usually go with him; these lectures are beyond me. But when I heard you would be speaking at the symposium I thought I really must come. I still remember your student talks.'

Laughter erupted from Dorlan's table. His friends were making the most of the evening. Carmelita looked towards them, smiling.

'Have your friends come to hear you speak?'

'More than that. They are taking part in my lecture. They are an integral part of it. Isn't that so Aniela?'

'Isn't what so?' Aniela looked towards them.

'I was just telling Carmelita that all of you are an integral part of my lecture.'

'Of course we are!' I shouted above the din, overhearing what Dorlan was saying.

'And here's to us!' Sam stood up, wavering on his feet with a glass in his hand.

Everyone raised their glasses in response. Dorlan looked around for a spare glass and poured Carmelita some wine.

'Say, Carmelita, what's with this Dracula stuff?' asked Aniela.

'Why don't you ask the count himself?' Carmelita smiled provocatively.

Dorlan blushed and again had to wipe his brow with his handkerchief.

'You've embarrassed him, Aniela,' said Carmelita. 'Dorlan was not always the distinguished professor that he now seems to be. In his student days he was wild.'

*   *   *

How embarrassing, all of us suffering from hangovers; I felt terrible, but driven by a sense of duty rose early and walked to Caffé dell'Ussero for the Italian version of a 'hair of the dog'. Dorlan's old flame gave me the recipe before we left the restaurant the previous night. I could not remember the ingredients but the barman caught on immediately the minute I rested my elbow on the counter. Was it that obvious? I retreated shyly with the concoction to one of the booths and unfolded the blueprint I had in my pocket. It was in a sorry state; there were so many folds and creases that I could not decipher my own drawing. I braced myself and downed the foul liquid in one gulp. It made me shudder. My head was throbbing. With difficulty I climbed out of the softly upholstered seat and staggered across to the door, hoping the fresh air would alleviate my condition.

The breeze blew through my hair, and by the time I reached the rectorate I was ready for work. This would be the last lap of our unusual adventure. Tonight Dorlan would stand on my podium and sweep the public off their feet. There was much banging and sawing in the hall; as I stood before the wooden framework, which was nearing completion, I felt great admiration for the dedicated workmen and students. The foreman showed me the scaffolding they had made for me to facilitate my inspection of the podium. I pictured Dorlan speaking from on high, down to the gathered scientists and academics; then, from beneath his feet there would . . .

'Avanti!'

The foreman nudged me and suggested I go up and look at the construction; otherwise we would not complete the work on time. Boldly I climbed the ladder; in my hung-over state I felt no fear. Everyone stopped working; their eyes were on me. I climbed higher and higher; then I hesitated and looked down. My head began to spin.

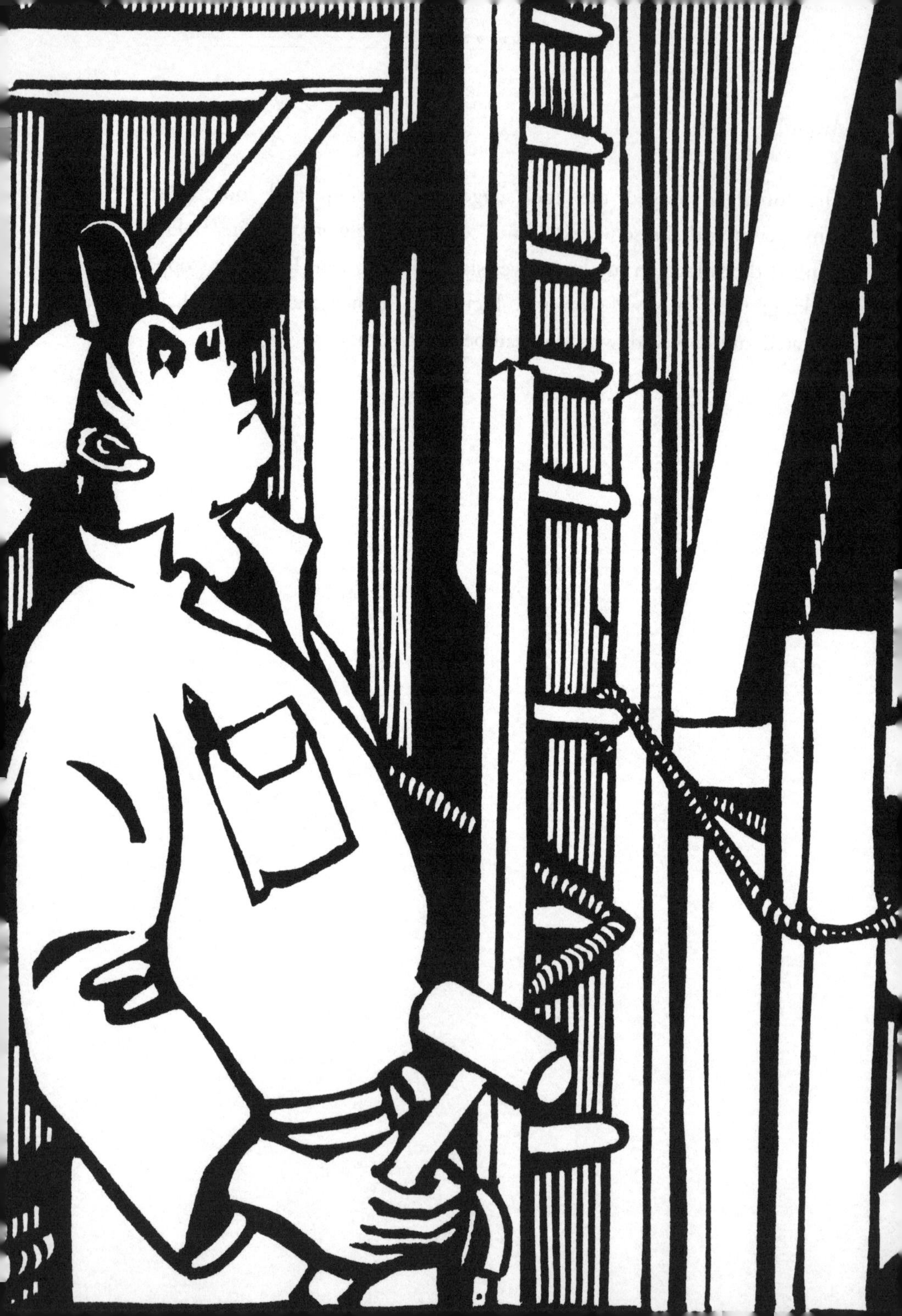

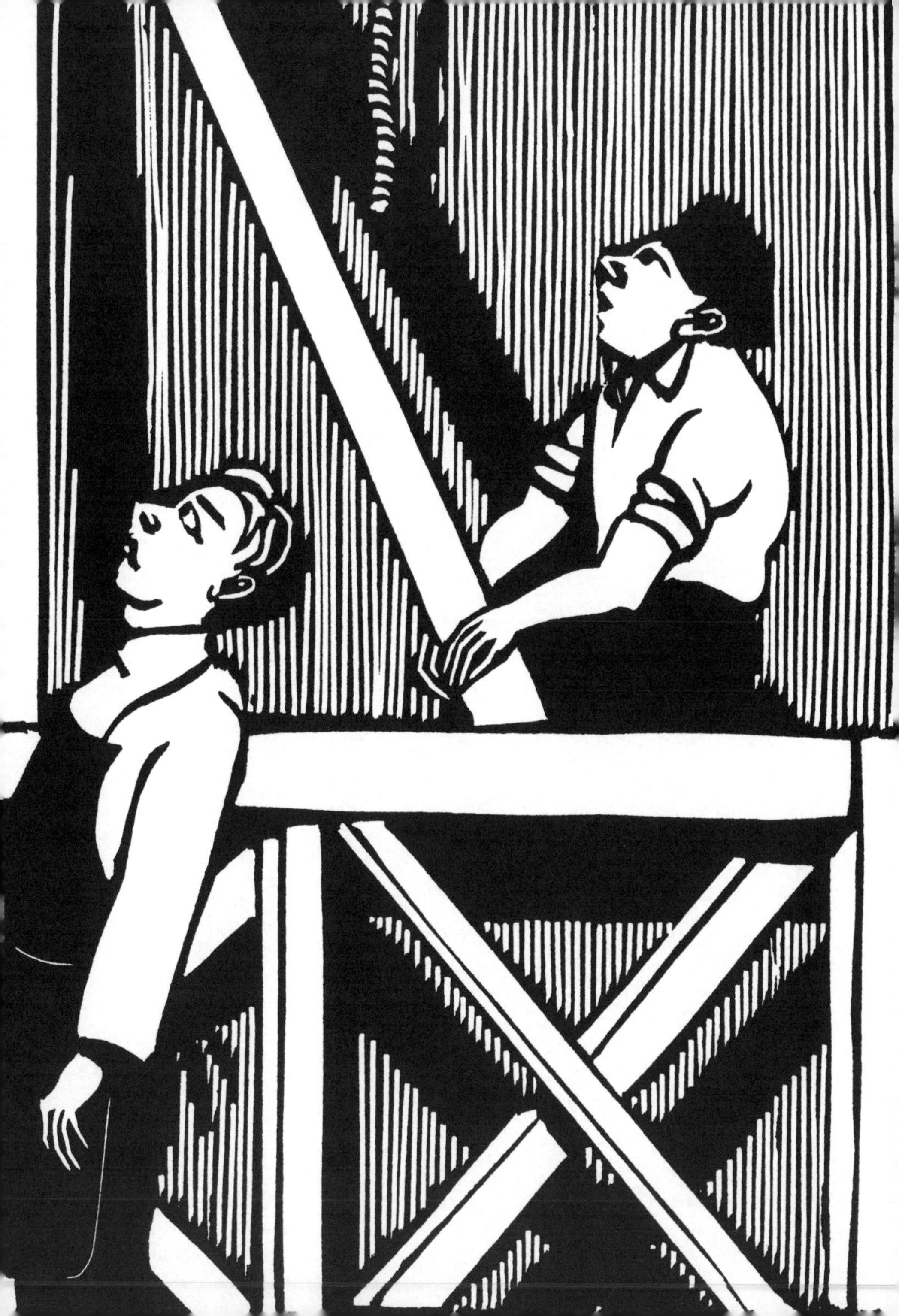

CHAPTER FIVE

Angela switched on the radio as Dorlan was shaving in the bathroom. Music drifted down the corridor and Dorlan started to sway to the rhythm and cut himself. He swore, then quickly pressed a piece of torn toilet paper to his chin to stem the flow of blood. He put on his horn-rimmed glasses and in his underwear and socks danced along the corridor in the direction of the sitting room, where he saw Angela doing the samba. On seeing her husband, she stretched out her arm towards him; he looked ridiculous within the door frame, in his horn-rimmed spectacles, dark socks, underpants, vest and the piece of paper stuck to his chin. Awkwardly he danced towards her.

'Horace, loosen up! Don't be so stiff!'

She waved her hand in the air. 'Listen to the music; let it flow.'

Her own movements were an example of how to do it, but Dorlan continued his own dance, as if in a trance. There she was, his goddess, Salome mesmerizing Herod. Half dressed, she was swinging her hips slowly one way, then the other; from her waist down she wore only black knickers and stockings which were held up by a thin suspender belt that Dorlan had bought her all those years ago in Warsaw, while away on one of his lecture tours. Angela had worn it for him on one or two occasions but then dismissed it as impractical in these days of wearing tights. Even when buying the belt he had felt guilty, knowing that it could be seen as an outmoded male fetish which a woman would only accept with resignation.

The moment of purchasing the item came back to him in all its detail in the few seconds that it took him to reach his dancing wife. He had discovered a minuscule, privately owned shop off one of the main streets. This was in the times of communism. The window display was old-fashioned but beautiful: pre-war dummies sporting outdated wigs displayed lingerie that was handmade, intricate, of high-quality fabrics. There were mirrors everywhere, around the window and behind the mannequins, showing off the items from all angles. It had taken Dorlan some time to muster enough courage to enter the shop from the street. His shyness had been noticed by the proprietor, for on entering he was made to feel at home immediately. Like her shop, she was also from a bygone age. She was old but well preserved, extremely elegant. It was obvious at a glance that she looked after herself; everything was in place: red lipstick, hair colouring, even her posture resisted the march of time. Dorlan spent a long time in the shop. He spoke French with the old lady, who allowed him to look at everything, taking great pride in her wares. He discovered that all the items in her shop were made by the proprietor herself, in the back room with the help of an old Singer sewing machine. In the end he bought only the black suspender belt. It appealed to him for its simplicity: its narrow zigzag pattern and gathered joins were beautifully crafted, far superior to the dainty, embroidered models. The old lady praised his choice and wrapped the item with great care in tissue and a black ribbon.

Now the belt had come to life again around Angela's narrow waist. Dorlan put his arms around her and was drawn into the living room. It took him a few seconds to fall into his wife's stride.

'Relax,' said Angela. 'Don't move so fast.'

Dorlan's hands slid down Angela's back into her knickers. She responded flirtatiously. He smiled and like a peacock towered over her. Angela wriggled away.

'Horace, we're dancing!'

At this moment the music quickened in tempo. She pulled her husband by the hand and they both laughed at his inept dancing. Soon he got into the swing of things; the greater the tempo, the more they enjoyed themselves. They moved from one end of the room to the other. Angela knocked into the antique radiogram. George Hanson fell over his double bass, which spun out of his hands. He crashed into Aniela, knocking the saxophone out of her mouth. Music notes spilled onto the studio floor.

Dorlan and Angela had stepped out onto the balcony; they were covered in sweat. Angela put her hands on the railings; Dorlan wrapped his arms around her.

They stood there for some time, looking out over the gardens. Beyond the gardens stood rows of suburban houses and beyond them the tall trees of the park. Together they stared into the distance. Angela pricked up her ears: there was interference on the radio; they had lost the station. She stepped past Dorlan into the room and went across to the radiogram. For a while she twiddled with the knobs, adjusting the tuner and changing the wavelengths until she found what she wanted. Dorlan remained oblivious to the slow tango coming from the radio, fixated by the view from the balcony, until his wife put her hands around his waist and lay her cheek across his shoulders.

'Let's dance again.'

Dorlan turned around, delicately kissing Angela on the lips as she lifted her eyes. He stroked her head and together they entered the room, where they danced slowly, floating across the floor in perfect harmony.

'There, when you don't think about it too much, you can dance well; none of those jerky movements and crazy poses.'

Dorlan responded by removing his spectacles and leaned towards Angela, pulling her back towards the floor. In his firm grip she yielded to a passionate embrace; the tango had come to an end. For a while the band did not move, as if momentarily reflecting on the music they had just played. Now they could relax; this was the last piece they had to record for the day.

'Did you know that Naco is playing at the club this evening? Perhaps we should go? Such a good dancer that you are.' Angela smiled.

'You mean Alexei Naco and his band? But he hasn't played since the accident.'

'What accident?'

'The time he electrocuted himself on his Hawaiian guitar. Did you not hear about it?'

'No.'

'But you must have noticed that he hasn't played for years.'

'Now you mention it, I assumed he was abroad or something. Anyway, he is playing, Emma told me. She even asked whether we might be going.'

'Emma? That means what's his name will be going, that fatso she hangs around with; and God knows who else.'

'Oh, Horace, you're such a bore. Even if they were going, we don't have to be with them. We can be alone together, just you and I.'

Angela caressed his bald head and with her fingers played with his ear. She knew how to disarm him.

'Very well. I'll pop over to the academy to tie up a few loose ends and I'll be back in time to get ready.'

'To the academy? But you've only just come back from your trip, surely the academy can wait. I thought we could go shopping; after all, I have to wear something tonight.'

'But you've loads of things to wear.'

'Look, Horace, who is more important, the academy or me? Well?'

'You are, of course,' emphasized Dorlan, 'but I have to debrief the research department on the symposium; it could influence our funding.'

'Funding? Research? Nonsense! The only thing that needs funding is me, and as for research, I have seen a dress in Joseph's that is perfect, but I rely on your opinion. You know how much I value your opinion. You have such a good eye. Without you, I could make a mistake.'

This last comment appealed directly to Dorlan's ego, and of course he fell for it. In any case, he was happy to see his wife wearing a beautiful dress, especially if they were to go out; and being in a relaxed mood, he agreed to visit the shops as long as it would not take all day, knowing how long Angela usually took to dress up and prepare for an evening out.

The day's frantic activity was worth the effort; Angela's dress was immaculate and it matched the shoes Dorlan had bought her in Pisa. Dorlan loved to observe his wife getting ready to go out; all that wriggling in and out of various outfits was so feminine. Clothes were strewn across the floor, articles on the ironing board ready to be pressed.

'So what can I wear with the dress?'

'The silver necklace and bracelet will do the trick,' answered Dorlan.

Angela put them on and pirouetted before the mirror, eyes scrutinizing her own figure.

'Mmm – I'll just see if the the blouse and those wide trousers might be more appropriate.'

Dorlan was horrified by the possibility of the new dress being discarded in favour of an old blouse and trousers, after all those tortuous hours in the shops. He took out his handkerchief from his trouser pocket and wiped his brow. He saw Angela fully dressed from the waist up, including her make-up and hair; from the waist down she was naked. In this state she was ironing her trousers. Dorlan approached her from behind and embraced her. Angela shrugged him off.

'Horace, we'll be late.'

'That's hardly my fault!'

'You must let me get ready.' She turned around, kissed him on the nose, then gave him a firm nudge.

Dorlan retreated like a wounded animal. He entered the living room, poured himself a drink and stepped out onto the balcony. The sun had already set and pleasant aromas drifted up from the gardens.

*   *   *

Dorlan opened the door of the taxi and helped Angela out onto the pavement. After paying the driver he took her by the arm and they climbed the few steps leading to the club. Angela left her bolero jacket in the cloakroom and went up to the bar, where Dorlan was already talking to the barman. He turned around and asked her what she would like to drink. Angela replied and the barman suggested they sit down at a table and that he would bring over the drinks. It was already quite busy in the bar area but they managed to find one free table. Angela whipped out her compact and lipstick; her husband sunk into a leather armchair. Only now did he realize how tired he was. It had been a busy time – so much to think about; so many things to organize – but it was all behind him now, he could just enjoy himself. He was staring at Angela as she was applying some more lipstick to her mouth, but his mind was elsewhere; he was back in Pisa crossing the bridge in the early morning sunlight and looking at a man on the balcony of an apartment block across the river. How strange that it happened to be the apartment he had lived in as a student; the very same place, all those years ago.

'Cheers!' Angela was holding her cocktail glass in the air.

'Cheers,' Dorlan replied automatically, awoken from his daydream.

Angela sipped her drink, leaving a red mark on the rim of her glass.

'What were you thinking about?'

'I was thinking of Pisa.'

'You mean about your lecture? I never really asked you how it went.'

'But you know . . .' Dorlan paused. 'I never had time to really think about it. It's always such an anticlimax after the event. So the honest answer is that I don't really know. I was pleased with it, as was my team. We all worked so hard and we created an event which was more like a vision than a scientific lecture. In no way did it resemble an academic event. It was more like . . .'

Dorlan paused for several seconds, as if he had lost his train of thought.

'More like what?' Angela was intrigued. Usually she could not engage with Horace's professional activities, his subject was so specialized and impenetrable. This time it seemed different. She instinctively felt that his work was undergoing a change.

'Theatrical. We created a sort of performance. But I don't think . . .'

'You don't think what? Honestly, Horace, it's so hard to make any sense of what you're trying to say.'

Horace, a little embarrassed, attempted to resume his train of thought. 'I don't think. That is to say, I don't really know what the public made of it. They applauded at the end of the lecture, but politely. I couldn't detect any enthusiasm or genuine engagement. I could just as well have been reciting logarithmic tables or reading out the dictionary.'

'Oh, I'm sure it wasn't that bad. People don't always show their true feelings. Maybe they were absorbing so much information; it's not as if it was an emotional event. Listening to a lecture is not like going to the theatre.'

'But that's it exactly. My lecture was like the theatre. It was an event. I would like to think it was a spectacular event. I was expressing my vision of things. It was an epiphany.'

'Listen, Horace, you shouldn't get so carried away. Epiphany! Small wonder they did not react as you expected them to. They simply did not expect something like this from you, an eminent scientist, someone who has always gone on about how important it is to be objective, pragmatic, even boring. Didn't you once tell me that the best academic lectures were usually boring?'

'What are you talking about?' shouted Dorlan, visibly irritated by Angela's statement.

'Calm down.' Angela looked about her, embarrassed by her husband's outburst. To her relief, no one was paying any attention to them; customers at the neighbouring tables were preoccupied with their own company. The din around them was now quite pronounced, as more people arrived at the club. The clientele at the bar proceeded through to the restaurant and their places were taken up by new arrivals. Cigarette smoke filled the whole bar area.

'I'm sorry, Angela. I really don't know why I'm getting so worked up.'

Angela leaned forward, touching Dorlan's arm.

'Do you know, I really wish I had come with you. This lecture of yours sounds so fascinating . . .'

'But you were with me,' retorted Dorlan.

'Are you all right, Horace?' Angela was not sure whether he was playing the fool. She was accustomed to his usual pranks, but this behaviour was not usual, it was worrying.

She tilted her head and looked into his eyes.

'Horace? Horace, are you feeling all right?' she said again.

'Of course. What are you trying to say?'

'I said that I wished I had gone with you to Pisa, and you said that I did go with you.'

'But you did come with me.'

The noise around them did not abate, but after hearing what her husband had said, Angela thought she had experienced an eternal silence before Dorlan resumed talking.

'And you were fantastic! Without your music the event wouldn't have worked.'

Angela could not believe her ears.

'You know, Angela, you're such a talented musician; no one plays the saxophone as you do. When those bats flew out as you blew into your instrument, keeping that high note, I felt so emotional I thought I would break down and cry. Why weren't the audience crying?'

As he was uttering these words his eyes were directed towards the ceiling. Angela did not reply, she just stared at Dorlan, Eventually she whispered.

'Horace, I don't play the saxophone; I play the piano. I wasn't playing for you in Pisa; I was here in London.'

Dorlan, with his eyes now closed, replied, 'You were playing for me in Pisa. Your saxophone brought out the bats. They flew from under the podium into the audience, then swooped up to the ceiling, swerving to the open windows and flew out across the river, making for the bridge like a cloud of locusts, barely visible in the night sky. The bats circled around the rectorate building several times before heading along the river, past the church of San Matteo, towards the distant bridge facing the park. They swooped down as they approached the bridge where the men in armoured suits had assembled some time before. As they made out the approaching bats, the knights started to panic, but as they were so tightly packed, they found it hard to advance to the embankments. A cacophony of sounds ensued as the bats crashed into helmets and armoured breastplates, simultaneously emitting their shrill cries. Some knights fell to the ground, others trampled over their comrades in a desperate attempt to flee the nocturnal creatures. In all the chaos the defence of the city was abandoned, no one kept their position. Should the invasion have taken place, the city would soon have fallen to the Moorish hordes. As it was, there were no boats making their way up the Arno; the long banners covered in Arabic script did not wave in the breeze.'

As he was unfurling his monologue a large figure towered over their table. It was Gus, Emma's fiancé.

'So you have come! To hear Alexei play?'

Angela was relieved by the interruption.

'Is Emma with you?'

'She has just gone to the Ladies to powder her nose. I don't think she will be long.'

'Well, why don't we make our way to the ballroom, we'll no doubt bump into Emma on the way.'

Once Angela got up from her armchair Gus tried to kiss her on the cheek, but his great bulk made the manoeuvre somewhat difficult. Eventually he managed to place a brief kiss on Angela's cheek and proceeded to shake Dorlan's hand, once the professor had drained his aperitif. Emma was already in the hall and the four of them climbed the wide, curving staircase to the first floor. As they approached their destination they were taken by surprise. The place was full of young people. The noise was overwhelming; there was no chance of speaking to each other and the lively crowd clutching bottles of beer pressed against them, forcing them precariously against the banister. Gus looked down past the chandelier towards the hall on the ground floor and felt faint. Not being able to communicate verbally, Dorlan signalled with his hands that they should follow him to the second floor. At that moment electric guitars burst out from the ballroom at such a volume that the building seemed to shake. Immediately the youngsters started to bob up and down, shaking their heads, with their arms in the air.

Dorlan's party were lucky to have made their escape when they did; the vestibule outside the ballroom now resembled a human wave. On reaching the next floor, they entered a large room through a set of double doors, which they promptly shut behind them; the heavy music abated, though its presence could still be felt through the vibrating floor. They had entered an oasis of calm. Groups of people sat at tables about the room, while in the corner, next to the bar, a man was playing a slow jazz number on a grand piano. They located a table in one of the alcoves. The soft music brought instant relief. The barman came up to their table and they ordered drinks; Dorlan and Angela repeated the order they had had in the downstairs bar, Emma followed suit. Gus, on the other hand, deliberated for some time, discussing at length with the barman the merits of one cocktail over another. As this went on Dorlan and Angela decided to dance. They excused themselves, leaving Emma at the table somewhat frustrated by her partner's indecision.

The couple danced slowly, immersed in the dreamy music. Dorlan whispered into his wife's ear.

'Don't look now, but I think the man at the piano is Alexei Naco.'

As the couple slowly turned to the music, Angela had the pianist in her sight. She raised her head from Dorlan's shoulder and fixed her eyes on the musician. Surely this was not him; he looked much too thin. She remembered Naco as being quite stocky. As for his face, and above all his hair, it was totally different. The man before her had a pale complexion and an unusual hairstyle. The hair that started near the top of his skull, revealing a large amount of forehead, was grey and wire-like. It was also long and frizzy, standing on end rather like that of Albert Einstein, as seen in so many photographs.

'This isn't Naco! What makes you think it is him?' she whispered.

'I'm sure it's him. Those sad eyes give him away. And he still has that thin moustache.'

The number came to an end. Angela and Dorlan walked back to their table, where they found Gus pointing to his drink.

'In the end I ordered a caipirinha, they make it just right.'

'Listen, don't look now,' Angela addressed her friends in a secretive manner, 'but Horace thinks that the man at the piano is Alexei Naco.'

The couple immediately turned their heads towards the piano. They scrutinized the man, then huddled around the table, conveying their opinion to Angela and Dorlan in a succession of whispers.

'It's not him. It can't be him. He's so different – look at his hair! It's more likely to be Albert Einstein on hunger strike than Naco.'

'That's what I told Horace, but he's adamant that it's him,' said Angela.

'Well, there's only one way to find out,' broke in Dorlan. 'I'll go over and ask him.'

The others felt uneasy about this and Angela tried to hold him back by placing her hand on his knee, but Dorlan got up and walked across the room, over to the piano. He reached it just as the pianist was about to resume playing. The man raised his eyes from the keyboard and looked straight at Dorlan. He smiled, 'Hello, Horace, it's been a long time.'

Dorlan asked him if he would join them at their table. Naco had to play one more number and then he would be taking a break. He would gladly join them then. Dorlan tapped his friend on the shoulder and walked back to the table with a broad smile on his face. 'It's him all right!'

'Well, well!' is all that came from Emma.

'I must say, I would never have guessed it,' added Gus.

'You were right after all, Horace,' said Angela. 'I find it hard to believe; he's changed so much.'

When Naco finished playing he went over to the bar, then, with a drink in his hand, he made his way to Dorlan's table. Dorlan rose from his stool and invited Naco to a seat which he pulled up from a neighbouring table. Everyone smiled and exchanged greetings. Angela promptly told her old friend how much he had changed and that only her husband had recognized him.

'But you, my dear Angela, have not changed at all! Always the young beauty.'

Naco may have changed physically but his gentlemanly manners were the same as ever. Angela lowered her head, shyly accepting the compliment, then asked, 'When was the last time we saw each other? It must be many years.'

'Do you know, I can't remember,' answered Naco. 'My mind's a blank.'

'Tell us what happened with the Hawaiian guitar,' interjected Dorlan. 'We heard you were electrocuted during one of your gigs.'

'That's true, I was,' answered Naco. 'There was some sort of short circuit. It was explained to me later in detail, but I wouldn't be able to tell you all the technicalities, it was such a long time ago. I do remember I was playing a Latin number and bam! The next thing I knew I was being sizzled. I felt oddly exhilarated. I was experiencing a kind of high, and that is all I remember. I was told that it was quite a spectacle. My eyes were popping out and my hair stood on end. As it does to this day, only in the meantime my hairline has advanced slightly; I regained some hair. I would have been happier if all of it grew back, but I can't complain.'

'It's certainly different to the suntanned bald head and black hair that I remember you having. With the pencil-line moustache, it gave you such a Latin look,' interjected Dorlan.

'Anyway,' Naco continued, 'I had collapsed and had been taken to hospital, unconscious. I must have experienced some kind of coma; I dropped in and out of consciousness and the hospital kept me in intensive care for several months.'

'Several months?' exclaimed Gus.

'That's what they told me.'

'What happened afterwards?' asked Dorlan.

'They released me; but it took me years to pick up the pieces. Needless to say, my group disbanded and I stopped playing. I drifted in and out of jobs. I worked in a factory, drove a delivery van. That led to working as a chauffeur. My client happened to be a composer and when he eventually found out that I too was a musician, he persuaded me to return to music. Which I did.'

'How fascinating,' said Emma, captivated by Naco's story.

'I'm glad you did,' this time it was Angela responding to Naco's tale, 'you play divinely. Don't you think so, Horace?'

'Yes, I do. There is something very melancholic about your interpretation of the melodies that we have just heard. They were deeply felt, as if they were reflecting your own life story.'

Naco looked at his old friend with some suspicion. 'You are being a bit philosophical, Horace. I'll play you something a bit more uplifting. But first I must finish my drink.'

Naco was genuinely pleased to see his friends again and the group talked for a few more minutes before Naco resumed his position at the piano. The barman was clearing the table nearest to theirs and Dorlan asked him for another drink. Sipping his drink, he started to daydream. Angela was in deep conversation with her friends, talking about Naco; Dorlan could abandon himself to his inner musings. He glanced towards the window; it was already dark outside. His gaze then fell on the radiator by the armchair nearest to the window, and there behind it he thought he saw an object wedged between it and the wall. He sat upright, taking a better look, and indeed came to the conclusion that there was something there. His getting up went unnoticed; only when he crouched down and began poking at the object, attempting to prise it out from behind the radiator, did Angela stop talking and comment on her husband's peculiar actions. Gus and Emma were at a loss as to what the eccentric professor was up to.

'Does your husband usually behave so strangely?' muttered Gus.

Angela shrugged her shoulders; she did not know what to say, but got up and walked over to the window.

'Horace, what on earth are you doing?' she whispered, curious but also embarrassed by her husband's manoeuvres.

'It's almost there. Just another inch and I'll have it!'

'What will you have?'

Dorlan was unable to answer because of his uncomfortable position. Cheek pressed against the wall, arm extended, he was waving his pen behind the radiator, up and down, loosening the trapped object. At last something fell to the ground. Dorlan, covered in sweat, was visibly relieved. He ran his handkerchief across his brow and straightened himself up, dusting down his jacket. At his feet lay a small notebook. He picked it up.

'It's my notebook; the one I had lost. Do you remember? I told you about it. It must have been months ago. I was so upset; it had all my diagrams and notes in it.'

'Yes, I do remember,' Angela stood close to him, looking over his shoulder as Dorlan flicked through the pages.

He stopped at one page; they both stared at it.

After a while Angela said softly, 'And there is the insect woman.' Dorlan turned towards her, removed his spectacles, placed them swiftly into his breast pocket and kissed her on the lips. Naco ended his melody; a few of the customers applauded and some of them got ready to leave the club. Naco remained perfectly still, his eyes closed and fingers on the keyboard.

Angela and Dorlan stayed motionless in their embrace.

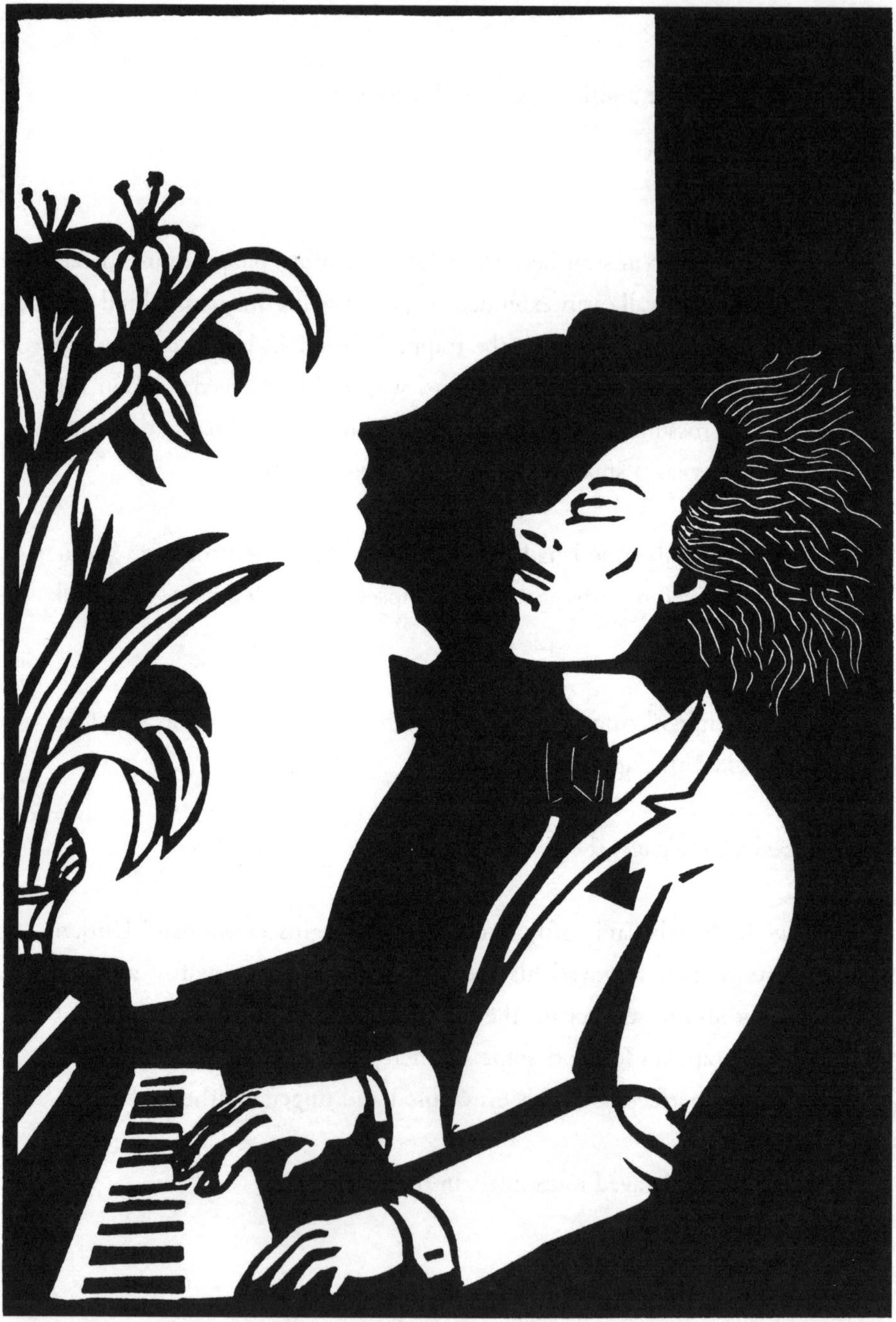

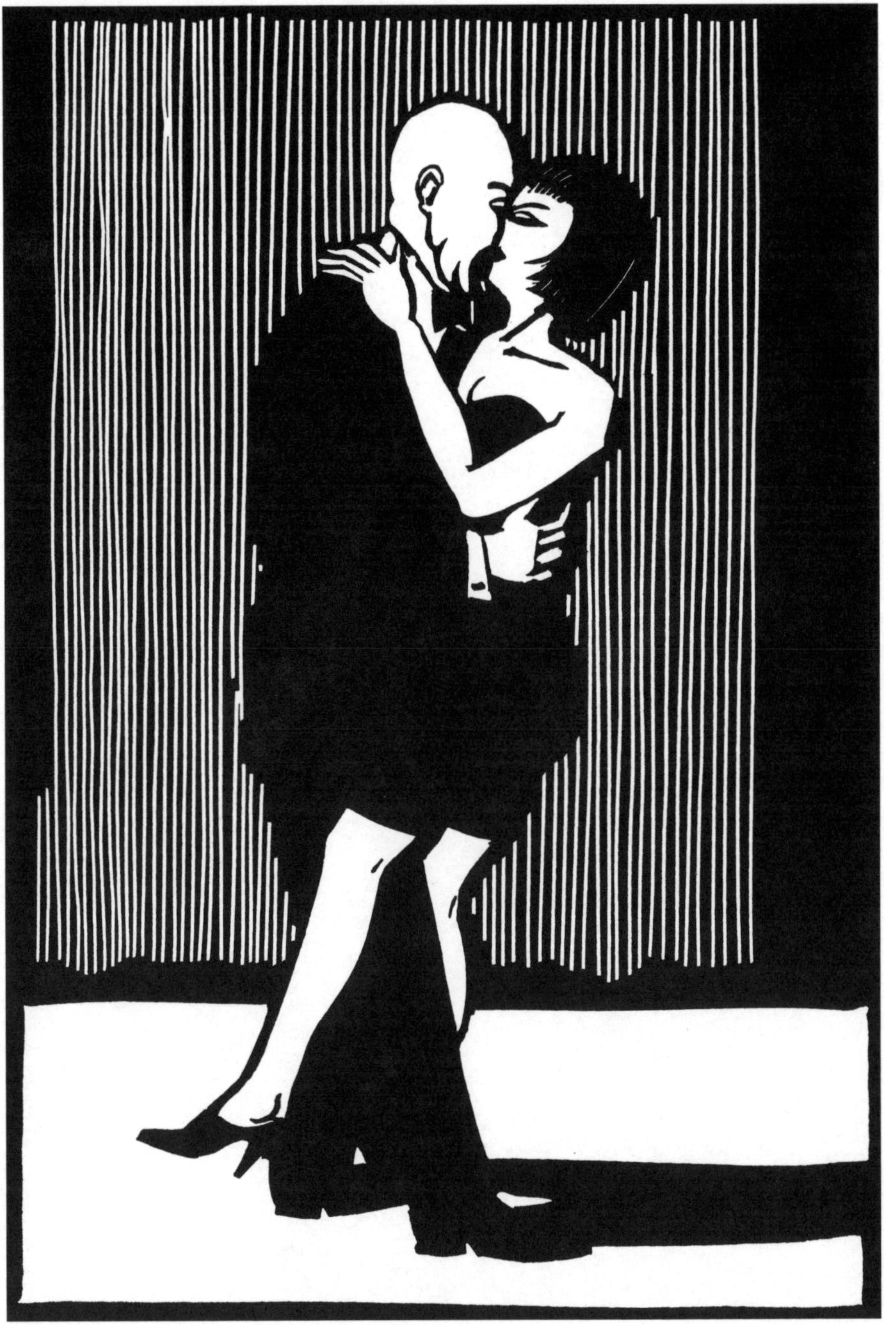

CHAPTER SIX

– You will listen to what he says and never contradict him. Should you not understand something, just nod your head and allow him to continue.

– I don't understand.

– You don't have to; it is important for him to express himself. I think we are close to solving the problem, very close.

– Well, if you say so, but . . .

– There is no but; I will see you afterwards and we will have plenty of time to go into the details. What you must remember is that we are expecting a great deal more. Much more will emerge; we will then be able to measure it, have a better idea of the past, as well as the future and the end. These are the things that interest us and we will know why those who have won shall be lost to memory.

– In order that everything can happen once again.

– Precisely so; in order that everything can happen once again.

*   *   *

I was glad that Angela decided to come with me; I was in no mood to be alone, not so soon after the radio recordings. It is one thing to work on pre-recorded talks, but to deliver a series of six lectures in front of a live audience is something altogether different. I wanted nothing more to do with insects and the ecosphere, at least not for a while. I wanted Angela; to hear her sweet voice.

We arranged to stay in Pisa for a couple of days; I promised to show her my old student haunts. Then I would travel north to the sanatorium while Angela would take a taxi to Lucca to see her friend.

Our flight was an early one and I fell asleep moments after take-off.

'I hope you don't mind, darling, but I have eaten your breakfast as well as mine. I did not want to disturb your angelic sleep. Were you dreaming?'

'Yes, I was; an intense dream. So intense that I've totally forgotten it.'

'It must have been intense; you're covered in sweat.'

I looked down to see my shirt covered in damp patches.

'I'll go to the toilet and freshen up.'

Just as I started unfastening my safety belt, an electronic gong signalled the pre-recorded announcement: 'Ladies and gentlemen, signore, signori . . .'

Too late.

'Here, let me use my napkin.'

Angela wiped my brow after removing my glasses. She then turned to the window.

'Horace, the view is magnificent, the sea is so transparent. Look, you can see the trails of small motor boats and the sails of yachts.'

I took my glasses from her hands and attempted to lean across her seat, somewhat restricted by the safety belt.

'We have crossed Liguria into Tuscany, and there's Viareggio. I used to work there during the summer holidays when I was a student. Lucca is just beyond, near the mountains.'

'Look, I can see the tower, and the Basilica, and the Baptistery; they look so small.' Angela was very excited and squeezed my arm.

When we landed I thought of Ed. The heat came as a shock when we descended the steps onto the tarmac. It was hard to believe it was almost October. Passport control was conducted swiftly and as luck would have it, our bags were among the first to appear on the conveyor belt in the baggage hall. We caught the first taxi and within ten minutes were unpacking in the hotel. Angela slipped out of her skirt and went to the bathroom; I opened the window and, with an outward gesture, parted the shutters, letting in a flood of light. I looked down onto the street; a few noisy Vespas passed by. Across the street in the facing window an old couple could be seen eating their breakfast. I turned my back to them and collapsed onto the bed. Angela emerged from the bathroom, looking radiant. Her eyes were sparkling and her mouth was exquisitely red.

I sat up. 'You look great, that lipstick suits you.'

'Then test it out!' She leaned over the edge of the bed.

It was my turn to freshen up before going out on the town. Dishevelled and covered in lipstick, I went to the bathroom.

By the time we left the hotel it was approaching noon. Together we took in the atmosphere of the city and enjoyed each other's company. I pointed out the cafés I had frequented as a student, the libraries and bookshops in which I spent so much time. We strolled through the park and along the river bank. After eating a light lunch we returned to the hotel; its cool interior was welcoming. I picked up the keys, and as the lift was occupied we decided to climb the two flights of stairs to our room. I followed Angela up the stairs, hypnotized by her swaying hips. I thought of the puffed-up pigeon trailing his female partner on the pavement outside the restaurant where we had just eaten lunch. On entering the room we made love and fell asleep.

The telephone rang. For a moment I had no idea where I was. The dark room and the unfamiliar chandelier hanging from the ceiling were disorientating. It was only when Angela stirred beside me that I realized I was in the hotel. I fumbled for my glasses and lifted the receiver.

'Pronto.'

'Is that Professore Dorlan?'

'Yes.'

'This is Dottore Inzaghi, from the sanatorium. I was wanting to know when you will be arriving to see Signor Green. Is it tomorrow morning?'

'The day after tomorrow, I think.' I was still very sleepy and found it hard to focus on the subject.

'Ah! I see,' the doctor responded.

'One moment, I will tell you exactly when I will be arriving'

I climbed out of bed; Angela wriggled a bit but continued sleeping. I took a few steps to the wardrobe and withdrew my diary from my jacket, flipping through the pages as I returned to the telephone.

'Thursday afternoon, five o'clock.'

'Bene, I will tell Signor Green.'

'How is Ed, I mean Signor Green?'

'He is improving.' After a short pause the doctor continued. 'He keeps asking when Professore Dorlan will be coming. That is why I am telephoning. I am glad I found you. I will be able to tell Signor Green you will be coming, Thursday afternoon, at five o'clock. Yes?'

'Yes.'

'Thank you, Professore,. Buona sera.'

I put down the receiver and lay for a while staring at the ceiling; Angela was still fast asleep.

We had the following day all to ourselves in Pisa. That allowed me to show Angela more of the sites. In the evening we went to the Ristorante Vecchio Teatro. Angela loved it; small wonder, as the patron lavished her with compliments and attention. We ended our night wandering aimlessly around the empty streets; the city was already fast asleep and the sky covered in stars, something we rarely see back home in London. Eventually we crossed the westernmost bridge and, walking along the river, returned to the hotel.

By mid-morning we were in Lucca. I placed a kiss on Angela's cheek and waved to her through the window of the taxi; she struck a fine figure standing by the San Paolino gate.

*   *   *

After spending some time with Ed, I left his room and walked across the corridor to the doctor's office. I tried to make sense of it all; it was obvious to me that Ed's fall had affected his mind. I knocked on the door. Dr Inzaghi let me in. We both sat down in silence, he could see that I was disturbed by what I had just seen. He asked if I minded him smoking. I had no objection. He lit his pipe and drew in the smoke in two short puffs, and then, removing the pipe from his mouth, he exhaled more smoke up towards the ceiling. He was going to tell me things I already knew. I listened carefully; outside it was getting dark. The lamp on the doctor's desk was the only source of light and it cast its warm glow across his face.

'Doctor, what is all this about a woman lying in the bed by the window?

There is no woman; the bed is empty! Yet Ed keeps talking about her as if she really existed.'

'Sssh! One moment.'

He rose from his chair and walked across the room. He stood for a while with his ear to the door.

'Professore, come this way.'

The doctor opened the door and we walked quietly down the dark corridor towards the large window through which moonlight was streaming onto the tiled floor. He whispered something into my ear.

In a recess near the window I could just make out the contours of a figure cowering over what I thought was a telephone. We moved closer, making sure to go unnoticed. There was little danger of that as the person was so absorbed in what he was doing.

'Hori?

Hori, we must help them.

We alone know. It is up to us.

We understand them.

They will disappear, like us, into thin air.

Never to be seen again. But we are tireless; therefore it can be done.

That is why I am talking to you.'

The silhouetted figure broke off as if listening to a reply, then repeated the same broken sentences.

Tears welled up in my eyes. I had to remove my spectacles and wipe them from my face, hoping the doctor would not notice. I did not have to worry; Inzaghi was transfixed.

He took me back to his office and we talked for a while longer about Ed's condition. The doctor spoke with great sympathy for his patient but I detected an air of resignation in his voice. Two months had passed without much improvement. Ed's behaviour was unpredictable and it would be irresponsible to release him from the sanatorium. However, Inzaghi believed that Ed's writing could prove to be his salvation. It was a motivating factor which allowed him to focus for short periods of time. On such occasions he was lucid. Even directly after a writing session his mind remained alert, and it was during these brief moments that the doctor was able to have normal conversations with his patient. What frustrated him was that these moments of lucidity did not last. The patient would soon be talking of the woman in the adjacent bed or be making more phantom telephone calls.

The doctor asked me to take Ed's manuscript to London the moment it was completed. I asked him how long that would be. He thought that Ed was nearing the end. It was inconvenient for me to stay much longer – I had hoped to join Angela in Lucca and spend a few days with her there before returning to London – but I agreed to stay. The doctor was delighted and offered to accompany me to my room.

The room was comfortable but spartan, just a bed, a wardrobe, a small table and two chairs. On the table two cups were positioned upside down on their saucers; next to them a tin of Chinese tea and an electrical appliance which was used for boiling water. It was a coiled rod with an extended cable and an electric plug. I thought of making some tea but I was fearful of the contraption; besides, I was tired, mentally exhausted. I went to bed and immediately fell asleep.

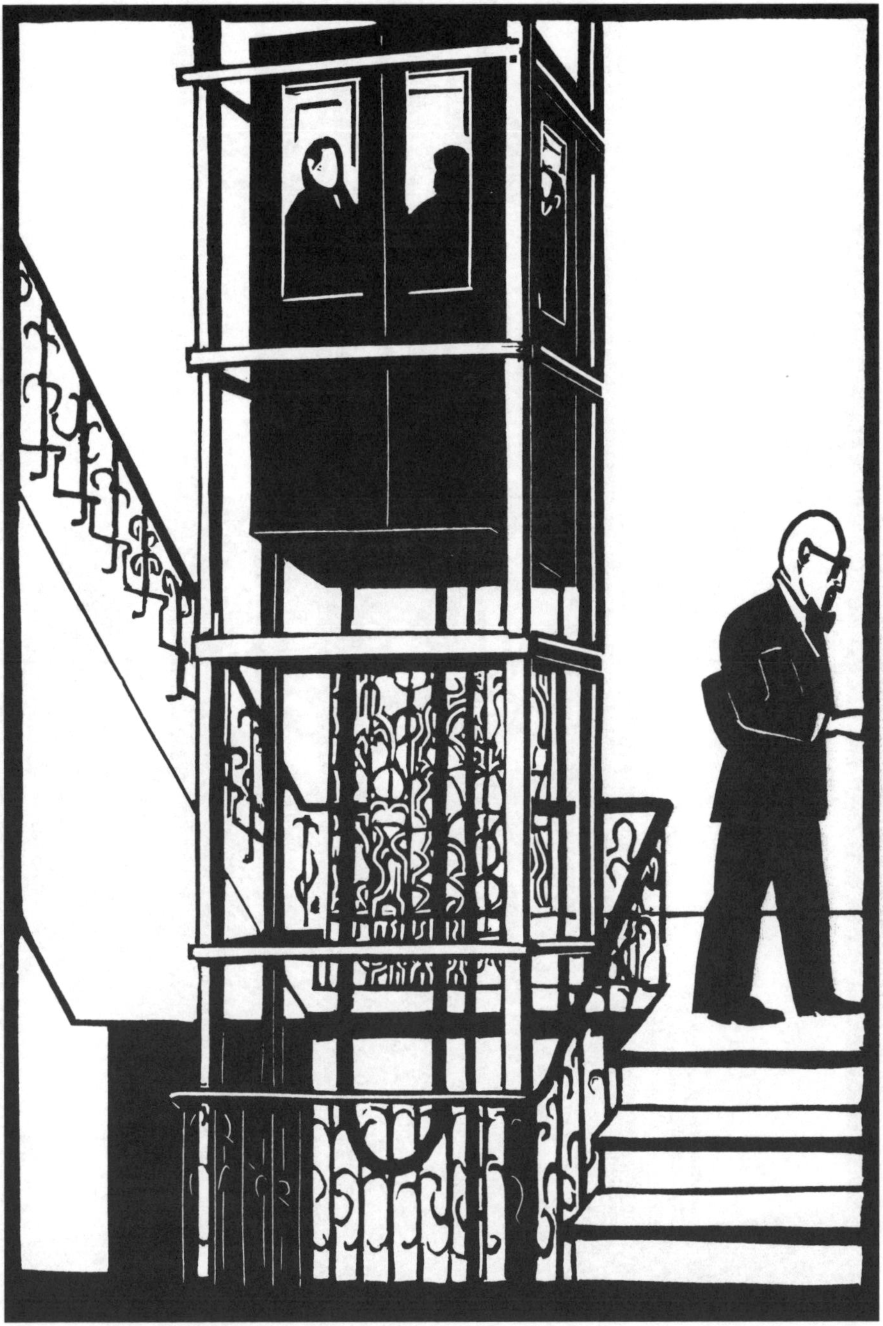

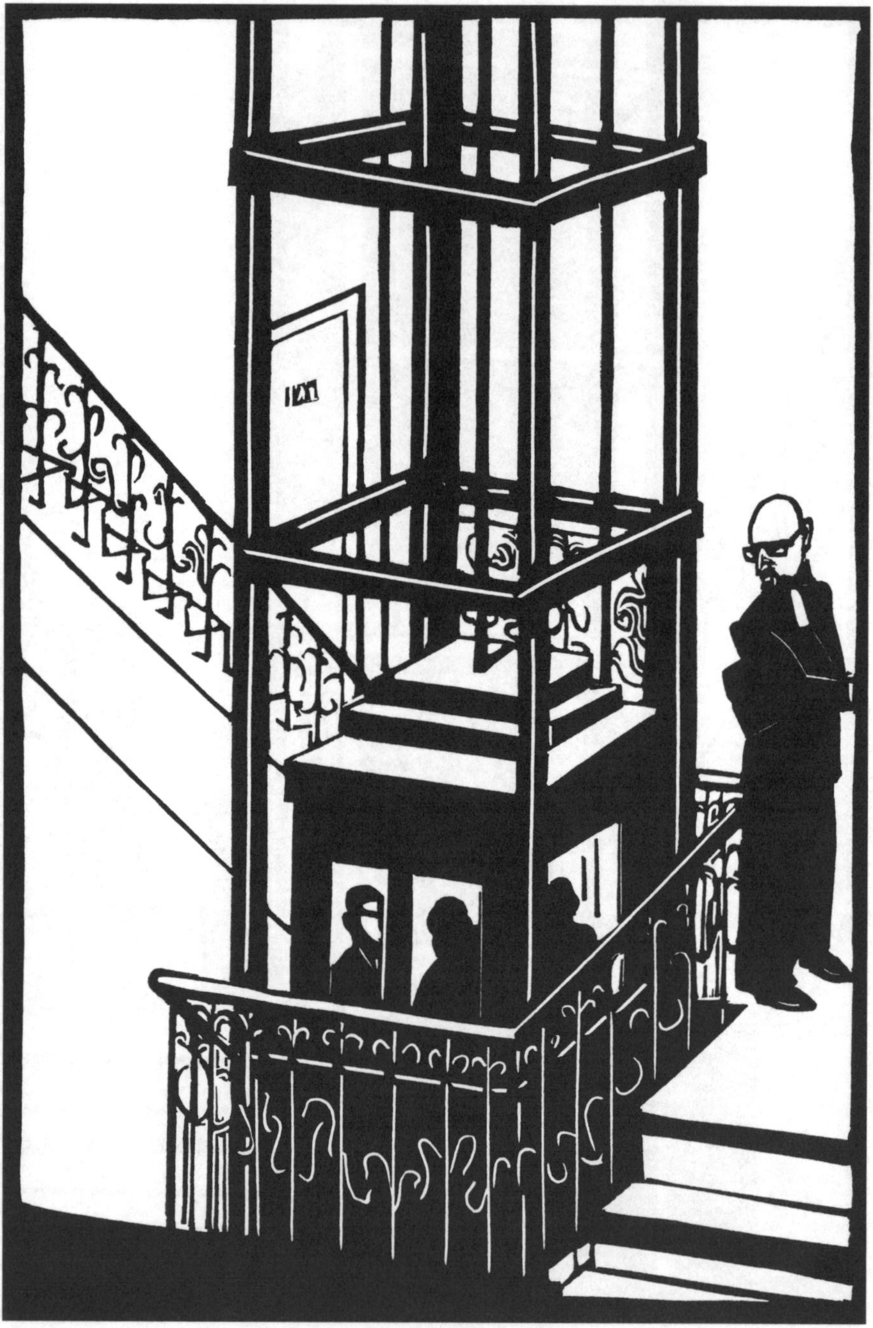

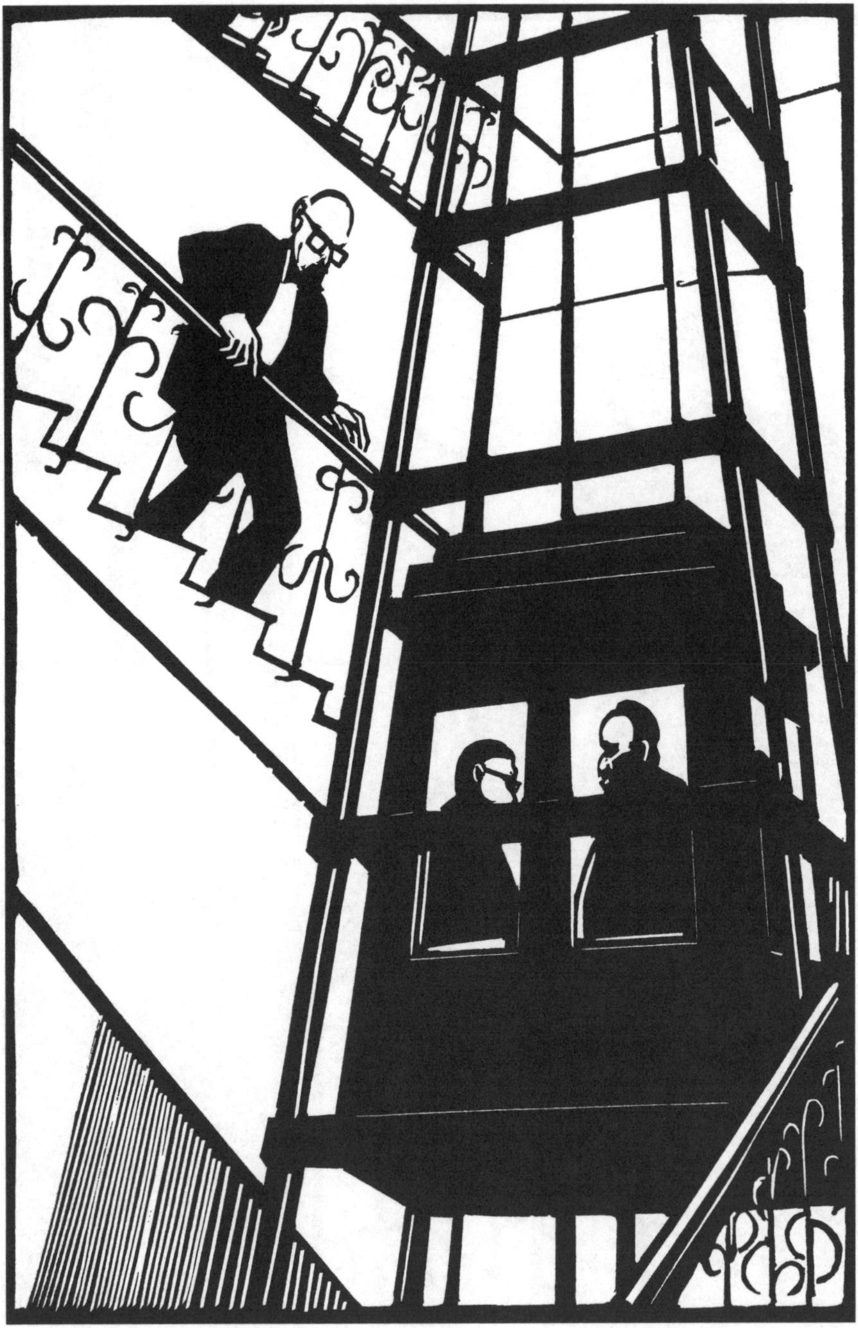

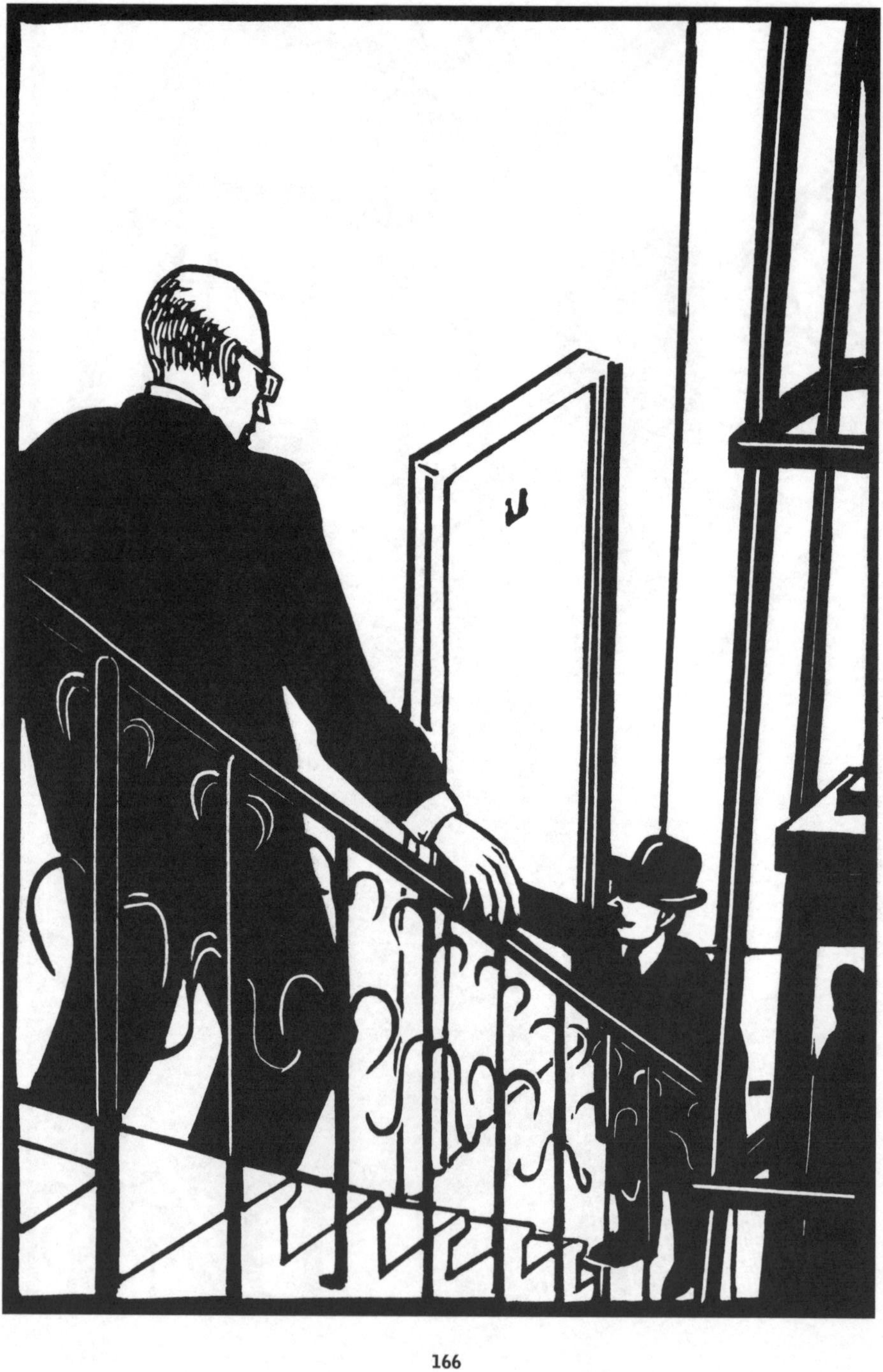

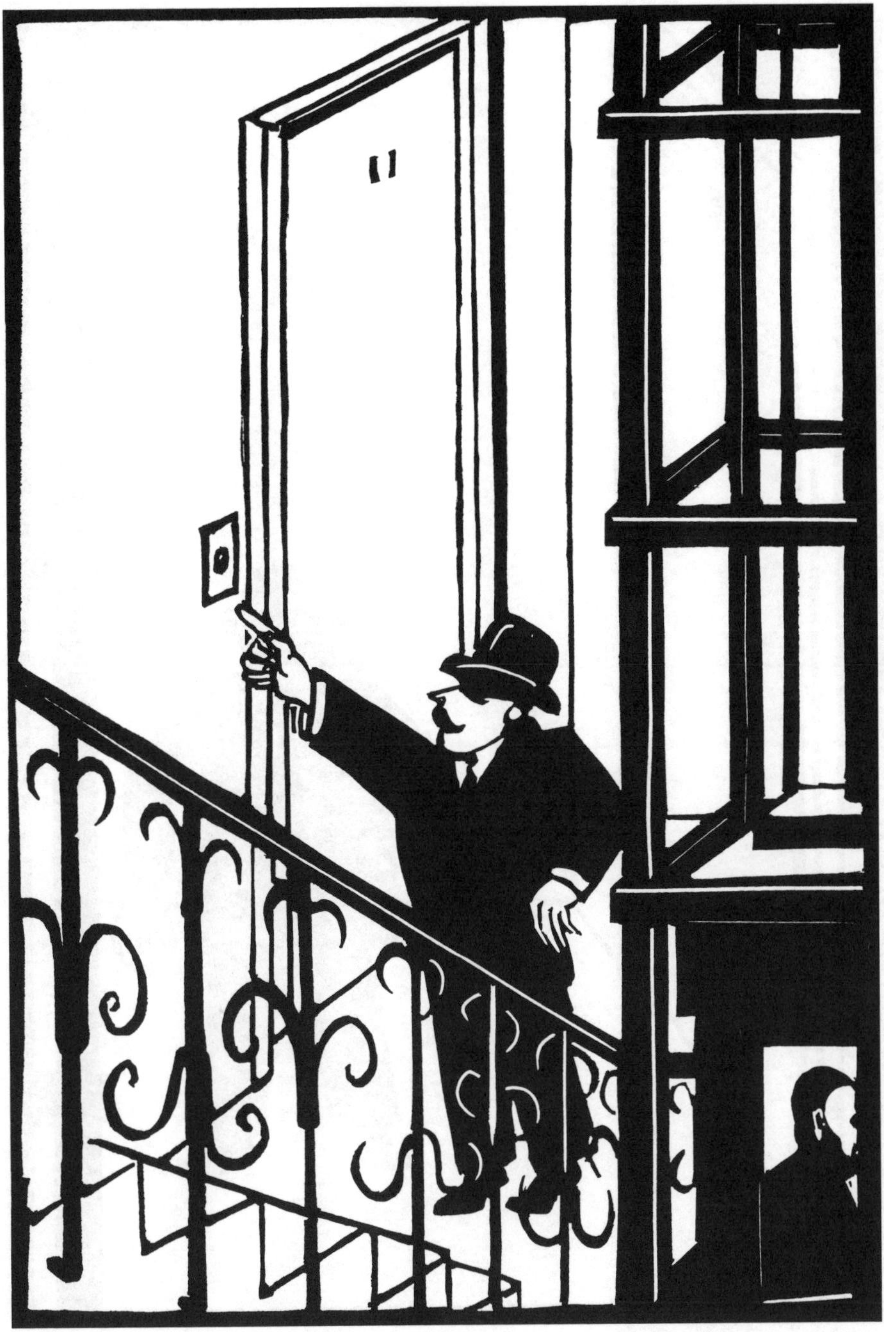

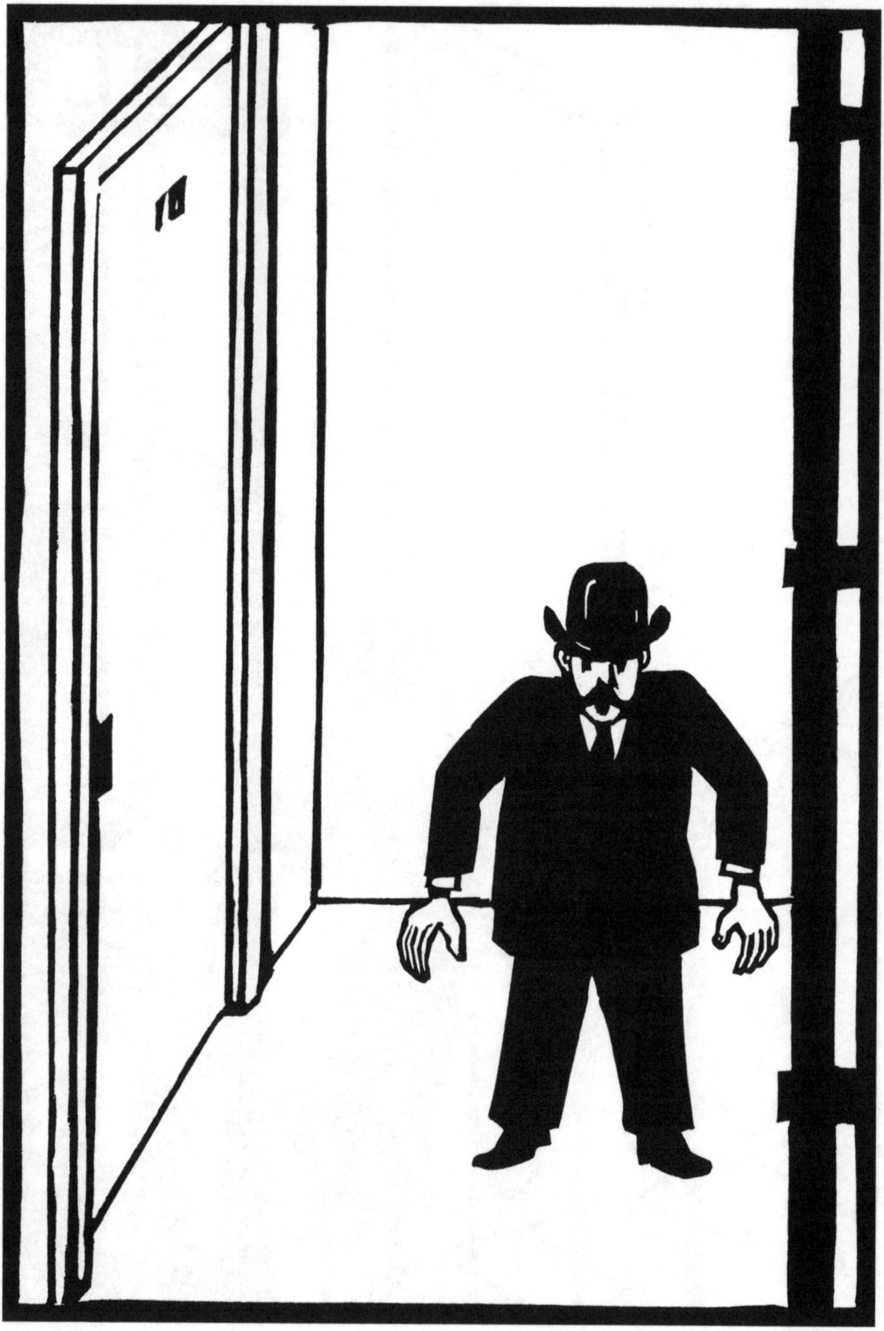

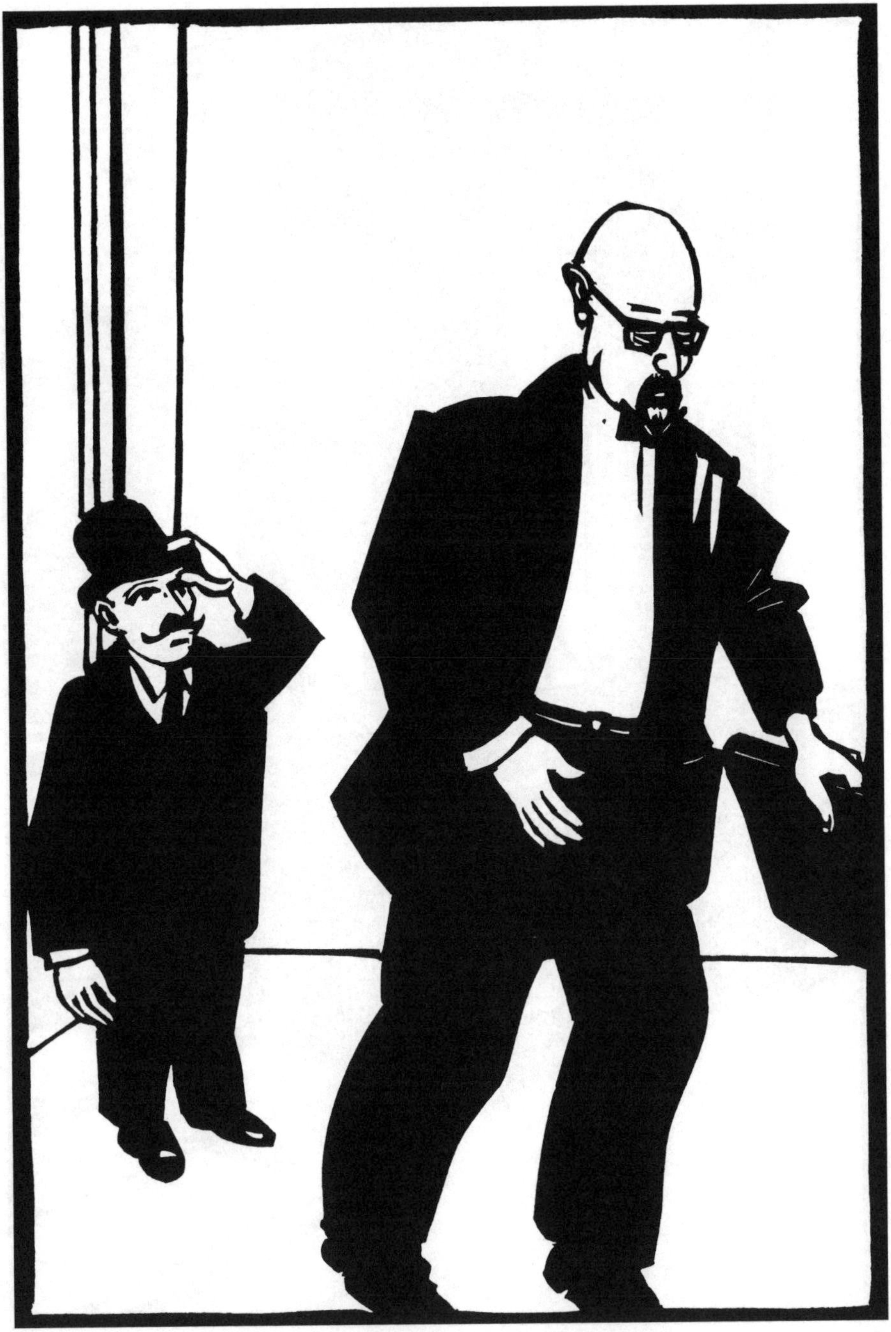

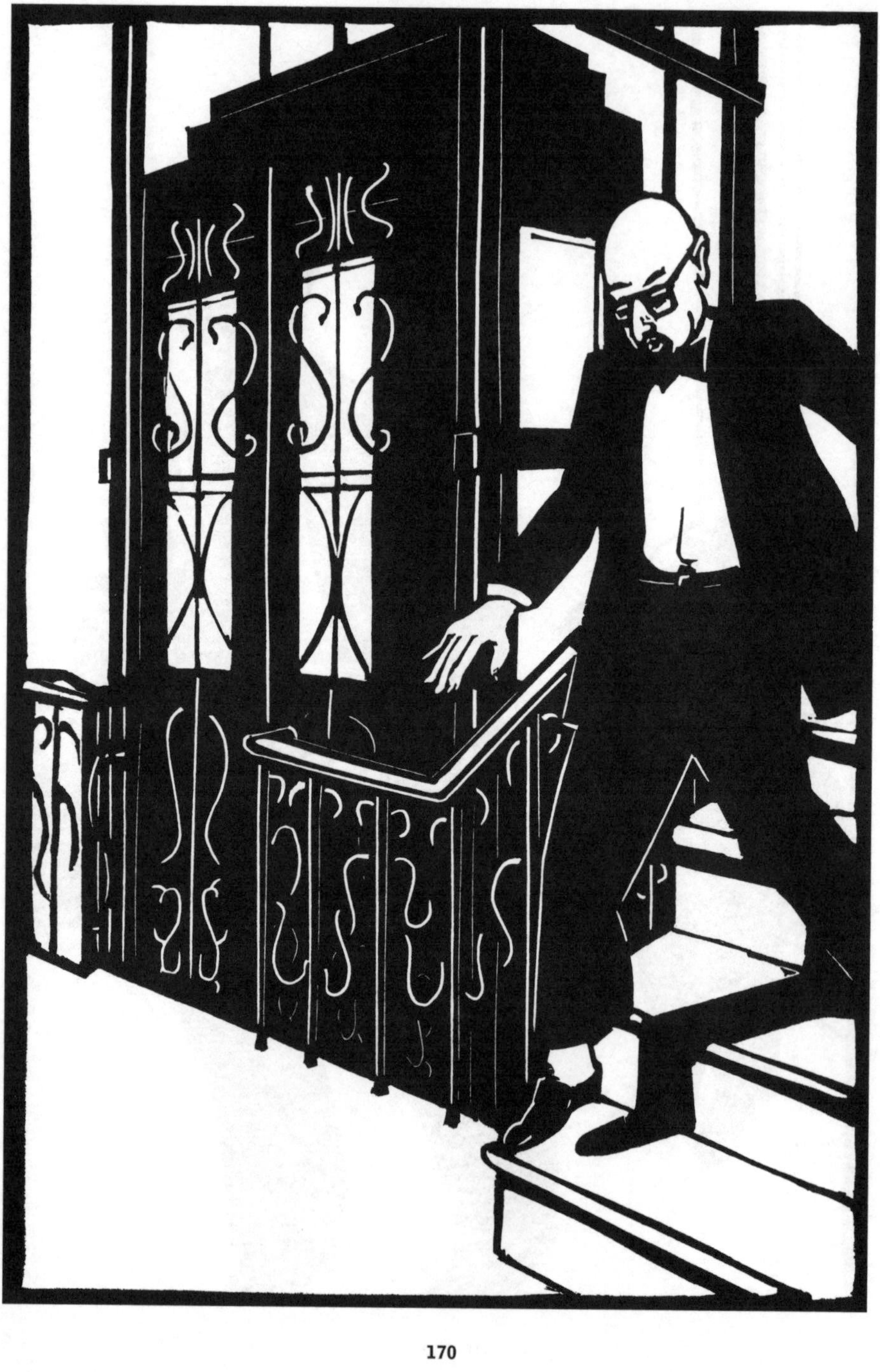

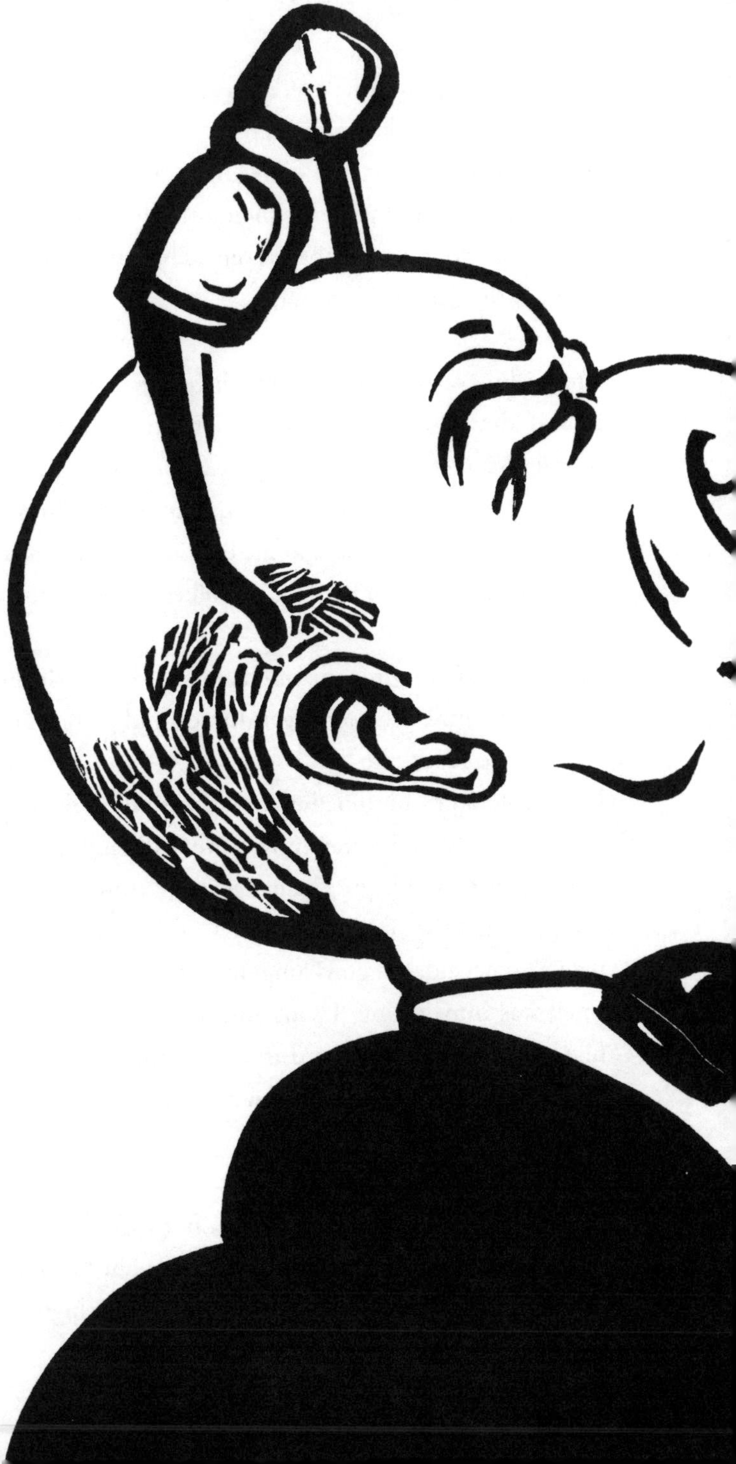

I was sitting up in bed, covered in sweat. The dream felt so real, but when I tried to recall it the vivid pictures were already receding, the scene that seemed so important had gone. Instead I felt the unpleasant sensation of cold sweat, of my pyjamas clinging to my body. In my slippers I shuffled across the floor to the bathroom. The grey light of dawn was seeping through the gap in the curtains.

After taking a shower I felt much better. I pulled open the curtains and looked down onto the gardens. The trees had caught the light of the morning sun, which was rising over the mountains. I poured some water into one of the teacups over the bathroom sink and inserted the electrical appliance. The water came to the boil in no time. I made some tea and, with the cup and saucer in my hands, walked across to the window.

In a short space of time the sun had risen clear of the horizon to cast its light into the room. I decided to get dressed and go out into the garden.

It was cold and I buttoned up my jacket, lifted the collar over my neck and walked briskly down the gravel path with my hands in my pockets. The grounds were well kept. The hedges were trimmed, the grass mowed, but as I approached the outer perimeter I noticed a deterioration of order. Here plants grew wild, the grass long, invaded by weeds and herbs; their pungent smell was intoxicating. I took in the panorama and breathed in the dew-filled air. I turned and faced the sanatorium. The building was run-down, but it had character; it was an example of modernist architecture from Mussolini's time.

As I walked back I thought of Ed, but on reaching the steps outside the entrance, food was on my mind and I thought I could smell coffee. My nose led me to the canteen, a vast sunlit hall with a high ceiling. The buffet was at the far end. Steam rose from the steel counter and covered the glass partitions with condensation; an array of culinary smells filled the air. I was the only person there. A cook eventually emerged from the kitchen and served me breakfast. With so many empty chairs and tables, I could sit anywhere, but I noticed the solitary figure of Dr Inzaghi sitting by one of the windows facing the grounds. Carrying my tray, I walked across and asked if I could join him. He was surprised to see me so early in the morning but he was happy for me to join him. We sat opposite each other, I laid out my breakfast, as he folded his papers.

'Please don't let me disturb you, Doctor.'

'Not at all, I was just re-reading Signor Green's manuscript. It is almost finished. He told me that by tomorrow he will have written the last page.'

This was good news; I would be able to join Angela earlier than I had thought.

'Professore, how did you get to meet Signor Green?'

'How did I get to meet him?' I had to think, although the answer was simple.

I had met him at the Academy of Arts and Sciences in London.

'And how long ago was that?'

'Two . . . no, maybe three years ago. I can't remember exactly. I think I may have bumped into him earlier than that. He's the chief carpenter at the academy; he runs the wood workshop serving all the departments.'

Dr Inzaghi did not say anything. I got the impression he wanted me to continue.

'He mainly works for the arts department. We in the science block have our own specialists. In fact the metal workshops are more relevant to our work, although on occasions we do get some woodwork done.'

'And Signor Green had some woodwork done for you?'

'Yes, he did. He helped me with a radio programme I was making. I was working in the field; in fact I am still working on the project. We had to record sounds, insect sounds, near some of the industrial estates and motorways surrounding London. Ed, that is Mr Green, was making wooden casings and containers for my recording equipment, which were to be placed strategically along the hard shoulders of the motorway and in a building specially designed by architecture students. It was all very exciting.'

'Did Signor Green complete the work for you?'

'He didn't. Everything was going well, but he had to go to Pisa. He was working on another project, also for the academy.'

'And that is when Signor Green had the accident?'

'I assume it was.' I turned my head and looked out at the garden.

'Professore Dorlan, would you say that Signor Green looks up to you? That he holds you in high esteem?'

'I don't know. I've never really thought about it.'

'Would you not say that he has been helping you with a rare enthusiasm? To put it another way, was he not overly engaged with this programme that you were conducting for the radio?'

'I don't know what you mean.'

'What I am trying to get at, is to understand why Signor Green was so fanatical about assisting you in the project.'

'Fanatical? I wouldn't call him fanatical. Dedicated, maybe. But fanatical . . . well, I don't think so.'

Inzaghi's line of questioning began to irritate me, yet he pressed on.

'His work was accurate and meticulous. He was more than your average assistant, wouldn't you say?'

'Very much so. Every day he had something new to show me, always a slight improvement on the previous day's work. In fact, many of the artefacts did not have to be made with such a degree of precision.'

'What about the adjustments he made for Edgetown?'

I stirred in my seat.

'Did you approve of Signor Green involving George Reyes on the Edgetown project?'

'Look, Dr Inzaghi, I am a scientist. I take readings and make experiments, and test them against those of my colleagues. From this I draw my own conclusions. I don't need to work with artists. I'm sure as a doctor you understand these things. Don't get me wrong, I value Ed's work, but sometimes too much proactivity can obstruct a simple task.'

'What about the sound machines, then?'

'What about them?'

'Are you denying that the machines Signor Green constructed for you played an important role in the radio programmes? Surely without them the programmes would not have worked. They were indispensable, but you could hardly call them scientific.'

What could I say? He was right. If it wasn't for Ed's machines . . .

All of a sudden the fire alarms went off throughout the whole building. The noise was unbearable. I could not hear what Inzaghi was saying. He pointed to the window. A man in a heavy overcoat was running along the lawn barefoot. From under the coat I could see his pyjamas. Two male nurses ran in pursuit.

The alarms stopped.

'Forsetti. He's back to his old tricks.'

'A patient of yours?'

'Yes, he sets off the alarms and then makes a break for it. Always unsuccessful, I might add.'

'One would think this was a lunatic asylum, not a sanatorium.'

This time the doctor looked irritated. He got up from the table and gathered the manuscript.

'Perhaps, Professore Dorlan, we can continue this discussion later. I have my rounds to do.'

We shook hands, then I sat down and watched him walk past the empty tables and exit the canteen. A sheet of paper lay on the floor by Inzaghi's chair. It must have fallen loose from the manuscript. I picked it up.

On it in an expressive hand was written: 'The Insect Woman by Edward Green'. I folded the page and slid it into my pocket.

Inzaghi's questions had somehow unsettled me. Why was he so curious about Edgetown? What had Ed told him? What was in the manuscript? I picked up another coffee from the buffet and returned to my table. For a while I remained immobile, staring out of the window. The coffee was too hot to drink.

Aimlessly I wandered down the corridors and found myself on a wide terrace. A group of convalescents were stretched out on chaises longues facing the sun, like sunbathers on deckchairs at a summer resort. They wore white robes and canvas caps, some were covered with blankets, all perfectly still as if posing for a photograph. In the middle distance pine trees swayed in the breeze, beyond them the mountains. I walked past the immobile patients and went through a door, which to my surprise led me to the corridor where the previous night Inzaghi and I were watching Ed make his nocturnal telephone call.

I went up to Ed's room and looked through the porthole window of the door; the curtains were drawn open but both beds were empty. I opened the door with some hesitation and saw Ed sitting at a table writing. He did not notice me entering; he seemed oblivious to the world around him. I sat on one of the beds and observed him from a distance. He continued to write, rarely pausing to reflect on or to read what he had written. Eventually he lifted his pen off the page and slammed it down onto the desk. 'Yes,' he exclaimed, 'it's done.' Only then did he become aware of my presence and he swung around in his chair.

'Horace, I didn't realize you were here.'

'I didn't want to disturb you; you seemed so inspired.'

'Well, I've finished.' He sat back in his chair and stretched out his limbs. 'It's done.'

For a while he said nothing more. Then he walked up to me and greeted me by putting both hands on my shoulders.

'Horace, you're such a good friend. I owe so much to you.'

'What do you mean?'

'Well, coming all this way to see me, to take my manuscript back to London, finding a publisher.'

'I haven't found one yet.'

'I know, I know. But even making the effort to find one. It means a lot to me!'

'You know, Ed, that I'll do my best, but I can't promise you anything. My contacts are limited to academic circles and your work, from what I can gather from Dr Inzaghi, is more like a novel.'

'It is and it isn't.' Ed started to pace up and down the room, hands clasped together with index fingers resting on his mouth, like a lecturer reflecting on what he had just delivered.

'You could call it a novel, but I prefer to call it a science fiction biography.'

'A science fiction biography?' I was baffled. What on earth did he mean? I could not understand a word of Ed's attempt to explain this, but, not wanting to upset him, I pretended to follow his line of thought.

'So you see my point, Horace?'

'Err, yes. I see what you are getting at,' I answered as convincingly as I could. It would not matter to Ed whether I was convinced by his argument or not, for he was, and he rambled on.

In my mind I saw Angela going in and out of shops, trying on clothes, looking at handbags. I thought of the suspender belt I had bought her all those years ago. I imagined putting my hands around her narrow waist; we would dance across the floor. I could see our old radiogram as clearly as if it was in front of me: its mock-antique veneer, curvy contours, dainty legs and the illuminated station panel staring back at me.

Ed thrust the manuscript into my hands. He looked me in the eye and smiled. Before I could respond he had already turned towards the window and gone over to the unoccupied bed.

'All right, I know, she's here.'

He leaned to one side, then bent down to look under the bed and started to talk to someone who was not there. I could not make out the words, but judging by his body language I thought he was whispering to a child. After a while he emerged from under the bed and introduced his phantom infant to the invisible occupant of the bed. I slipped out of the room, clasping the manuscript close to my chest, and quietly closed the door. Through the porthole window I saw Ed talking to his imaginary companions. What now? I made my way back to the canteen where I had eaten my breakfast.

This time it was busy. The patients from the terrace were queuing up by the buffet. In their white robes they looked like monks in a refectory; I imagined them saying grace before tucking into their breakfast. Only it was not breakfast, the clock on the far wall indicated quarter to one. This puzzled me; I was here just a short while ago and then it was well before eight. How could all those hours have passed so quickly? I was hungry and so joined the queue, feeling like an intruder among the white-robed, cloth-capped patients, some of whom still wore dark glasses. I was hoping to catch sight of Dr Inzaghi, but there was no sign of him.

As I ate lunch I began to look through the manuscript, 'The Insect Woman by Edward Green'. The first pages described an empty city, completely abandoned, not a soul on the streets. The deadpan description made it eerie; I read on. It was early morning, summertime; a breeze blew down a wide street, shifting an open newspaper along the pavement until it wrapped itself around a lamppost. The author described one urban district after another, all of them deserted; then, in a park, the first sign of life.

A group of patients politely asked if they could sit at my table; the canteen was very full by now. I had no objection and drew the manuscript closer to my plate. The noise of conversations and the clatter of plates and cutlery filled the hall.

Among the bushes, alongside the park fences, men clad in white suits, wearing masks and breathing apparatus, were spraying the shrubbery with a fine white foam. They were very focused on their task; every so often they would rummage in the undergrowth, parting branches with their gloved hands in order to insert the nozzles of their long rods into the vegetation, then squeeze a pad with their elbow, releasing the foam through a tube from the canisters on their backs. They conducted this work with great concentration, but one of the men stopped to look beyond the park fence. He was looking at a tall woman crossing a footbridge over the dual carriageway running alongside the perimeter of the park. The tall woman stopped in the middle of the bridge and, leaning over the railings, looked down onto the empty lanes of the motorway. She remained perfectly still for some time, as did the man watching her from the park. Then, quite unexpectedly, she removed her shoes and extended her arm over her shoulder to unzip the rucksack on her back. With some difficulty she extracted a fragile wing from the opening in the bag until it fully unfurled, protruding from her back. She executed the same manoeuvre with her other hand. The two iridescent wings shimmered in the sunlight. They shone so brightly that the man in the park had to shield his eyes from the reflection. Then just as unexpectedly, the tall woman climbed onto the railings, balancing herself like a tightrope walker. The man in the park alerted his colleagues, but when he pointed to the bridge, there was no one there.

Two more patients joined our table; it was difficult to continue reading under such conditions and I excused myself. I looked for a quiet place to go and once more found myself on the terrace. The sun was now directly overhead; I could feel its heat. Taking off my jacket, I settled down on one of the chaises longues. I was alone. With the manuscript on my lap, I looked up towards the sun, delighting in its glow. I closed my eyes.

In no time I was fast asleep.

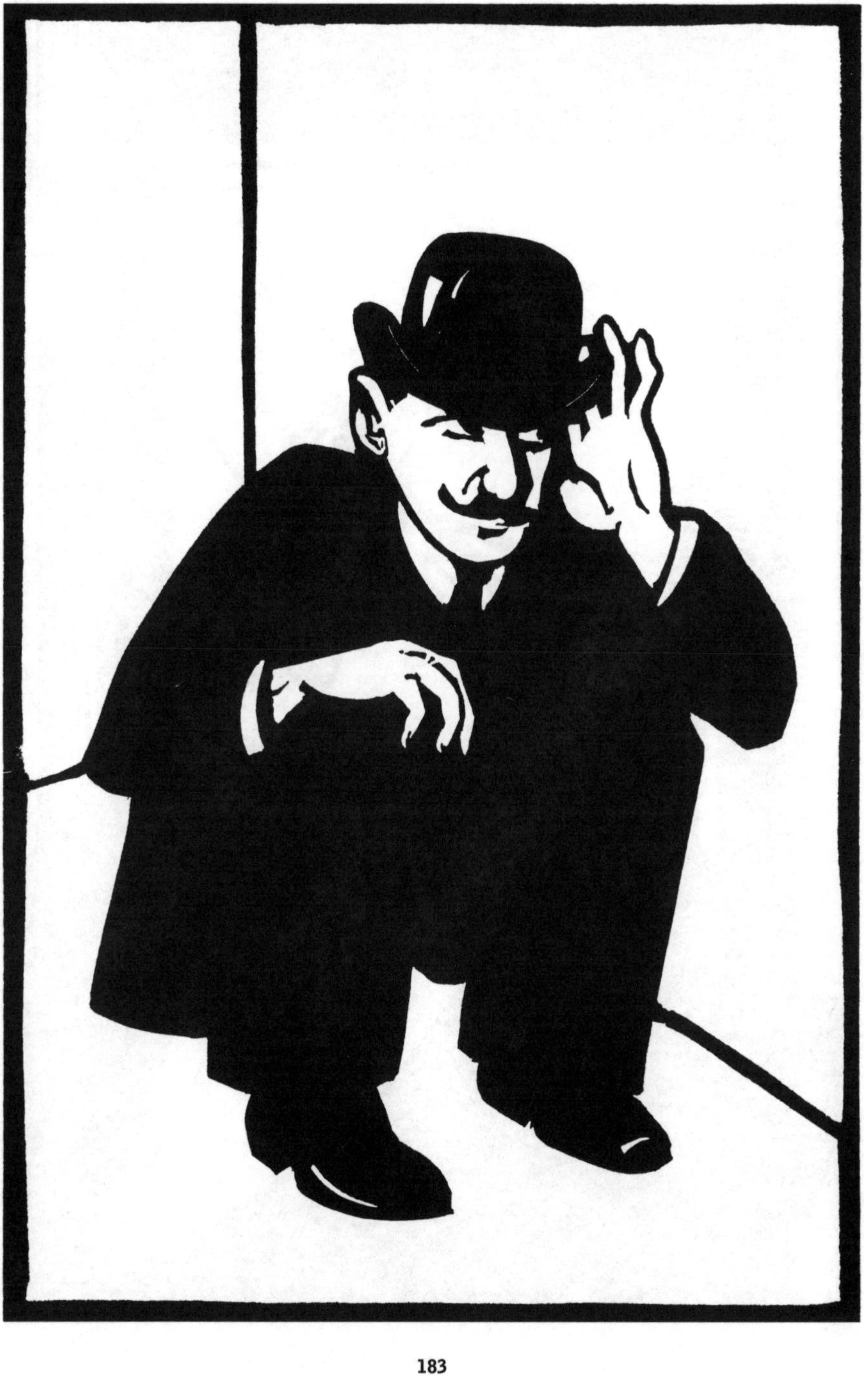

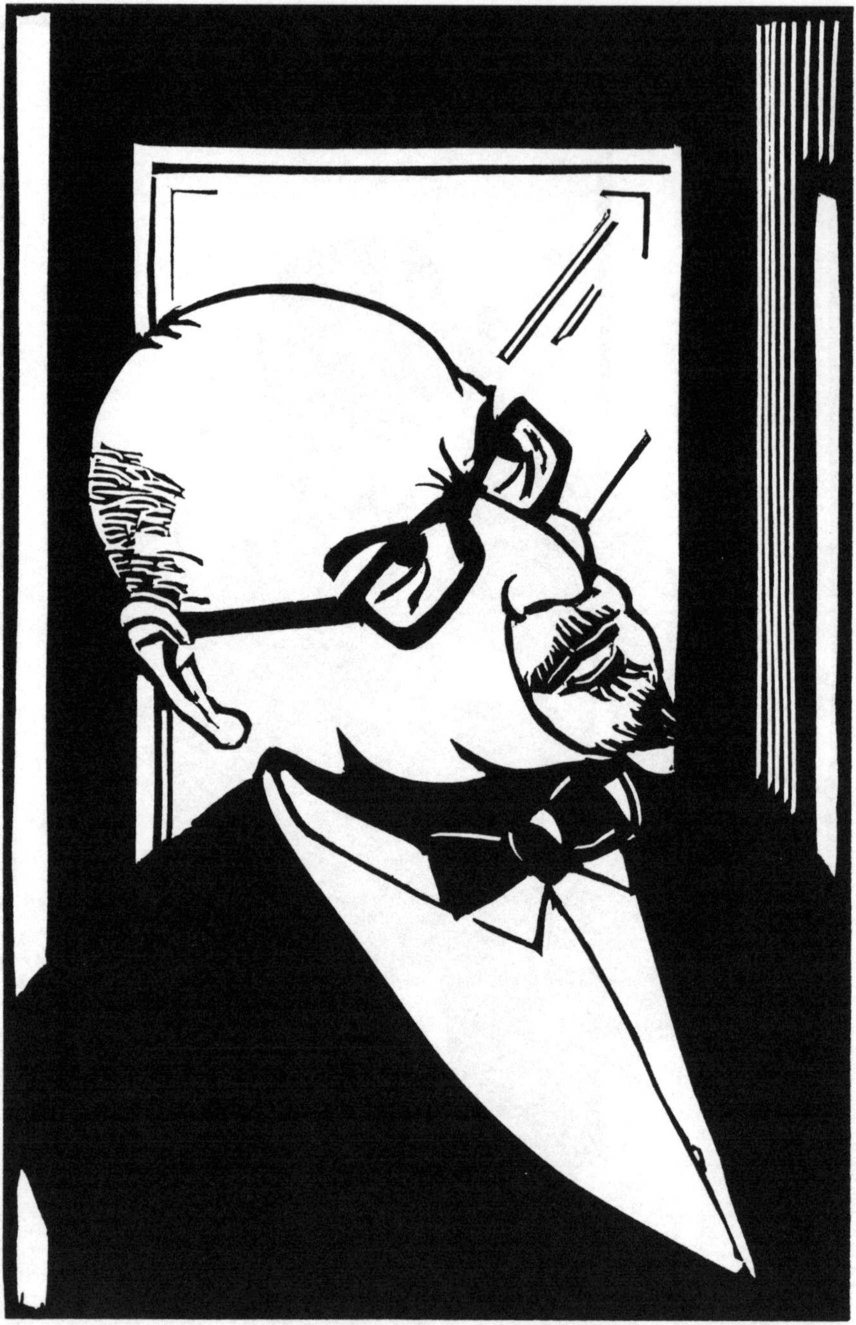

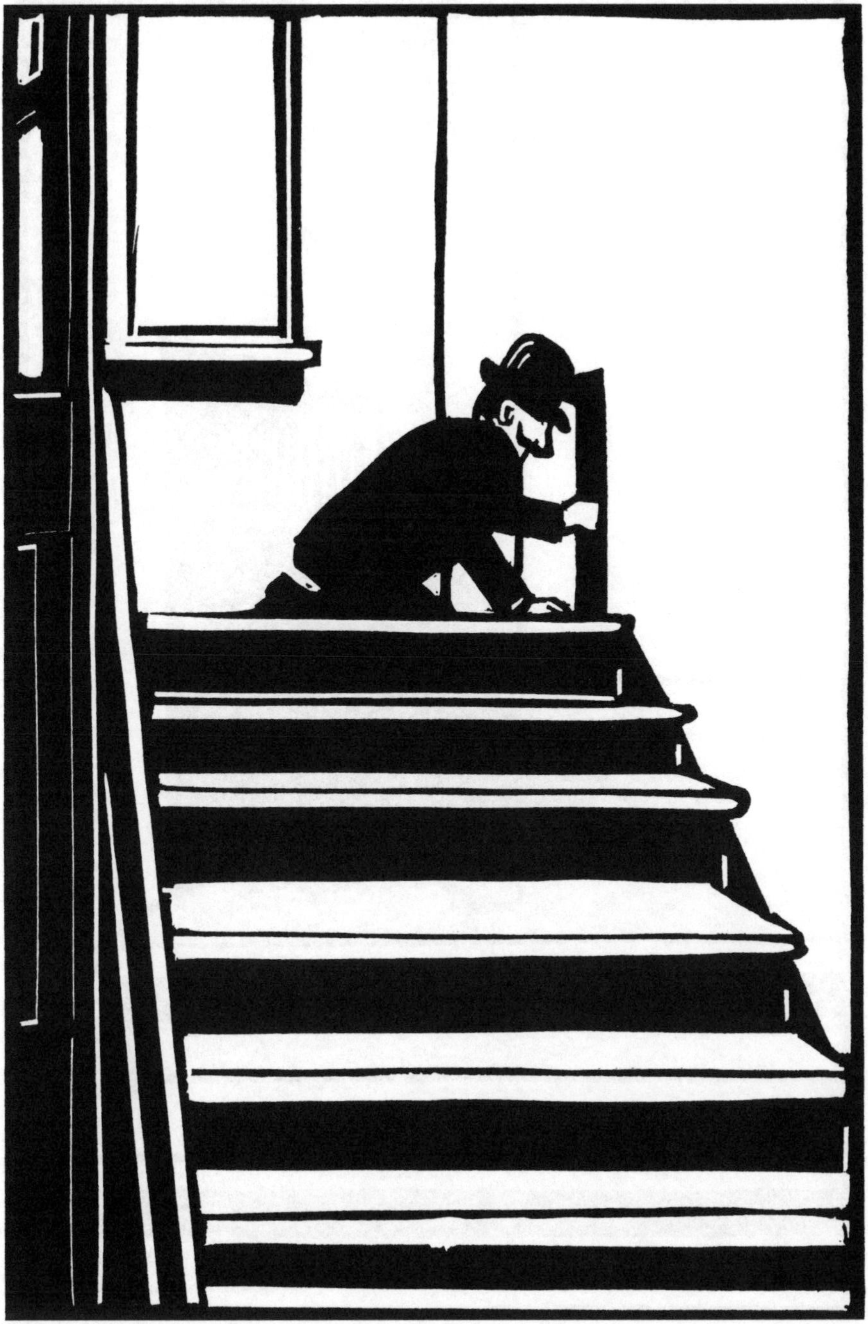

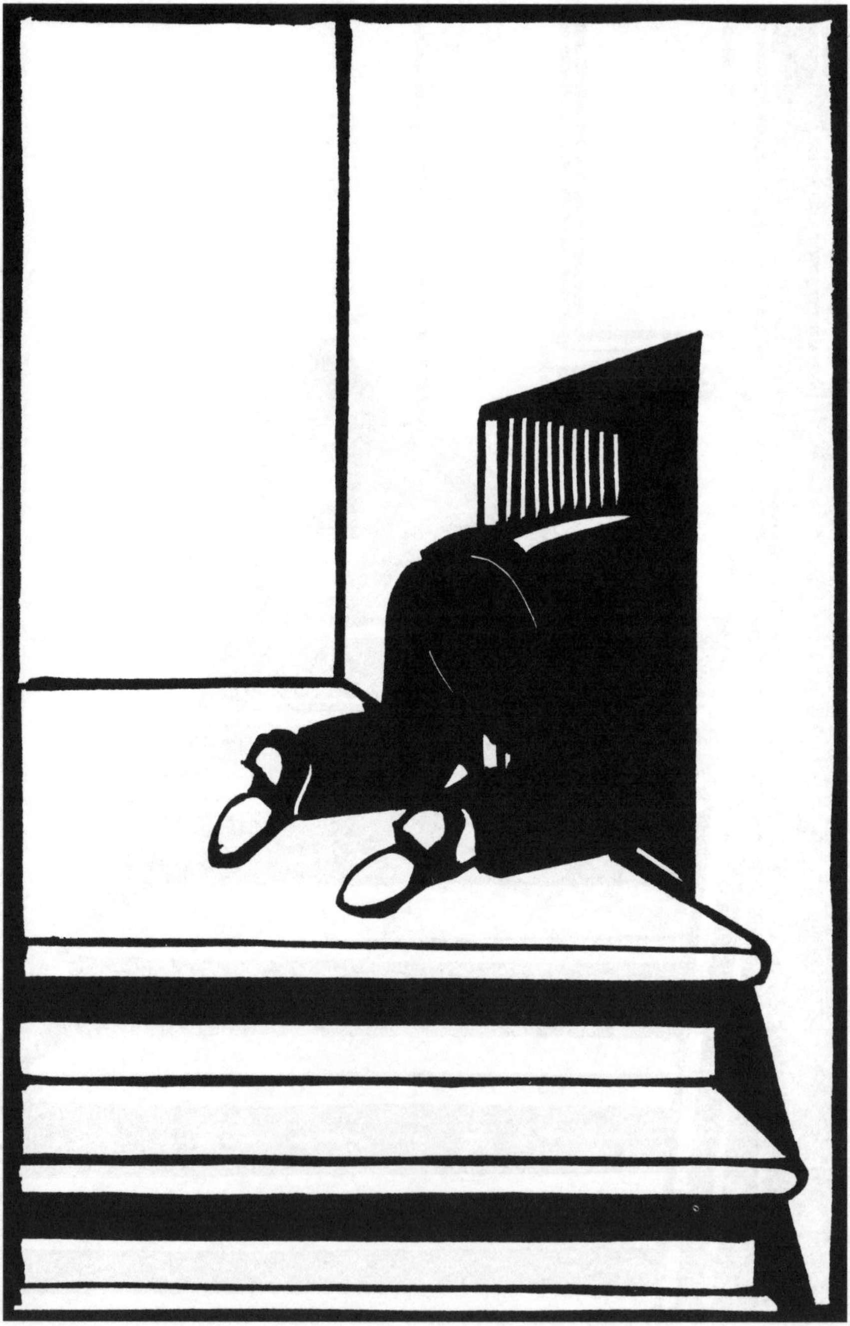

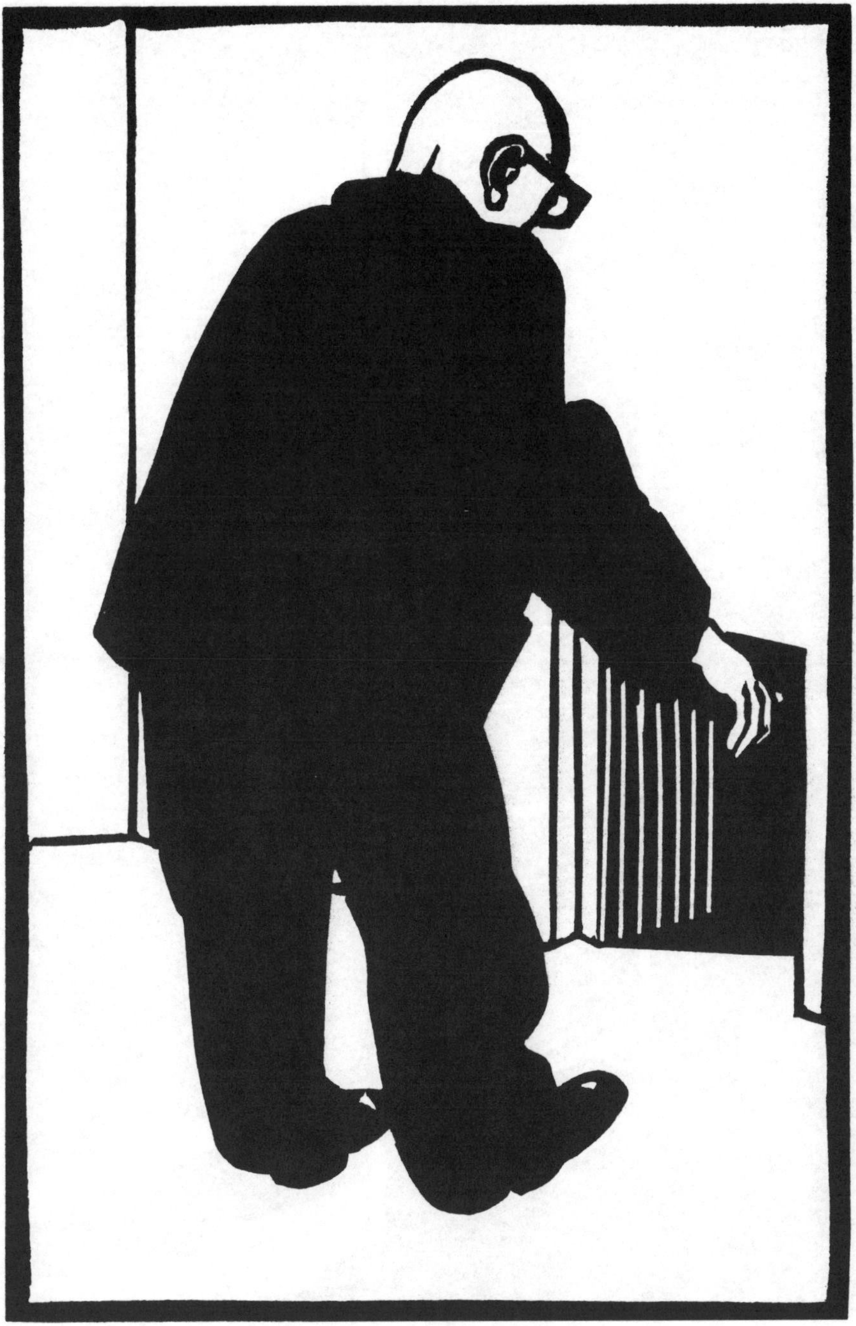

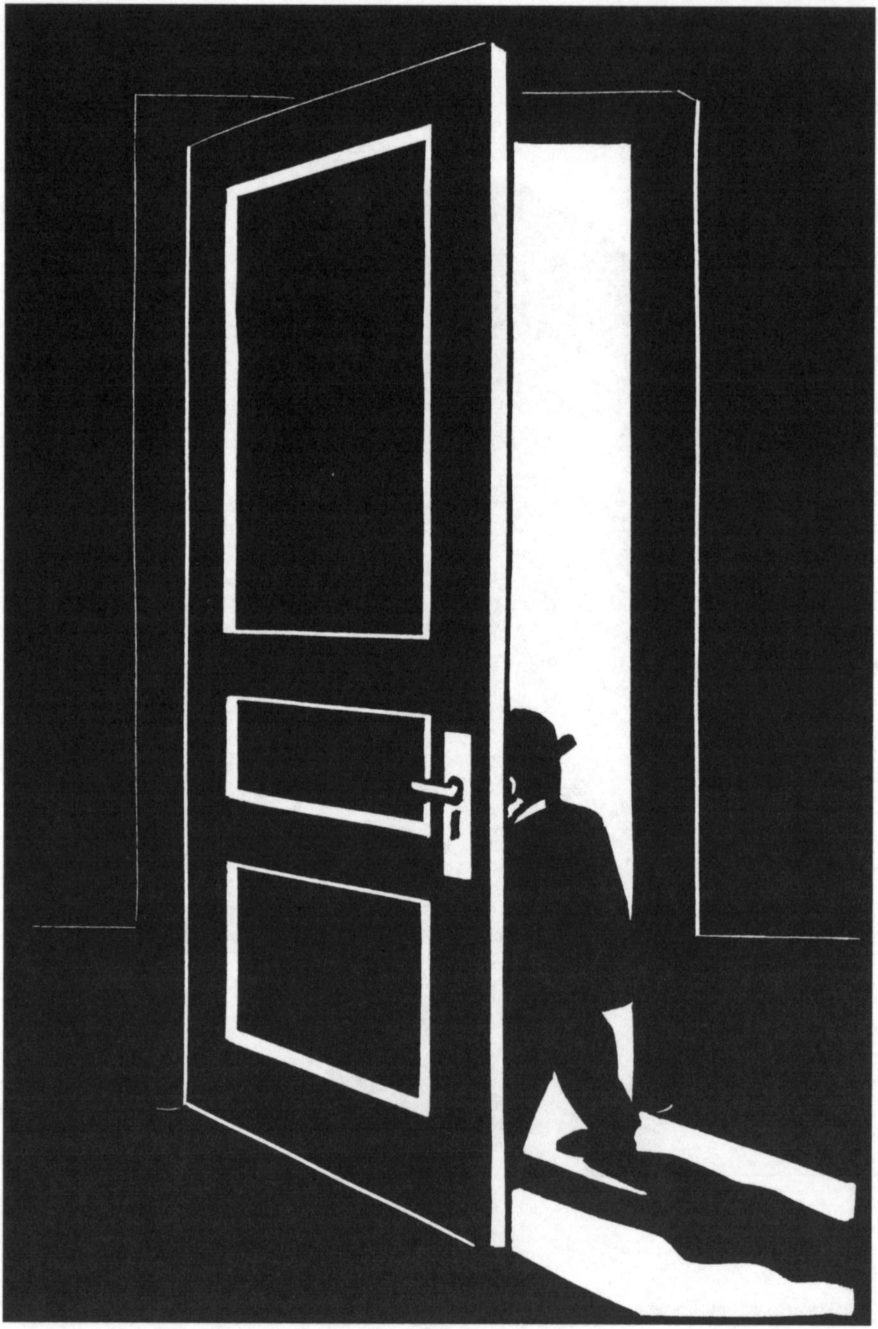

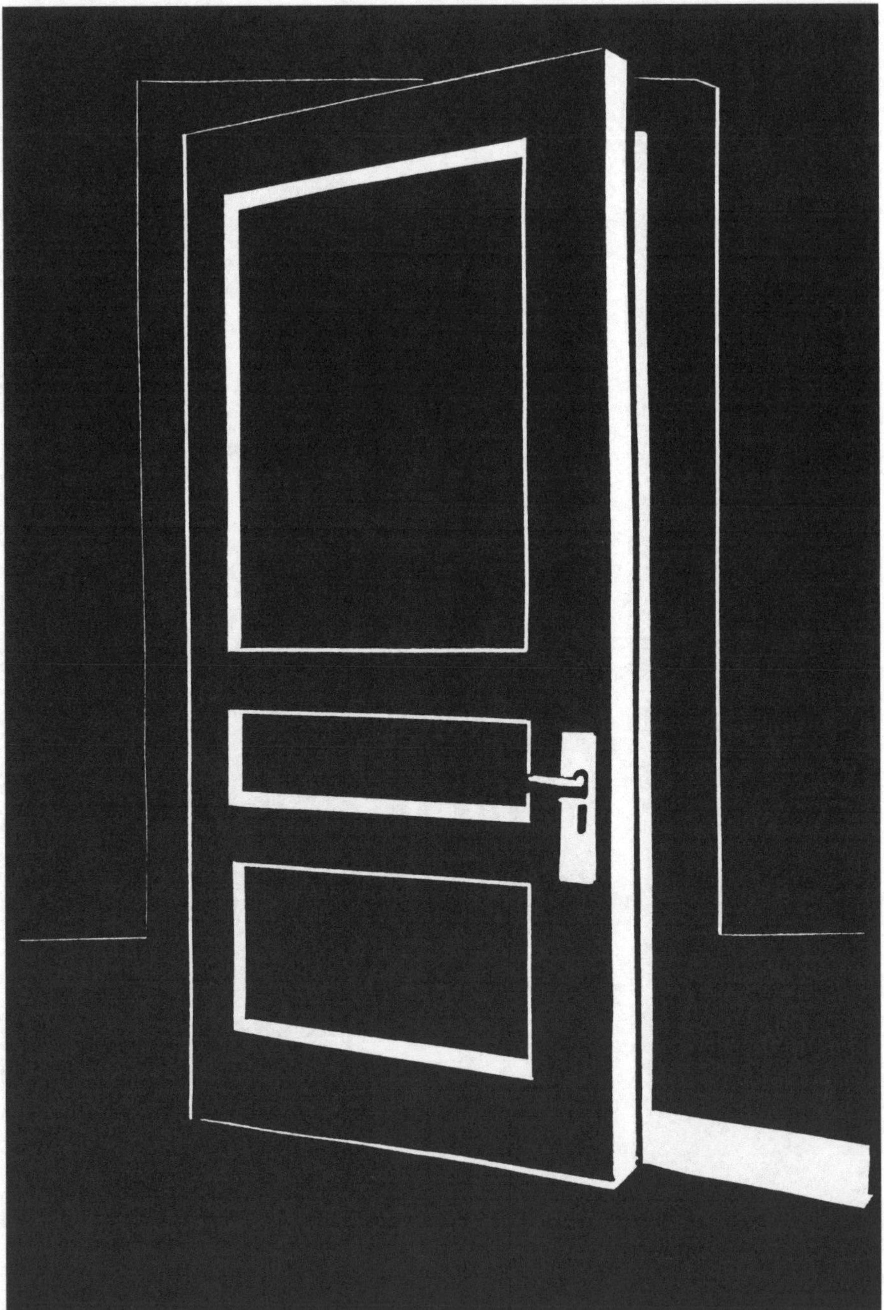

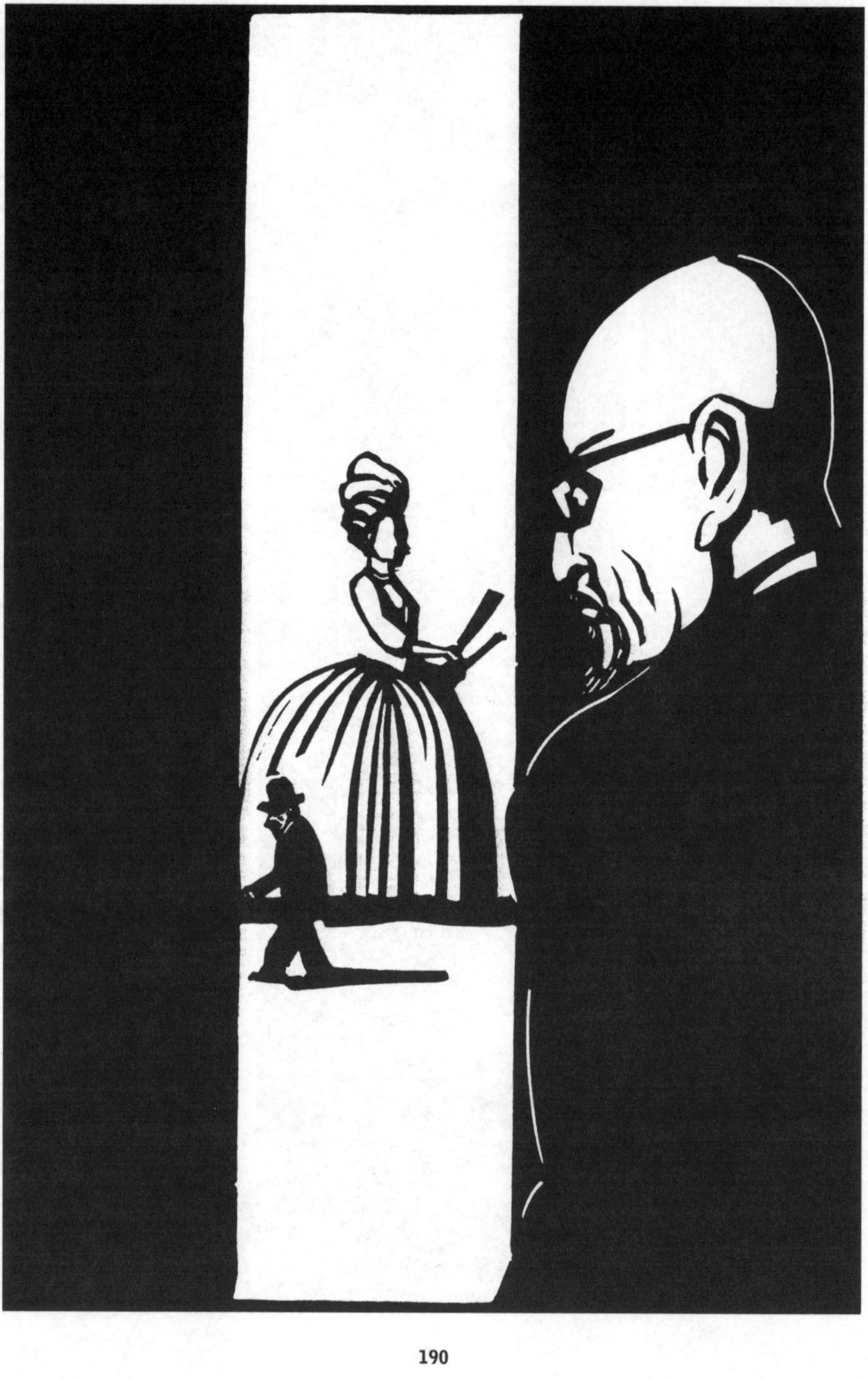

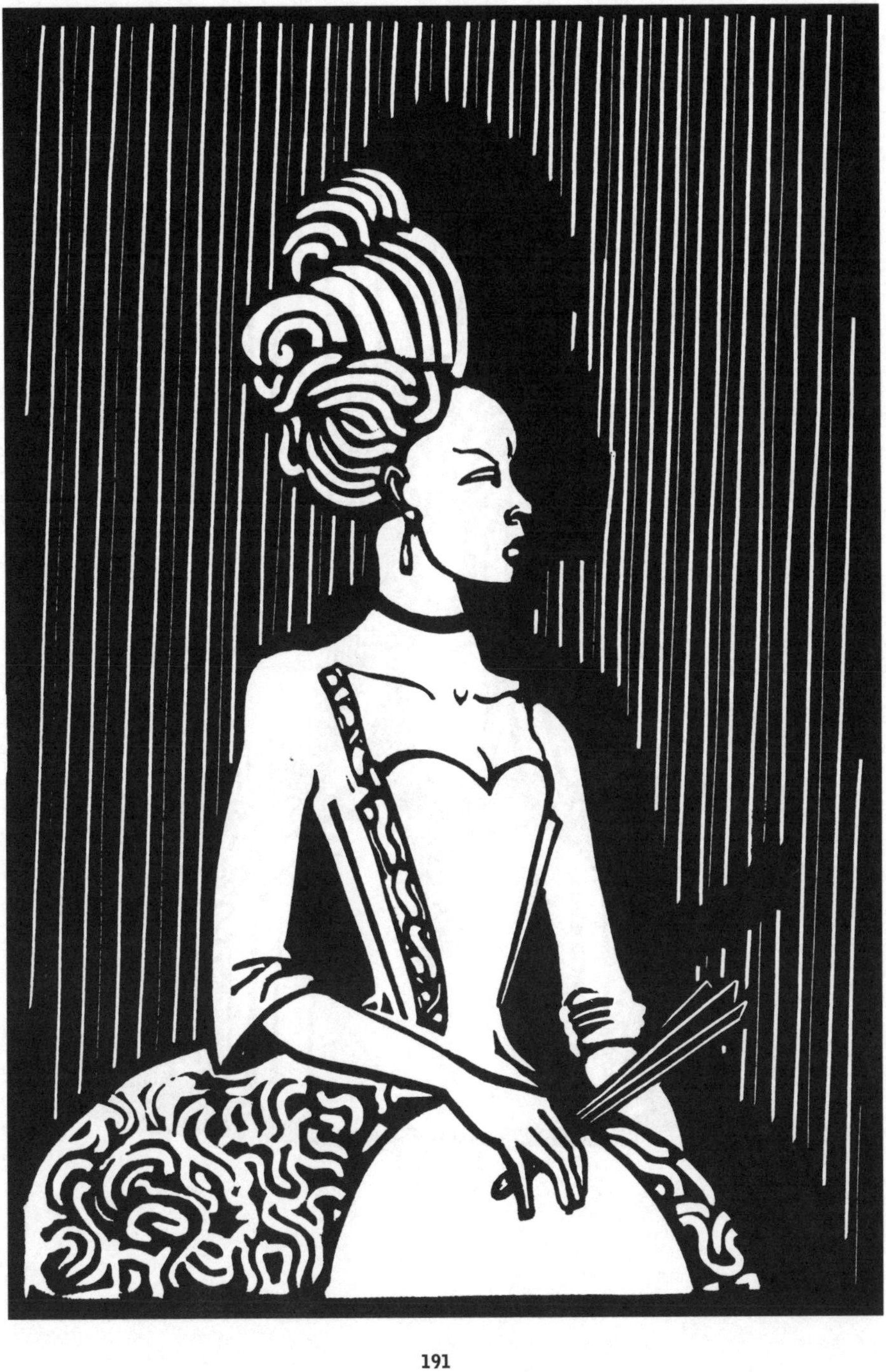

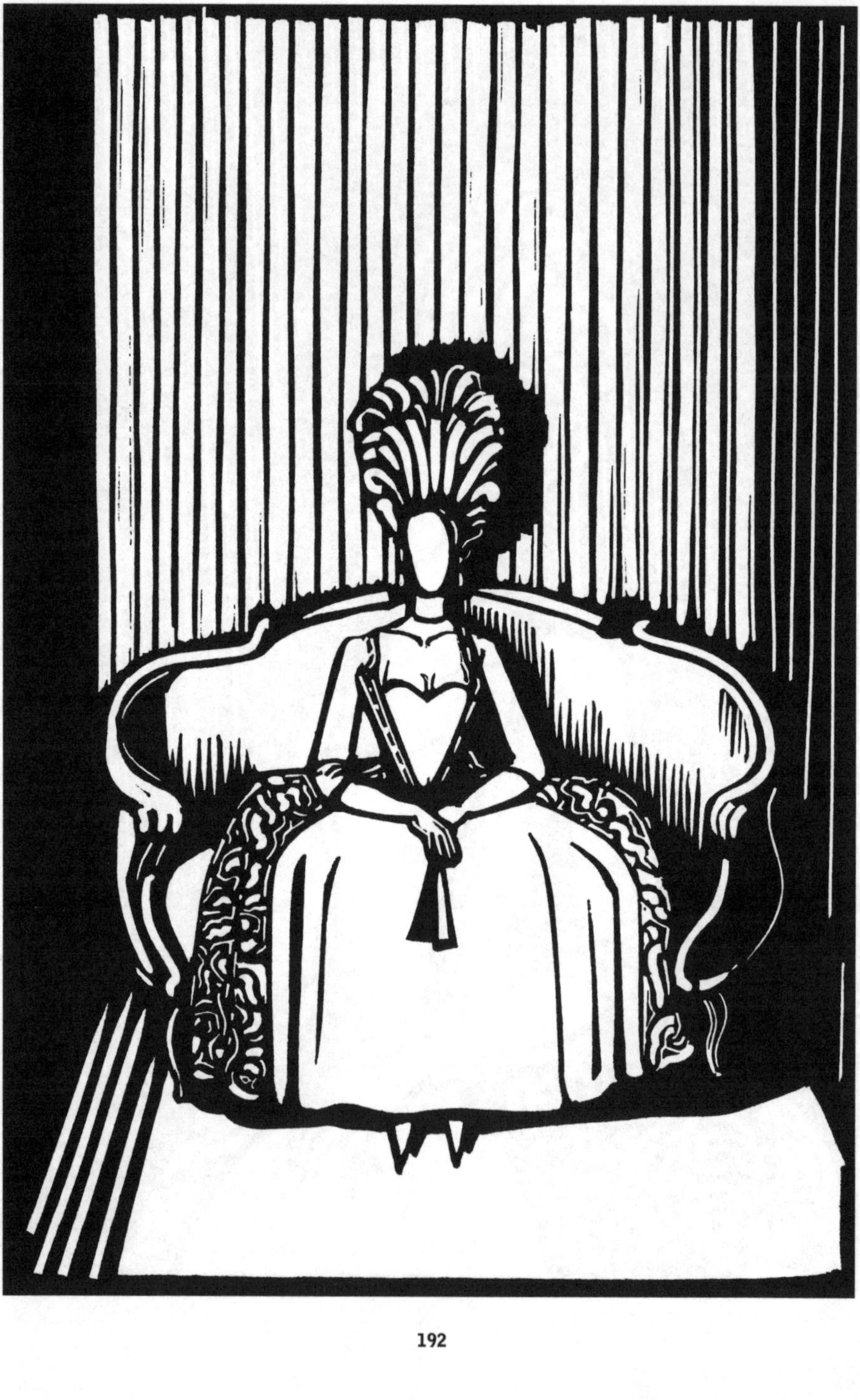

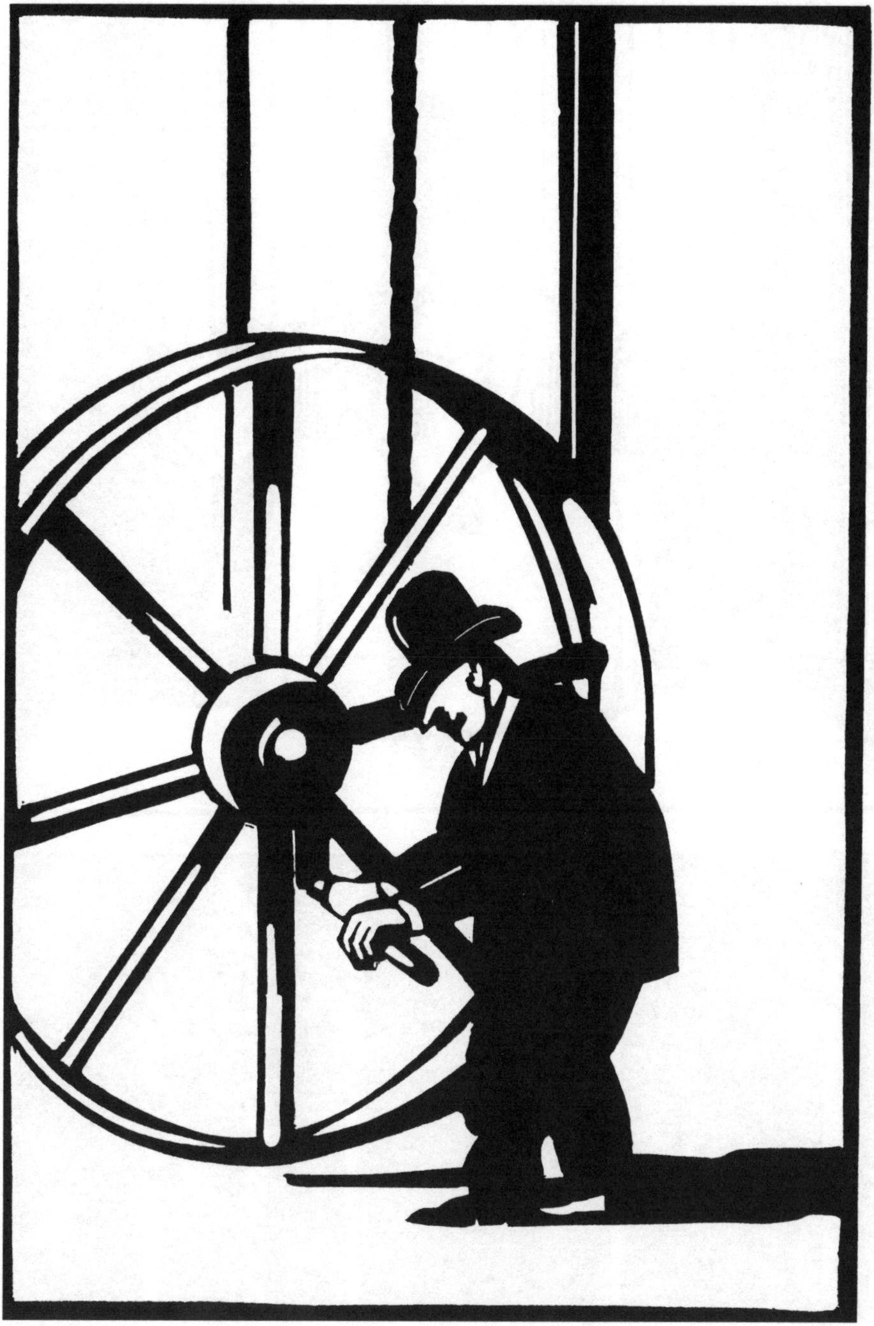

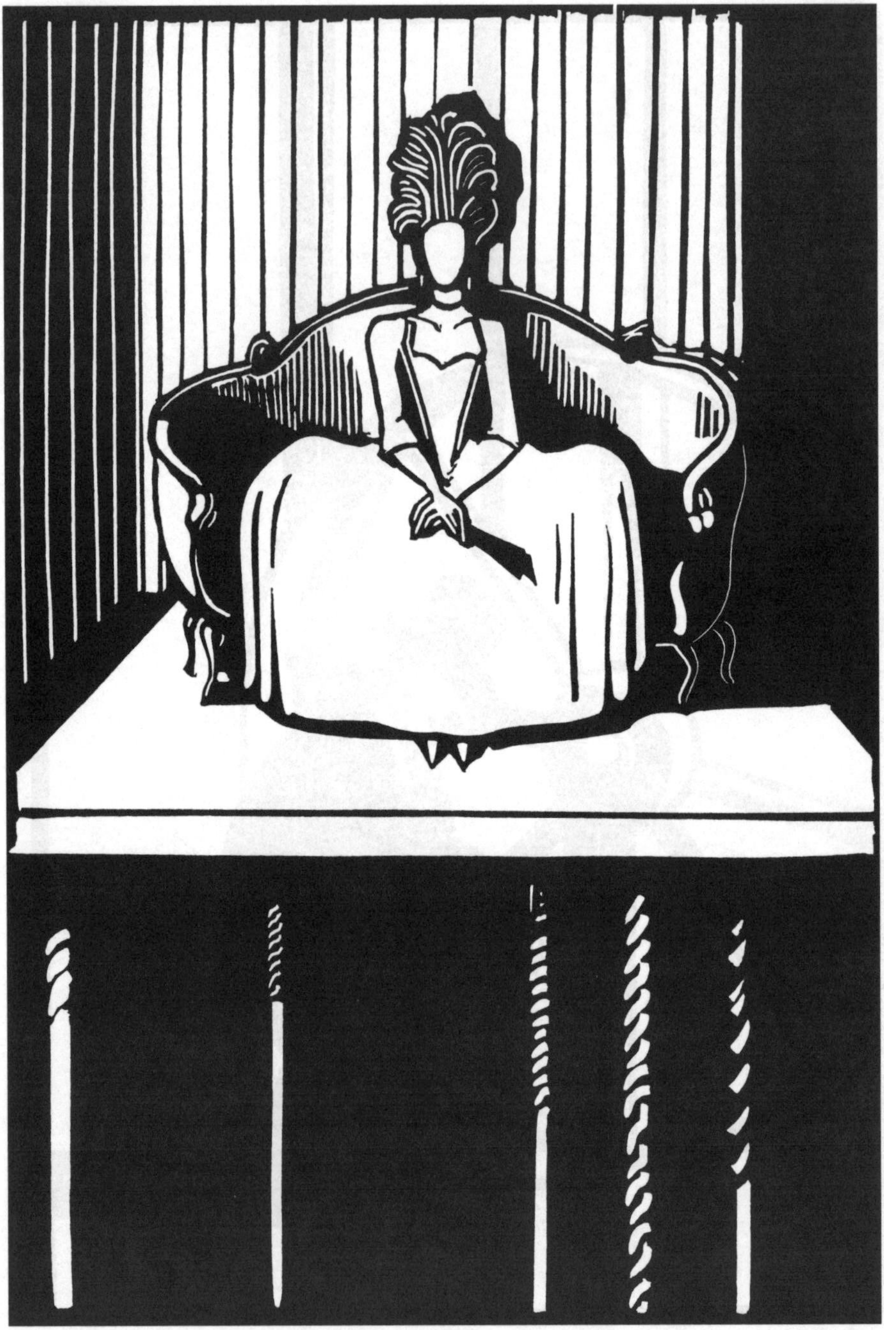

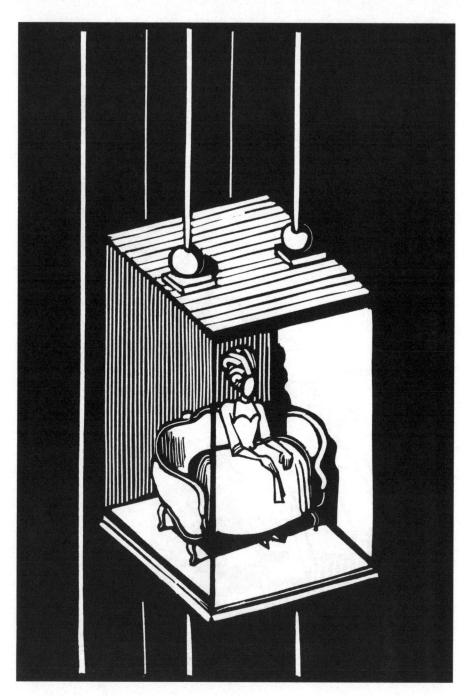

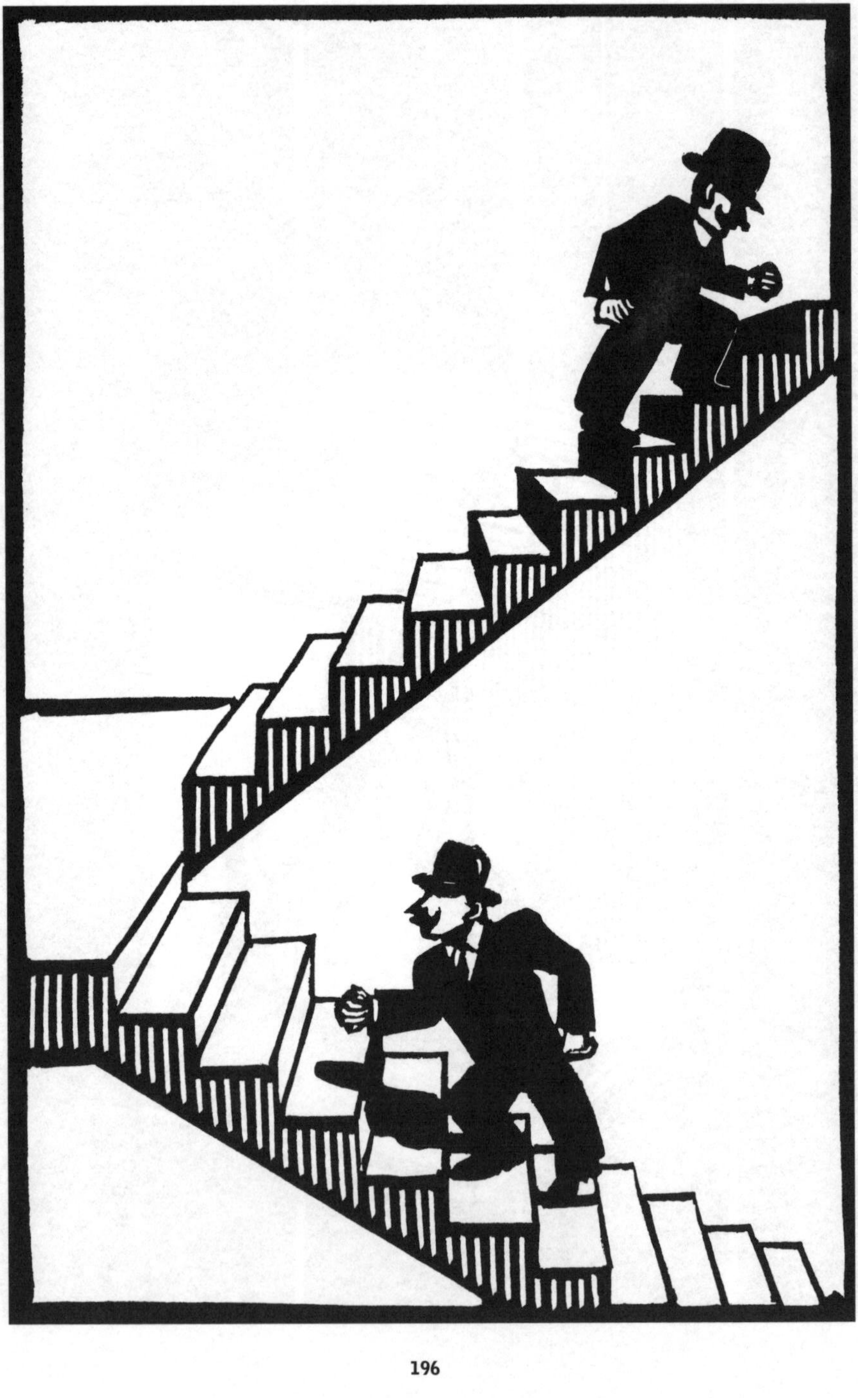

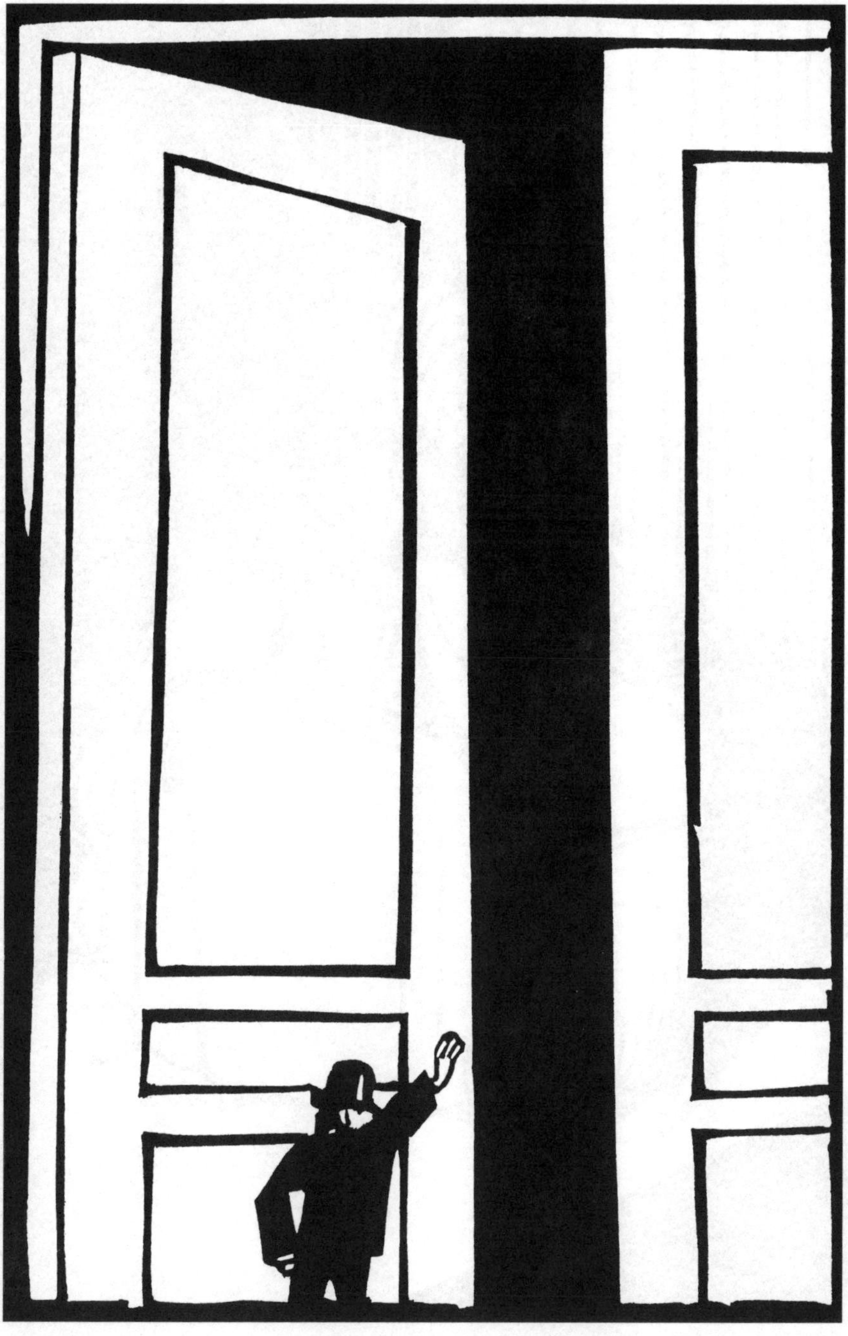

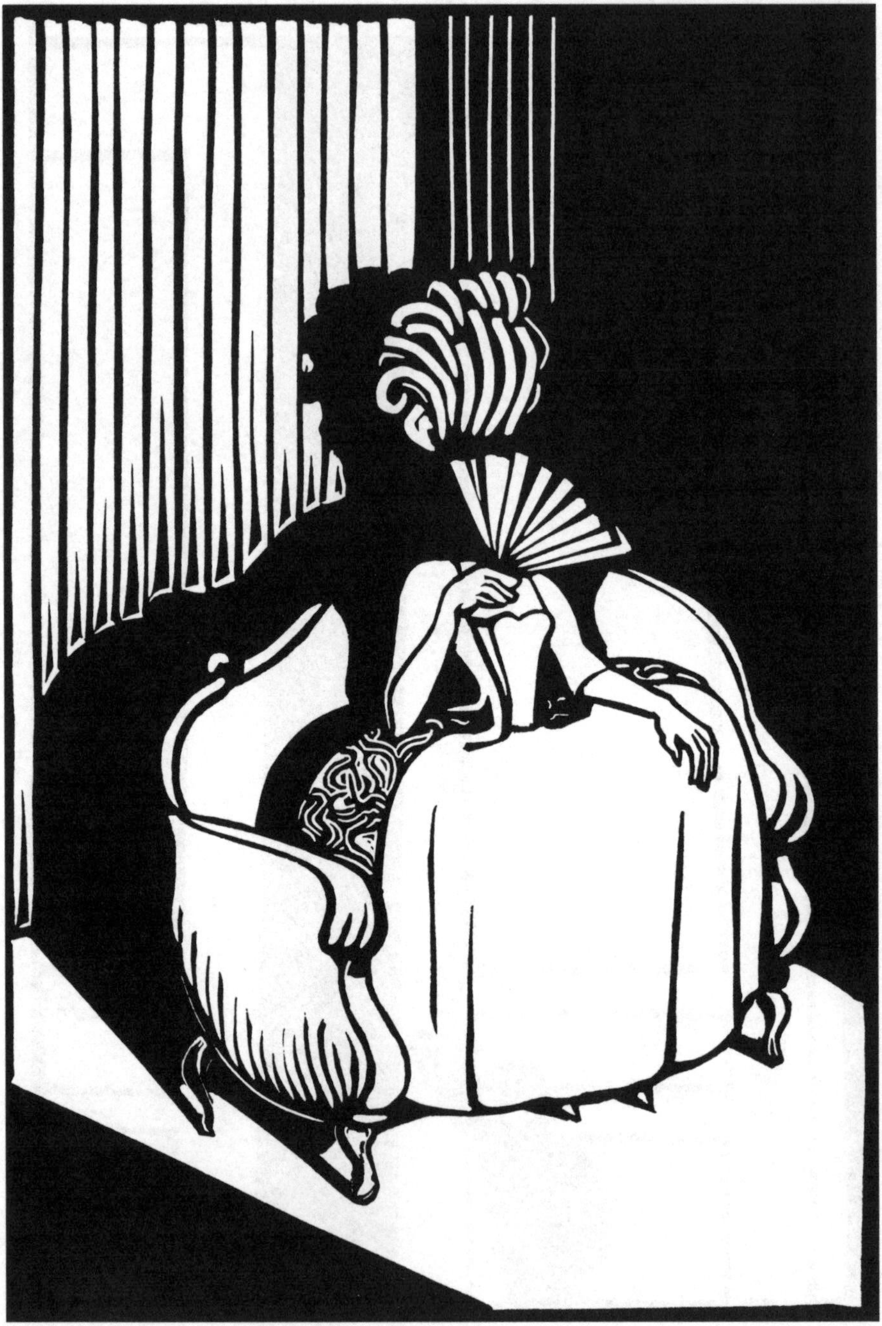

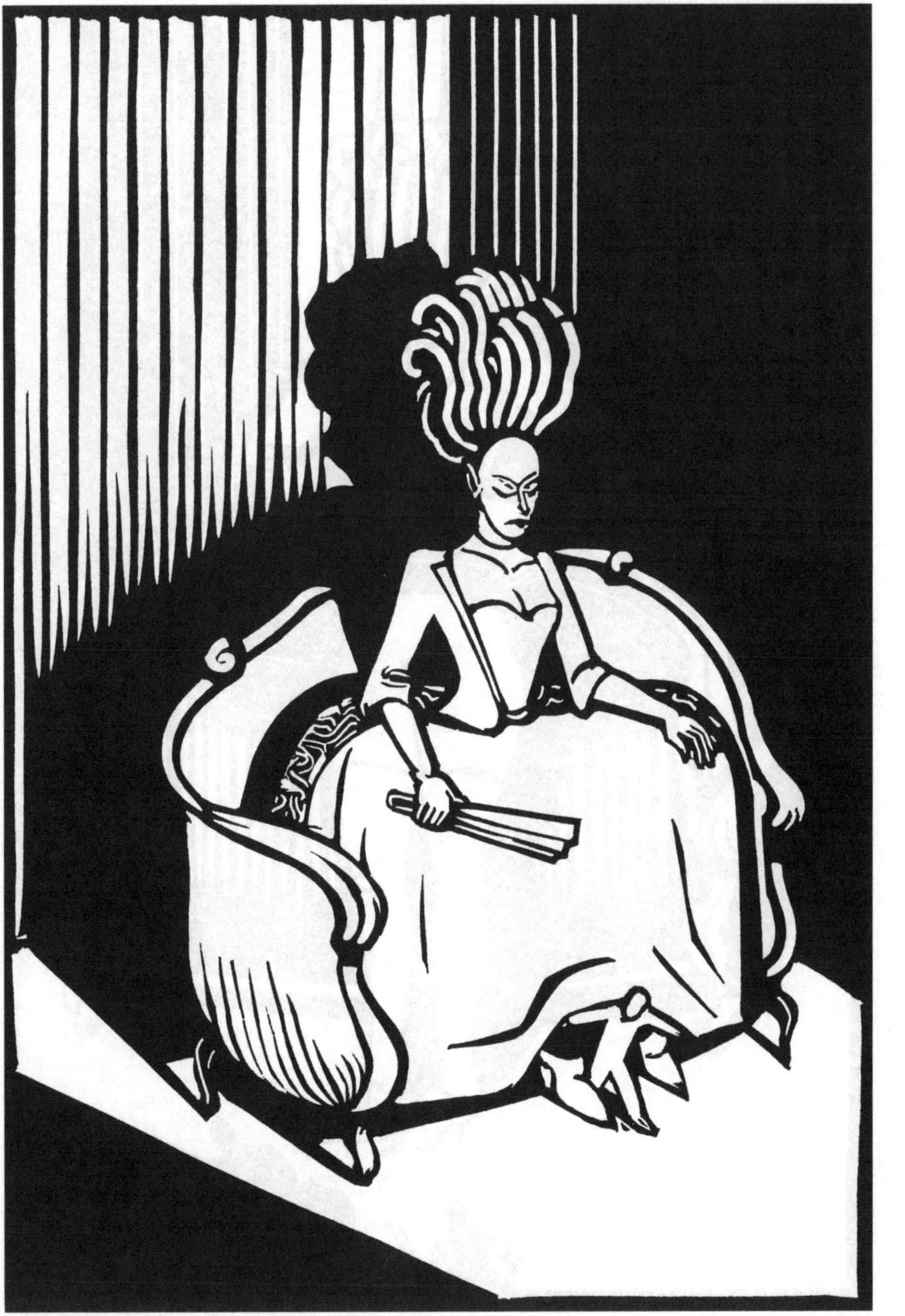

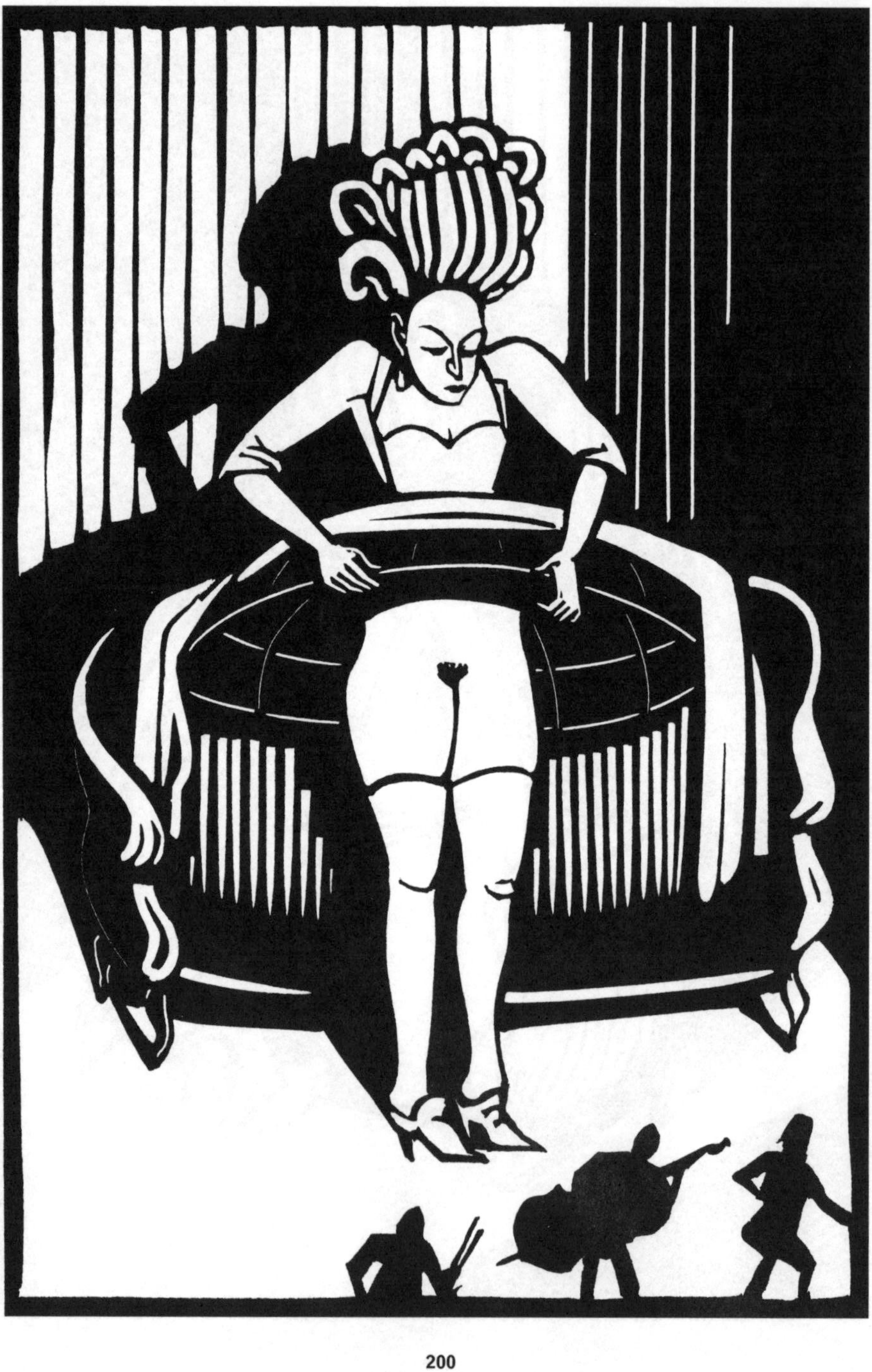

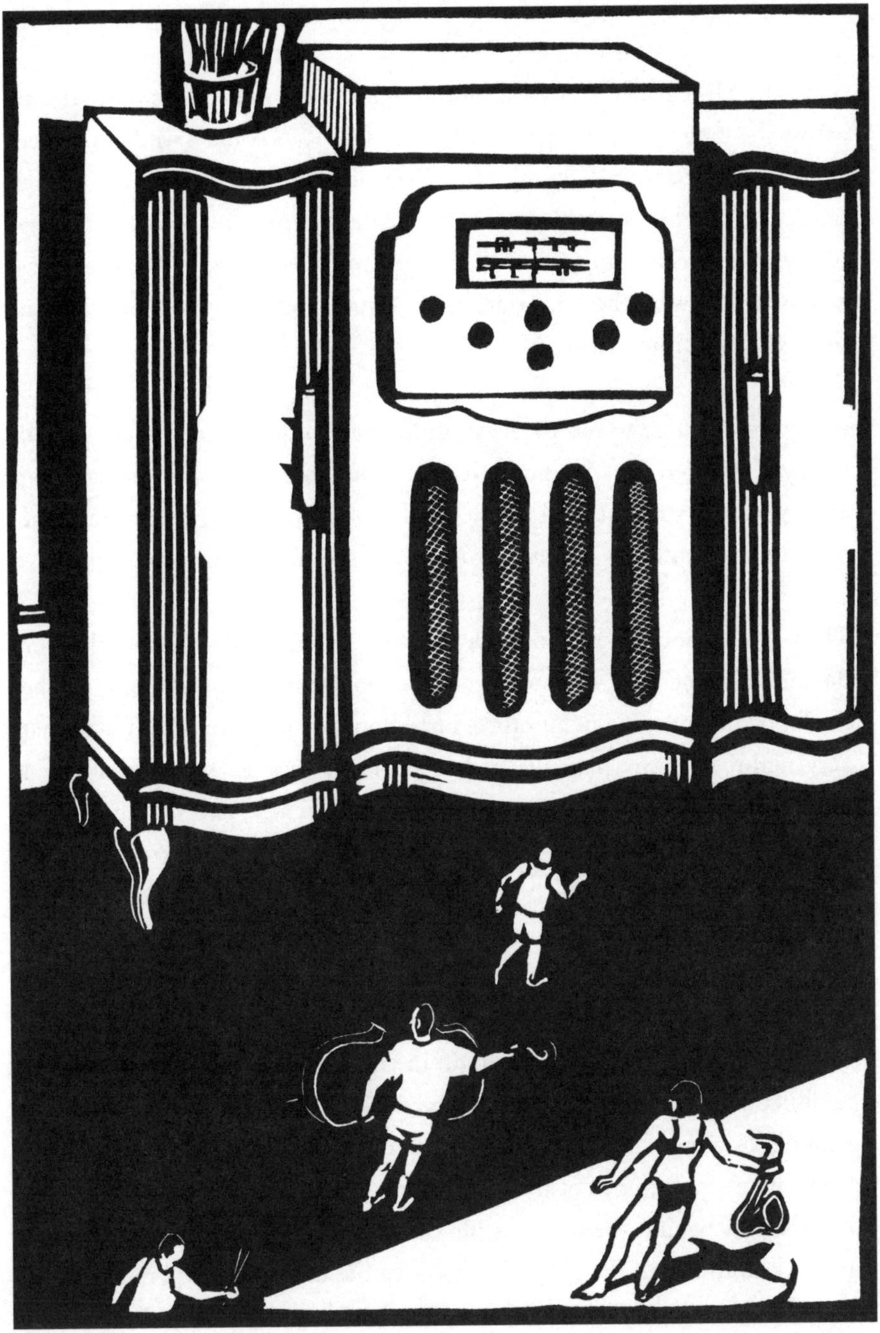

Sheets of white paper were floating through the air; some more were strewn across the terrace; the rest remained in my lap. It took me a while to realize what was happening. I sprang up and ran in all directions, gathering the papers before they were blown away over the balcony. I was lucky. I clung to the manuscript, happy to have salvaged my friend's work. My heart was beating fast; I was relieved. I stacked the papers together into a pile and sat on it as I put on my jacket.

In my room I tried to put the pages in the right order. On all fours I started to lay them out on the floor. It was a much harder task than I had anticipated; not all the pages were clearly numbered and I had to read the first and last sentences of many of them in order to establish continuity.

There was a knock on the door. Dr Inzaghi's secretary informed me that the doctor had to go on a visit away from the sanatorium, but wished to see me the following morning in his office. I had hoped to join Angela in Lucca that very night; now my plans were dashed. There was no sense brooding; I continued with my work, but my back started to ache and my knees were sore from crawling around on the parquet. With difficulty I lifted myself off the floor and hobbled out of the room, I wanted to phone Angela. The corridor was already dark, but without locating any light switches I still managed to find the doctor's office. It was locked; the secretary had already gone home. Once more my sense of time had deserted me. I descended the main staircase; moonlight reflected off the marble walls at all angles, making it difficult to establish a sense of direction. Once I found myself on the landing, however, the remaining steps were clearly illuminated by the light from the main entrance of the sanatorium. The reception was to my right, but the seat behind the long marble counter was vacant. A soft light from beneath illuminated the chair's battered leather cushion; it still retained the round indentation of its recent occupier. By a desk diary I could see an old telephone. I cleared my throat and coughed a number of times, hoping to attract attention. No one emerged from the back room. I was reluctant to help myself to the phone; ever since my interview with Inzaghi I had felt like an intruder, even though I was in this institution for a valid reason. Eventually I brought myself to utter the words.

'Hello, anybody there?'

No reply. I looked around. On either side of the main staircase two sets of stairs descended to the basement. A sign at the top of the right stairs showed an arrow and three words, the last of which I could understand. Telefono. I followed the sign, but walked down with apprehension, clinging onto the brass handrail for fear of falling in the dark. I experienced a shock on reaching the landing, thinking there were more steps before me. As my eyes adapted to the dark, though, I was relieved to make out a set of glass-panelled doors in front of me. They were also locked and so, turning around, I continued my descent down the next flight of steps. Here it was pitch black; I could not see a thing. Keeping close to the wall, with my right hand firmly on the handrail, I inched my way down the steps like a blind man. The handrail ended and my hand guided me further across the marble surface of the wall until it reached a sharp edge. I took one more step and realized that to the right was a doorway. My hand left the wall and for a second was suspended in the void until I was touching glass, then wood and finally a metal handle. The door gave way; as it opened, a light switched on automatically, blinding me for a second. It was a telephone booth: a cabin neatly tucked away under the staircase, with a low-wattage light bulb installed in the ceiling. Dust covered all the fittings and there was a faint smell of stale tobacco; I felt like an archaeologist stumbling upon a long-forgotten site. Now for the phone call to Angela! I lifted the receiver; the phone was in working order. I had to find her hotel number and rummaged through the pile of telephone directories that lay discarded on the floor underneath an empty shelf. Some pages were torn, others missing and I soon abandoned any hope of finding what I was looking for. I would have to phone the operator; but what number should I dial? I sat down on the seat, which was so low that instead of seeing my face reflected in the glass panel of the door, all I saw was the top of my head, a shiny dome. I had to laugh, who was this bald dwarf reflected in the glass? The light bulb flickered a few times, and then went out. This was all I needed. I took a handkerchief out of my pocket and attempted to adjust the bulb, hoping it was just loose in its socket. But it was of little use, I heard the filament tinkle; the bulb was gone. I slumped back into my seat, dejected.

Something kept me in my seat; I had no desire to move. Slowly my eyes began to register a dim haze of light outside the telephone booth. It came from the bottom of the stairs. I thought I could see a dark figure, a faint silhouette. Was it staring at me? I stared back, first in fear, then with benumbed fascination. Was I looking at myself? Never before had I experienced such a sensation. I could hear my own heart beating; I could hear the blood run through my veins, every involuntary muscle spasm or nervous twitch registered upon my brain with magnified force. New to such a heightened awareness, I did not even notice that the phantom form I was staring at was no longer there.

*   *   *

I opened the door to my room and lingered for a while on the threshold before entering. Moonlight poured in and the sight of Ed's manuscript strewn across the floor made me feel tired; I would have to complete the work in the morning. I walked carefully around the edge of the floor towards the bed, accompanied by my shadow on the wall. With heavy abandon, I collapsed onto the mattress and fell asleep.

But my sleep was not deep; I felt somebody's presence. I did not dare open my eyes when a hand touched my forearm. I was being lifted out of bed; we were moving across the floor and out of the room without touching the ground.

*   *   *

The light in the living room was so bright that I had to pull down the blinds; even then I chose to sit down on the armchair in the darkest corner of the room. It was the longest day of the year, Angela's birthday. Ever since I first met her we had always spent her birthday together. Why was she not with me now? I kept staring at the telephone. Was I really awake? It was so quiet, yet I was aware of a faint sound in the apartment. I listened, then got out of the armchair and walked over to the hall. The sound of running water; I had left the tap on in the bathroom. In my felt slippers I slid across the floor to the bathroom. Then it was the coffee noisily percolating on the stove in the kitchen. The bathroom was steamed up; the coffee pot was spilling over, its dark liquid hissing on the gas plate.

The newspapers landed outside the front door. I would let the bathwater cool down. The time was right to recline on the sofa, drink coffee and read the newspapers. I had to take it easy, sit back, put my feet up and slow down. A momentary shiver passed through my body.

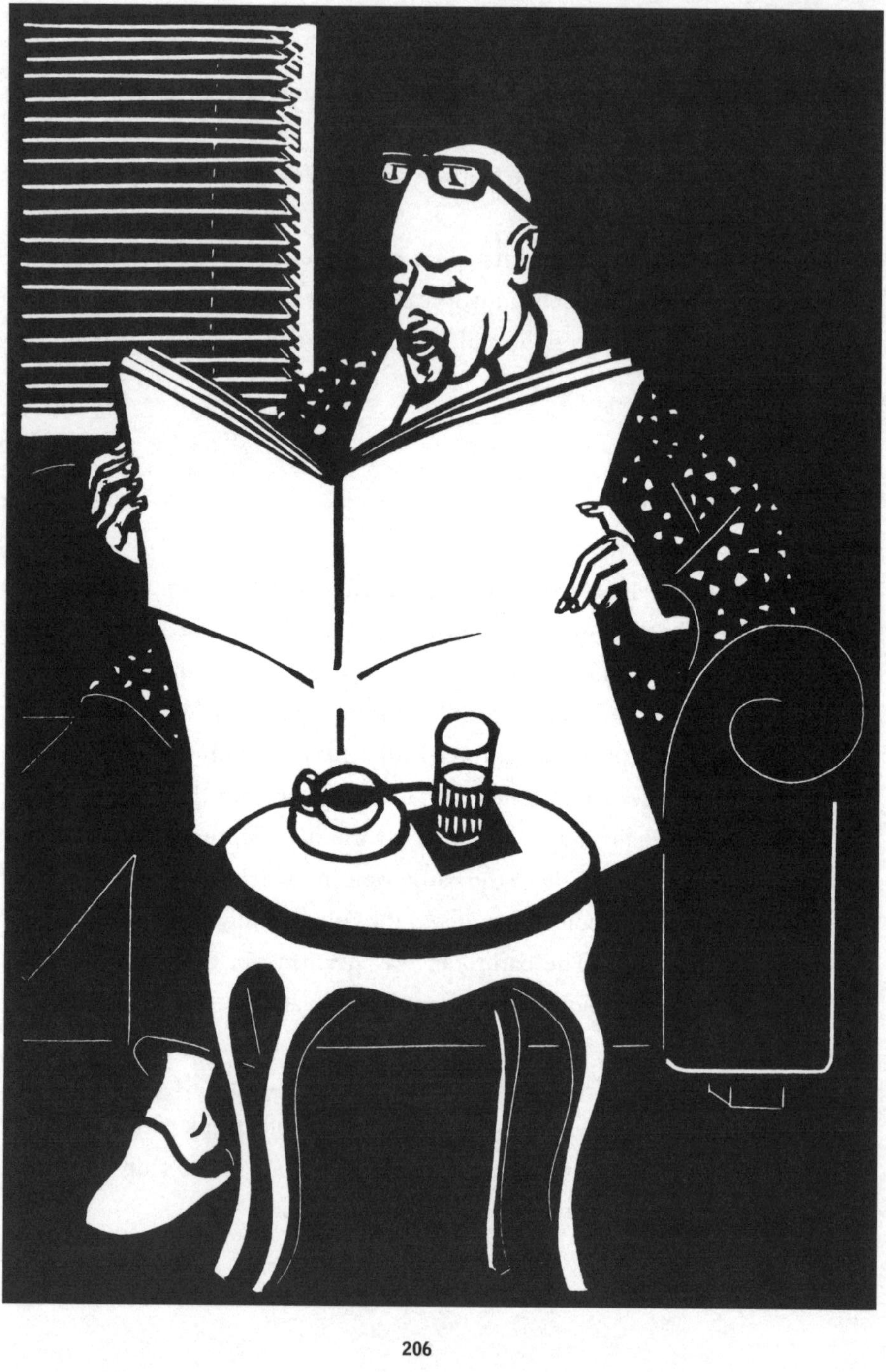

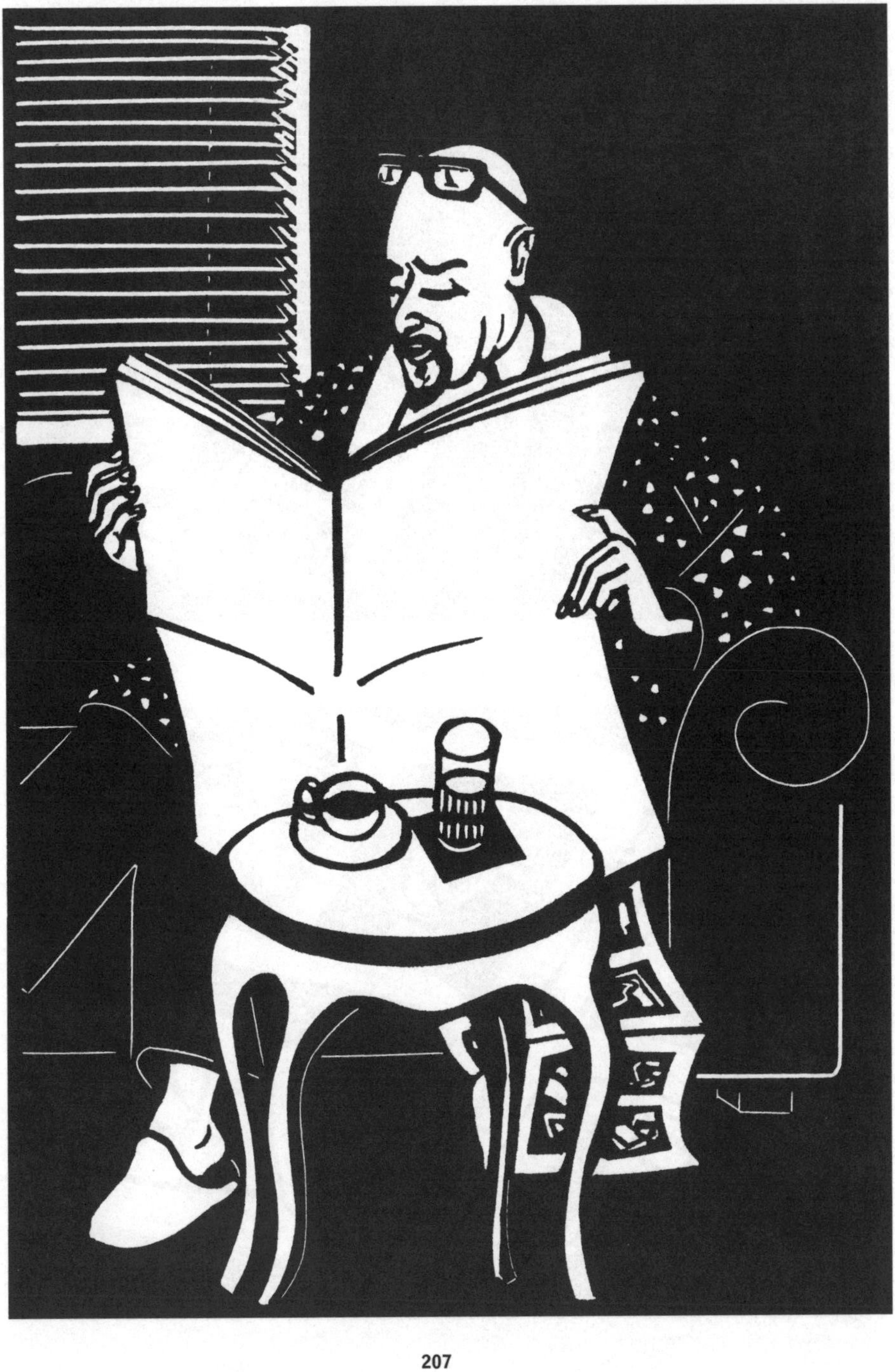

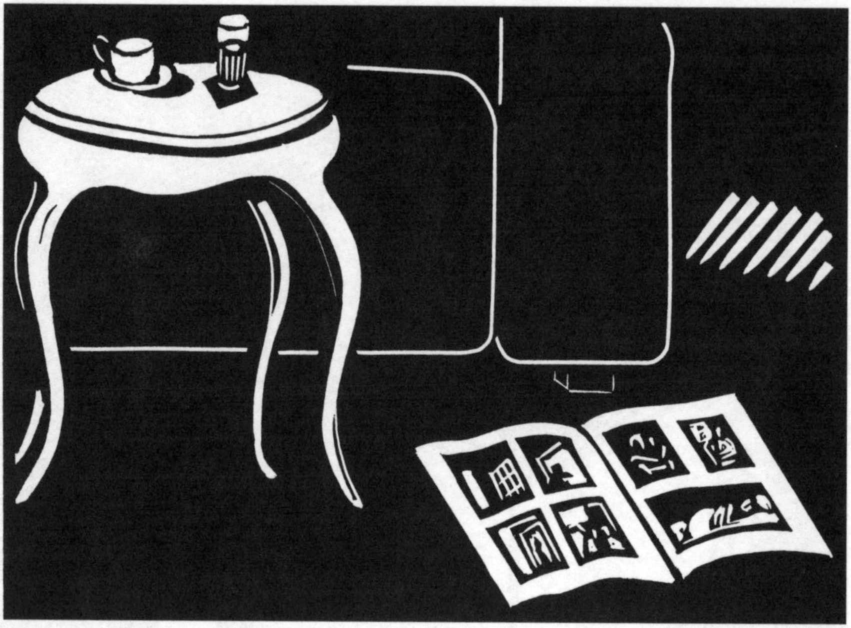

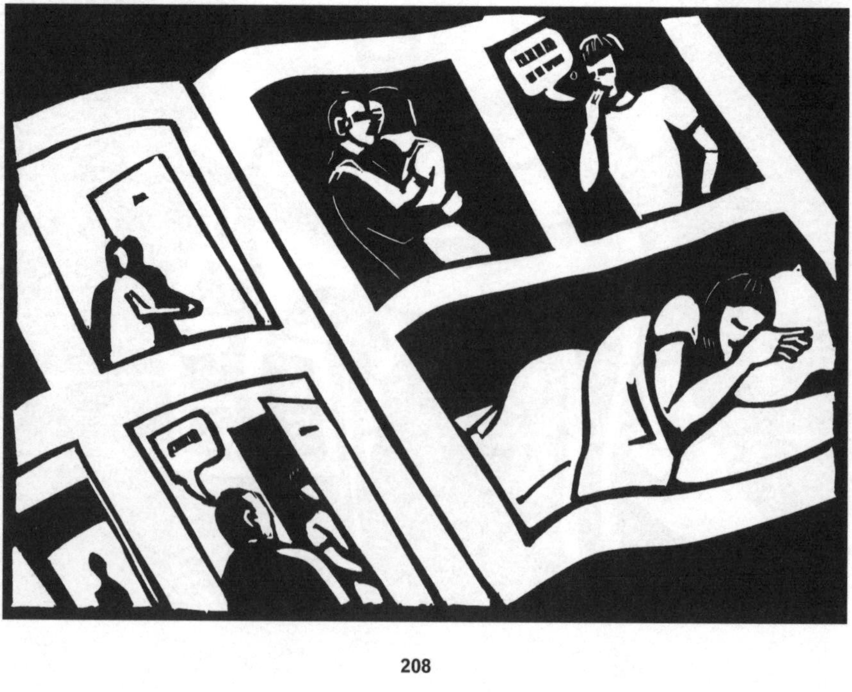

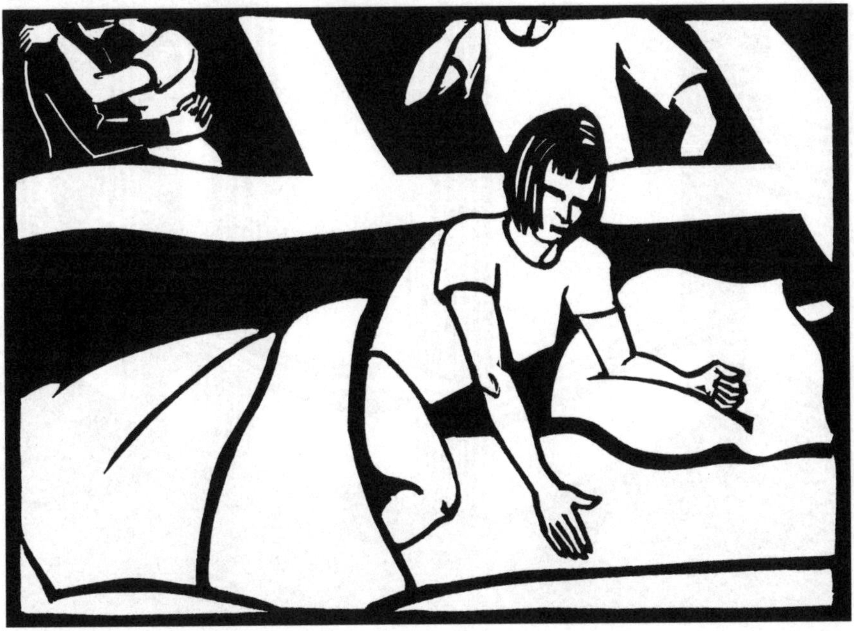

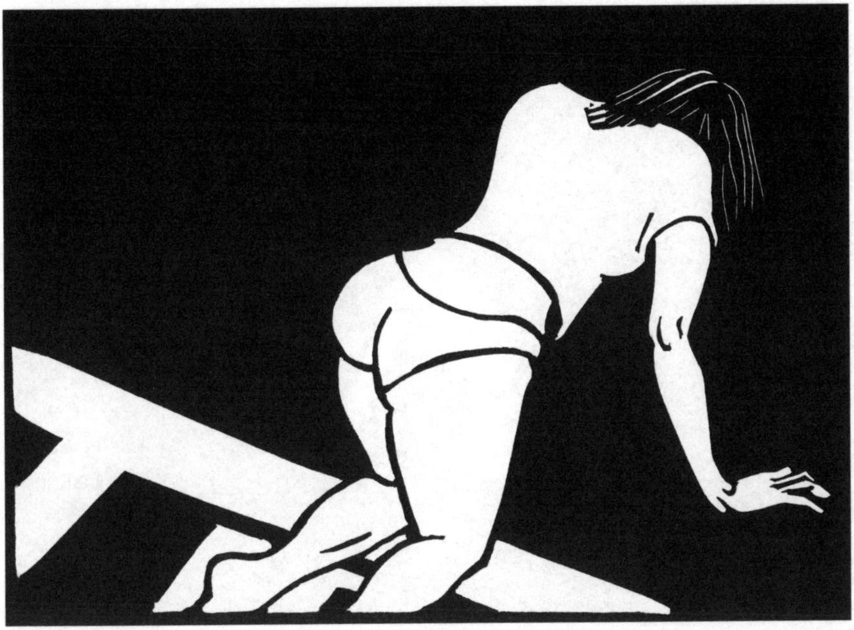

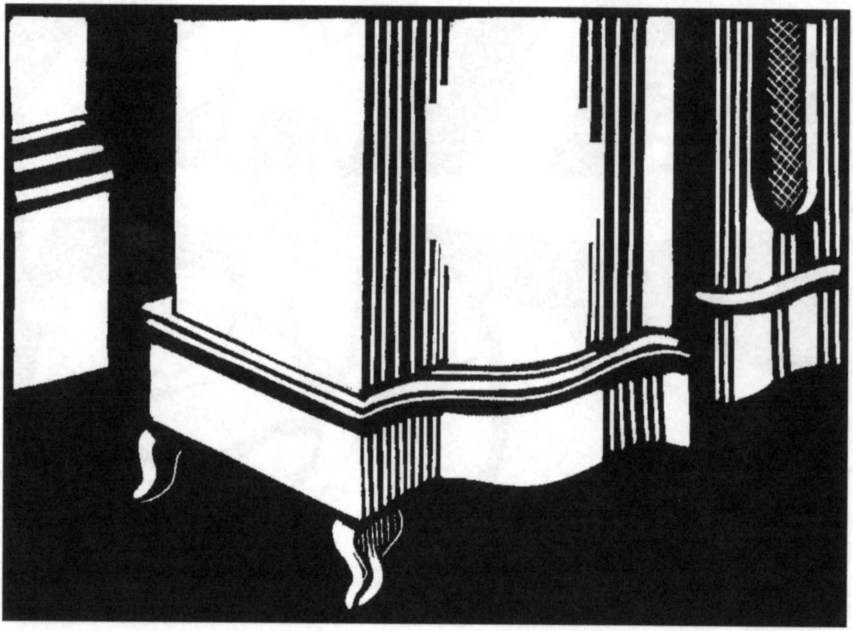

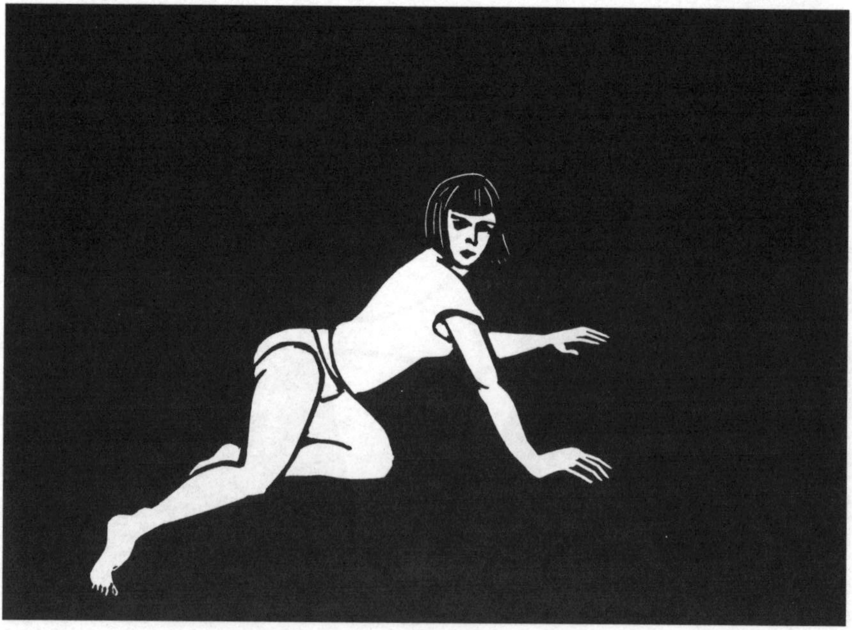

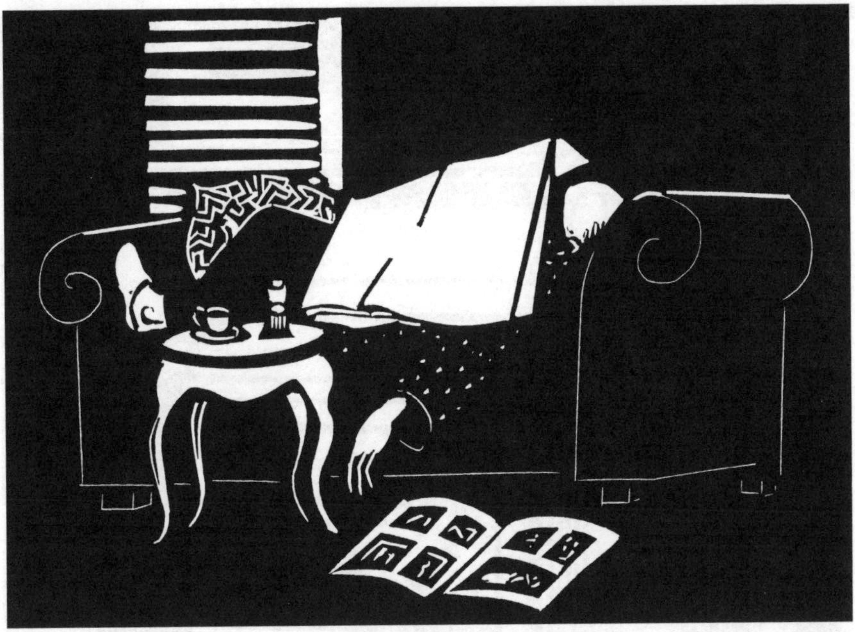

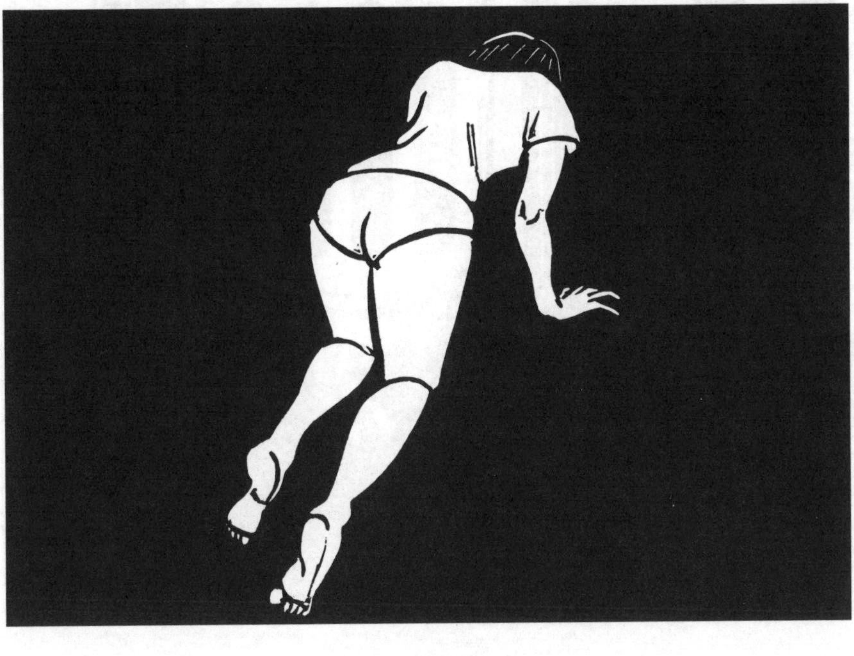

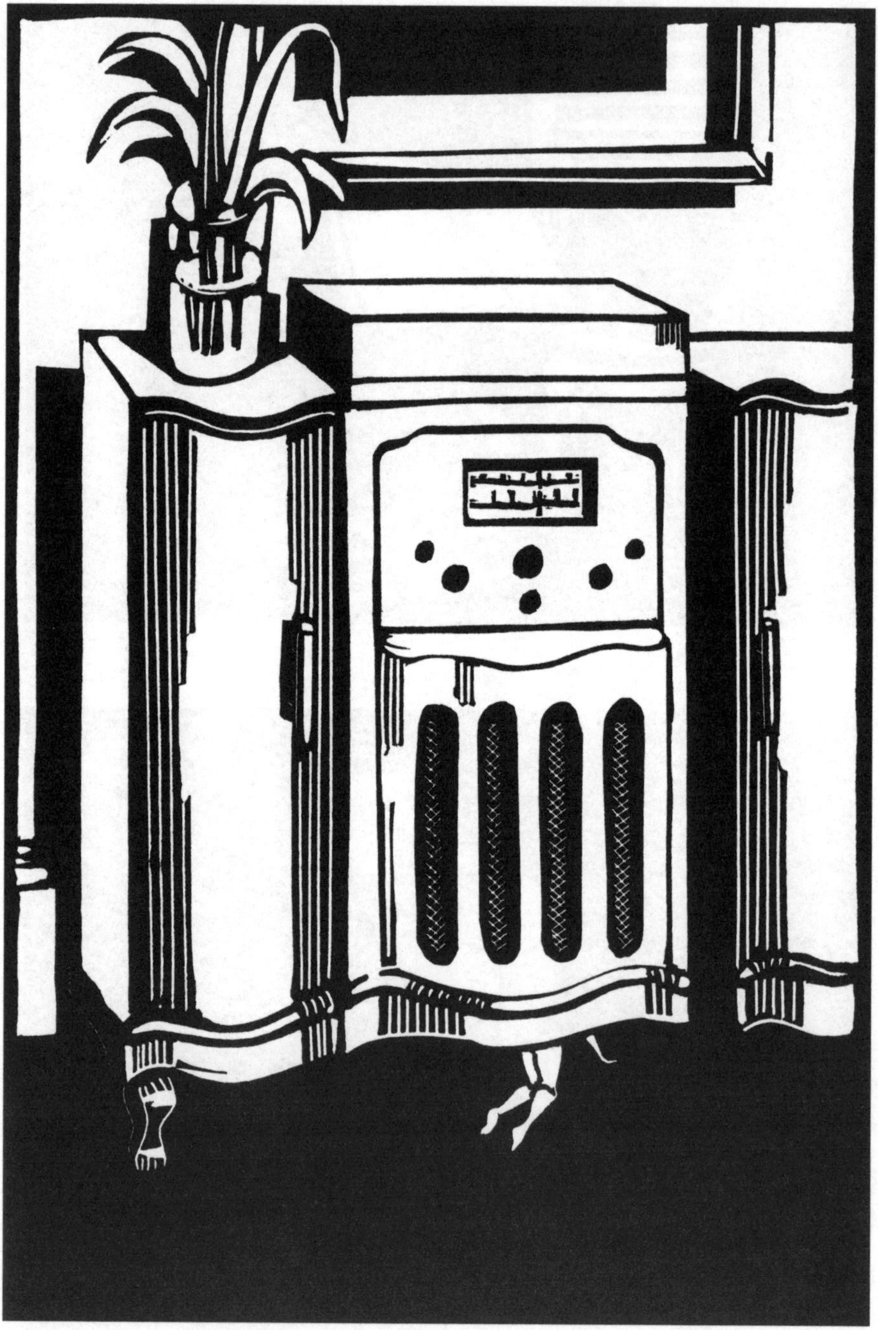

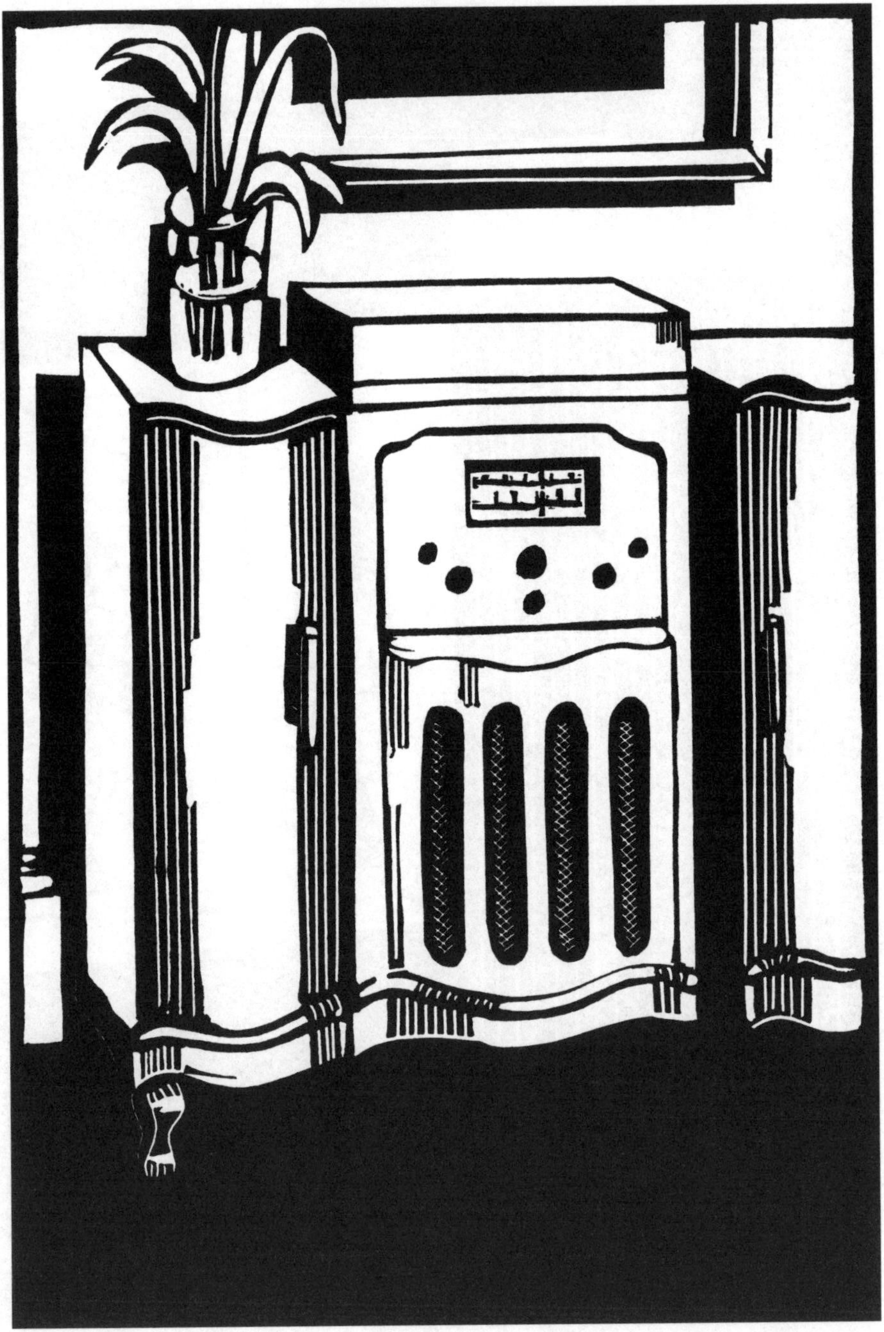

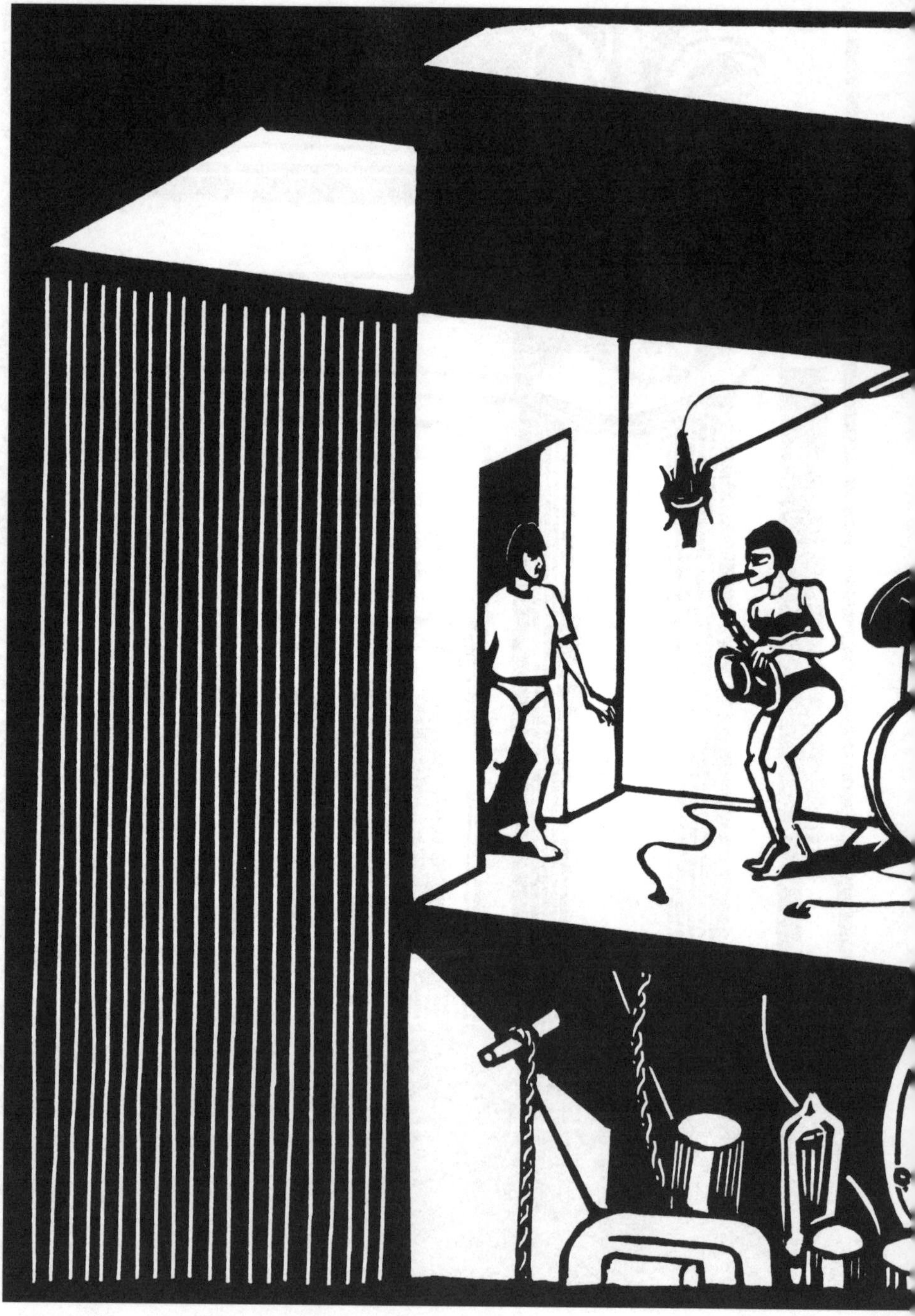

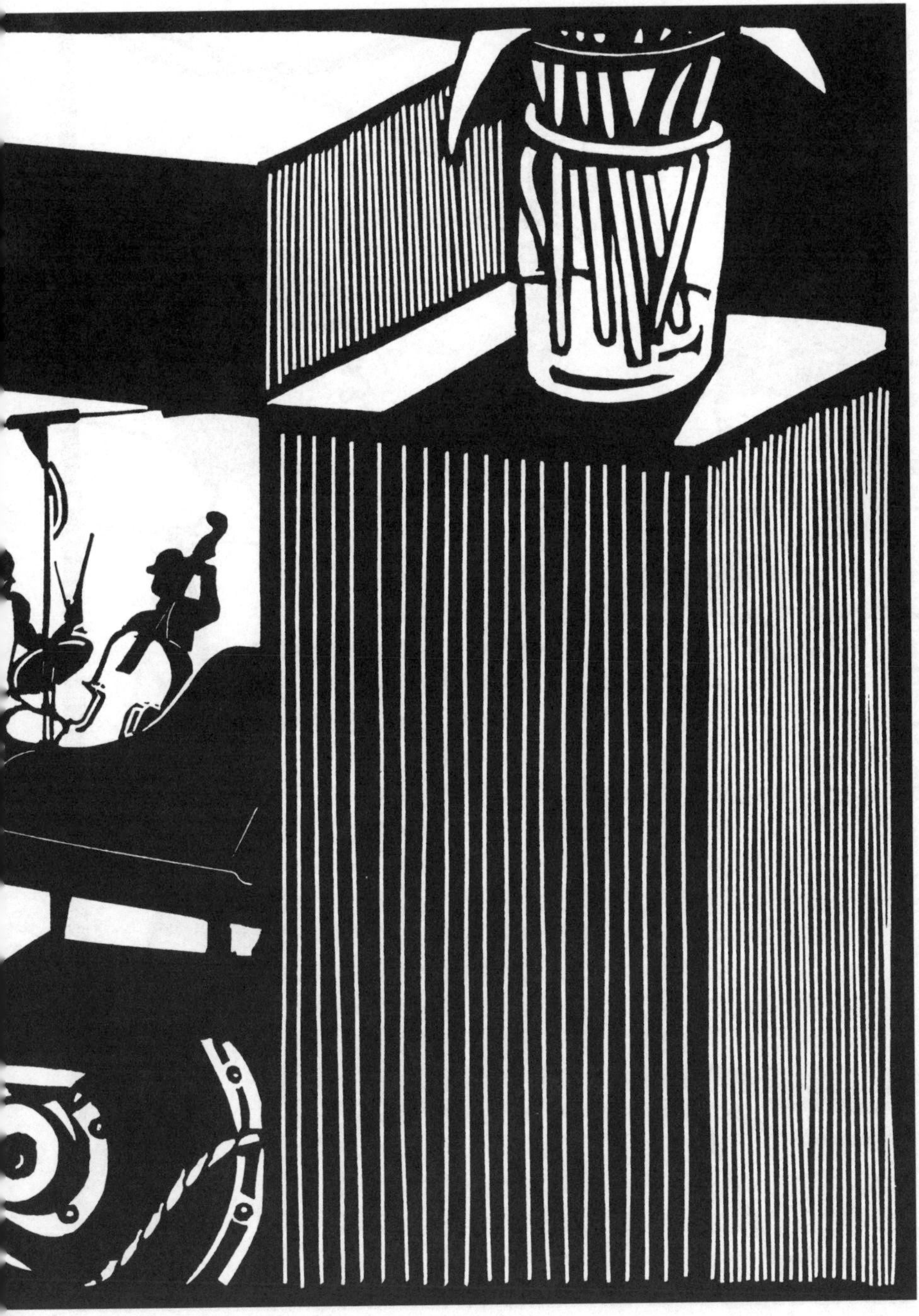

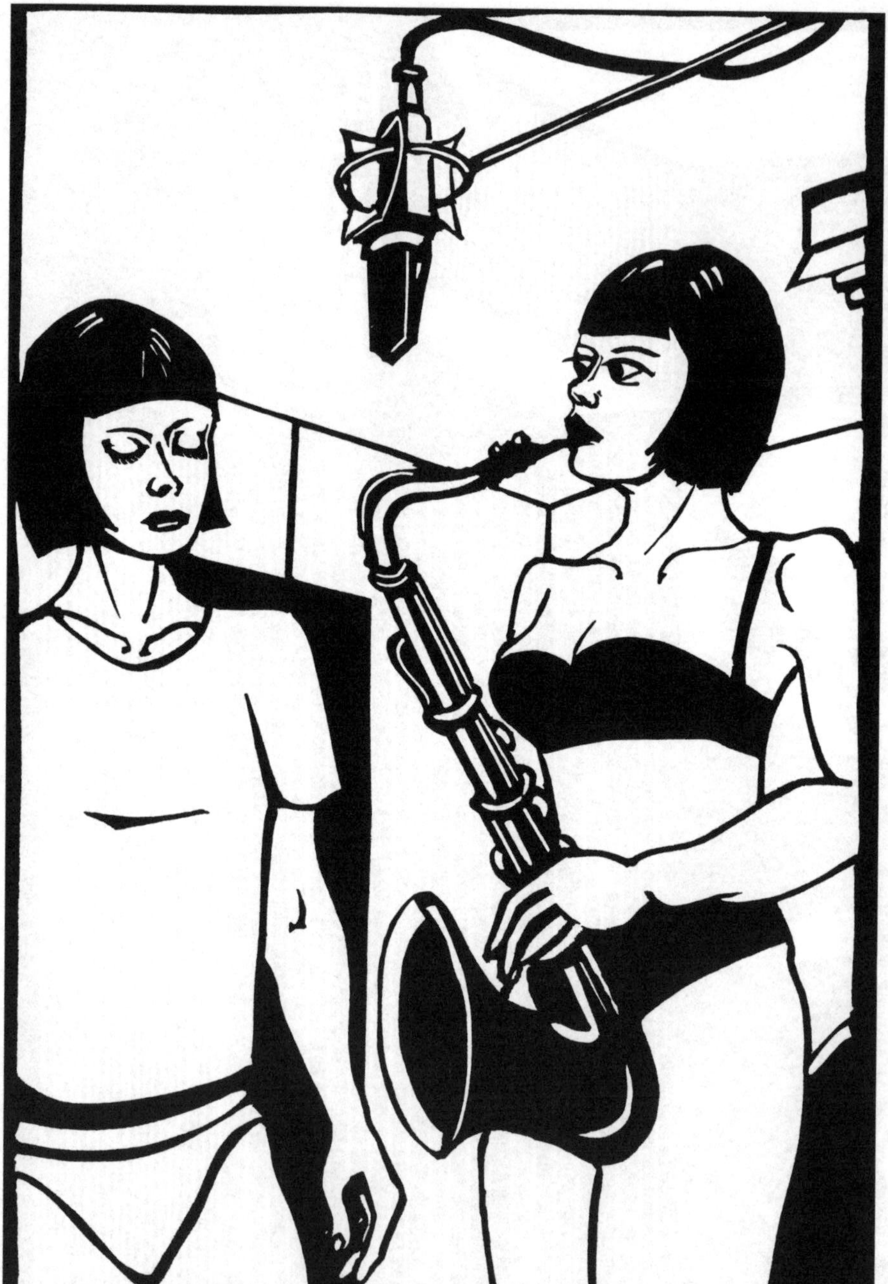

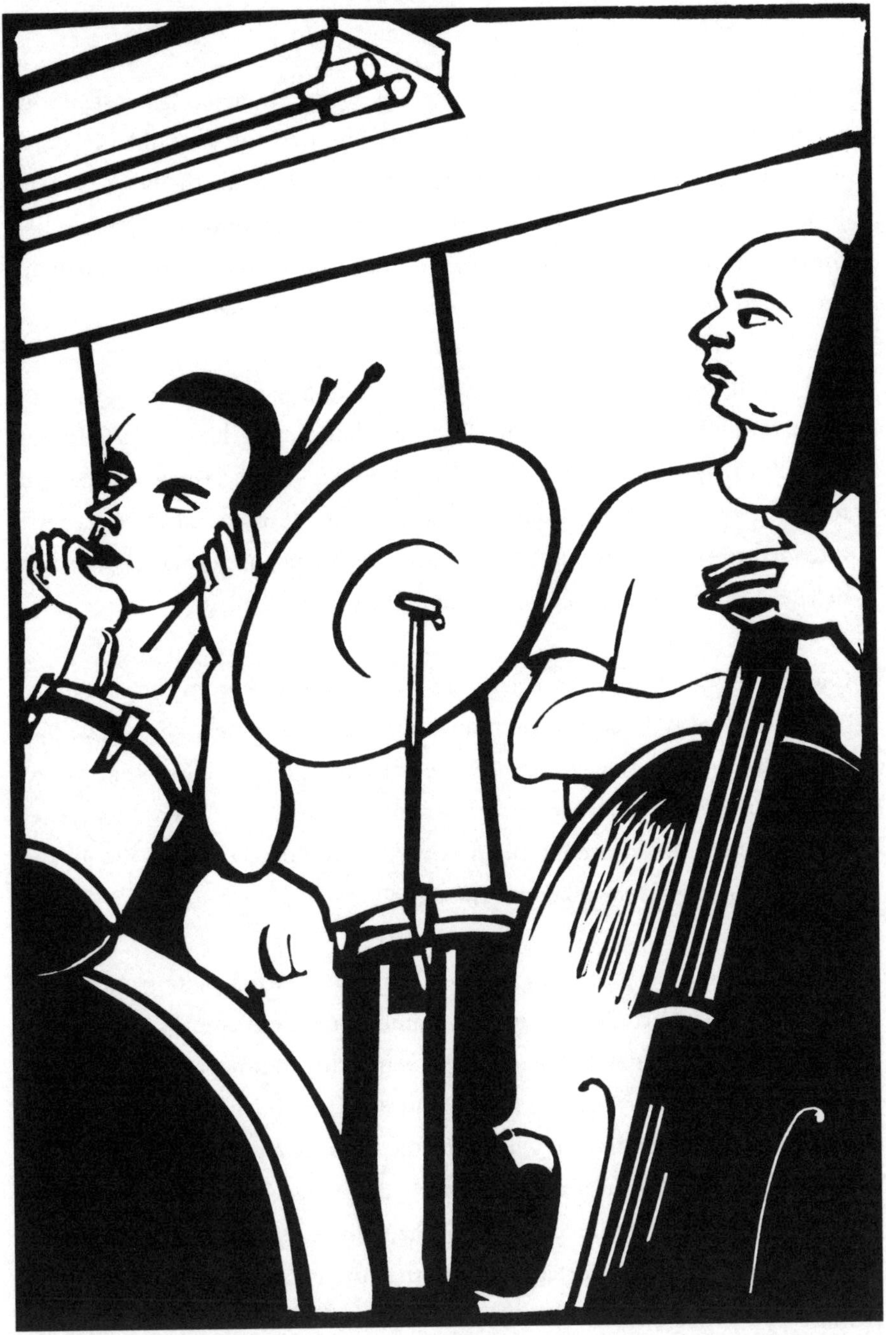

A momentary shiver passed through my body; something brushed my forehead. it was Angela leaning over me. She told me I would be late; I would have to start off soon if I were to make it back for the book launch. I looked into her eyes, at her mouth, and then down into her cleavage; her breath was sweet. I made her sit on my lap. There was no time for that; breakfast was on the table. Yes, the smell of coffee reached me.

Did I really want to borrow her car? Yes I did. She gave me the keys with some misgivings. After all, when was the last time I had driven? It was difficult to say when, but she knew, for she told me; it was when we travelled to Budapest. But there would be few cars on the roads; that was why I intended to start so early in the morning. Under no circumstances was I to be late. I promised. I squeezed Angela tightly and then left.

Outside it was grey; a thin drizzle descended invisibly from the sky. Once on the motorway I had to switch on the windscreen wipers; the drizzle had turned to rain. There were very few vehicles on the road; those that passed me left a dirty spray in their wake. It was one of those days when the weather would remain bleak; a constant murky hue would accompany me all the way to Edgetown. I switched on the radio.

East of London, the motorway was even emptier. I started looking out for the road signs; soon I could see Edgetown among the destinations. I glanced at the digital clock on the dashboard; there was plenty of time. I could even stop over for a coffee at the next petrol station. The rain had subsided and I switched off the windscreen wipers. In the distance I could see a pedestrian footbridge stretching over the lanes of the motorway. I slowed down; on the bridge I could see a figure leaning over the railings. As I was approaching the bridge I had an uncomfortable feeling that the person was about to jump. Once past the bridge I drew into a lay-by and looked into the rear-view mirror. There was no one on the bridge. I stepped out of the car and looked back. On the other side of the motorway a person was walking briskly along the hard shoulder away from the bridge, in the opposite direction. I moved over to get a better look. It was a woman; she seemed unusually tall, although from such a distance it was hard to tell. On her back she was carrying a small rucksack; her hair was pinned back and I think she wore glasses, but she was walking so fast that I could no longer see her clearly. It was drizzling again. I ran back to the car; Elvis was singing one of his old songs.

My students had left everything in perfect order. All I had to do was to remove the tapes from the various pieces of recording equipment, and take them back with me. I put new reels into the recorders and checked the gauges of the transformers. I did not bother to inspect the filters and did not take down any readings; I would leave that for another time.

With the tapes in my briefcase, I was ready to return home, but Edgetown fascinated me. I had only seen it as a scale model at the academy; in reality it was something altogether different.

From the motorway the building could easily be mistaken for a lay-by restaurant, only more austere, without the neon branding. It consisted of three chambers. The end chamber was suspended on pillars over two of the motorway lanes. The middle chamber cast its shadow over the concrete gradient that eventually levelled out with the embankment, which supported the first chamber with its entrance from the slip road. This was the domestic quarters. The floor of the chamber overhanging the motorway was of a transparent material reinforced with iron girders; standing on it was like standing on air. It was disconcerting to see cars pass directly beneath one's feet. A metal rack, carrying rows of TV monitors, transformers and recording equipment, ran down the middle of the chamber; cables protruded from the machines and meandered like snakes across the floor to the second chamber, the control room, which was stacked with computers. Here the walls were solid and opaque; all the illumination came from the flat skylight.

For a while I stood over the motorway, looking into the distance through the tinted-glass wall. It was dark but I did not switch on the lights. I turned towards the monitors, which were throwing up images from the closed-circuit cameras; they gave a kaleidoscopic impression of the immediate surroundings.

The flickering grey images revealed parts of the motorway, the vegetation around it, even the woods beyond the footbridge. Other monitors showed close-up images. The macro-lens cameras focused on insect and animal life in the wasteland bordering the road. I could observe the behaviour of insects trapped in some of the containers that I had designed with Ed. The sound of a solitary car would occasionally disturb the otherwise perfect silence. I was hypnotized by the image of a stick insect crawling to the top of the container, where it would drop to the bottom, only to repeat its laboured ascent over again.

All of a sudden a much louder sound came from nowhere and a gigantic shadow crossed the floor. I raised my head to see the underbelly of a Boeing pass over the skylight towards the airport. Vibrations passed through my body. In the ensuing silence I fiddled with the controls; random images appeared on the screens. I discovered that I could view the recorded footage retrospectively and turned my attention to the monitor that was linked to the camera by the footbridge; a hazy picture flashed up onto the screen. The tall woman with her antennae pigtails was descending the stairs of the footbridge. I took off my spectacles to get a better look, but she was already out of frame; I replayed the footage.

A second aeroplane flew over, the dials on the sound recorders flickered nervously like seismographs. They levelled out as the noise receded, but I could hear a bell ringing faintly in the distance. I went through to the control room and then the living quarters, following the sound, finally stopping by the chair over which I had thrown my jacket when entering Edgetown, and took my mobile phone from the pocket. I rarely carried my mobile and was surprised to have taken it with me.

'Hello.'

'Hori, darling.'

'Angela, is that you?'

'Are you on your way?'

'Yes, I'm just about to leave.'

'Well, don't be late, or we'll miss the launch.'

The clouds disperesed, revealing the sun low on the horizon in the gap between the north and east apartment blocks; a red glow bathed the street. I breathed in the air, so fresh after the rain, before following Angela into the taxi.

'Are you excited?'

'Yes, but I am a bit nervous.'

'Why should you be nervous? You've done everything you had to do.'

I told Angela that, had I read the whole of Ed's manuscript, I would at least know what we were in for, but the call from Inzaghi put an end to that. If only I hadn't fallen asleep on the plane and read it all there and then.

'I wouldn't worry, Horace. You're a loyal friend; you kept your promise.

You don't think I'm overdressed for the occasion, do you?'

We stopped at the traffic lights; Angela took out her compact and started to re-apply her make-up. It still puzzled me why Ed should have requested that no one should read his text except for the prospective publishers themselves. What was the purpose for such secrecy? Anyway Territories had taken it, so they must have liked it; no one publishes a book they do not believe in. I was mulling over the subject when Angela asked me about Edgetown; she was curious to know what it looked like. I pulled out my mobile phone and played around with the keypad. Once I had programmed the photographic images, I handed it over to her.

'Is that it?'

'Yes.'

'But this is just a building; I thought it would be a town.'

'The students named it Edgetown. Here, there are a few more.' I pressed the keypad.

223

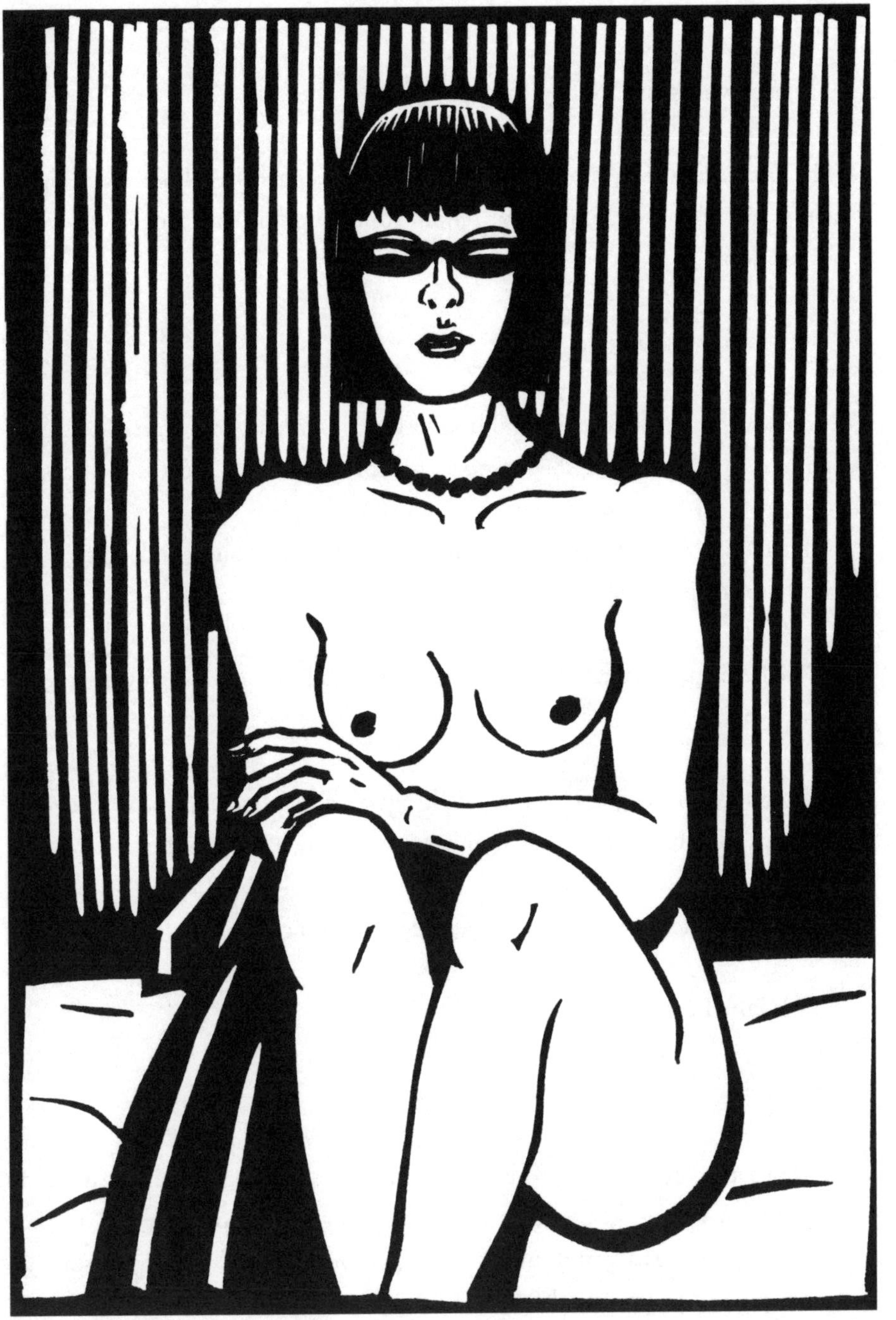

'Horace, what's this? When did you take this one?'

The taxi swerved abruptly into a side street. Angela's eyeliner went right across her forehead; I could not refrain from laughing, but Angela gave me a stern look.

'Don't worry, darling, let me.'

I took out my handkerchief and, moistening it with saliva, I started to clean her face. She looked into her compact mirror; it was clear she was not happy.

'I'll have to wear those glasses in the photo,' she said, and started to rummage through her handbag.

'We're here guv,' the taxi driver addressed me, sliding back the glass partition behind him.

I closed the door to the taxi and caught up with Angela, who was already on the steps. She had put on her sunglasses and turned towards me.

'I thought you said the launch would be in a library?'

'In Sir Ian's library.'

'At least I won't be overdressed.' Angela smiled.

Without ringing the bell, the door was opened by an elegantly dressed young man who indicated that we should proceed through the hall to the main room. It was a grand interior and I felt out of place, but once I started to recognize a few people I felt better.

'Angela, you look divine, and you, Horace . . . I am really looking forward to your next radio lecture; the first one was superb.'

Leaving Angela with Emma and Gus, I moved over to Professor Rignoli and his wife. I did not expect to see them here. In fact I was surprised to see so many familiar faces, some of whom I had not seen since my student days; it was like going back in time. I automatically took a glass of champagne from a waiter and walked over to a stack of books; I had to see Ed's book, but before I was able to flick through its contents I was besieged by friends and acquaintances. Everybody was wondering when Ed would arrive. A band started playing; the saxophonist was a beautiful woman whose features were uncannily similar to Angela's: their hairstyles were exactly the same. I was looking around for Angela when someone started tapping on an empty glass. It was Sir Ian, the chairman of the publishing group. He struck an elegant figure against the bookshelves full of leather-bound volumes. As he spoke I scanned the crowd. I could see Inzaghi clutching his pipe. Ed's uncle was there; next to him a tiny man in a bowler hat. Sir Ian spoke for several minutes about the unique qualities of Ed's book, how it would break new ground, but my mind was elsewhere; I was fascinated by the exotic guests. There were many people from the academy who were barely recognizable without their laboratory coats. George Sudok was standing on the lower rungs of the ladder attached to the bookshelves; dressed in a tuxedo, he looked as stiff as a tailor's dummy. The only person missing was Ed himself.

Ending his speech, Sir Ian raised a toast to the author. At that moment the doors swung open.

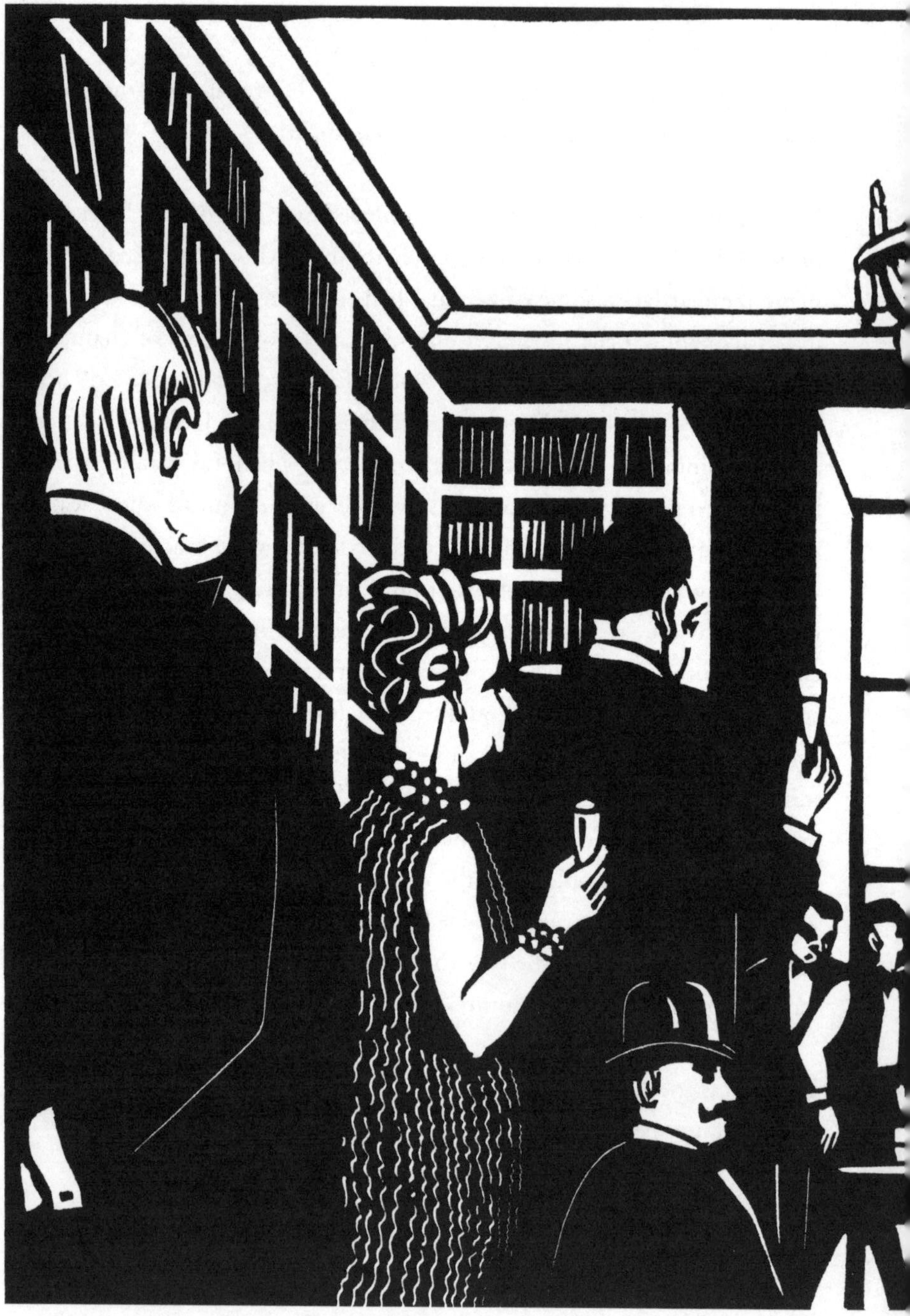

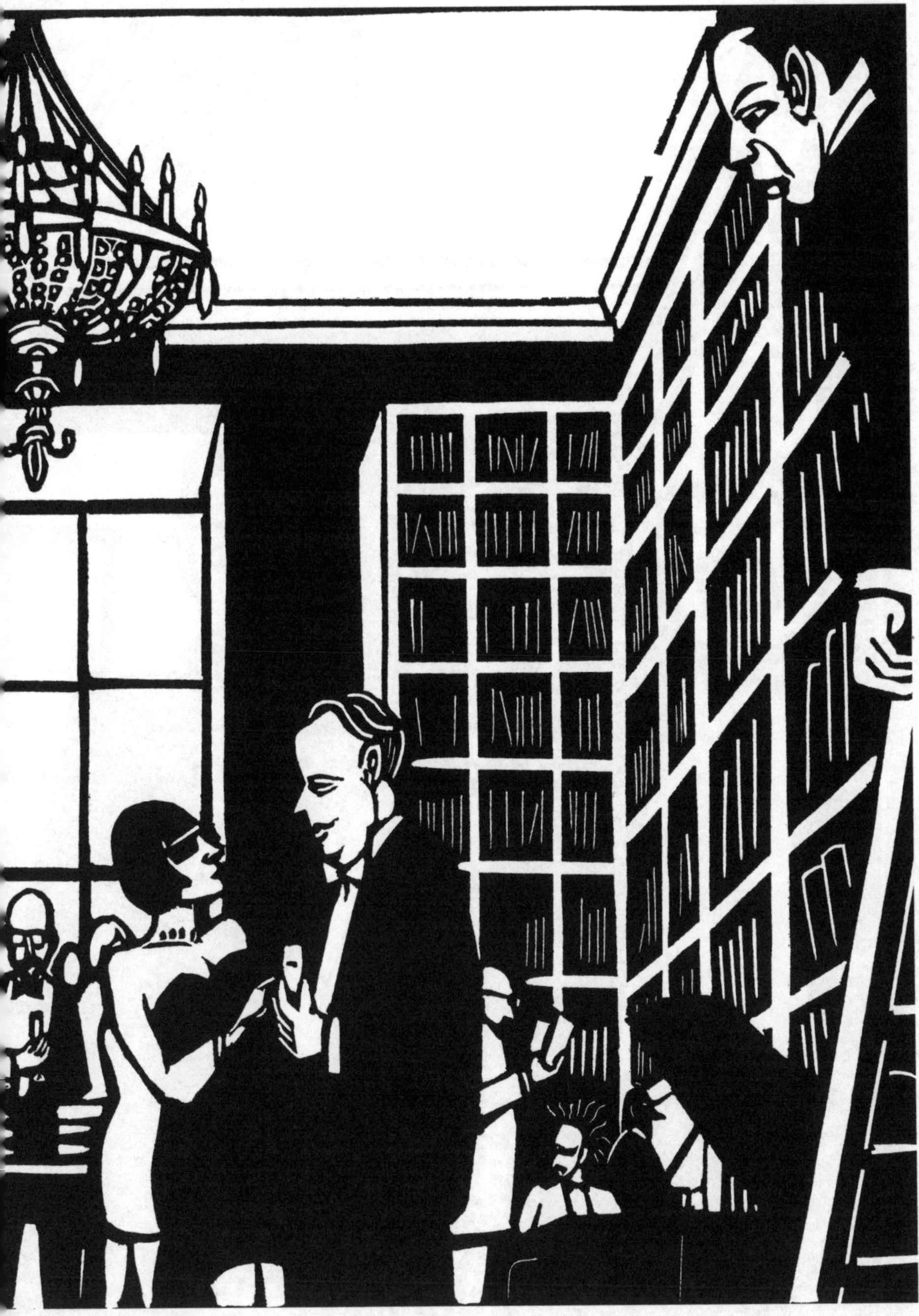

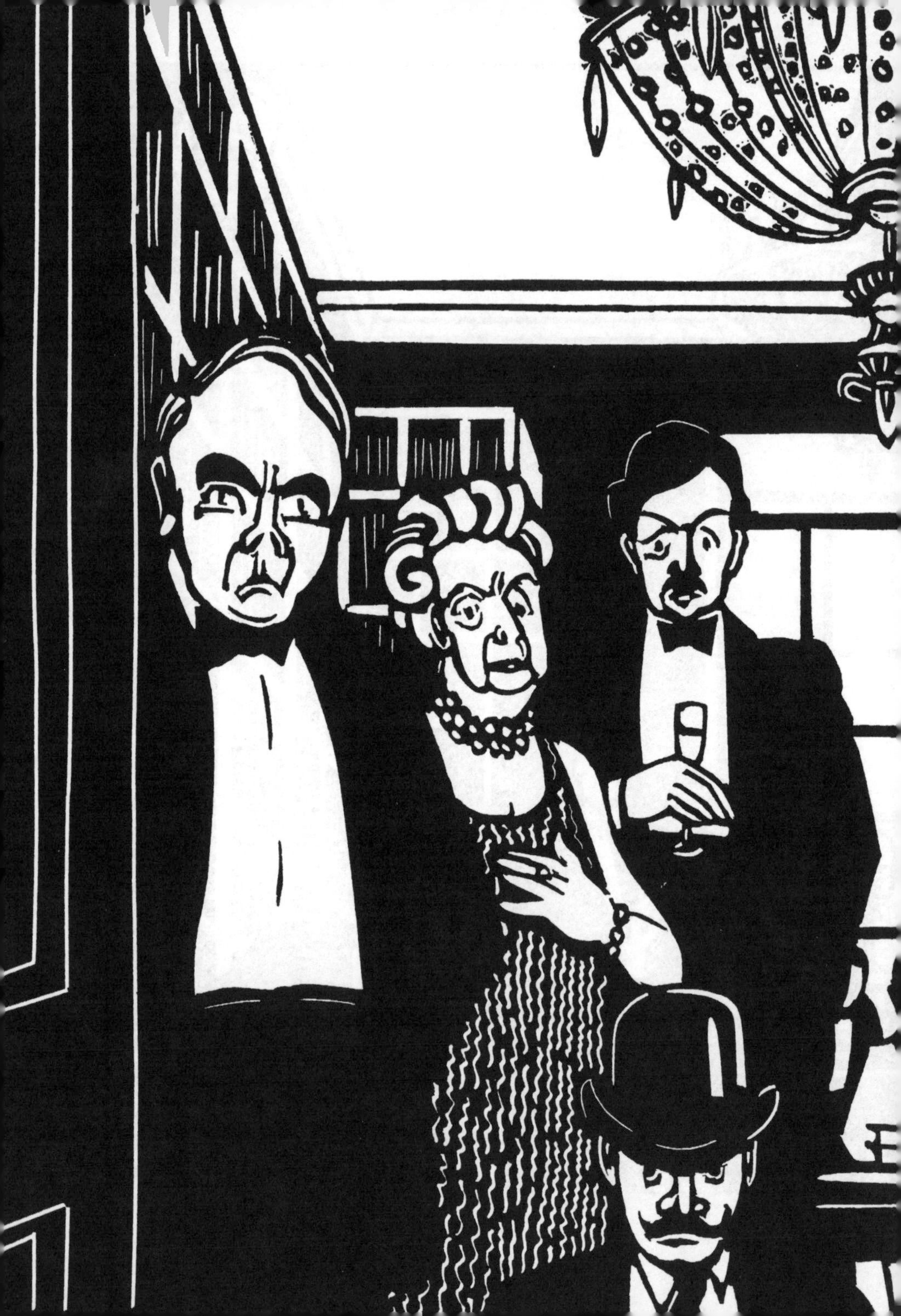

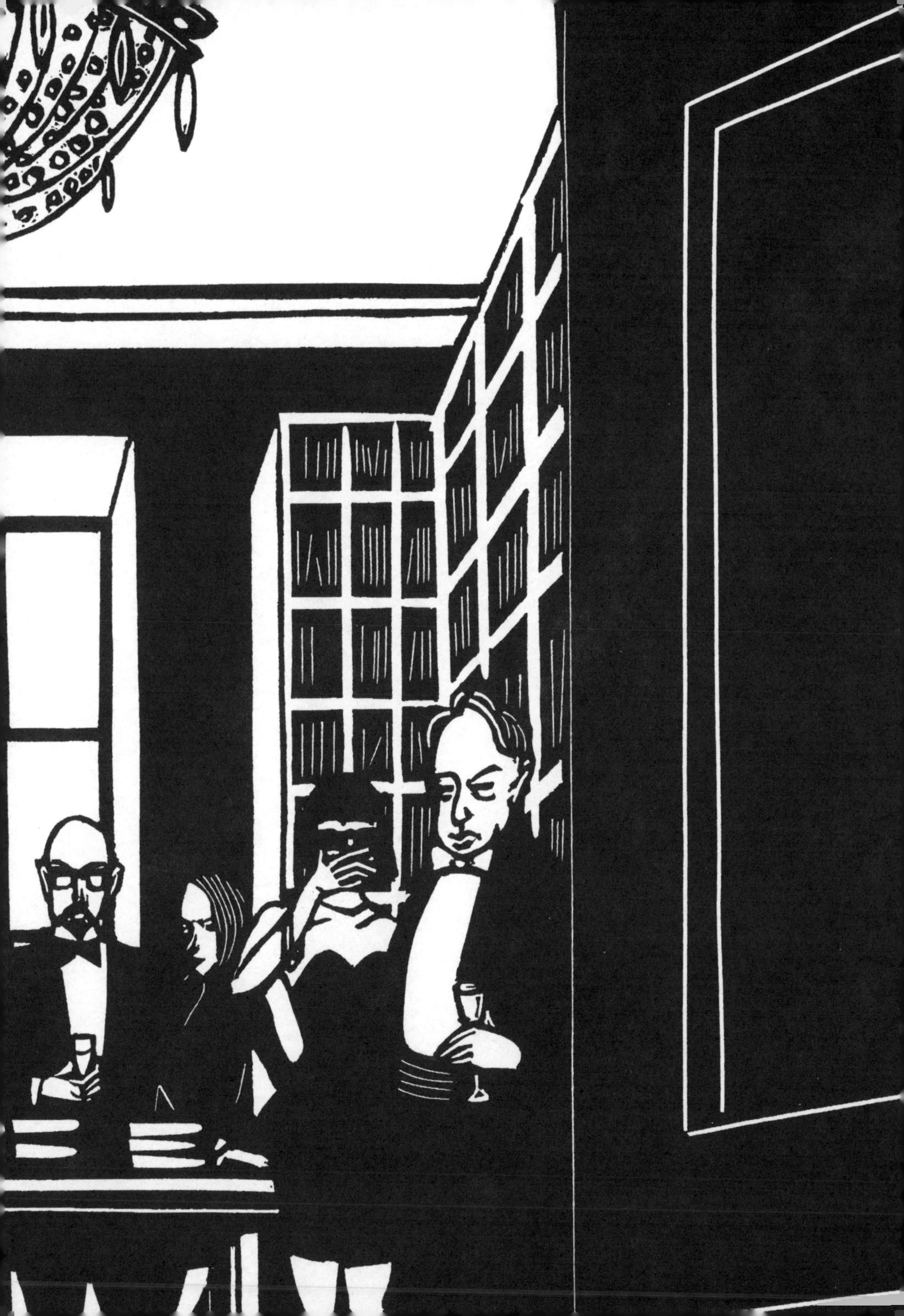